BEC McMASTER

SHADOWBOUND

THE DARK ARTS SERIES

Shadowbound: A Dark Arts Novel
Copyright (c) Bec McMaster

Edited by: Hot Tree Editing
Formatting by: Cover Me Darling and Athena Interior Book Design
Cover Art (c) Damonza.com

ALSO AVAILABLE BY BEC MCMASTER

LONDON STEAMPUNK SERIES
Kiss Of Steel
Heart Of Iron
My Lady Quicksilver
Forged By Desire
Of Silk And Steam
Novellas in same series:
Tarnished Knight
The Curious Case Of The Clockwork Menace

DARK ARTS SERIES
Shadowbound
Bloodbound (Late 2016)

BURNED LANDS SERIES
Nobody's Hero (May 2016)

OTHER
The Many Lives Of Hadley Monroe

CHAPTER ONE

'Sorcery is a vile practice. The work of the Devil. And we shall not rest until those devil-worshipping practitioners who reside in society are driven to repent—or driven out of our fair city of London.'
- Grant Martin, Chief of the Vigilance Against Sorcery Committee

London, 1894

"COME NOW, my lady, it's not safe."

Miss Ianthe Martin pressed the delicate handkerchief to her nose as she looked around the cell. Steel bars cut the gloom, delivering stark stripes across the stone floors. A shadow curled up beneath the barred windows, light striking the plain buff breeches covering his knees, and the bare soles of his feet. Large feet with carefully delineated toes. She stared at them, as her vision slowly adjusted to the gloom, remembering the feel of those bare feet against hers, once, shockingly long ago.

The prisoner looked up slowly, through the dark curtain of brown hair that surrounded his face. Dangerous, topaz eyes the color of molten gold watched her coldly, beneath harshly slanted brows. They flickered to her right, as if taking in the attendant who escorted her, then back again. Like a cat lashing its tail.

Secured, yes. Chained and beaten down. But instinct stirred, a smoky hot shiver low in her stomach. The long-subdued, primal part of her recognized danger when she saw it. "How long has he been kept in such solitary confines?"

"Ma'am." The attendant coughed reproachfully. No doubt he thought this completely beyond the pale.

Ianthe took a step closer as the attendant cleared his throat. His silence rattled her temper. "Damn you, how long?"

"Three months in solitary, ma'am."

And another nine before that, locked in with the writhing sprawl of humanity in the other corridors. New Bethlem Hospital—or Bedlam to most—had more than earned its reputation. Home to the criminally insane, the mad, and the Devilish Lord Rathbourne. The press had named him all three.

"Rathbourne?" One hesitant step into the cell. "Do you know who I am?"

There was a pentagram carved into the stone floors. New, from the look of the chisel marks. No doubt inspired by her father's work, and his precious committee. Though the Order of the Dawn Star that she belonged to served its Queen and country, there were always citizens superstitious enough, or too foolish, to understand what sorcery was.

"Rathbourne?" She hesitated, then added, "Lucien?"

Blast it. She'd hoped to find a sign of the man she'd once known. She could see more of him now; those stark cheekbones delineated even more clearly from the straitened circumstances, and the harsh, almost-black beard that lined his jaw. No sign of the elegant man who'd once melted her seventeen-year-old heart... and then ripped it out of her chest with barely a smile.

She hadn't even known his name the night she laid with him.

Not that he had any inkling of the reason for her dislike of him. That long-ago Equinox, she'd been masked, like all of the participants. Just a young woman—a girl truly—wanting to know more about the hot lick of power within her... and finding herself in perhaps deeper waters than she'd anticipated.

Rathbourne's affliction and subsequent incarceration had stripped all of the gilt off him, and cut him down to little more than taut muscle, furious eyes, and simmering animal fury. A chained beast, the shackles pinning him to the pale, limestone walls. Even one around his throat, as if even chained they'd still feared him.

As they should have. Rathbourne was a dangerous man.

The hand holding the handkerchief lowered. There was no sign of recognition in his eyes. No sign of the lucidity she'd hoped to see. Her last hopes dashed. A flicker of cold disappointment burned in her throat. What the devil was she going to do now?

Firstly, she had to get him out of this squalor.

"Are you aware that this man is a peer of the realm?" Ianthe turned on her heel and pinned the attendant with her best glare.

"His lordship is dangerous. Mad as hatters. Tried to choke a man with his own chain. Kept on about the shadows, how they were coming to get him..."

Ianthe's gaze flickered. The shadows didn't shift here. That didn't mean they couldn't. She knew better than that. The gleaming emerald around her throat threw off a splash of vibrant green against the bare walls as the sun caught it. Rathbourne flinched, as though the light hurt his eyes. No doubt the visiting cell they stood in was far different to the merciless pit they called solitary.

"You will remove him immediately and see him washed. New clothes. And shoes." Those bare feet bothered her.

The attendant opened his mouth.

"Don't argue," she said coldly, "or I shall see you dismissed."

Stepping through the door, she stared down the long, white corridor and pressed a hand against her temples. This was a nightmare. What was she going to tell the Prime? That the man Drake sought to free was long gone, lost in a mire of madness brought on by the backlash of his own powers. That sorcery had cost the Prime his bastard son's wits?

"Wait."

The sound rasped through a dry throat.

Ianthe's head jerked up, her breath catching. Slowly she lowered her hand and turned around.

Rathbourne's glittering eyes locked on her. "You."

Throwing himself against his chains, he strained hard. Muscle gleamed in the tattered remnants of his shirt, his biceps tightening as he fought to free himself.

"Shadow-lady," he whispered, yanking again and again, until blood shone on his dirty skin. "I remember you."

Despite the chains, she felt not at all safe. "Stop it." Ianthe forced her voice to remain hard. He'd not take well to kindness, not from her. "This exercise is pointless. You shall only hurt yourself."

8

The gleam of his bared teeth was the only answer.

Ianthe took a step inside the cell. Show even a hint of fear, and he'd tear her apart. She let her aura flare, dropping her wards for a brief second. Rathbourne froze, his eyes showing white as he saw power fill her. It was a sign that at least his mental acumen and abilities had not been entirely broken.

"Serve me," she whispered, "and I shall let you out of your chains."

"I'd rather rot."

"And let your enemies win?" she asked, stretching out one petite, white-gloved hand.

He flinched, and Ianthe forced herself to stretch those last few inches to touch him. "I know you think me an enemy," she murmured, stroking her gloved thumb along that roughened jaw.

"You put me in here."

"I did. Do you remember why?"

Those dangerous eyes dropped away, losing their focus. "I–I–There was a fire."

Not a fire. Not quite. This close to him, she could see the marks still. See where they'd burned their way into his flesh, gleaming scar-slick through the tears in his shirt. Perhaps it was best to let him believe that flames had scored those marks into his chest, and not a demon's wrath.

"I will let you out, Rathbourne, but you must do this one thing for me first. You must let me bind you, to make certain you're no danger to myself, or anyone—"

"No! I remember you, shadow-binder. I know what you are."

Shadow-binder. She stroked her other fingers along the floor, and caught the edge of the nearest shadow, letting it trail closer, the shadow-web trapped by the edges of her fingertips. "You know nothing, Rathbourne." If he denied her this, then she would stand alone against her enemies, alone against all who tried to destroy her cause.

And the cost... the cost of losing was unacceptable.

Louisa... Oh, God.

His thigh flinched away from the shadows as they drew nearer. Ianthe leaned closer and whispered in his ear. "I need a Shield, and you need an Anchor. Allow this binding, and once we are done, you shall be free to exact your revenge on all of those who saw you placed here. I swear."

His head turned, breath rasping. "Even you?"

No matter what the price... "If you help me find what I'm looking for, then I shall release your bond at the end of our terms of service. You may do to me as you will. Or you can attempt it." She was not without her own forms of protection, after all. She was no longer the foolish young girl he'd entranced that long-ago Equinox.

Those tiger-eyes turned thoughtful, watching the shadows under her touch disperse. "Two weeks of service."

It should be enough time. "I'll need your oath that you will agree to the binding once we are quit this place."

"By my Power, I shall let you bind me. I shall not hurt you, or yours, and I shall obey all directives."

Ianthe let out the breath she'd been holding. Thank goodness. Tears pricked at her eyes, but she couldn't let him see how much she needed him. "I accept." Leaning forward, she pressed her lips lightly to his, tasting the vow on his tongue and drawing it within her mouth.

The bite of the oath stung her lips, leaving them bloody. It mingled with his own oath, the power-spat words tearing over her tongue. So he was still strong enough for this. She could practically feel the hum of his power throbbing beneath his skin.

"You have two weeks of service," he said. "Use it wisely. Now get me the hell out of here."

Hot water. *Good lord.* Lucien pressed the flannel to his face, wiping away the last of the shaving foam. His face gleamed back at him in the reflection from the mirror, his newly shaven cheeks flushed and pink. It did little to soften the harsh look of his face; the sharp slash of his cheekbones and the golden, almost feverish gleam of his eyes. His body had fared no better. Hard, lean, stripped down to bare muscle, he looked somewhat like a caged tiger. Bedlam had changed him. A little shudder rolled over his skin as the power in the wards in the room brushed against him. *In more ways than one...*

The carriage ride to Miss Martin's establishment had been horrendous. Bright lights, the harsh blare of an omnibus horn, and muffled shouts. He'd had to drag the curtain on the carriage down, shielding his eyes from the inch of light that managed to creep in below it. Three months in the liquid dark of solitary had made him horrifically sensitive. The world was too bright, too loud, and full of noise, ripe scents, and the jarring scream of babbled conversation.

When Miss Martin had glanced at him, a question in those dangerous blue eyes, he'd simply curled his lip in a silent snarl. *That's right, darling. You wanted a madman. You got one.*

Dragging on the shirt one of her servants had placed out for him reminded him a little of the man he'd once been. A stranger. His fingers fumbled with the buttons, but he finally managed to make them work. The creature in the mirror was transforming before his eyes, resembling the man he'd once been.

Still... Not the same. Never the same again, no matter how much he looked like it.

This was what came of trusting the man he'd called a father all his life—agreeing to a wellspring bond that had allowed Lord Rathbourne to take control of his powers for a certain ritual. It was the only reason he was still alive. Unable to repel Lord Rathbourne's controlling collar, he'd been forced to summon a demon *against his will*. It was those last few words that were the important ones. A capital crime became incarceration, instead of execution.

Memory fractured in his head. The demon's foul, gloating smile as Lucien's mouth formed those damning words, Lord Rathbourne pulling his strings much as a puppet-master might. Fighting it. *No... No, I will not command it to do this! I will not ask it to murder the Prime!* And those fatal words as he realized there was no way free of this: "I bid thee to kill my father."

He'd meant Lord Rathbourne, of course.

And the demon had smiled, its bulbous lips splitting over ragged teeth. "As Master commands."

Then it had vanished.

Lord Rathbourne's mocking laugh was the only thing remaining, and in that moment, he'd speared Lucien with the truth, the reason he'd been such a cruel bastard all Luc's life. "Who do you think your father *is*, boy?"

The pain of the memory slashed through him, and Lucien returned to himself, bent over the vanity and gripping the polished oak veneer as if his life depended on it. Sucking in a huge breath, he could barely see, his vision shattering into a million different colors.

Lord Rathbourne. The Prime. Miss Martin. This was upon their heads. He would have his revenge, the way he had Lord Rathbourne. The thought served to soothe some of the violence of his nerves, to let all of those dancing colors flicker away to nothing.

Lucien looked up, meeting his own expression. Lord Rathbourne was dead, obliterated by the backlash, as Luc tore himself free of the bond forged. Now he had a chance to repay the Prime's so-called *mercy* in sending him to Bedlam, and Miss Martin for being the one to capture him. He wouldn't forget the callous way in which she'd cut him off from his sorcery and dragged him before the Prime.

Ever.

Thumbing his braces over his shoulders, he fixed a tie over that damning scar at his throat, and shrugged into his coat. The tie looked a mess, but he was breathing too hard to let anyone else in here to help him with it. Silence and peace. That was all he needed, for the moment. How ironic that after months of dreaming of people, of touch, of conversation, all he wanted now was to hide away. Ignoring his shaking hands, he straightened the tie and examined himself. He wasn't going to get what he wanted.

Time to deal with the Devil herself.

If he found the courage to leave the dark, shuttered bedchambers she'd delivered him to at her small set of apartments.

Christ. Lucien scraped a shaking hand over his mouth. He felt like half a man. *Pull yourself together, you lily-livered toff.* Dragging on the copper bracelet they'd taken from him when he first arrived at Bedlam, he instantly felt soothed. He'd spent months working runes to shield and protect into the metal; it was a device that could protect him from sorcery, even with his power still so raw.

Miss Martin. If he focused on the devilish-sweet memory of her face, he found he could breathe a little. *Revenge. Freedom. To forge himself anew.* The litany grounded him.

Lucien found Miss Martin in the conservatory, led there by the indomitable Mrs. Hastings. The black crepe of the housekeeper's gown gave an irritating rustle that set Lucien's teeth on edge.

Set between a pair of rooms on the upmost level, the conservatory wielded a view of the city. Nothing dangerous lurked within it, only a slender young woman with her raven-dark hair curled up in an elegant chignon and pearl earrings dangling from her ears. In the years since their disastrous first meeting, Lucien had begun to think of her as cold and frigid. It was somewhat disconcerting to come face-to-face with her again and realize how lovely she was. Younger than he'd remembered, too. Dangerously attractive, with that full, stubborn mouth that drew a man to think of kisses, and the tiny beauty mark on her cheek. She sat on a white wrought iron chair, at a similar setting, and sipped a steaming cup of tea as she peered through the glass walls of the conservatory. She didn't seem to have noticed his arrival.

Before he could look his fill—assess her, in truth— Mrs. Hastings cleared her throat. "Madam," she said, "his lordship has come to take tea with you."

As if either of them intended anything so civilized.

He'd sworn to serve as her Shield Companion, which meant he was bound to protect her with his life and his power. Bound to obey her too, which would leave him at a distinct disadvantage. If he tried to break his oath, his own power would consume him and leave him little more than the shattered hulk they already thought him to be. Cold sweat dampened the back of his neck at the thought of being under her command. Lord Rathbourne had taught him what being under another's control meant, but what choice did he have? To rot in Bedlam?

The moment Miss Martin's blue eyes locked on him, he felt a jolt all the way through his body. They were very nearly violet eyes, in this setting, with rain dampening the windows, and her lavender gown bringing out the highlights in her irises. He could remember the first time he'd ever seen her, at a gathering several years ago. She'd taken his breath away, for a moment, and he'd *had* to meet her, begging an introduction from his friend, Wetherby. She'd been cool then, and very nearly discourteous, though Lucien hadn't understood what he'd done at the time. Still didn't know, in fact. For some strange reason, she'd taken an instant dislike to him, and they'd never moved past that fact.

Now, it was his turn to dislike her.

He needed a means to balance the bond and gain some sense of control.

"Thank you," she said to Mrs. Hastings. "Would you care to take a seat, my lord? We have matters to discuss."

My lord. How strange, but then, technically, he *was* the Earl of Rathbourne now. His cousin, Robert, had been fighting to have him declared *non compos mentis* in the courts, the last he'd been aware. Evidently, the case must have stalled, which was something he would have to see to.

"Do we?" Lucien crossed his arms. "I have to admit, I'm surprised to be offered the honor of being your Shield. You're the last person I ever expected to free me from that hellhole, and there are dozens of men who would kill for an opportunity like this."

"And you're not one of them. I know." A flicker of dark lashes obscured her pretty eyes. "This was your father's doing, not mine. Drake insisted."

"He's not my father."

"Your *sire* insisted," she corrected.

And it was widely rumored that she was his sire's mistress. Perhaps that was why she did not care for him. "Do you always dance to his tune?"

"Drake has earned my respect and my trust, so when he asks me for a favor, I am always pleased to help him."

"My, how this one must have rubbed you the wrong way." Lucien prowled around the room.

"I've had easier missions to contend with, yes." Her eyes narrowed. "Why are you staring at me like that?"

That earned a faint smile from him. He'd give her this, she certainly didn't back down. "Perhaps I'm simply admiring the scenery." It gave him an idea, a way to haul the reins of power out of her hands and into his. "You need me for something."

"Perhaps you should sit and take some tea. We'll discuss matters."

"Unless it's got brandy in it, I'm not interested."

"Somewhat early for hard spirits," she countered, pouring him a cup of steaming brown liquid. "Perhaps lemon would suffice."

In another woman, he would have admired the gall of her. Instead, he sat and watched, rubbing his thumbs over the pleat of his trousers. Touching something helped to anchor him, to stop the overriding morass of sensation that constantly made his mind drift these days, until he wondered if he were truly going mad.

A tabby cat wended its way through her legs, its tail trailing her lavender skirts across the paved floors. Setting her cup on the tea service, Miss Martin reached down and scratched under his chin, eliciting a throaty purr. "Shall we cut to the point, Rathbourne?"

He arched a brow and waited.

"What do you know of the Blade of Altarrh?"

"It's one of three relics." Every sorcerer worth his salt knew that. "They were created by the Prime himself, his ex-wife, Morgana, and friend, the Earl of Tremayne." His mind shied from the memory of what the blade had been created for, and somehow he managed not to lose himself to the sudden narrowing of the room. *Focus on the facts.* "They were created in an attempt to summon and control a Greater Demon."

"It's missing."

Lucien's fingers tightened on the arm of the chair. He breathed out a half-laugh. "Missing?" Suddenly his mind was supplying pieces of the puzzle. "You want my help in finding it."

"Your talents in scrying would be of tremendous assistance," she concurred. "Few have the depths of your ability."

If he could manage to control them. He hadn't wielded his power in over a year. The backlash caused from trying to halt the demon he'd summoned at the bequest of his so-called father... It had scarred more than his body. "Why haven't you used the Prime's pet seer?"

"The relic was removed from a locked and warded case, in the heart of the Prime's mansion. Drake laid the wards himself. There were no signs of a break in to the manor, no strangers sighted in the vicinity—"

"Someone on the inside then." It all made sense now. "Which is why you're using me. How many others are working the case?"

"Only us."

Lucien started. There were men and women available within the order who dabbled in darker arts than he did. Sorcerers called the Sicarii, who policed the occult world, though few knew their true identities. "The Prime is playing his cards very closely to his chest."

At this, Miss Martin stood, crossing restlessly to the windows, looking toward a ruddy glow in the east. "You've been incarcerated for a long time. I forget what little you would know of the world. Come here."

A simple enough request. Lucien unfolded his long length and crossed toward her. For a second, he wondered how brazen she was, leaving him at her back like this, but a glint of those brilliant blue eyes in the window reassured him that she was not quite as trusting as she seemed.

"Yes?" He stopped directly behind her. The spill of her elegant, swagged bustle kept him at a proper distance.

Close enough, however, for her to turn her head slightly, her shoulders stiffening as she sensed his proximity, his threat. "Do you see that?"

Following her finger, he focused on the ruddy glow hidden behind cloudbank. Sucking in a sharp breath, he stepped forward, forgetting himself. Miss Martin stumbled against the window, her fingers splayed on the glass, and his reflexes being what they were, he found himself holding onto her waist, chivalry not quite as dead as the rest of him.

"The Dawn Star," he whispered. The feel of her tightly bound waist flexed beneath his fingers, the press of whalebone giving some hint of her stays. Despite that, he could sense the heat of her body, the sweetly curved line of her hips.

"Rathbourne," her voice warned.

"How long has it been in the skies?"

"The red comet appeared two days ago."

Little wonder the Prime was so nervous; the comet signified a change of the guard, whether he willed it or not. It had hung in the skies during the end of the reign of three previous Prime's, reappearing every thirty years, or so. Ascension was coming, a new Prime to sit on that carved ebony chair the duke maintained.

"No wonder the bastard's using us. Ascension is coming, the Blade of Altarrh has been stolen by someone he trusts, and most likely, he's facing a mighty tumble himself."

If not death.

Miss Martin pressed her back against the window as she turned. "I am going to do everything in my power to see that doesn't happen."

Anything to protect her lover. "Of course. And I have given my word to help."

Her shoulders slumped in relief. She didn't point out that he was standing far too close to her, but he could see the nervousness in her eyes. "Precisely. Now would you care to sit? I would like to proceed with the binding."

"Not yet." Instead, he reached out to brush a strand of dark, curling hair behind her ears. Miss Martin flinched. Her skin was softer than silk, though perhaps that was only because he'd grown used to roughened, limed walls and coarse canvas shirts.

Colors skittered over her skin, the pastel wash of chalk against a footpath, shimmering wetly. Or at least, that was how he saw it these days. Emotions became colors. The problem was in his mind, he had slowly discovered, not his eyes. Whatever that backlash of power had done to him, it had broken a piece of his mind, and he feared he didn't understand the full extent of it yet.

"Rathbourne." Her voice held the faintest hint of a growl in it. "Don't mistake me for some frivolous bit of muslin. You're in a warded room. I can have you dancing straight back to Bedlam before the hour is out, bound, gagged, and naked, if I wish it."

Bedlam. The threat made his heart kick painfully in his chest, his fingers tightening just a little, leaving small dints in her plump cheek. He'd do anything to remain free of such a place. Anything. Just the thought almost unmanned him.

You're free, he told himself. *But for how long? After all, you're of no use to her... Not like this.*

Their eyes met.

She could never know.

"You wish to remain free of such a place." Her voice became softer and smokier, though her eyes were still hard little chips of violet ice. "Do not presume to put your hands on me."

"I have no intentions of hurting you." Not physically. Revenge was a far more intricate puzzle. She wouldn't understand how many nights he'd considered how best to destroy her and the Prime. It was the only thing that had kept him sane during those long, silent hours, with not a single word spoken to him, no sign of another human, not even a glimpse of light... Just a plate shoved through his door at rough intervals with gruel slopped across it. He'd thought himself truly mad then. When the people of his bloody fantasies were the only companions he had.

But now...

She seemed softer somehow, far less certain than the cold, battle-warded woman who'd broken into his rooms at the Grosvenor Hotel and surrounded him with a circle of thirteen. He'd been half-blinded then, his skin tight and slick, still stinking of the burning reek of brimstone. Knowing that he'd committed one of the greatest crimes against the Order. A death sentence usually. Barely even a trial. But the Prime had had him dragged before him. Examined him for long, slow moments, as if trying to find some remnants of himself in Lucien's face.

And then he'd turned his back on him and exiled him to Bedlam.

"No?" The wariness never left Miss Martin's eyes, as if she found it difficult to believe he meant her no harm.

"No." *I have plans for you.* Something far more interesting than anything he'd previously concocted. After all, he was the one who'd learned that death was kind. He stepped away from her, letting her suck in a deep breath. Heat flushed through her cheeks, but she mastered herself as if such a moment had never existed between them.

"I intend to strike my own bargain with you," he told her, returning to the table and picking up his lukewarm tea.

"Bargain?"

"You need me far more than I need you, I think." She'd added the barest hint of sugar, but after so long without, his throat rebelled, and he was forced to swallow it without gagging.

"Debatable."

"You threaten to send me back to Bedlam for the slightest infraction, but how long must I wait until a new Prime sits at the head of the Order? How long before the comet's appearance fulfils its prophecy?" He tossed the tea unceremoniously into the pot of the lime tree. The cat padded toward it, sniffing to see if it were something edible. "Who else can you use, Miss Martin?"

"And would a new Prime see you free of Bedlam?"

His smile told her more than words ever would. He could wait. She couldn't.

Eyes narrowing, she crossed her arms. "What do you propose?"

"You need my assistance," he told her, "and I have promised to give it, but there is a difference between grudgingly helping, and doing everything within my means to assist. I can slow your quest to the point of incompetence if I choose, or I can complete it very quickly.

I am very, very good at what I do when I choose to set my mind to a task."

"Go on." The slant of her eyes told him she was waiting for the axe to fall.

"I will give you my days," he said. "I will obey your every command whilst bonded and serve as your Shield. I will help you to the best of my ability, protect you, and do my best to see the relic swiftly found. But... my dear sorceress..." his voice lowered, "your nights are mine."

For a moment, she looked as if she didn't quite comprehend. Then her eyes widened, her full mouth parting in surprise. Color bloomed in her cheeks, pinks and reds, blending in to each another. "I beg your pardon?"

"You want my cooperation? Then that is my price."

"Getting you out of Bedlam is the price I paid. You swore you would come with me and obey my directives."

"I will obey," he said, leaning back in the chair, as he enjoyed the moment. "I will obey to the very letter of your statements. No more. No less. I'd suggest you choose your words very wisely."

He had her. He saw it in her shocked eyes, in the riot of colors that danced across her skin. Her composure was only skin deep; some hidden well of emotion threatened to spill over her, which made her game for his plans.

Concern for her lover, the Prime? Somehow he had the feeling concern would be a different color to what he read now. The greens, blues, and violent indigo that swirled around her were muted and draining. Fear perhaps, if he could put a color to an emotion. Weariness. Desperation.

Hot pink desire.

Lucien stilled, his cods drawing tight. *Bloody hell.* That was something he'd never expected.

Miss Martin took her seat opposite him. The silence stretched out between them, and she looked slightly shaken, a little tremor in her fingers, the rattle of the saucer as she jarred it... Taking a deep breath, she finally stilled, staring at the gold-rimmed porcelain of her cup before lifting her eyes to his. "Why?"

"Because I want you in my bed."

She sipped her tea in response. "After all that I have done to you, you wish me to believe this isn't motivated by revenge?"

"Partly."

Her eyes narrowed. "I won't allow you to hurt me."

"My dear..." He pushed the sugar bowl closer to her. "What makes you think I have any intentions of harming you?" All of the heat he was feeling filled his voice. "You might even enjoy it."

"Of course. How foolish of me. Why would I ever doubt your intentions?"

Lucien merely smiled. It was easier to converse with her than to deal with the rest of the world. Some of the overwhelming press of sensation went away, leaving him to deal with only one; the hardening of his cock. "Make no mistake. I intend to make good use of that sweet little body of yours. It won't all be kindness. Some of it will be the most delicate kind of cruelty."

Violet eyes blinked at him over the rim of her cup, as she choked down some more of her tea.

"But I promise you this." He leaned forward and caught her lace-gloved hand. "You will enjoy it. You might even beg me to be a little cruel."

Tea slopped down her wrist, and Miss Martin swore as she jerked her hand away and snatched up her napkin. Lucien went to his knees beside her, plucking the napkin from her hand and using it to soak up the tea stains on her skirts. Their eyes met as she put her cup down.

"So be it." A proud look tipped her chin high. "I can, and have, endured a great many small cruelties over the years. What is one more?"

"Perhaps you might get your case of inks then, to mark the runes on our skin for the bond?" A smile curled over his mouth. "Before we both run out of daylight..."

Where she would pay the price before he earned his service.

Ianthe's heart beat madly in her chest as she slowly unfolded herself onto the stone slab. The conservatory seemed a distant memory as Rathbourne eased his way around the cellar she'd led him to, lighting the smoky wicks on numerous candelabrum. Wax dripped down the sides of each candle, creating leering faces.

This was her chamber of sorcery, an enormous magic circle set into the floor in solid silver. The pair of double circles—one inside the other—contained numerous runes, set to keep outside interference at bay so that she could perform her major works.

The last candle flared to life and the circle's energy was suddenly palpable, trembling over her skin and dancing between her thighs. She was trapped in a magic circle with the one man she wanted above all others.

A man whose touch she could only too clearly remember. Ianthe wet her lips. She knew the scent of his body, the satiny glide of skin over each muscle and sinew as he'd buried himself inside her.

And the pain that single act had caused her...

Concentrate. Rathbourne is the means to an end.

"Do you wish to close the circle? Or shall I?" Rathbourne seemed to be easing back into his skin with every minute, becoming more and more the man she remembered from the hotel. Bolder and far more arrogant than he'd been as a youth. He spoke of gentle cruelties now, but he'd known none of them then. Indeed, he'd been mesmerizingly gentle as he laid her back upon his cloak that night, so long ago. Kissing her as if he sought to steal the very breath from her, his fingers trailing under her skirts and seeking the heart of her desire. It had hurt, of course, for she was a virgin, but the hurt of it had soon dissolved, her body wrapping around his as he ground himself into her and whispered shocking, delicious words in her ear.

"If you will," she replied.

Taking the ritual blade, he carefully ran it across his finger, squeezing out several drops of blood onto the first silver circle. A silvery dome flickered to life, locking them inside. As his blood dripped over the inner circle, another could be sensed, this time an invisible, but no less dense protection. A dome built to keep magic out.

Rathbourne's eyebrow arched, and he tipped his chin to her. "Exquisite work."

"You expected less?"

Toying with the knife, he circled her, eyes gleaming hotly amber. "No. It reminds me of the Prime's work."

"It's an echo. Since he was my master."

"In all matters," Rathbourne murmured.

The remark stung, though she knew it was commonly believed rumor. After all, how could a healthy young woman such as she not have a lover, when her lack of marriage, career choice, and decision to live alone marked her clearly as someone of lesser morals?

It didn't matter what he thought of her. Only that she found the people who wanted the relic. For a moment, she almost felt ill, the prick of tears threatening.

Rathbourne's slow circling had stopped. "The thought upsets you."

"What?" Ianthe turned her head to the side to look up at him. Perhaps some part of the man who'd once been her lover still existed.

Or perhaps she was looking too hard for an ally that didn't exist.

"We haven't got all day." Ianthe turned her face away. "Make your blasted marks, and let us finish this. The trail is growing colder by the minute."

Rathbourne knelt on the edge of the stone slab. "So be it." Reaching out, he plucked at the buttons of her high-necked dress.

The touch was shockingly intimate, and her fingers caught his, trying to knock them aside. "I can manage."

Rathbourne held up his hands. "Merely trying to hurry the task along."

Swallowing hard, she managed to undo her gown all the way to the top of her breasts. Rathbourne reached out and flicked the collar open, baring her décolletage. Those lazy, lion's eyes warmed as he looked his fill. Cold air pricked her naked skin, reminding her that she wore little more than her chemise and stays beneath her dress. Breath quickening, she stared up at the ceiling overhead, trying to ignore the heat of his presence. It had been like this ever since the day he stalked into Drake's ballroom and presumed to seek an introduction with her.

As if he hadn't been the man who'd claimed her virginity, all those years ago.

"Blood to bind," he whispered, and the sharp coppery scent of blood filled the room as he cut his finger again and let his blood well into the small lead bowl she used for that purpose. "Saliva, for the breath of life." Running his finger inside his mouth, he sucked hard on the cut. "Ink to mark the flesh."

Spitting on the block of ink, he rubbed his bloodied finger through it, and Ianthe felt the first small stirrings of magic tighten inside her. She stifled the urge to squirm restlessly. An inability to focus was the mark of a mere acolyte.

Not even Drake would deny that you've enough to unsettle any mind... Rathbourne himself, the relic and... the debt of guilt and grief.

Tears pricked her eyes. *Don't think of that now.*

"*Hecarrh cairedh mi caratha...*" Soft, whispering words so excellently nuanced that they had to be his personal Words of Power.

The candle flames all flickered, then flared higher in a singular wave. The pull of power became a warm, tugging knot in her abdomen, a gentle pressure between her thighs. Sorcery had always felt slightly sexual in nature for her. It wasn't always, depending on the person and the elements of power that attuned more strongly to them. Some preferred the stir of blood, the anticipation of cutting the magic from their skin. Some found their link in the grave and the power of death.

From the feel of the pull between them, she knew precisely which aspect Rathbourne attuned to. The muscle in his thighs clenched as he leaned over her, dipping a finger into the mixture of ink, saliva, and blood. His erection strained against the cambric of his trousers, and she swiftly glanced away as he straddled her hips.

"That's hardly necessary," she protested.

Soft fingers stroked a loose strand of her hair out of the way. "Shush." The moment he touched his blood-wetted finger to her chest, Ianthe felt it, as though he'd plucked the strings of a lute. Sorcery shivered through her; vibrations that set her blood on fire and forced her to bite her lip. She pressed her knees tightly together. *Merciful heavens.*

Magic of the most intimate kind glimmered to life with the bond between them, leaving her wet and aching, trapped beneath him, the press of his knees on either side of her hips pinning her skirts.

When the power faded, Rathbourne was straddling her, the press of his body pinning her hips to the stone slab. Breathing hard, his dark hair tumbling over those shocked eyes, he looked down at her. One hand splayed over the stone near her head, the other was resting lightly on the rune he'd drawn on her skin, fingertips barely grazing her.

All it would take would be one move.

Hers.

A fist curling in his cravat as she dragged his weight down atop her... A perfectly legitimate way to finish this ritual, but if this were the result of a single rune, then what would happen if she let free all her inhibitions and took this to a conclusion they both desired? Just how powerful would their spell craft be?

And what would be the result?

There were three types of bonds that two sorcerers could use; a wellspring bond, where one sorcerer gave control of their power over to another; the bond between Anchor and Shield, which was somewhat more reciprocal, though the Anchor typically held control; and a soul-bond, that rare bond that could be created between lovers and could never be broken.

Ianthe wasn't quite romantic enough to believe in it.

At least this Anchor bond could be broken by choice when the time came.

Even if the desolate ache between her thighs left her feeling strangely unsatisfied.

Tonight, that ache would be assuaged. She'd given her word for it.

"Are you done?" she demanded, both frightened and titillated by the idea of being in this man's bed, under his control, his power.

"Of course." Rathbourne traced his fingertips across her collarbone, eliciting a shiver, then stood and began unbuttoning his shirt, golden candle flame highlighting the stark line of sinew in his shoulders and muscle. "Now it's my turn."

CHAPTER TWO

THE PRIME'S RESIDENCE was a far cry from Miss Martin's, which had been located in the heart of the theatre district. Not too far from the Rathbourne family manor, actually, though Lucien had no reason to go there whilst the courts held his case. Surely the Prime could afford to put her up in a more affluent section of town?

"I assume the Prime has had the manor searched?" Lucien asked, as the carriage began to slow as it pulled into the circular driveway, the jingle of the bit ringing and the horse's hooves crunching over the gravel.

"Of course he did. Discreetly." Not a sign of concern showed in Miss Martin's comportment, though her foot tapped with restless ease, her fingers scrunching the corners of the newspaper she'd been perusing.

"Is it safe to presume that the theft has gone unnoticed by others?"

"We've managed to contain the spread of rumor so far. The butler alerted Drake to the empty case sometime this morning, and he sent to wake me at dawn. The few servants who know are under a suppression rune, and there were only two guests for the evening, neither of them suspect."

...*sent to wake me at dawn*... Where precisely? It sounded as though she hadn't been in the duke's bed. "Were you staying at the manor?"

"Yes. I only returned from the north yesterday afternoon, and Drake asked me to stay and dine with the Ross's. By the time we'd retired to the sitting room, it was late and I had no desire to venture out into the rain." She put the paper down and sighed.

"Who are the Rosses?" The stamp of her own magic was lanced into his chest, pulsing with quiet discord. If he didn't know any better, he'd suspect Miss Martin was a mess of steadily growing nerves.

"Mrs. Ross and her niece, Adeline, are old friends of Drake's."

"That means nothing. Either could have done it."

"Addie is barely fifteen and considered a wallflower. Her aunt, Eleanor Ross, was accounted for at the time of the disappearance. You might as well accuse me, whilst you're at it."

"No." His smile was grim. "It's exceedingly clear where your loyalties lie. You're the only one I don't consider to be guilty."

"I would strongly advise you not to accuse either of the Rosses without due cause. Drake is exceedingly fond of them."

He ignored her. "So, servants, the Rosses, and anyone familiar with the wards. You mentioned there was no sign of a break in. Could someone have gotten in without anyone noticing?"

"Anything is possible. Unlikely, but possible. Until this morning, I should not have thought anyone capable of breeching Drake's wards."

Wards were an intimate magic. Only one well attuned to a sorcerer's style could have any hope of touching them without sending them blazing, let alone getting through them.

Still, he had the sensation she was keeping something from him. How in blazes did she expect him to be able to help if all of her information was grudging?

A dark figure limped into view as the carriage pulled up, leaning heavily on a silver-handled cane. Wings of silver highlighted the man's black hair, and his heavy-set figure was no less powerful or imposing than it had been a year ago, when Lucien had been dragged before the Prime in spelled chains.

Drake de Wynter was a powerful foe, but Lucien couldn't stop looking at the man's cane. The Prime hadn't had that the day they'd dragged Luc into the study upstairs. Instead, he'd been seated behind his desk, his face ravaged with weariness. The demon had manifested directly in the center of the duke's Equinox ball the night before, scattering screaming acolytes and launching itself upon the Prime.

The only reason it hadn't done more damage was because Drake had somehow managed to bend it to his will and sent it back to its master.

Fire. Lashing along his chest as if someone had wielded a whip made of pure electricity. Lucien's fingers dug into the carriage strap, and he clung for dear life as he tried to force the image down. "What happened to his leg?"

"The demon. It took quite a large chunk out of him, once it realized he was magically compensated against any of its attacks. He almost bled to death."

Small comfort. Lucien's nostrils flared, and he offered her his hand as the footman opened the door. "Shall we?"

Ianthe looked surprised, but in truth, he liked the feel of her small hand in his. The moment their fingers touched, the world seemed to slow down around him, its edges becoming crisp and defined, instead of a constant blur of sensation and color. He hadn't realized how much he needed an Anchor to ground him at the moment.

Handing her down onto the damp gravel, Lucien examined the man who had sired him. They shared the same dark hair, but that was where the similarities ended. Lucien took after his mother, with her exotic amber eyes and thick wealth of hair.

A thousand questions filled his mind. What had driven the Countess of Rathbourne into the arms of the Prime so many years ago? He'd done the math. His birth followed almost a year after his parents' marriage. A rather finite amount of time for his mother to cuckold her husband, though his experience with Lord Rathbourne over the years meant that he didn't bother to ask why she'd sought another man's arms. Merely, why the Prime?

Silk bunched beneath his hand as he slid it firmly over the small of Miss Martin's back, needing the peace her presence wrought. A somewhat possessive gesture, and one that the Prime's sharp gaze didn't miss.

Choke on that, he thought viciously, gracing the Prime with a smile. "We meet again."

"Rathbourne," the duke intoned.

"It seems you have a problem you wish my help with."

The Prime took that moment to glance at Miss Martin. "You bonded him?"

"It seemed wise," she replied, her expression gentling as she looked up at the man. "He could be dangerous, Your Grace."

The Prime's silvery eyes lanced Lucien to the soul, searching for something, an ancient sadness lingering about his aura. "You have your mother's eyes—"

"Let us dispense with the pleasantries," Lucien cut in angrily. "You and I mean nothing to each other. I'm merely here because you offer something I want. Freedom. So let's not pretend this is anything more than it is."

An awkward silence settled.

Drake de Wynter slowly nodded, looking tired, more than anything. Lucien almost felt sorry for him, but then the Prime turned and limped toward the house. "So be it."

Lucien grit his teeth. He was letting his own emotions get the best of him. What had she said? That the duke suspected someone within his inner circle? That meant he ought to keep his bloody eyes and ears open, rather than focusing on the back of the Prime's head, his fist clenching. Revenge would not be taken out in such a bloody, confrontational way. No, he had better ideas. Lure Miss Martin into his bed. Steal her away from the bastard, perhaps. Return the relic and then watch as the prophecy did the rest.

I will enjoy seeing you brought to your knees...

"We're going directly to Drake's private wing." Miss Martin handed her hat and gloves to one of the footmen, giving him a reproving look. "Time is against us. Do you require anything?"

"I'd like to see the place where the Blade was kept first."

The upstairs wing was silent and still, evidently the Prime's private quarters.

"This is where the relic was kept," the Prime said, his deep voice echoing in the marble-floored hallway.

Half a dozen Chinese urns lined pedestals along the wall, with glass cases interspersed between them. Magic pulsed in the air, thick shivery fingers that brushed against Lucien's skin. He could almost see waves of it, like heat shimmering in the distance on a hot day.

"It's an athame blade, isn't it?" He blinked through the pain of exposure, circling the empty glass case in front of him. A red velvet cushion rested forlornly on its pedestal, the shape of a dagger crushed into the material, but no sign of the actual implement itself. The case looked undisturbed.

"There were three of them: The Blade, the Chalice, and the Wand. Together they form the Relics Infernal. The Blade was forged from the iron of a fallen star and an obsidian hilt; the Chalice is carved from ivory and bone; and the Wand was cut from whale bone."

"Why create them?"

"Curiosity on my behalf," Drake replied. "And power on the others. I was eighteen and rising swiftly through the ranks of the Order. The previous Prime was a bastard of the most unimaginable depravities. My friend Tremayne meant to see himself in this seat." His eyes dwelled on the empty case. "The spell craft was learned from a grimoire that Tremayne had purchased in his travels in the Orient. It made sense to me to wield it, even knowing the dangers, and my ex-wife, Morgana, always craved power. It is said that demons taught us the secrets of sorcery, opening our eyes to the power that we could wield. What else could they teach us? What could a Greater Demon know?" A faint grimace. "At that stage, I had not yet learned the consequences of dabbling in the darker arts. Just because one can do something—"

"Doesn't mean that one should," Miss Martin murmured.

They shared a faint smile. It spoke of a long familiarity.

"Without the other relics...?" Lucien asked.

"By itself it is still powerful, still dangerous," the Prime replied. "One of the secrets none of us understood, or I hope that none of us understood at the time, was that the Relics Infernal need a Grave sacrifice to work, not just blood. Once cut by the Blade, it's very difficult to stop bleeding." He held out his wrist, unbuttoning his cufflinks. A faint silvery scar traced his olive skin. "We all sacrificed blood to the original attempt of the ritual. It was my first inkling that all was not as it seemed. I told the others, then and there, that I had no intentions of continuing."

Death magic. Despite himself, Lucien was fascinated. "And?"

"They agreed, but I saw the look in Tremayne's eyes. The Blade can be used to steal another's power for a brief time, by draining their blood and using it to fuel spell craft. At that stage, my ex-wife and I decided it was too dangerous to leave the objects in his care."

"You mean, Morgana wanted them in her own hands," Miss Martin said wryly.

"As I said, I had not yet learned certain consequences associated with power." The Prime stepped back. "She was a master of illusions, her particular talents running to deception. She created copies of the relics, and I switched them. Tremayne had no inkling of what I'd done until it was too late, and...by that time, the Prime, Sir Davis, had begun to hear word of our little experiments."

This was the part of the story Lucien knew well. Sir Davis had sent his Sicarii assassins for Tremayne and de Wynter, dragging them before the entire Order at the Equinox where he'd demanded one of them give him challenge, or he would see Morgana executed first. Tremayne had demurred, not yet having the experience to fight a man of the Prime's worth.

And de Wynter would have done anything for his wife at that stage.

"Once I became Prime, Tremayne was furious," the duke explained. "He tried to use the Blade against me, and of course, not even Morgana's illusions could conceal the fact that I wasn't bleeding as I should be. He realized what we'd done and demanded the relics back. In the quarrel, I cast him from the house and warned him never to set foot in my sight again, or I would kill him myself."

The case was perhaps three feet wide and four foot long. Lucien ran his fingers along it, the instant thrum of the case's wards almost blinding him. For a moment, the hallway was full of dancing colors. The duke seemed mainly made of saddened greens, whilst Miss Martin had an almost sickly tinge of yellow mixed with desperate grays.

Lucien touched his nose to see if it was bleeding.

Miss Martin's hand slid through his and relief was instant. Serving as his Anchor, she effortlessly dispersed the overwhelming taint of sorcery between them so that it wasn't concentrated solely on him. It let him breathe again.

"You're a Sensitive?" she murmured.

Such sorcerers could feel the very thread of a spell, working out how to manipulate it, though it often left them overwhelmed. He couldn't tell her the truth though, so he just shrugged.

"Perhaps we should adjourn somewhere quiet, where you may prepare yourself?" the duke interrupted. "What shall you need?"

"A bowl of purified water, an athame, and..." He glanced back at the warded case, wondering why the spell craft surrounding it hadn't changed, as it should have if it had been opened and the wards displaced. "That piece of velvet should suffice."

The Arts of Divination were a gift through his mother's side of the family. She'd been the Cassandra at the time, the strongest seer in a generation. Though Lucien didn't have her abilities to forecast, he could scry over a particular distance and had a certain amount of control over psychometry, the ability to divine an object's history.

Both the duke and Miss Martin were silent as Lucien prepared himself, sitting on the ground and forcing his breath to ease until he was aware of every single aspect of his body. The Void washed through him, leaving stillness in its wake and his senses focused to pinpoint accuracy.

Lucien reached out and picked up the athame the duke had provided for him, slicing one of his other fingers. Blood dripped into the bowl, and he plunged the piece of velvet into the stained waters, whispering words of power under his breath. Instantly, his mind connected to the piece of fabric, images flashing at him one after the other—the dagger, hands stroking the fabric, magic twisting around it—then back further to the fine nap and weave, as someone worked unfinished threads to create it... Lucien tried to push all of that away, trying to focus on what had happened in the early hours of dawn.

Where are you now? he scried.

There was nothing, only the vibrating image of the house painted onto the back of his eyelids.

Panting hard, Lucien released the skeins of vision. Divination unraveled, as though it had never occurred. Everything distracted him. The hair on his arms, each individual pore standing to bright revue. The swirl of dust motes through the air, circling around the Prime, as if he'd moved, and the man himself... Harsh grains of freshly shaved stubble, a tiny scar under his lip, and the glints of silver in his irises... Lucien could almost feel the beginning of a scrying lock on the man, images swirling up in his mind.

A woman laughing, the sound echoing in his ears. A child's voice calling out, '*Mama*!' And a somewhat watery version of Rathbourne Manor in Kent, though it seemed as if it had come directly from before the renovations of 1862. Lucien pulled away from it. A grave sprang to mind. The Prime standing guard over it in the snow, staring sadly down at the words on it. A handful of words carved into the granite. *In memory. The son I never knew. 1868.*

Wincing, Lucien clapped a hand over his eyes. Miss Martin hurriedly drew the drapes, plunging them into darkness.

"What did you see?" she demanded.

Too much. That had never happened to him before. Usually he could read only objects, not people. Reading people was a very rare talent and unpredictable. The effort made him stagger into a nearby chair, his stomach revolting as it threatened to disgorge Miss Martin's overly sugared tea onto the Prime's Turkish carpets.

"What was it?" Miss Martin knelt by the chair, her fingers clutching his own.

"Give him air, Ianthe." The Prime squeezed out a rag over the bowl of water he'd been using and stepped forward, leaning the cane against his desk. He reached out and undid Lucien's poor attempt at a cravat, draping the wet rag over the back of his neck. "Keep your head down and focus on the ground. Your vision shall return to normal within a few minutes."

How did he know that? Lucien obeyed, too wrung out to argue. "I saw... *Christ*—"

"Me," the Prime said grimly, "or flashes of my past. I caught the edge of it."

That made his head jerk up, a fact he regretted instantly. The Prime shoved it back down, his callused palm firm on the back of Lucien's skull.

"My son was miscarried, so I'm told." The words were quiet with grief. "The grave is his. A final parting gift from my ex-wife when I threatened her with divorce. I saw that much." A hesitation. "Was there anything else?"

"Rathbourne Manor. My mother's laugh." And a little boy crying out her name. "Me and you."

The pressure of the Prime's hand eased just a fraction. "I was never meant to see you, but she allowed it, just the once."

"What of the relic?" Miss Martin insisted. "Did you see it?"

Nothing. Lucien had hoped that his gift for divination hadn't been affected by whatever the demon or Lord Rathbourne had done to him. He'd been wrong. "No. All I get is an image of the house." A glance toward the Prime. "Perhaps your wards are affecting me."

"They shouldn't," the duke replied, "but it's possible. All I know of divination came from your mother, and it was her area of focus, not mine."

Miss Martin's shoulders slumped. "No sign of it." The words were soft. "I shall send for my trunks then. We'd best get moving. I need to see Remington. We'll work from there." Her pale hand slid over the duke's and squeezed. "We'll find it."

"One can hope." The duke rubbed at his mouth.

"Hopefully before the comet disappears," Lucien said, though it lacked the malice he'd owned before his visit. None of this made sense. The duke had asked to see him as a boy?

"Hopefully before either of the other two relics go missing," the Prime corrected. "If someone is setting out to summon a greater demon..."

No need to say more. That alone inspired Lucien to complete this task. The demon he'd summoned himself, whilst under Lord Rathbourne's control, had been a greater demon. Imagine someone evil controlling a creature like that? London would be destroyed. "Do you know who holds the other two relics?"

The Prime nodded, giving nothing away. "I have warned them."

Miss Martin caught his wrist as he swayed. The scent of her sultry perfume was almost dizzying. "Come. We've no time to waste. You can rest in the carriage." She glanced at the Prime. "I assume we may take it?"

"Whatever you need." The duke slowly stood, gripping the silver-handled cane. His gaze flickered to the small feminine hand that rested on Lucien's sleeve. Their eyes met. "Don't let her get hurt."

"I won't." He had the strength for one last retort. "Miss Martin owes me entirely too much, and I fully intend to collect on the debt."

Her cheeks pinkened beneath the duke's enquiring gaze, and whatever question had been asked was answered.

"Good luck," the duke said, with another unfathomable quirk of the brow, and Lucien wasn't certain whether he meant her, or the pair of them in their search.

Ianthe oversaw the loading of her traveling trunks from her recent trip to Edinburgh. Resting a hand on the largest, she let a flicker of magic, carefully concealed, trail over the timber panels. There was no answering tug. No sign of anything magical. The manufacturer in Scotland had done his job to her precise specifications, lining the hidden compartment with lead, a substance known for its magic-dampening abilities, and sealing it with *look-away* runes.

Slowly, Ianthe released the breath she'd been holding. *I'm so sorry, Drake...*

She slid her gloves back on, locking down all of the emotion that threatened to show on her face. A trick she'd learned at her father's knee. Rathbourne gave her a strange look, but she merely gestured at the coachman. "Take them back to my apartments and see them unloaded in my bedroom once you've delivered us to the theatre."

It ached to let the large trunk out of her sight, but what was she to do? She couldn't allow any suspicion to fall upon herself.

Once upon a time, she would have said that nothing could have made her betray her master. *But we all have our weaknesses, don't we?* She only hoped she could discover a way out of this mess before Drake discovered her treachery.

Fingering the locket at her throat, Ianthe watched the trunk, and its magically sealed compartment, vanish into the city, her heart feeling like lead in her chest.

Thank all the gods that Rathbourne had failed to scry out the Blade.

CHAPTER THREE

'The purpose of the Order of the Dawn Star is twofold; one, we seek to understand the Great Mysteries of life and the divine; and two, we aim to serve our country. To protect it from malevolent forces that exist in other planes, and those who seek to use them.'

- 'Understanding the Divine', by Sir Anthony Scott

THE BUSTLING STREETS of Covent Garden were their first stop. Ianthe alighted from the duke's carriage with effortless grace.

Lucien raked the streets with a hard glance. "You think someone here took the Blade?"

"No. But this is where I'm going to start my search."

"That makes little sense."

"All will be revealed, Rathbourne."

Bright theatre posters screamed their headlines to the world as she paused at the entrance to the Phoenix Theatre. *Behold: The Great Remington Cross and, his beautiful assistant, the exotic Sabine.* Tugging her key out of her reticule, Ianthe let herself through the theatre doors.

Lucien prowled past her, his dark hair brushing against his collar, as he lowered the smoked glasses he had taken to wearing. Absurdly long and unfashionable, that hair, but her eyes lingered.

Damn Drake for saddling her with him, when she needed all of her wits.

Ianthe followed him over the plush red carpets. The walls here were yellow-striped wallpaper, a far cry from the entrance the working classes used to keep them separate from the rich. That entrance led directly to the galley, the tier in which the poor were allowed to inhabit. There was no wallpaper there, no plush carpets. Illusion was everything in this world she'd once known.

Lucien unfurled a faded poster, straightening out the rolled up edge until he could see the painted figure upon it, with her blonde curled wig, devilish smile, and spangled gown. The Mysterious Sabine. Those unusual golden-brown eyes cut toward Ianthe, and she had no difficulty interpreting the look.

"It was an occupation," she said, preceding him toward the auditorium. "One that an occultist excels at. We don't all have vast inheritances to fall back upon."

"You use sorcery to entertain?"

Ianthe turned on her heel, the abruptness of the move leaving her face-to-face with him. He jerked back before he could slam into her. "Go ahead," she said fiercely, "mock me. All I have to do is order you to hop on one foot for the rest of the day. You know you'll have to do it." Her eyes narrowed. "Or perhaps you'd like to wear a dress?"

He'd given his word to obey her, sealed in blood. Even now, the mark between her breasts tingled.

"And tonight, you'll be mine." Leaning closer, Rathbourne reached out and brushed the backs of his knuckles against the smooth skin of her décolletage, branding her with the touch, his lips thinning with anger. "Imagine how I'll seek my revenge."

Ianthe could imagine it. All too well. Wickedness had been her downfall once, and it proved to be her weakness now, for she felt that tremor of sensation all the way through her.

And so did he, judging by the heated look in his eyes.

Suddenly, it wasn't anger that marked the air between them.

"Be careful what you ask for." Ianthe reached up on her toes to whisper the words into his ear, her hands hesitantly pressing against the roughened fold of his coat collar. "Revenge can be the sweetest thing. If you think I won't surrender to you, you're wrong. If you think that I can't twist you around my little finger whilst submitting to your desires... then think again. I'll brand myself on your skin, Rathbourne. I'll make you forget every other woman you've ever been with." This, the enticing words, were something she had learned over the years as Sabine. To warp the taste of a man's desire until he was panting at her feet, breathless for the want of her. "And when this is over," she drew back, glancing up beneath her lashes at him, "when we break this bond... You'll beg me to take you back."

Hard fingers manacled her wrists. Rathbourne lowered his face to hers, his breath caressing her sensitive lips. Interest flared in his eyes. "Are you challenging me?"

The sensation of her perceived helplessness ignited her body. All she had to do was tell him to stop. She knew it. So did he. "What kind of challenge?"

"The kind that will show you who your master is." Lips slid along the curve of her jaw, teeth nipping at the heated flesh of her earlobe. "Who can bring the other to beg the soonest?"

A thrill lit through her. "I thought you wanted to bed me."

"Oh, I'm going to bed you, Ianthe. I'm going to fuck you as hard and as often as I can, but I'm not going to kiss you. Not unless you ask me, until you're on your knees begging for it."

"Do you hold the quality of your kisses so highly?" Nervousness trembled in her voice, along with desire. The way he said '*fuck*' made her whole body jerk. She'd never been spoken to like that before in her life... and some dark part of her liked it.

Another slow heated smile. Rathbourne pushed away from her, letting go of her wrists. "A kiss is the measure of a person's soul. If you think them overrated, then you haven't been kissed, Miss Martin. Not well enough. That is how we shall know who's won. By whoever succumbs first."

Wisdom insisted she say no, but her eyes narrowed and she lowered her arms, feeling the sensation of his hands still manacling her own. "I think you'll kiss me first, so I shall accept your challenge, my lord. If anything, it should make this agreement of ours somewhat more intriguing." That earned a rise out of him, but she held up a hand. "Come. As fascinating as this is, we're late. Cross will have my head."

"Cross?" he arched a brow.

"My other savage, bad-tempered master," she replied.

He didn't like that at all, she noticed, as she swished toward the auditorium, putting an extra little swing to her hips.

The hollow, echoing silence of the auditorium was clear relief against the tumult of the streets. Lucien followed on the heels of Miss I-Shall-Make-You-Beg, knowing that he pressed too close to her.

The challenge in the entry had been a revelation. His gaze slid to the nape of her neck. Miss Martin had a seductive side that was well-nigh irresistible, though from the forced serenity of her expression one could barely tell.

Tonight... Tonight he would get to reveal that side of her again, even though she'd seemingly buttoned it all away. As she said, revenge could be incredibly sweet, and he was looking forward to it.

A sharp crack filled the air, an explosion of smoke and sparks onstage. Luc didn't think. Simply threw himself into Miss Martin, carrying her to the floor beneath him. The Shield hummed to life around him, the copper band around his wrist tingling icy cold as power flowed through it. It was one of the first workings he'd ever done, and relief flooded him as he realized the shielding bracelet still worked.

"Rathbourne!" she cried.

Ears buzzing with the heavy echo of silence, he looked up. A man had appeared out of the smoke, clad in shirtsleeves and a black silk waistcoat. A blood-red scarf was tied at his throat, and his pinstriped trousers were neatly pleated and immaculate.

"He likes to make an entrance," Miss Martin murmured, wriggling beneath him. Lucien realized he was crushing her a little.

"As do others," the man onstage called out, his voice ringing through the theatre. "Are you done mauling my assistant?"

Rolling to his feet, Lucien held out his hand to her. "I haven't yet started."

Miss Martin blushed at the innuendo. "Remy, meet Lucien Devereaux, the Earl of Rathbourne. Rathbourne, this is Remington Cross, The Great Conjurer."

"Delighted," Cross said flatly.

Lucien recognized the man from the posters now, though the picture there tended toward flattering, rather than realistic. In truth, the man's piercing dark eyes and aquiline nose were more hawkish than handsome. Though one couldn't doubt the overwhelming nature of his presence. Luc was dealing with a Master of Sorcery, if he wasn't mistaken, though he'd never encountered Cross among the Order's gatherings, and there were no rings on his fingers to indicate Cross's rank. "Likewise."

"And I'm retired, Remy." The words held some hint of fondness in them, as Miss Martin used his hand to gain her feet. "Remember? It's been three months. And Rathbourne wasn't mauling me, he was..."

"I thought it was an attack." Lucien scowled.

"How much?" Cross demanded, taking the stage in sharp strides and thundering down the stairs to meet her.

"How much what?" she replied.

"How much will it cost to get you back?"

"Annabelle does just as well onstage as I. You should be thankful that someone else is willing to put up with you."

"Aye." The man took her fingers, pressing a kiss to the back of them, as if Luc didn't exist. "But she lacks your presence."

"She lacks my rather impressive bosom," Miss Martin shot back. "You know my reasons. They haven't changed."

Something silent crossed between the pair of them. "Bah," Cross sneered. "Respectability is little more than a sham."

"Not to me, it's not. Besides, I'm busy," Miss Martin added. "I have my studies to attend to, before I take the next level tests, let alone my duties as Drake's seneschal." As if the matter were dealt with, she buffed her lips against

Cross's smooth cheek, and gave him a wry smile. "I miss you too, Remy."

"Is that why you're here?"

"I wish it were," Miss Martin replied, and she meant it, which was somewhat baffling, for Lucien couldn't find many redeeming traits in the man.

"How's that pup, de Wynter?"

"As well as can be," Miss Martin answered obliquely.

"Trouble?"

"Brewing, but not here yet." Taking Cross's hand, she tucked her own through his arm. "I need to speak to you privately. Are you coming, Rathbourne? Or would you like to guard the theatre?"

"Wouldn't miss it," he replied, and followed the pair of them into the darkened bowels of backstage to Cross's private rooms.

"Well?" Cross asked, pouring them all a finger of whiskey once they arrived. "What brings you to my door?"

"Bad tidings, unfortunately," Miss Martin said, tossing her pretty hat on a chair and turning serious as she accepted the glass he offered.

"Whiskey?" Cross challenged, and Lucien accepted the glass, sniffing at the amber liquid as he surveyed the room with all its various accouterments.

There was a sarcophagus shaped item in the corner, painted to resemble an artifact from ancient Egypt. Lucien crossed toward it, the gaslight lengthening his shadow so it loomed over the wall. A pile of artifact lay dusty on the shelves—a small mini portrait of a man in Tudor fashions, a set of gemstones, and a coiled snake that almost seemed to watch him—

"Don't touch it."

Lucien froze, violence notching each muscle in his outstretched arm as he met Cross's stare. Something about the man rubbed him the wrong way.

"Don't touch anything," Cross added, pouring himself another dram, his fingers wrapped around the neck of the bottle. "You never know what might bite you."

Lucien looked at the lifeless statue of a cobra, which he'd been about to touch. Oriental scrawling's tattooed its skin in black ink. Or what he hoped was ink. As he stared at it, he almost felt like it moved, the jewel in the center of its forehead shimmering.

"There's sorcery here," he said, tucking his hands into his trouser pockets, as if of his own accord. "Though it's foreign to me."

"It's Hindu magic. That of the Nagi," Cross explained, sounding as if he was settling in for a lecture. "Used to protect against the rakshasa."

"Indian demon spirits."

"In a simplistic version, yes." Cross set the glass to his lips, his eyes glittering. "I consider myself somewhat of a collector of relics and artifacts."

"Which is precisely why I came to you," Ianthe cut in, before he could elaborate. "I need to know, if a particular relic went missing, who might have taken it? Or commissioned the theft? You belong to the Dark discipline. You should know."

"I haven't been a part of that Order mess for years," Cross snorted, though his interest looked piqued. "Which relic?"

She stayed silent.

Cross scowled. "It would highly depend on the relic, but if it's something that tends toward the darker studies, I'd say Magnus Cochrane, Lord Tremayne, Lady Hester Lambert, and the not-so-Honorable Mr. Elijah Horroway.

If you're simply after information, I'd direct you to talk to Lady Eberhardt first, however. Tickle the tiger's chin before you stick your neck in a snake pit. She has an unsurpassed collection, apparently, and might know who to deal with, though if it's on the black market, Cochrane's your next best bet."

Lady Eberhardt. Even Lucien arched a brow. Tickling the tiger's chin was putting it mildly. There were a few people in the order whom he wouldn't cross, and Eberhardt's name was on that list. But still... "I thought Horroway was dead."

"Some say he is. He studies the Gravest of Arts, does he not?"

A pun, the likes of which apprentices uttered. There were three disciplines within the Order; Light, Dark, and Grey. The Light discipline was primarily inhabited by healers, astronomers, and diviners. Lucien's natural affinity was for the Light, thanks to his divining talents, whilst the Grey was Ianthe's discipline, as indicated by the chip of hematite in her rings. It also held the most practitioners of any category, considering the broad spectrum of their talents. Being of the Dark did not automatically mean that one was inclined to mischief, but Luc privately thought most of the Dark adepts pushed the boundaries of that. The Dark was where you found those who sought power beyond their own, and they were often the strongest sorcerers, though not always. The darkest of all arts was necromancy, and the Prime had been forced to set certain policies in place regarding the use of Grave Magic.

Necromancers were rarely stable, at best, nor did they own the purest of motives, and Elijah Horroway was the strongest necromancer around.

"I thought it was impossible to defeat Death," Lucien said.

"Some still try." An indecipherable look penetrated Cross's gaze. "It is an inescapable truth, that where a man is tempted by power and mysteries, he will always try to halt Death."

"And it never works out well," Miss Martin muttered. "One is not intended to live forever."

Both she and Cross exchanged a look.

"No. It doesn't." Cross tipped his head to her. "So a relic has gone missing, and Drake has sent his right hand scurrying after it. Which one is it? The Circlet of the Dawn Star? The Pentacle of Merlin? The Blade of Altarrh—" Some expression must have given her away. "That's it. That's the one, isn't it?"

"Remy," Miss Martin warned.

Ignoring them as they bickered, Lucien glanced at the miniature portrait again. There was something familiar about it. Nothing tingled when he reached toward it, and frowning, he blew the dust from it.

He was right.

Remington Cross looked back at him, but Luc's psychometric abilities were tingling, plunging him back through images of wet paint and an Italian estate, fat grapes, a painter dressed in renaissance dress as he licked the brush, a pretty blonde woman opening a present and finding the miniature, then blood, darkness, jealousy, and death... Lucien gasped and nearly dropped it. This portrait was over three hundred years old, and Cross didn't look a day older. How—? He looked up sharply, only to find Cross staring at him.

"Nothing good ever comes of it," Cross repeated softly, before turning to Miss Martin. "If you need me, you know where to find me."

"I thought you didn't like meddling in Order affairs."

"Not since the 18th century, at least," Cross's eyelids drooped, "but I would make an exception this one time, just for you. I can feel a vortex of power moving out there, somewhere in London, sucking in mass amounts of energy. It's flares at odd increments of time before vanishing, but it's been there for a week. I've never felt anything like it."

Colors danced over Miss Martin's skin; uneasiness, fear, and something else that he couldn't quite put a finger on. A yellowish-gray color. "Drake knows nothing of this."

"Drake doesn't have my depth of experience," Cross replied, then caught Lucien's gaze, holding it there through sheer force of will. "Nor does he have my scrying abilities. There is a knot of shadows woven around the pair of you, and it has something to do with the Blade and this mysterious vortex of power. Swear to me that you'll keep her safe."

That was the second time someone had asked this of him. "I swear."

"Good." Cross relaxed somewhat, then frowned. "Something dark is stirring in London, and I don't know if either of you are going to come out of this alive, but I do know this—you need each other if you have any hope of surviving."

CHAPTER FOUR

GOLDEN LIGHT suffused the air around the mansion as Lucien stepped down from the carriage, hinting at a glorious sunset within an hour. He turned and offered his hand to Miss Martin, her skirts swishing around her ankles as she stepped onto the curb and looked up at Lady Eberhardt's home. The black wrought iron fence encircled the property like a warning, and the gardens were lush and overgrown, with faint chittering sounds whispering from within its bushes, as if something lay in wait.

"Charming," Luc drawled. "It has the welcoming ambiance of an ambush."

Miss Martin's voice was hushed. "I would be careful with your words here. Lady Eberhardt is somewhat... eccentric. And powerful. We don't wish to offend her."

Lucien pushed the gate open, its hinges squealing. The chittering in the bushes stopped. *Not at all eerie,* he thought, with a shudder. "I thought the correct term was 'mad as hatters'?"

"Yes, well. They said that about you too, my lord." Miss Martin swept past him, slanting a sideways look up at him from beneath the brim of her jaunty lavender hat. Its black ostrich feather trailed behind her, like a war banner. Everywhere she went, she strode briskly, as if to make her presence known to the world.

Luc followed, allowing himself a tight smile. "And do you find their assumptions correct?"

"I think... that there's a little bit of madness in all of those who choose this path."

"That's not an answer."

"It's the only one you're going to get, just now."

Miss Martin rang the buzzer at the door, and an enormous *ding-dong* sounded from within, its echo vibrating. Their eyes met.

"I've had little to do with Lady Eberhardt over the years, though I know of her reputation," he said. "She's buried three husbands, all in suspicious circumstances."

A frown furrowed Miss Martin's brow. "The first two I'll grant you, but what was suspicious about the third? I believe it was a fall, was it not? He broke his neck."

"He fell off the chamber pot at a brothel."

Those eyebrows rose. "I hadn't heard that part of the story."

"Innocent ears, and all."

Miss Martin snorted.

The door swung open. A somewhat cadaverous butler appeared. "This way, my lord. Ma'am. Lady Eberhardt is expecting you."

Which was somewhat disconcerting. At the lilt of Ianthe's brow, Lucien gestured her forward. "Ladies first."

The door slammed shut behind them with little evidence of the means, making both of them jump. A lion's head leered off the wall, a tiger stuffed beside it. The entire hallway was a display of some hunter's prowess, and Lucien had the eerie suspicion that some of those glass eyes were staring back at him.

He'd been in creepier places—Bedlam sprang to mind—but there was something about the detonating silence here that made him feel watched.

Voices murmured from behind the sitting room the butler led them to, but when he opened the door with a flourish, there was no one inside.

"If you'll wait here," the butler murmured, "her ladyship should be with you momentarily."

A dozen candles sat on a mirror on the small table, their wicks still smoking, as though they'd been blown out but an instant before the doors had opened. A Wedgewood tea set sat beside them, smoky shadows filling the teacup, shifting as though in a slight breeze. Lucien peered into them, catching a glimpse of something... Lady Eberhardt was an acclaimed mistress of the Divination Arts, but he'd never seen the like before. He leaned closer, making out small images. The dark smoke seemed to suck at him, drawing him in, until he fell into Vision.

An older woman he didn't know was lying back on red silk sheets with her raven hair spilling across the pillow as she curled an adder to her breast and laughed up at him. *"Three sons,"* she whispered. *"Three brothers. Three sacrifices."* Her smile turned vicious and triumphant. *"One relic in hand and one to come. And one that is lost. Where is it?"* Those slanted green eyes became distant, as if she stared into nothing. *"There,"* she breathed. *"There it is. Right behind you."*

Lucien glanced over his shoulder into the room, and the woman vanished, leaving nothing more than her laughter echoing in his ears.

"I'm coming for it."

The vision twisted, leaving him watching from above as a man strolled out of an alley, swinging an ivory-handled cane. The Prime's face stared back at him, only he was younger, devastatingly handsome, and his eyes were as dead as liquid mercury. For a moment, those silver eyes turned as if peering up from the depths of the cup and seeing him looking back. Chains bound his wrists, though they were made of shadows, and the Prime didn't seem to be able to see them. Then something tore the center of that handsome face apart and a demon crawled out from within, discarding the fleshy husk like a piece of abandoned clothing. A demon he knew.

"*Hello there, Master,*" it hissed, and Lucien cried out, though he couldn't move all of a sudden. Couldn't escape. Cold speared out through his body, but he was locked in stasis, that awful whisper branding itself on the inside of his mind in burning letters.

"Lucien?" someone called, and he felt a tug at his arm.

"*Revenge is a dish bessst served cold...*"

Then flames were roaring over his skin, burning away at him from the inside, burning him to nothingness. He screamed—

A hand dashed between him and the teacup, shattering the vision.

Lucien staggered back, and Miss Martin's hands directed him onto the nearest daybed. He collapsed there, panting, slapping at his clothes from where they still smoked. *Bloody hell.* The demon was still out there, somewhere. Somehow. Perhaps he hadn't banished it after all? Agony lanced through his head at the thought, and he pressed his palm into his forehead, trying to stop it from splitting his head open. He felt like there was something within him, trying to tear him open from the inside, like the demon had done to the Prime in his vision.

"*Mercurah abadi di absolom*," Miss Martin murmured in a hollow voice that rang with power, growing louder with each word, as she traced glowing sigils in the air around him with her finger. They shone brightly, then sank into his flesh, like menthol brands, both hot and cold. *"Mercurah abadi hessalah di abscrolutious."*

"You are not welcome here, creature of darkness," someone else intoned. "Begone, begone. Take thy foul self and leave this place."

Someone blew a candle flame out with a clap, and the pain and pressure in his head abruptly disappeared, leaving him shaking and sweating.

The world began to leech back into him. There was a warm weight on his lap, one that smelled like lilacs and rustled as she moved. Miss Martin. Her arms curled around him, drawing his face against her shoulder, and she stroked her fingers through his hair. "Shh. It's all right. It cannot touch you here. You're safe. It's gone."

Luc shuddered, clinging to her as he fought his way back to sanity.

"You should know better than to look into another's living dreams, boy," said an older woman, not unkindly. "What did you see?"

He couldn't stop shaking as Miss Martin drew back. Was this the vortex that Cross had mentioned? "*Bloody hell.*" A hand through his sweaty hair did little more than dislodge its style.

"Rathbourne." Another small hand took his and laced its fingers through his own. The hematite and emeralds on Miss Martin's fingers winked up at him. "It cannot get to you here."

"What was that?" he asked hoarsely.

"Shadows of Night," the other woman murmured, pouring the smoky not-quite-liquid back into the teapot where he couldn't see it. She owned a mannish, husky voice. A voice quite used to command. "Impenetrable, unless one has a gift for Divination, and you, my boy... have quite a gift."

Taking him by the jaw, Lady Eberhardt tilted his face up to examine it through eyes as black as pitch. "Ah," she murmured. "Now the wheels are turning. No wonder Drake sent you here to me."

Hers was an arresting face, strangely ageless. Broad cheekbones hinted at an exotic beauty once upon a time, and the straight patrician nose hearkened back to Roman days. She would never have been a pretty woman, but he could see men stopping in their tracks as she walked by, not quite able to take their eyes from her. Knowing that here walked a woman of power, someone who owned every inch of herself, and probably them too.

"Tell me what you saw," she commanded again. Black crinoline whispered about Lady Eberhardt's legs as she walked to the opposite chair and settled into it. Her feet were bare, long toes sinking into the carpets, which was shocking. Her large, angular eyes seemed to hint at secrets. If not for the curtain spill of silvery hair around her face, he would have been quite unable to pick her age.

Lucien ground the heel of his palm against his forehead. It was aching again, but he tried to work through the multitude of images in his head and translate them into sound.

After he'd finished, Lady Eberhardt simply stared at him, chewing on one of the figs that sat on a plate on the table. "Interesting," she murmured, looking inward. "Describe the woman."

"I think the greater concern would be the demon, would it not?" he replied.

"Describe the woman," she said again.

Miss Martin gave him a nudge.

"She was possibly the most beautiful woman I've ever seen, though there was no blush of youth upon her. Dark hair, with a few strands of grey that looked like they'd been dyed, and green eyes." He thought about it. "She looked mysterious, as though she knew secrets that I didn't—as though she enjoyed knowing such secrets. And I'm fairly certain there was a tattoo on her inner wrist. A snake, perhaps. Or Ouroboros. She said she was coming for the last relic."

Lady Eberhardt paled. "That's not possible."

"You recognize her?" Miss Martin asked.

Lady Eberhardt found her feet, swishing to the cold fireplace and staring into the coals. "Maxwell!"

The butler appeared at the door, as if by magic. "Milady?"

"Send word to Bishop. Tell him I want him here immediately."

A slight arch of the brow, and then the butler disappeared again.

Lady Eberhardt rubbed her hands together. "Three sons," she muttered. "Three relics. Bloody hell. Now this."

Miss Martin rose and went to her. "You're not making any sense. Who is this woman?"

Lady Eberhardt's mouth thinned. "Morgana de Wynter, by the sounds of it, though I'd not thought to see her on this side of the Channel again, after the scandal of the divorce."

A tiny itch of distress lanced through the bond between them, and Lucien looked up sharply. Miss Martin had paled. "The Prime's ex-wife," he said.

"Yes," Lady Eberhardt replied grimly. "That bitch is back."

Ianthe knew the story, of course, though only from hearsay. Drake never spoke of his ex-wife, or the scandal of the divorce.

Only once had he breathed word of Morgana: *"Her Arts were that of Illusion, and what is illusion but deception? What I did not understand when I married her was that her very nature was that of illusion too. She gave you exactly what you wanted to see, and underneath lurked the deception. Underneath..."* His face had grown somewhat sad then. *"Underneath was a stranger who you didn't even know."*

"It all started nearly thirty-five years ago," Lady Eberhardt said. "A young girl had come to the Order a couple of years earlier, begging for sanctuary. She would not reveal her name, only that she knew sorcery and that she wished to be called Morgana, after Morgan le Fay." A faint arch of the brow dictated her thoughts on that. "That should have been the first warning sign.

"After her years of apprenticeship, she met Drake at one of the Equinox balls. The pair had something in common, an interest in those that we call demons and the dimensions, or planes of existence, from which they came. Morgana was a great flirt, toying with the emotions of those around her, including Drake and his then-friend Tremayne. One moment, it seemed certain that she would accept Drake's suit, the next she'd be gadding about with Tremayne." Lady Eberhardt snorted. "I never trusted the little bitch, but Drake won her over. The competition between he and Tremayne hadn't ended, however, and both were determined to be the first to safely control a Greater Demon. The Relics Infernal were created, and it was only then that Drake began to realize how dangerous such a creation could be.

"This was the first step in the downfall of his marriage. Morgana helped him steal the relics from Tremayne, but the cost of the events had taken its toll. Morgana was now married to the Prime of the Order, a worthy position in her eyes, and certainly one in which she used every opportunity to lord it over the rest of us mere adepts. But Drake was beginning to assert his authority and could not be so easily swayed by his wife. Morgana began to grow flirtatious again, seeking to control her young husband through jealousy." Lady Eberhardt rolled her eyes. "It was a constant battle of wills between them, often ending in the bedchamber, but over time... Drake grew tired of the battle. He threw himself into a new direction for the Order, offering to serve the young Queen and her cabinet. Anything to allay the common people's fears toward sorcery, especially after Sir Davis's reign of secrecy. It was a worthy cause, but Morgana was furious at his lack of attention. There was no heir conceived between them, and her husband was spending more and more time away from her. Even rumors that she'd taken a lover could not bring her husband back to her. Another young lady had caught his eye. One who shared his ideas and helped to guide his vision with her talents of Divination. One who rarely fought with him, a true meeting of minds. The only unfortunate fact was that she was already married."

A prickling silence entered the room. Lucien lifted his head, those golden eyes blazing. "My mother."

"Your mother," Lady Eberhardt said, with some satisfaction. "I liked Lady Rathbourne. She told me once that she'd always known she would meet the man she would fall in love with, when it was too late. That's the problem with being able to see hints of your future, but not enough of it. Lord Rathbourne, of course, did not appreciate the fact that his wife was swelling with another man's bastard. Drake was forced to give your mother up, but Lady Rathbourne's pregnancy infuriated Morgana. She wanted her power back, her control."

"And so she schemed to poison Drake's nephew," Ianthe whispered, knowing the story well. She couldn't even fathom how a woman could do that to a child.

"Unfortunately, yes," Lady Eberhardt replied. "I think Morgana realized that a child could be her route to power. She began working on potions to bring life to her barren womb, but the problem was, her husband had no interest in her bed, following the death of his nephew, Richard. Drake was... shattered. I watched that little bitch worm her way back into his good graces, all sympathy and consolation, and then barely three weeks later, Morgana starts crowing about her pregnancy. That was when I began to grow suspicious. Who had the most to gain from Richard's death? She did. Who knew the Darker Arts? Who knew poisons? Morgana. The trail slowly began to lead back to her, and the woman was arrested. The first thing she did was tell Drake that he'd never see his child alive, if he tried to press through this divorce or her verdict. Drake was furious, of course, and presented his case to the Order. They ruled in his favor, and the Queen granted him his divorce in parliament." Lady Eberhardt's eyes grew sad. "None of us truly thought she'd go through with her threats. The next day, her guards were found murdered. Morgana had vanished, and a week later, the body of Drake's unborn son arrived in a box. Drake swore then, that if Morgana ever returned to these shores, she would be arrested and executed immediately by the Order for treason. The order is still signed."

The room fell silent.

"How on earth do you know all of this?" Rathbourne demanded.

Lady Eberhardt sipped her tea, looking amused. "Before I married my last husband, I served as one of the three councilors for the Order. I signed that execution warrant, my boy, and I'm privy to an entire host of secrets that nobody else knows."

"So if Morgana is back on this side of the Channel, then she's here for a reason," Ianthe murmured.

Rathbourne stroked his chin, his eyes hard and flat. "I wonder what that reason is?"

A little chill started, somewhere in the middle of Ianthe's chest.

A chill that said: *Louisa.*

A chill that remembered the man who'd quite rudely bumped into her in the street but two weeks ago and slipped her a piece of the little girl's black hair, and said, "We want you to bring us the Blade of Altarrh. Otherwise, you will never see your child again."

Ianthe had raced home to gather herself before she told Drake, when she'd found a note in her *room.*

'Tell anyone, and she dies. We have eyes watching you and the Prime to ensure you behave. Trust no one. Expect anyone. You will receive further instructions, when you have stolen the relic. We will contact you. We will know.'

Ianthe fingered the locket at her throat, where her one portrait of the girl resided. She was barely a mother—she could never claim that—but they had struck her where she was most vulnerable, and now she was playing a dangerous game of trying to keep a half dozen cups in the air. She had to wait until her blackmailers contacted her before she could give them the relic, but in the meantime, Drake had saddled her with Lucien as a partner.

"Morgana," she said, in a somewhat hoarse voice. She'd never recognized the man in the street and had wondered who this shadowy organization was who had stolen her daughter and murdered poor Jacob and Elsa, Louisa's adoptive parents.

Could Drake's ex-wife have anything to do with this?

If so, then what was Ianthe going to do? There was no one to help her. No one. Not even Drake. She couldn't trust any of the sorcerers around her, for if the note was true, and there was someone close to Drake who was watching her, then she might do something inadvertent and reveal her hand. Then they'd kill her daughter. The only one...

Her thoughts stalled as Ianthe looked up in horror at the hard edges of Rathbourne's face. The only sorcerer she knew who couldn't possibly be involved was Rathbourne.

Could she trust him? He'd said himself that he wanted revenge against both Ianthe and the Prime. Would the safety of an unknown child matter to him? *His* child?

The truth was that Ianthe didn't know. She didn't know Rathbourne well enough to trust that he would help her win her daughter back over the possibility of taking revenge on his own father.

Wait, a little part of her whispered. *Wait a few more days and see what kind of man he is...*

But what if they wanted the relic before then?

"Are you all right?"

Ianthe blinked and realized that those hawkish amber eyes were watching her as if he'd picked up on her emotional distress. She froze, the pretty locket trapped in her fingers as she stared back at him. "Yes. Yes, I... I'm just surprised to learn that she's back. What if Morgana set this in place? What if she gets her hands on the Blade?" Her voice became particularly strident toward the end, and Rathbourne's brow arched as if he noticed.

What if I have to give her the Blade in order to get my daughter back?

"One relic in hand," Lady Eberhardt mused. "Did the vision mean that she already has one in hand and the Blade would make two? Or that the Blade is in her hand and she needs to find the other two?"

"I don't think she would have the Blade yet," Ianthe replied quickly. "It's barely been twelve hours. Whoever stole it would have to lie low for a while, and there was no sign of anyone leaving the estate in a hurry."

"So we might presume she has one in hand, with the Blade soon to join it," Rathbourne murmured. "Which means that whoever holds the final Relic Infernal is in danger."

Lady Eberhardt met his stare. "Perhaps."

A second later, a ripple of chimes flooded through the house, growing more intense in noise and stridency. Lady Eberhardt's head cocked, her face paling.

"What was that?" Ianthe asked.

"Is that a tripped ward?" Rathbourne added.

"Yes," Lady Eberhardt erupted out of the chair, twitching aside the curtains at the window. "Someone is on the property. Or some*thing*. Either it is sorcerous in nature, or created of sorcery, and it doesn't intend to knock."

Ianthe rose. Her heart started to beat a little faster in response to the wary flash of the whites of Lady Eberhardt's eyes. Lady Eberhardt was eccentric, but fiercely invulnerable. She'd hunted a demon singlehandedly over the course of a year, or so it was told, so why would she be frightened now? "But why would they attack us?"

"Because," Lady Eberhardt met her gaze, "*I* am the protector of the third relic—I am the guardian of the Chalice."

CHAPTER FIVE

'Sorcerous constructs are creatures of power with no autonomy, no will of their own, animated by a Word of Power, and their master's will. But beware, for all of them hunger for life, and if they slip your control they will try to drink it from your veins.'

-Sir Justin DeFino, Sorcerer Royal and Master of Constructs

THERE WAS a pregnant pause as that knowledge sank in.

"Bloody hell," Lucien swore. *What a rotten coincidence. And dreadful timing.* He strode toward the window to see what had tripped the wards. "Where is the Chalice now?"

There was nothing outside, just the faint drift of fog through the gorgeous rose gardens out back. Tendrils of it crept this way and that toward the house, as if slowly hunting for something.

"Hidden—" Lady Eberhardt turned and rang the bell pull "—and protected."

"Your house is well warded, I presume." Miss Martin tried for reason.

"As was Drake's."

"Do these still work?" Lucien demanded, striding to the cabinet where Lady Eberhardt's hunting pistols remained.

Both women shot him a surprised look, then Lady Eberhardt nodded. Lucien armed himself, priming a pair of pistols and slinging a couple of rounds into his pocket.

By that time, both women were halfway through the door. Lucien cursed under his breath, then hurried after them.

"Allow me to go first," he said, catching Miss Martin by the wrist. "I'm the one with the shield bracelet."

Those blue eyes widened; then she gestured him into the lead. Her skirts swished behind him as they took the stairs. Lady Eberhardt strode ahead, drawing a blade across her widened palm. Blood welled in a neat gash, and she curled her fingers into a fist and then flung them wide, spraying droplets all across the entrance. Blood spattered on the glass in the door and the gleaming marble tiles, and the second each droplet hit, Lucien could feel a prickling along his nerves.

"Arise!"

The door rattled in its casement, as did the windows, as if the house slowly awoke to Lady Eberhardt's cry. Long dormant protection spells sprang to life, shimmering in brilliant gossamer spell veils along each window and doorway that he could see. Lady Eberhardt must have spent months weaving them into the surface of the house. He could barely see for the cascade shimmer of spell craft, a piercing ache echoing in his left temple.

Would this ever end? He couldn't deal with this weakness of his right now, not with so much sorcery spilling through the air.

Dragging a bloodied hand over the marble lions in the foyer, Lady Eberhardt strode on. The first lion tore its head free from its marble paws, its eyes gleaming with golden light. Chips of shattered marble scattered over the floor as it shook out its mane and gave an enormous roar. Its twin, standing in silent entreaty across from it, stretched, shaking free of its casement. They bounded after Lady Eberhardt, their heavy paws leaving cracks in the tiles behind them.

Sorcerous constructs were creatures of power with no autonomy, indeed no mind, no will of their own. He'd heard rumors of golems created out of clay by rabbis, with a Word of Power carved into their foreheads to animate them, and these were somewhat similar.

Constructs could be formed of anything—leaf and mud, metals, stones, shadows, sometimes even blood and flesh, if the sorcerer in command belonged to the Grave Arts. Those were the hardest to control, for the flesh still remembered what life was and craved the taste of it. Nine years ago, Sir Alastor Walton brought over a dozen zombie constructs to life, and when he lost control of them, they'd torn half of the East End to pieces. It took forty sorcerers to destroy the zombies since the cut off pieces kept trying to reform, and eventually they'd had to burn them all. Sir Alastor had been tried by the Order and executed, and the Prime had pledged to the Queen that creating constructs of flesh were now forbidden and that it would never happen again.

Bam. The first assault against the wards shook the entire house. *Bam. Bam.*

The sheer weight of the sorcery nearly drove Lucien to his knees. Slamming up his inner barriers, he clung to the bannister for a moment as dust trickled down from the roof and eerie green light flooded through the windows.

"Are you all right?" Miss Martin demanded, and as his vision returned to normal, he found her clutching his sleeve and staring up at him.

He couldn't let her see his weakness. "I'm fine," he replied gruffly, staggering as something else hit the house and rebounded from the wards. An explosion of actinic light blazed like a corona outside, and he slammed his eyes shut, clapping a hand over them. Sorcery fired through his blood, setting his mind afire, as he cried out.

Mother of night. "What in all the hells is out there? Hell spawn?"

The light touch of Miss Martin's skin against his hand eased the overwhelming sensation as their bond swelled. Lucien caught her fingers as she moved to retreat, and her gaze swept to his as he blinked, her lips parting gently. It felt like they were trapped in a bubble that silenced everything around them. It felt like he could breathe again.

"I'm concerned that I won't be able to protect you very well at this juncture in time," he admitted, though it galled him. "It's too soon since my release. I'm weak from lack of food and the effects of my incarceration. I haven't used sorcery in over a year, or at least, before this morning. It's... overwhelming."

The dark slash of her brows softened. Her fingers curled around his. "Then let me act as your Anchor. You should have said something earlier."

Lucien gave a careless shrug. Surrendering this much control to her went against every grain of his fiber, but the relics were more important. Even he, who wouldn't shed any tears to see the Prime fall, knew that they could be dangerous in the wrong hands.

Cool sorcery slid over his skin like a whisper, beneath his clothes, forming a ward around him. The instant it locked into place, the overwhelming sensation of magic vanished. He could breathe again. See again. Lucien let out a breath of relief. "Thank you."

"You're welcome." They stared at each other for a long, drawn-out second.

The front door crashed open, and Lucien swept in front of her, flinging the blade he kept in his sleeve, before he could blink.

A stranger flung both arms up in front of his face in a cross, and the blade struck an invisible ward around him with a flare of green that shot through the entire shield, then vanished. The knife clattered noisily to the floor.

"Some kind of welcome," the stranger drawled, lowering his arms. He wore a great coat that smothered him and a beaver hat perched over his brow. Parts of his coat still smoldered, and a conflagration of power crackled over his shoulder as something launched itself up the front steps, and then vanished in a crackle of searing white light.

At Lucien's side, Miss Martin caught Luc's sleeve. "Don't. He's one of ours. Mr. Bishop, how do you do?"

"Any idea why the house is under attack by imps?" Bishop had the sort of smile that no doubt stole hearts by the handful, and a face that looked younger than he probably was, but Lucien didn't mistake the rasp of his voice, as if something had scarred his voice box, or the cold blackness of the man's eyes. Shadows lurked there, whispers of darkness and sins unknown. Combined with the heavy rings on his fingers with their chips of obsidian that stated him a seventh level adept, there was no doubt this Bishop was a dangerous man. The seventh was the highest level one could achieve, below that of the Order's Councilors, or the Prime's ninth level.

"Some idea," Lady Eberhardt's voice echoed through the entry as she returned. Only one of her lions stalked at her heels. "Shut the door and step lively. The wards are about to fall, I believe, and we're going to be inundated with hell spawn. Someone's dragged them straight out of the Shadow Dimensions."

The stranger stepped over the lintel, his heavy boot landing on the floor. It felt momentous, as if the shiver of that landing echoed through the marble in an underground fault line that slithered its way toward Lucien's boots and ended there.

What the hell? Lucien looked down. Nothing had happened, but he couldn't shake the feeling that he'd been here before, seen this moment played out in slow, time-catching movement, again and again—or perhaps, as if he'd been heading toward this moment his entire life.

Even the stranger paused, no doubt aware of it too. "What are you?" A hand slid to his belt, as if Bishop touched a knife there for reassurance.

Their eyes met and the air grew sharp with wariness, danger, and the underlying black current of sorcery as both men gathered themselves.

"What are *you*?" Lucien demanded in return, taking a step forward.

"That's enough, you two. We'll deal with this little mess later. Right now, we have over a dozen imps on hand," Lady Eberhardt commanded, striding forth with the fire poker in her hand. "Your timing is impeccable, as usual, Bishop." She peered out through the side panels of glass by the front door. "They've taken down my first ring of wards." A hand slid over the stone lion's head at her side. "Mounting an assault at the front door, it seems. They must have sensed the crack in the second ring after that last assault."

"Is there anything we can do?" Miss Martin asked.

Lady Eberhardt's smile was dangerous. "Stay out of my way and keep them off my back."

Glass shattered somewhere near the side of the house. "I've got it," Bishop declared, striding toward the noise. As he went, a pair of blue-white daggers formed in his hands, flickers of lightning dancing off them.

Dangerous. Lucien watched him go. He wasn't sure who, or what, the man was, but he knew a predator when he saw one, and he could still see the after-image of the man stepping inside the house, flashing again and again in the back of his mind, as if it had been burned into his retinas.

More glass erupted, this time from the back of the house.

"Go!" Lady Eberhardt told them, and a ball of pure energy began building in front of her, a mage globe of red light.

Definitely time to leave Lady Eberhardt to her own devices. She clearly knew what she was doing.

"Guard my back!" Miss Martin panted as she grabbed Lucien's wrist and hauled him past the stairs and toward the back of the house.

Lucien primed one of the pistols he'd confiscated, feeling incredibly useless. What was he supposed to do? His magic was useless to him in this situation, his legs felt like lead, and an imp would swallow his bullet and spit it straight back at him. "Can you handle this?"

"Watch me." Miss Martin flashed a grin over her shoulder before she pushed a door open and strode into the kitchens, her lavender skirts swishing around her legs.

An imp leapt on top of the kitchen table, hissing at them. Its skin gleamed a dull bronze color, and though it wore the coat and trousers of a boy, there was no mistaking those all-black eyes, or the razor-sharp teeth in its face as it leered at the pair of them. A thin tail lashed out behind it, back and forth, like a cat anticipating its prey.

A Lesser Demon, it could still wield an enormous amount of power from the Shadow Dimensions it came from. Lucien aimed his pistol directly at the creature's forehead and fired.

The imp hissed as the bullet slammed into its skull, a black hole glaring back at them like a third eye. Then the hole began to mend itself, vanishing into smooth, unblemished skin.

"What part of 'guard my back' did you not understand?" Miss Martin took a stance in the middle of the room, flinging her arms out to the sides and muttering power words under her breath.

The room turned cold, and the imp hissed as a mage globe the size of Lucien's fist sizzled to life in front of her. It gleamed like blue lightning. Dangerous, but not bloodthirsty, the way Eberhardt's mage globe had been.

Lightning lashed off the globe, spearing toward the imp. It sprung, claws clinging to the hanging pot rack above it, then twisted as another spear of lightning arced toward it, and leaped toward the sink. As it went, it threw a variety of utensils at Miss Martin. Lucien grabbed a frying pan, using it to bat away the knives and pots that the creature flung. He was less than useless, but at least he could do this. Miss Martin needed to concentrate.

"Where did you learn... that?" he gasped, as more lightning sizzled, leaving smoking welts on the scarred timber benches. Most battle globes were simply balls of energy to be flung at one's opponent. Her grasp of telekinesis was impressive.

"Drake." Her eyes gleamed with power. "My affinity is with telekinesis, as opposed to telepathy."

Where his own strengths lay. He had learned how to manipulate telekinesis, but telepathy was his first natural calling and his strength.

The imp cast cunning eyes their way, then grabbed an enormous cast-iron pan. Instead of throwing it at them, it launched the pan like a discus toward the mage globe. Electricity sparked and crackled, staggering them both backward, as the mage globe collapsed in upon itself at the touch of metal.

"Miss Martin!"

"I'm fine." She blinked at the magical backlash, then shoved him out of the way, "Watch out!"

Claws *thunked* on the wheeled kitchen trolley and it hurtled toward them from the force of the creature's momentum. The imp launched itself into the air, leaping over Miss Martin as the trolley took her legs out from under her.

"Ianthe—"

Miss Martin went down. The imp sprang off the wall, aiming for her back.

Lucien didn't think. Just reacted. An enormous battle globe of flickering red flung toward the creature from his hand. The plaster cracked as the imp exploded into nothingness, and Lucien staggered as power leeched out of him and he realized what he'd done. Every piece of glass blew out of the windows, and pots and pans and knives *thunked* into the wall or onto the floor. Coppery ectoplasm was smeared across the plaster.

The world swayed, and he was leaning heavily against the bench. Lucien blinked. His entire head felt stuffed full of molten lava, and his nose was numb. Ears ringing. The world... too bright. Too loud. Miss Martin's gloved ward that had blocked out his sensitivities seemed to have faded.

"Get down! There's another one!" Skirts fluttered, and then a warm body collided hard with his. He went down in a spill of violet silk, just as an imp sailed past where he'd been. It skittered on the tiles, its claws slicing into the floor and peeling up curls of terracotta tile as it slid to a halt.

It launched itself at them. Lucien tried to roll Miss Martin out of the way, and—

An enormous stone lion leapt out of nowhere, its teeth crunching over the imp's head and shattering it. Shaking its head, the lion sprayed droplets of molten, coppery liquid up the walls and on the roof. Ectoplasm sizzled against Miss Martin's flickering wards, sliding down the transparent dome that protected them and forming small puddles on the floor.

"That was close," she gasped beneath him.

Lucien looked down. There was a blind spot in the vision of his right eye and a sharp aching numbness behind it. He wiped at his nose, and his hand came away bloody.

"Are you all right?" Miss Martin asked, reaching up to touch his cheek. Fingertips grazed the stubble there. Her ward slid over his skin again, blocking out the worst of the pain.

"I'm fine," he replied crisply, levering himself up onto his knees as the world stopped spinning. He could see again too, no more double impressions of everything. *Christ.*

"Rathbourne... You used Expression."

It had been a desperate surge of power he'd flung at the imp, rather than the carefully formed ritualistic sorcery they were taught to practice. Expression was tied to emotion, and hence, dangerous. But which emotion had overwhelmed him, stripping away all of his years of study and ritual?

He saw it again. Miss Martin knocked off her feet, the imp bouncing off the walls toward her, its claws extended, his heart in his throat—

Lucien shook his head, forcing it to subside. He'd sworn to protect her. That was all, but the very violence of his thoughts at the time shook him a little. He didn't like the idea of her under attack, but that was something to digest later.

"It won't happen again," he told her. "I need time to recuperate my strength, and meditate."

"Do you think—?"

"Are we done in here?" Lady Eberhardt flung the door open and peered inside, viewing the carnage, and saving him from Miss Martin's questions, thank goodness. "Look at this muck. Poor Maxwell and the maids shall have quite the day of it."

The lion butted its head against her thigh, nearly knocking her over.

"We're done," Lucien replied, offering a hand to Miss Martin to help her up. The look she returned him said she hadn't quite finished with what she was saying and that they'd revisit the conversation later.

Over his dead body, perhaps. The last thing he wanted to confess to her was his fear that he'd never wield sorcery properly again. Or perhaps explain that something about that image, about her under attack, had driven him to regress back to his youth, when Expression was all he knew.

Reaching out, Lady Eberhardt grasped the hilt of a knife and tugged it from the wall. "Good. Perhaps we ought to convene in my library again? Now that the immediate threat is out of the way, I think we all need a spot of tea and some cake and biscuits. I don't know about anyone else, but I'm famished. Nothing like battling beasties from the Shadow Dimensions to give one a good, hearty appetite, no?"

"If you give us a moment to clean up, we'll meet you there," Miss Martin replied.

Lucien however, pushed through the doors with an eagerness to escape that wasn't lost on any of them.

The library looked like the scene of some great safari rampage. One of the marble lions lay in shattered pieces all across the room, its shards embedded in the roof and walls, as if it had exploded, and there were three molten puddles of coppery ectoplasm that betrayed the fate of some of the imps.

"Poor Aurelius," Lady Eberhardt murmured, sweeping marble gravel off the daybed. The other marble lion laid a sad head upon her lap as she sat, as if sensing her grief.

Lucien exchanged a look with Miss Martin, whose face remained impressively smooth.

"That's the last of them accounted for," Bishop said, striding into the library. It was unnerving how silently he moved for such a large man. Lucien watched him like a snake. There was no sign of that sensation he'd felt earlier when the man first stepped into the house, but a certain *knowing* fused his blood, a taste of Foreboding.

This man was dangerous, and whatever Luc was about to learn here, would set them both on a dangerous course.

"Tea, sir?" Maxwell asked.

Lucien nodded, but didn't take his eyes off Bishop as the other man sat directly opposite him. Bishop's hands rested on the arms of his chair, that black chip of obsidian in his prime ring winking at Luc. An adept of the Darker Arts then.

"I feel as though we've met," Bishop said in that scar-rough voice he owned. "Though I'm certain I'd remember you."

"You haven't met." Lady Eberhardt's hands moved briskly as she served them all thick slices of ginger cake with clotted cream. "It was decided that it would be best if you were kept apart until necessary."

"Kept apart?" Lucien asked.

"This is Adrian Bishop, the Prime's bastard son by Mrs. Amelia Bishop, born several years after Drake's divorce," Lady Eberhardt purred, sitting back with her tea and staring him down. "Adrian is one of the Order's *Sicarii*, and was my apprentice once upon a time."

"Agatha," Bishop said sharply, as if betrayed.

Prime's bastard. Lucien froze. The words echoed in his head like ringing steel, a sense of incredulousness raining about him. Lady Eberhardt *had* to be joking. She had to be. For that meant that this man was his younger brother.

Not only a... a brother, but a dangerous one too.

A sickle in the shadows, an assassin. Something Luc had never encountered before, but heard plenty about. There were said to be five of them within the Order, those sorcerers whose calling belonged to the Grave arts, who dealt death to serve their Prime. Few knew their identities.

Bishop's lips thinned. "I presume that was necessary?"

"Oh, indeed." Lady Eberhardt clearly hadn't finished yet and gestured toward Lucien in a way that made him suddenly nervous. "And this, Bishop, is Lucien Devereaux, the Earl of Rathbourne and the Prime's firstborn bastard son." Lady Eberhardt's smile was positively cattish. "Say how do you do to your brother, boys."

Bishop's gaze cut sharply toward him, incredulousness sliding over his features and twisting the scars at his temples.

Scars... It was the only resemblance the pair of them had.

"What do you mean, he's my brother?" the other man demanded.

"Why was it decided that they should not know each other?" Miss Martin added. "Who decided such a thing?"

"The Cassandra at the time, Lucien's mother, laid a foretelling upon his birth. Drake would seed three sons, but never know them until it was too late, nor would they know each other. The moment any of his sons met, disaster would begin to befall the Order and the boys." Lady Eberhardt took a sip of her tea, watching them all over the rim of the cup.

"Disaster? Why on earth did you allow this meeting?"

"Because the disaster is already here," Lady Eberhardt replied, her voice deepening until it sounded not at all her own: "*When the red comet rules the skies, the Prime shall fall. A new Prime shall Ascend to the head of the Order. Three sons. Three relics. Three sacrifices. Only then can the Prime be torn down.*

"*There is but one chance to save them. The Snake at the Breast shall cast the first roll of the die, setting the Game into motion, but might be all that holds back the pall of madness. The Thief shall wear a false face, but wield a true heart; and only the Blind One can see how to save the heart of the Mirror.*"

Silence settled over the room like a mantle, highlighting the steady tick of the clock on the mantle.

"And all of that means...?" Bishop asked.

Lady Eberhardt shrugged. "Clear as muck, I know. Divination usually is. I've been meditating on it for years, and the only thing I've been able to clarify is the fact that the sons refer to Drake's children, and that if they are sacrificed, presumably using the Relics Infernal, then Drake shall fall."

Silence fell.

Over the course of the last year, since discovering the truth of his birth, Lucien had dreamed of one day seeking his revenge. Sometimes those dreams had seen his father fallen at his feet, but now, upon hearing the words, he wondered if they had truly been dreams, or merely his Divination coming into play.

His father, crawling over a field of skulls, his skin drawn and ragged as he clutched at Lucien's boots. Three altars dripping the blood of two men whose faces he could never see. "Run," the Prime would whisper. "You should not be here. You should never be here to see this."

Always the same dream. Lucien swallowed. It was one thing to wish his father ill, quite another to realize that he had a part to play in it.

Miss Martin paled. "Drake said the ritual to invoke the Relics Infernal required a grave sacrifice to open a Gateway to the Shadow Dimensions. If they bring a Greater Demon through into this world, without the usual limitations, they could easily tear Drake down. Nobody would have the power to stop it."

"Indeed," Lady Eberhardt said enigmatically.

"Who is the third son?" Bishop's dark eyes narrowed.

"Alas, he was forced from his mother's womb many years ago." Lady Eberhardt set down her teacup with a sigh. "Too early to live."

"Then one son has been sacrificed," Bishop said thoughtfully, as if unconcerned by the fact that he was possibly next.

"Two to come." Lucien's voice thickened and their eyes met.

"I am not so easy to kill," Bishop replied.

No, but right now *he* was. "Everyone can be killed."

"Time for that later, perhaps." Lady Eberhardt's fist curled tightly around her pearls. "I called you here for a reason, Bishop. Morgana is back, and she's after the third relic, the Chalice, of which I happen to be the current guardian. I need you to take it and protect it with your life."

"And what about you?" Bishop demanded. "She'll come again, if she thinks the Chalice is still here."

Lady Eberhardt waved a dismissive hand. "I can handle myself. You just worry about your own hide. It is precious to me, dear boy. I would not see you harmed, but it seems that there's nobody better suited to handling the relic than yourself."

"Agatha..." he warned.

It occurred to Lucien that there was a great deal of fondness between the pair of them.

"It's decided," Lady Eberhardt said, and her voice had a ringing sound of finality to it. She turned those piercing eyes to Lucien and Ianthe. "Good luck finding the Blade. I think you'll need it. And keep me apprised. If it comes time to hunt down Morgana, I've got quite a bone to pick with her."

CHAPTER SIX

SHADOWS LENGTHENED, the sun turning into a thin gold line on the horizon for several seconds before it stretched out and vanished.

"Night," Lucien murmured. His eyes glinted gold in the darkness of the carriage, full of secrets... and truths.

There was a faint twist within Ianthe's chest, the magic leash she wore streaming back the other way. Toward him. Ianthe clapped a hand to her chest with a faint gasp as her corset seemed to tighten.

"And now you're mine."

Ianthe licked dry lips. He didn't move, but tension tightened the muscles in his thighs, the fabric of his trousers rustling as he shifted slightly. All day she'd been too distracted by her dilemma to think of this, but images sprang to mind following his words—of her on her knees in the carriage, her gloved hands sliding up the lean muscle of those thighs whilst Lucien watched impassively. What would he ask her to do? She could only imagine.

"Summon a mage globe," he told her, stretching both arms along the seat back, "so that I can see you."

A small white orb stirred out of the shadows, just large enough to brighten the carriage. Reaching out, he tugged the blinds down. Just the two of them now. Locked together. Her body felt flushed and full, threatening to burst at the seams.

"You have kept your word today, so I will keep mine. I'm no gentleman in bed, Ianthe, but if you truly do not wish to perform any of the acts I ask of you tonight, then all you have to do is say so."

"I will insist upon a sheathe," she replied.

"I—"

"It's not open to discussion, Rathbourne. I will not risk a child." Her heart stirred dully in her chest.

A slow nod. "That suits me as well."

Breath catching, Ianthe rested her hands on her lap, waiting. Every second stretched out the tension between them. Her pulse began to race as her body remembered what it had felt like to have him kneeling above her in her secret chambers, his fingertip painting that blasted mark between her breasts. Even now, the mark began to sink into her flesh, as if some sort of sorcery worked its magic between them.

"Pull your skirts up."

So he liked to be in charge, did he?

Ianthe breathed in, then out, making her own quiet decisions, and then slowly, slowly curled a fistful of her skirts in each hand.

This was a new game. The challenge was to see who broke first.

If Rathbourne thought her in any way squeamish...

Her smile had edges to it, she was positive, and when she met his gaze with an arched eyebrow, dragging her skirts higher, she could see her ploy had struck its mark. She wasn't the only one tested by desire here.

Rathbourne's mouth hardened, though his eyes turned to pure fire. Hungry. "Well?" he said, leaning on his fist and flicking a bored hand at her, as if to say: *Any time you're ready, my dear.*

"But we've got all night, have we not?" she all but purred. The drag of her skirts against her knees and then thighs rustled in the sleek compartment. Cool air whispered over her sensitive skin. Obeying left her wet and aching.

"Perhaps I've got plans."

"Oh? Do tell?"

The smile he gave her was dangerous. "No, I don't think so. I think I like it when you don't know what I intend. Remove your drawers."

Her breath caught. "Don't you want to do it yourself?"

Those amber eyes glittered furiously. "If I wanted to do it myself, then I wouldn't be sitting here watching you."

So be it. Submission could be merely another means of controlling the situation. Ianthe shifted and wiggled them down her legs, her petticoats spilling down to hide herself. They were pale pink linen. Clenching them in her fist, she stared at him. What now?

Rathbourne held out a hand, and her cheeks burned as she deposited them in it. He never took his eyes off her as he tucked them in the inner pocket of his jacket.

"Touch yourself."

That shocked her. "What?"

"I want to see you please yourself. Surely you know how."

Of course she did. When a sorcerer's energy was driven by sexual means and one didn't have a lover, one had to be resourceful. But that was private. From the smoldering look in his eyes though, he knew that.

Damned if she would give him the satisfaction. Parting her legs, Ianthe slid tentative fingers up her inner thighs. The ache inside ratcheted tighter, made her wet her lips, her teeth sinking slowly into the flesh of her lower one. Those fingers traced slow circles on her inner thigh, sending tingles shooting through her. It was the way he watched her that made her wet, an intense look in his eyes. The way tension rode his hard frame. He was one step away from reaching for her... Ianthe shuddered.

Lucien's eyes were heavy-lidded, and he rested his chin on his hand. "Are you trying to tease me, my dear?"

"Am I succeeding?"

He shifted slightly. A faint smile traced his hard mouth. "What do you think?"

Ianthe slid her fingertip lightly against her clitoris. Sensation shivered through her. "I think one of us is more patient than the other."

Those hard eyes softened lazily, as if she'd said something that amused him. "Do you want to see who it is? Is that the game? Whoever lasts the longest?"

"You enjoy the play of power, don't you?" Again, she let her fingertips brush against her secret flesh. He couldn't see it. Her skirts saw to that. But she could see the flare of his nostrils as he took a sharp breath, and the tightening of his pupils. Warm light from the mage globe bathed the two of them.

"One could say the same, madam. First you challenge me not to kiss you first, now this... Who's playing games, Ianthe?"

Ianthe. The hot stroke of his tongue over her name sent shivers through her. A sudden wicked urge overtook her. He had ordered her to touch herself: he was not unmoved. And she wanted to win this. She wanted to move him.

Using her telekinesis, she lightly stroked him with her senses, 'caressing' the broad planes of his chest, as if with her own hands.

Lucien went still. His gaze locked on hers. He was actually shocked. And heavily aroused.

Ianthe smiled as she stroked the lush, already damp folds of her secret self. She pulled her skirts just a little higher, revealing herself. Her breasts heaved, pushing against the constraints of her bodice. "I do wonder," she whispered, as her psychic touch trailed lower over his abdomen, "who will last the longest?"

The touch was light, a whisper of sensation over his skin. Temping, teasing, and twisting him tighter, until he was almost ready to explode.

And the little devil watched his reaction, her teeth sunk in her fleshy lower lip, as she slowly stroked herself between the thighs, eyelashes fluttering lower and her cheeks painted a pretty pink. "I thought you wanted me to please *you*, Rathbourne?"

"This does please me. I want you wet," Lucien told her, leaning against the window and watching her. Feigning an unruffled demeanor, though a muscle tightened in his jaw as those invisible hands caressed the inside of his thighs. He couldn't stop his hands from clenching. Bloody woman. He was rapidly losing track of this seduction. He just wanted inside her. Now. "When we get inside, I want you to go upstairs to your bedchamber, bend over your bed, and lift your skirts. I want you to be ready for me, Ianthe. I plan to take you then, with no preliminaries."

Her fingers paused, her eyes springing wide. "So be it," she whispered. Her fingers resumed their work, and he could see now, see the blushing pink depths of her and the paler flicker of her fingernails.

Fuck. Lucien ground his teeth together, trying to stifle the raging erection in his trousers. She knew it too, the devil, her eyes laughing at him as she fingered herself. Her flesh all soft and flushed and peeking out every now and then from beneath the exquisite mound of her petticoats.

"Harder," he whispered.

Again, a flicker of uncertainty danced through her eyes; then she slid one finger inside herself. As if to compensate, a phantom fingertip stroked down the length of his cock. Lucien groaned. He'd never been with a woman who could do that.

"Are you thinking of this?" he asked, cupping his cock. Fabric strained over it, the shape brutish and straining. He needed to touch it. "Of how I'm going to fuck you? Would you like it to be soft and slow, Ianthe? Or hard?"

There'd be no time to ask later.

Her head lolled back, her teeth sinking into her lower lip. The flush of desire painted her body, a soft moan easing from her lips. A firm fist of pressure locked around his cock, taking him to the edge.

"Stop," he commanded.

That hand stopped, her fingers buried deep inside her wet opening. Luminous, half-dazed eyes opened, locking on him incredulously.

He smiled, relishing the moment. "Remove your hand and stop touching me."

"Why?" she breathed.

"I intend for you to reach your pleasure, my dear, but not alone. I'll let you come later, when I'm buried inside you." His words turned dangerously soft. "*Only* when I'm inside you, Ianthe. You're not to touch yourself from now on, not unless I allow it. Not even during the day."

With visible agitation, Miss Martin thrust her skirts down over her knees, leaning back and pressing the back of her hand to her lips. She wouldn't look at him, though her heart was racing, visible in the flickering pulse at her throat.

"Besides," he murmured, "we're almost home."

Taking her hand, still slick from her body, Luc pressed it to his mouth, his tongue darting over the musky taste of her and earning a shocked flinch. "Are you ready?"

"More than ready." Those violet eyes challenged him. She'd recovered herself with exquisite aplomb.

"Good," he said, stroking her knuckles as the carriage pulled up to the curb. "Now go make yourself ready and wait for me."

Lucien took his time, sending the butler for some brandy, as Ianthe glared at him then made her way upstairs.

It felt strange to be in this place, going through the daily routine as though nothing had changed, as though Bedlam had never happened. He sipped his brandy, savoring the taste and the scent of it, but he couldn't pretend much longer. The only scent he wanted to smell right now was the musk of Ianthe's body. The only taste he needed was her skin beneath his mouth. She'd been gone for almost five minutes. Long enough to show her who was in charge here. Need itched beneath his skin.

Cock raging, he drained the glass, then left it on the mantle in the parlor. He'd intended to drag this moment out, but there was no point in pretending he could think about anything else but the temptress upstairs.

"A light dinner," he told the maid as he passed her near the stairs, "to be delivered at the half hour. Precisely."

Climbing the stairs left him almost trembling with need. He didn't bother to knock on the bedchamber door. Instead, he opened it and stepped inside swiftly, shutting the door with a gentle click. The swift intake of a breath behind him indicated she'd heard him. Lucien's mouth went dry, and he slowly turned, reaching up to drag his cravat away from his throat.

He was transfixed by the sight before him. All he could see were the wicked pink stockings Miss Martin wore, ending at mid-thigh, and the exquisite lace of her garters. Hands fisted her skirts into a bunch over her back, revealing the smooth globes of her bottom and the flushed pink wetness he was about to devour. Luc's hand fisted in the cravat, the room shuddering a little around him. He forced himself to hold onto control, tightly winding the cravat around his fist to remind himself.

Ianthe's breath was a soft sob. She couldn't see him.

Lucien poured himself another brandy from the decanter on the sideboard, gulping it down with a dark look in her direction. Each chink of glassware made her shift on the bed. Her fists quivered, and her skirts started to slide down.

"Don't," he told her, dropping the cravat and crossing the plush Turkish rugs. Reaching out, he traced a finger over the smooth curve of her bottom. "You're exquisite."

The brandy burned as he swallowed the rest of it, needing it to slake some of the ache of desire. He was close to spending in his trousers just at the sight of her. And that wouldn't do. He needed to break her with desire first.

Putting the glass down on the small bedside table, Lucien returned to her. There was a small packet laid on the bed beside her, an oiled sheathe. He picked it up. "You never answered my question," he said, slowly unbuttoning his trousers. His cock sprang free, and Luc's lip curled in a silent snarl as he fisted the head of it, wiping the slickness of a bead of pearly cum across the throbbing tip. He sheathed it swiftly. "Hard? Or slow?"

"Damn you," she whispered into the mattress, her dark curls hiding her face from view as he stepped behind her. A soft moan made her squirm. "Just do it. Hard. Take me hard."

The softness of her panting gave the illusion that she was begging. He liked it. Still fisting his cock, he traced his dampened finger between her legs, circling the softened bud of her clitoris. The first touch of her almost undid him. Ianthe moaned, one fist grabbing at the bed spread, her fingers turning into claws as that half of her skirt threatened to slide down.

"Say please," he whispered, taking hold of her hips. His fingerprints left little marks in her pale, perfect skin.

She shook her head.

Lucien pushed her onto her knees on the very edge of the mattress, her ankles dangling off it. He thrust forward, letting his cock graze her tender flesh, parting her just a hint.

"I can wait all night," he told her. A lie. *God.* Just the feel of her satiny skin drove his teeth into his lip. No matter what she begged for, he could not take her as he'd wanted. If he fucked her now, he'd be done in seconds, and he wanted this to last. Wanted to brand himself deep within her. Wanted to beat her at her own game.

"Please." It was a whisper torn from a reluctant throat. "Take me. Now."

"As you wish."

He sank into heated flesh, and a gasp tore from his own throat. The tight clench of her body was exquisite. A vein throbbed in his temple as he held onto her hips, grinding himself deep within her.

Burying his fingers in the fabric that tightened over her hips, he ground his teeth together and plunged into her hot, willing body.

A feather light stroke touched his balls. Lucien flexed hard, an unexpected thrust. His fingers curled around her hip, sinking through the soft folds of her gown until he found the molten core of her. He wanted her loose and undone, absolutely destroyed beneath him. Fingers dancing over her wet flesh, he fucked her with sweet, short strokes, taking them both to the edge of pleasure. Every surge of his fingers was rewarded with the tightening of her body, until he was so close to exploding, he had to bite his lip to stop himself.

But something was stopping her from taking that plunge.

"You're beautiful," he whispered. "So beautiful."

That touch danced over his balls again, a soft caress that made him throw his head back and see stars.

"Damn you," he groaned. Heat shivered at the base of his spine, working its way right through him. Giving into the urge, he sank his other hand into her disheveled chignon and tilted her head back. "Come for me, darling. Come."

She bit her lip and shook her head.

"This dance isn't over until you do."

One last flex of his fingers, a hesitation, and then Ianthe cried out, her entire body milking him. "Oh. My. God." She gasped, "*Rathbourne!*"

He hissed, thrusting one last final time as he came.

Breathing hard, Lucien let his head fall forward, still grinding small circles with his hips. Her body quivered beneath him. They both breathed heavily, trying to find the ground beneath their feet. A minute ticked past. Then another. Slowly, her skirts fell, hiding their joining from view, and with regret, Luc pulled free of her, taking the sheathe in hand and disposing of it neatly before tucking his cock back into his trousers.

His first glimpse of heaven. Every inch of his body felt alive and flushed with power that rejuvenated him. It should have been enough, but he burned still, as if he could spend all night fucking her and still not be sated.

Dragging her skirts down, he slid his hands around her waist and drew her up onto her knees. "Are you hungry?"

Tendrils of silky black hair clung to her damp forehead, and her glassy eyes flinched as they met his. Lucien leaned down and pressed his lips against the soft spot just beneath her ear, hands drinking in the sensation of her crinoline gown as he drew her back against his chest. From this angle, he could see directly down her bodice and feel the soft curve of her abdomen hidden behind its confining stays. All woman. Made to be desired. A goddess.

"Hungry?"

"I've sent for dinner." Stepping back, he forced himself to stop touching her. He could wait. The swift coupling had eased some of the harsh edge within him, and they had all night.

Lucien dragged a plush armchair from the hearth and settled a small table in front of it. Ianthe dragged her knees up to her chest on the bed as she watched him, her cheeks hot and rosy. "Since when did you commandeer my staff?"

"Forty minutes ago," he replied, "when the sun set." Pouring a shot of whiskey into his glass, he offered it to her, capping the flask again.

Miss Martin sipped at it, watching him warily over the top of the glass. The fine hairs at her temple had curled in the heat of their passion, though the rest of her looked like a dignified lady. Only he knew she wore no drawers, her knees crossed tightly against the slick wetness between her thighs.

A sharp rap at the door drew his attention. "Come in," he called, stepping over his crumpled cravat.

One of the maids bobbed a curtsy, pushing a small trolley into the room with several silver domed trays upon it. The scent of fileted lamb made his mouth water, and he directed her where to set the trays. Miss Martin had shifted from the bed, crossing to stand by the window as she stared out into the night, sipping her whisky. None of the staff would be ignorant as to the circumstances between them and whose bed he was going to be sharing, but both the maid and Miss Martin gave a good show of acting as if this were any normal night.

"Would you care for anything else, my lord?" the maid murmured.

As she left, he told her they did not wish to be interrupted. Dragging a napkin off the table, he handled the cork of the champagne bottle. Drops of moisture clung to its green-tinted glass, and it gave a loud *pop* when the cork dislodged, frothing up over his hand. Miss Martin jumped at the sound.

"Come here." He cradled a champagne flute for her in his palm as he poured it.

"I think you like giving orders," she said, setting the empty whiskey glass down as she crossed the room. Candlelight dappled her gown and face, warming her creamy skin. The soft swish of her skirts was a seduction in itself.

"And I think you like me giving orders," he countered, handing her the flute. Their fingers met as she took it, her eyes darting to his.

"Champagne on an empty stomach? What are we celebrating?"

94

"Perhaps I'm merely feeling somewhat... relaxed." Folding his long body into the armchair, he extended a hand to her. Confusion distorted her brow, but she took it, and Lucien drew her into his lap, brushing the tendrils of wispy-fine hair off the back of her neck. Miss Martin tensed, a half-glance back over her shoulder revealing her nerves.

Revenge had never seemed sweeter, though his means of seeking it had changed. There was just one little problem. Lucien brushed his mouth over the soft skin where her neck sloped into her shoulder, fingers working at one of the buttons that fastened her gown in the back. Pearl, of course.

He'd always enjoyed the mysteries of a woman's body, the sensations of learning every inch of it. One ex-mistress had even accused him of being a sensualist, and it was true.

With a sidelong glance at her, he tugged more of her buttons free as he leaned up to press his mouth against the bare skin revealed. Tracing the edge of her chemise and stays, his lips rippled over the indentation of her spine. Warm firelight set her skin to a softened gold.

Time to confront that little problem.

"You didn't come," he murmured, tongue darting out to trace the sweat on her skin.

Miss Martin glanced back. "Yes, I did."

"No lies," he warned, meeting her gaze. "You gave a good approximation of it, but you didn't gain your pleasure." Which meant that she had won. In the moment, he hadn't been sure, but now...

Miss Martin's cheeks burned. "It's not always easy for a woman," she murmured. "I have a lot on my mind. It... It's harder to lose myself in the moment."

"Is it the way I touched you?"

"No." The light struck her fine face as she turned, revealing shadows beneath her eyes. "To be honest, it has nothing to do with you. Your touch is... pleasing. Orgasm simply eludes me at the moment."

He considered that. "I prefer honesty in all things. If you cannot seek *la petite morte*, then don't pretend you did."

"I won't." It was a bare whisper, but her shoulders relaxed, as if some weight had been eased from them.

"Then I'll continue to seek to wring soft cries of pleasure from you," he murmured, brushing his mouth across the smooth slope of her bare arm as he turned his attention back to her buttons. "I like a challenge, after all."

And everything about her was challenging. Revenge would be sweet, now that he'd fixed his mind on the method of it. *I'm going to steal you away, my dear. Make you crave me, just as much as I crave you... I'll make you forget his name. Forget your loyalties to him...*

The last button popped free and he slid his hands up the curve of her back, separating the gown over her shoulders. Miss Martin made a soft sound in her throat. "Dinner is cooling," she whispered.

"We shall eat soon," he replied, sliding her sleeve down her slender arm and tugging it over the tips of her fingers. "I'm just making you comfortable."

Soft light revealed the swell of her breasts thrust up by the pale pink stays she wore. A little tracery of Venetian lace drew his gaze, and then his fingers, absorbing the roughened fibers of the lace. Lucien let his mouth rove across the bare curve of her shoulder, his cock hard and firm beneath her rounded buttocks, as he drew her other sleeve clear.

She sat in a puddle of skirts, breathing hard. Desire danced over her skin in flushed pinks and reds, and this time he didn't mistake it. The problem then, was clearly not with his skills or her interest in him. Lucien flicked his fingernail beneath the sleeve of her chemise and slipped it from her shoulder, leaving her soft and disheveled.

"Perhaps you are the meal," he suggested.

"I'd rather liken myself to dessert," she replied, and her stomach chose that moment to growl fiercely. Miss Martin flushed a becoming pink and pressed her hands to her abdomen.

Lucien paused, pressing a kiss to her neck. "Eat," he said, reaching past her shoulder and lifting the first tureen to reveal the white soup. "I wouldn't want to compete with your stomach's attentions."

Miss Martin looked thoroughly out of her depths. "Should I fetch another chair?"

"No." He rather enjoyed her right where she was.

"But how shall you—?"

"I'm not overly hungry," he replied, which was the truth. They'd dined at the Prime's, and he'd only managed a couple of mouthfuls, as delicious as they'd been. At first, the meals had been of better quality and frequent in his incarceration, but during the last two months, after he'd attacked the prison guard, they'd come barely once a day and were little more than gruel. Hunger had been one of the hardest elements to deal with, though his body had grown accustomed. Strange what one could learn to deal with.

He fed her with his own fork, cutting pieces of the minted lamb and sliding it over her plump lips, then spearing a sliver for himself. The richness of the sauce was delicious, but somewhat overpowering. Lucien contented himself with the bread, breaking pieces of it off with his fingers and ignoring the butter. He'd dreamed of hot buttered rolls when he was in Bedlam, but the last thing he wanted was to upset his stomach. Too used to nothing but gruel and water, or perhaps the hard stones that they called bread, he didn't particularly wish to spend his night writhing in pain.

Instead, he took his enjoyment in watching her eat. Most gently bred ladies had the appetite of a bird, but Miss Martin evidently enjoyed her meals. Granted, sorcery burned through a lot of an adept's energy, so she would need it.

Lucien contented himself with stroking the silky texture of her stays and watching her. She finished the lamb and he placed her knife and fork down precisely, as her head lowered. "What's wrong?"

"I cannot work you out."

Lucien let his smile show. "Oh?"

"This hardly seems like revenge." He caught a glint of the blueness of her eyes, smoky and violet-tinged in the near-dark. The type of lower-lashed look that stroked a hot hand through his groin.

And I am working you out, my dear. Miss Martin was an accomplished flirt, well used to taking the measure of men. She didn't like that she couldn't do so with him.

Hands petting her hips, he slid them lower, bunching up fistfuls of her skirts. Miss Martin sucked in a breath as he dragged her gown up over her head and raised arms, before throwing it across the room.

"Are you trying to distract me?"

"Is it working?" he asked.

A faint smile hovered around her lips, but then it died. "Perhaps." Something sad seemed to flicker in her eyes. "Perhaps I want to be distracted."

It arrested him, that small sign of loss in her eyes. He felt jubilant, but she was hiding something. "What is it?"

"Nothing." She shook her head. "Everything. I'm worried about Drake."

Of course. "He'll earn his just reward, I'm sure."

The look she shot him was razor sharp. Lucien tapped her on the nose, and she bit his finger. A reminder that she might have submitted, but she wasn't completely under his control.

And wasn't that just fascinating.

"You've been a very obedient lover," he replied. "If you behave, then you shall be rewarded."

Her eyes flashed fire, and Lucien laughed as he resettled her on his lap, reclining in the armchair with his legs stretched out in front of him and Miss Martin's head resting against his shoulder. Gossamer fine petticoats danced around her legs. He seized a fistful, and with a jerk, tore them clear off her.

A gasp. Then she settled again, her fingers twirling in the lapels of his coat. "You're going to owe me a new wardrobe, Rathbourne."

"I'll dress you in whatever you like," he murmured, brushing his lips against her breasts. "Just as long as I get to remove it all."

That earned him a wrathful look. "I'll dress myself, thank you very much."

Flicking one finger under the edge of her corset, he slid her nipple free and smiled at her. "You're proud and independent." Peaked, rosy flesh met his gaze. Watching her expression, he licked it, then drew it into his mouth.

"You would do well to remember that," she whispered, but her defiance died as he suckled hard. Ianthe gasped.

Lucien lathed attention on her breast before turning to the other. Every gasp she gave was just reward. The hand that caught his and began to drag it south made him smile. Then she cupped his fingers over the wet-slick flesh between her thighs.

"What do you want?" Lucien murmured, trailing kisses up her arm.

"Touch me."

"Please," he commanded.

"Please."

And so he did. She was incredibly responsive, incredibly wet. A flush of desire swept through him.

"Fetch another sheathe," he told her, pushing the dinner cart out of the way.

Clutching her loosened corset to her breasts, she did so. When she returned, Luc caught her fingers and directed her to her knees in between his legs.

"I like your obedience."

"Don't presume it will last," she warned.

Lucien smiled. "I don't." Reaching out, he plucked a handful of pins from her hair. "Put it on me."

The look she shot him was dangerous. Easing open the flap on his trousers, she curled her pale hands over his cock. Lucien's hand slid through her hair. With gentle pressure, he directed her down until her lips brushed against the tip of his cock.

"Suck it," he whispered.

Her tongue darted out. Tasted it. Lucien bit his lip. Watching him the entire time, she lowered her head, her warm, wet mouth curling around his erection and taking him almost to the base.

Oh, God. *Heaven*. His eyes rolled back in his head, his hand on the back of her head controlling the depth of her mouth. Miss Martin was no expert, but she was enthusiastic and that counted.

"Enough," he finally demanded, a shiver running down his spine.

Those firm hands slid the sheathe down over his cock, and she gave him one last suck, as if to prove that her compliance only stretched so far, before she let him draw her back into his lap.

Backward.

White, milky thighs straddled his. Miss Martin glanced back, almost curiously, as if wondering what he meant by this. Lucien pressed her forward, her hands resting on the dining cart as he gently eased his cock between her thighs.

"And down," he whispered, as she sank back onto him.

A shiver ran through her spine, and she flexed her hips, settling her hands on her thighs. "You like to take me from behind."

"I do. There are reasons, of course." He smacked her bottom as she rose.

Miss Martin jerked up before impaling herself again. Luc rubbed at the reddened mark of his handprint on her round arse, licking his finger and then tracing it down over her smooth skin, teasing at the puckered rosebud there.

Her fingernails dug into her thighs as she gasped, the muscle in her thighs rippling as she lifted.

"Down," he whispered, and she impaled herself twice, each exquisite muscle clenching around him.

"Rathbourne!" Her body shuddered, little pinpricks of gooseflesh erupting up her bare arms.

All you have to do is say no. But she didn't, rising again slowly, then increasing the pace.

Hot and clearly flustered, she raked her hands down her face as she rode him, moaning a little as he worked her with hands and cock. The tension in her body tightened.

"Touch yourself," he demanded, hand curling over her hip as he thrust up into her, feeling his balls clench hard up into his body. *Fuck*. He'd meant to stay aloof, to enjoy her surrender, but it was becoming harder to keep his mind clear. Harder to think at all. Lucien threw his head back, his lip curling in a silent snarl as she slid gentle fingers down between her thighs. Perhaps her own touch would stimulate her.

She moaned, her body tightening as she sank her other hand into her hair and she cried out, her upthrusts slowing, slowing, body quivering...

Then she shook her head, curling her fist in the hem of her chemise instead. "I can't."

Frustration edged through her tone.

"It will happen," he assured her.

He couldn't restrain himself any longer, mouth falling open, as she wilted forward. Catching her hips in both hands, he drove himself up into her. Miss Martin caught at the table, scattering plates and silverware in her desperate fingers as she clung to the edge. He let go of control, let himself drown in her, and it was the sweetest moment ever. Waves of pleasure washed over him as he spilled himself within her.

It seemed like forever until the world stopped spinning. Lucien let out a breath he hadn't even realized he was holding and eased from her body. Miss Martin threatened to slide off his lap, but he caught her and dragged her back against his chest and rumpled coat.

Picking up her fingers, he pressed a gentle kiss there. "You, Miss Martin, are exquisite." Turning her hand in his, he placed a deeper kiss in her palm. Sleepy-lashed eyes looked up at him.

Beautiful eyes.

For a moment, his head lifted and she lowered her face up to his. Those tempting, utterly delectable lips were barely an inch away when he realized what he was doing.

Luc drew back and her eyes opened wide. He forced himself to smile. "Ready to lose our bet?"

Realization dawned. Miss Martin sat up in his lap. "And here I thought *you* ready to succumb."

Picking her up, he carried her toward the bed and spilled her onto the covers. Ianthe tumbled onto her back in a mess of her chemise and stockings, with her hair tumbling down around her shoulders, and just the right expression on her face. "Do you know, Rathbourne, I think I rather enjoy your style of revenge."

Part of him was tempted to tip her onto her back and kneel over her again, to lick the sweat off her skin and rip all those pretty little bits of silk off her body. He wanted her to come.

Patience. He had plenty of nights to unwrap this delicious present, and he needed sleep. He could already feel the long stretch of the day sinking into his bones like lead, the use of his long-denied magic draining him.

One couldn't appreciate a woman like this when his hands were starting to tremble.

Reaching out, Lucien pinched the candle out by her bedside. Miss Martin leaned back on her hands with her knees knocking together and her feet splayed, eyeing him as if she were mentally undressing him.

His abdomen hardened. No one was ever going to see the mess the demon had made of his body; it was bad enough letting them catch glimpses of his madness.

"Dream of me." He turned, starting toward the door, but not before he caught a glimpse of her mouth dropping open.

"Where are you going?" she called.

Bending to snatch his cravat off the floor, Lucien didn't pause. "To my bed chambers. You didn't think I was actually going to sleep here, did you?"

It was probably for the best that Rathbourne hadn't stayed.

Seconds ticked into minutes and slowly began to stretch into hours. Ianthe tossed and turned, trying to keep her mind off matters, but it was no use. Here in the warm, silent dark, she had nothing to occupy her busy mind. Nothing to distract herself with. It wasn't so bad during the day, when she could *do* something, anything, to try and get her daughter back... But at night? All she could think about was Louisa. What was her little girl doing? Was Louisa hungry? Cold? Was she hurt?

They'd sent her a letter that first day.

Dear Aunt Ianthe,

I am having such a wonderful time on my holiday.

Cousin Sebastian is teaching me about his roses. He likes roses, he says, but he won't let me touch them. I like the red ones. He does not do tea parties very well, either. Not like you do. He says the cups are too small for his hand, and he is very bad at charades. And I miss Sir Egmont and Hilary. It's not the same without them. And mama and papa and you. And Tubby.

Sebastian said I must write to you. I don't know why because it's your turn to visit in a week, isn't it? You always visit on the last weekend of the month.

I hope I am home by then. I miss mama. Sebastian says we will see. He said it depends upon you, so hurry up and come take me home! I want to see Tubby again. He'll have grown so much!

Love,
Louisa

The tears came then, the ones that she fought all day to hold back. The words were Louisa's. She just hoped her daughter was as oblivious as she seemed. She mustn't have been there when they killed Jacob and Elsa. That was some small measure of peace, at least.

There was no use crying; that wouldn't bring her daughter back to her, but Ianthe succumbed in a fast storm that left her face hot and flushed against her damp pillow. She curled Louisa's small, ragged bear, Hilary, against her chest and fought to conquer her breathing.

What was she going to do?

She couldn't go to the Prime. She'd been warned away from doing such a thing, and didn't dare, not with her daughter's life at stake, but this... waiting... was doing her head in. She'd spent the first three days following Louisa's abduction doing everything she could think of to find her. She'd tried to scry her whereabouts, she'd haunted London, hunting for traces of the little girl, spent a small fortune hiring men to hunt for her, searched for this Sebastian... and then she'd finally collapsed when it became clear that she had pushed herself past the brink of exhaustion. Thus had come the second part of her plan—to do as Louisa's abductors asked and steal the Blade for them.

At least now that Drake had given her the task of finding the 'thief,' she could make subtle moves without fear that the nameless, faceless kidnappers who had her daughter would punish her for it. If they did threaten her again, then she could claim that she'd been forced to cover her own tracks.

Or were they nameless?

Morgana de Wynter. A name she knew well, but a woman she'd never met. Morgana was a dangerous foe, but at least if Morgana was behind this, then Ianthe had an enemy to aim for.

And Ianthe could be dangerous herself when need be. When she thought of it, a tidal wave of rage swept over her, threatening to drown her. She was barely a mother, but if they thought for one second that they weren't facing an enraged mother bear with her stolen cub, then they would regret it.

Rage was better than grief. Action was better than sitting around, waiting incessantly. And tomorrow, she would begin tracking this new thread of information, teasing at it to carefully discover if Morgana was the one who held Louisa.

Tomorrow, she told herself and let her swollen eyelids flutter closed. She needed sleep, or she'd be worse than useless.

CHAPTER SEVEN

'Sir Geoffrey Mellors, a sorcerer during the Georgian era wrote of his belief that for every sorcerer, there was another out there in the world—the missing half of their soul—and that, if the two should ever meet, it would be a glorious joining, a union of two equals. Lovers whose hearts beat as one and who shared the same breath, till death did they part.'
- Lady Eberhardt's transcription on Soul-bonds

THE NEXT MORNING, they breakfasted swiftly at the dinner table. Miss Martin wore a day gown of burgundy velvet that covered her from throat to toes, and yet was somehow dangerously sensual. The color suited her dark hair and pale skin, and frequently drew Lucien's gaze. Silence lingered, broken only by the swish of that velvet and the metallic ting of knives and forks. It sounded somewhat like someone was fencing, and from the swift dart of stealthy glances between them, Lucien wondered if it were them and if silence had become the weapon of choice.

Only, this time the silence was filled with all kinds of wicked imaginings, at least on his behalf. With every smooth glide of her hands, he could see her body surrendering beneath him, her willowy limbs supple and fluid as he fucked her. As she bowed her head to eat, the long line of her nape showed, a submissive posture that reminded him of others. Lucien's blood burned, but her distracted gaze as she stared across the table at nothing, told him he was alone in such imaginings.

His brows drew together. Now that he was looking at her—truly looking, not just admiring—he had to note that her eyes were slightly swollen.

As if she'd spent half the night in tears.

A gut-wrenching blow, for when he'd left her, she'd been utterly ravished. What could have moved her to tears? Had he hurt her? He'd not been gentle, but his reading of the situation at the time had told him that she'd liked it.

"Did you sleep well?"

Miss Martin took up her teacup in both hands, meeting his eyes over the rim of it. "I snatched a few hours."

Which told him nothing. "You look tired... I didn't hurt you?"

That brought her full attention to bear upon him. She blinked in surprise, then a faint, weary smile curved over her pretty mouth. "Would it bother you if you had?"

"I'm not in the habit of abusing the fairer sex. Of course it would bother me."

They stared at each other, her gaze curious and faintly wondering, and his defensive.

Miss Martin gave him a respectful tilt of the head. "My exhaustion has nothing to do with you, Rathbourne. My mind is busy at the moment. Too much to dwell upon. It keeps me from sleep. Your demands are but a welcome distraction, a chance to forget... for a moment."

Sadness painted a pale, milky blue across her face, like a watercolor that swiftly dissolved. She shook her head, as if setting herself to rights. "But enough of that. I have been thinking about yesterday afternoon and the events at Lady Eberhardt's mansion."

"Yes?" He poured himself some tea, wondering where she was going with this.

"You didn't use your power, Lucien, except for that one act of Expression."

Lucien. It was the first time she'd called him that. The word was somewhat... intimate, but then he supposed that last night had been infinitely more so. The rest of her words, however, bothered him. "It's been a long year, Ianthe"—he too could use her name—"and my strength had waned. There is little energy to be gained in the cold stone walls of the isolation ward or in meager fuel supplies."

"Good." Her eyes sparkled. "Last night between us should have restored your power reserves then. It's the least I could do." She gestured toward his clean plate, where he'd buttered his toast lightly and smeared the faintest hint of jam across it, as compared to her breakfast of beefsteak, fried ham, and eggs. Sorcerers often ate heartily. "Would you care for another helping? I desire you strong and whole."

"I fear my stomach wouldn't tolerate it," he admitted. "It's used to deprivation."

"You spoke of being overwhelmed. I had wondered if your mind were blocked and you couldn't access your powers."

"A... little."

Sympathy flashed in blues across her features. "That's to be expected, following a severe psychic assault, such as what occurred with the demon."

Lucien looked away, the teacup rattling as he set it down, memory assaulting him for a brief second. "I barely remember it."

Ianthe pushed back her chair and stood, those skirts swishing around her ankles as she circled the table. Her fingertips rested on his shoulder, instantly affirming the bond between them. It was stronger today, knotted tightly around the two of them; a result, no doubt, of their carnal relations. "I could help you, if you wished it—"

"No." He could deal with it himself. He just needed time.

"Lucien, I could see your aura bleeding all over the place that day in the Grosvenor Hotel, after the demon savaged you. That you've managed to heal it to this degree in such a short time as twelve months is incredible, but it's entirely possible that you won't be able to manage more on your own, or without long periods of calming meditation, and unfortunately, we don't have such time up our sleeves. There's a sorcerer I know, a man who can heal maladies of the mind to some extent. Or, perhaps... Drake could—"

"I'll think about it."

She released an exasperated sigh. "I should think you would be inclined to pursue every avenue, considering that prophecy has predicted your death."

"I said I would consider it, and the prophecy wasn't so specific, I noticed," he replied, pouring himself more tea. "It predicted only that my death would be part of the relics spell, if it were to succeed. Not that it was a definite. Considering everything that occurred yesterday, I'm surprised that *that* is the line of questioning you've chosen to pursue."

Dark eyelashes lowered. She was hiding something, and he had a sudden gut-wrenching suspicion that he knew what it was.

"Did you know about it? About Bishop?"

"I knew."

His nostrils flared. "And you didn't think to mention it: *Oh, by the way, you have a brother.*"

He'd spent half the night brewing on the subject, and he was angry now. The Prime had pushed and pulled him throughout his life, like a pawn on a chessboard. *He'd* been the one to decide if Lucien should be in his life, and *he'd* been the one who'd thought both brothers should not know each other. The teapot clattered against the table as he set it down rather abruptly.

A brother. Hell. A stranger. How many times had he watched other children playing nearby and wished that he could join them, when Lord Rathbourne decreed that he attend his studies instead. He wouldn't have been so bloody lonely if he'd known that there was someone else out there, someone just like him. It would have been easier to cope with the truth when he realized that he was the Prime's bastard son, not Lord Rathbourne's, and that the Prime wished nothing to do with him.

"I'm sorry. I didn't realize... It wasn't... I've had so much on my mind of late, that it didn't occur to me."

"It feels like my entire life has been a lie, Miss Martin." What else didn't he know? "And every time I uncover a little piece of the truth, it unlocks a dozen more strands. My reality, as I know it, is unraveling. I stand on shifting sands every day, with not a single ally, nor anyone who truly gives a damn about me."

"Your father—"

"Sentenced me to this life. Don't use that word for him. He is not a father. His debt to me ended the moment he spilled his seed, and I won't forget that. If you think for one second that I would allow him to... to help me with this... *God*." Turning away, he fought hard to bring his emotions under control. "What else are you keeping from me?"

She made a choked sound in her throat. "I–I–"

He made a slashing motion with his hand. "Forget it." This was what came of letting her get under his skin. When he'd seen her swollen eyes, he'd begun to care. When she laid her hand upon his shoulder as if to offer comfort, he'd begun to forget she was the Prime's tool first and foremost. A lie. It was all a lie, and he couldn't forget it again. "The enemy of my enemy is my friend," he told her. "That is all we can be."

"I'm so sorry, Lucien—"

Heavy footsteps thundered down the stairs, and then a young woman appeared, her pale cheeks flushed with youth and her hazel eyes gleaming. "You're back! I didn't even hear you return. I did it, Ianthe! I froze my cup of tea!" Holding said cup upside down, she shook it firmly, then seemed to realize that Lucien was sitting there.

Miss Martin somehow appeared perfectly serene, as though their argument hadn't occurred. However, she couldn't quite hide the brittleness in her voice when she said: "Lucien, this is my apprentice, Miss Thea Davies. Thea, this is Lucien Devereaux, the Earl of Rathbourne, who is serving as my current Shield."

Thea's eyes widened. She bobbed a curtsy. "My lord. How do you do?"

"A pleasure to meet you," Lucien greeted.

Miss Martin gestured to a chair beside her for the young woman as she returned to her own. "Excellent progress, considering the fact that you were only supposed to be studying your books while I was gone and not using sorcery."

Thea's smile died. "I was careful."

"And what happens if your temper flares, hmm?"

Thea squirmed.

Miss Martin held out for long seconds, making her disapproval clear. "Now make it melt."

Thea's lips pressed together mulishly. "Can I not have breakfast first?"

"Melt your tea and then you may dine."

Thea set her teacup on the table in front of her and stared at it. Nothing happened for a good two minutes, though Lucien could feel the girl's energy reserves turning molten within her. Thea would be a powerful practitioner one day, perhaps even more so than him. Even being in the same room as her was starting to set off an ache behind his left eye.

"Thea's natural affinity is Telepathy," Ianthe explained a little proudly. "She struggles with Telekinesis, however, and her control is limited. She's so determined to do something, that she can often do it once out of frustration, but rarely at will and never whilst calm."

Thea's lips pursed, her fingers clenching into fists as she glared at the cup. It took almost a minute, but the iced lump of tea gradually pooled into water, until a miniature iceberg floated in the cup and then bubbles started floating to the surface, slowly, then faster, until the tea was boiling.

It was an impressive display, relying on sheer force of will, rather than ritual and Words of Power. Or it would have been, if the room wasn't so cold. Lucien had to stand and move away, the girl's power bleeding all over him.

"Now freeze it again, but this time, I want you to focus on your meditative techniques. Remember what we discussed about building your sense of ritual? You were angry again, which means you were able to melt the tea, but you cannot allow that to form a block in your mind, which ties your power to emotion, or else you'll never be able to advance."

"I will advance." Thea took a steady breath and closed her eyes, but emotion painted rainbows of color across her face—anger, defiance, frustration, hope, perhaps even fear, if he was reading that dark, indigo blue correctly.

The tea stopped bubbling, but even when Thea began murmuring her ritual words, it remained stubbornly steaming. Her lashes flickered, those hands beginning to curl into themselves.

"Stop," Ianthe instructed. "You're getting angry again. Let it all go, Thea. Release all of your emotions and your power and have some breakfast. You can begin again afterward."

When Thea opened her eyes, mutiny burned there. "I can do it."

"How do you form ice?" Lucien found himself asking, his voice calm and cool.

"Absorb the energy in the water," Thea explained. "Energy and friction compel the water to heat, yet by removing all of the energy and absorbing it yourself, you force it to cool."

"Yet emotion drives us to expend energy, which is why boiling water is easier than cooling it."

"Yes, but I froze the water, even when I was using emotion as my driving force of will!"

He smiled faintly, sharing a glance with Ianthe. "I'm starting to feel some sense of kinship with my own mentor."

Ianthe sipped her tea. "And I believe I'm starting to understand why Drake passed her apprenticeship onto me. I'm learning rather a lot myself, most particularly the fact that His Grace has an odd sense of humor. He's probably been waiting for this moment ever since I first began my apprenticeship."

"I thought it was rude to discuss someone when they are sitting right there at the table with you." Thea stabbed a kipper with ruthless intent. "I don't understand why we cannot simply use the tools we already own. Expression works! Why does it matter if I'm angry, or scared, or—"

"Has your mentor never explained why we tie our sorcery to ritual and power words instead?"

Ianthe glanced his way. "Lucien—"

"The girl should know the truth."

Ianthe's lips thinned. "I didn't wish to frighten her."

Thea's eyes widened. "What do you mean?"

"Most of our first forays into sorcery are caused by emotion," he said. Like his yesterday, which was an uncomfortable truth. He pushed it aside. "A girl is beaten by her father so often, that one day some mental block in her mind snaps and she wants him to stop hitting her so much so that he does. Her desire and her emotional energy force the laws of nature to her will, just for a moment and often uncontrollably. Perhaps she throws her father across the room? Perhaps she breaks every bone in his body or chokes him to death? Sometimes the girl can even force her father to never lift a hand against her again by placing a compulsion in his own head, though such a thing is extremely rare. It's most often telekinesis or pyrokinesis, something destructive, something that is relatively easy for the will to perform. Sometimes these girls or boys are so afraid of what they can do that they form a mental block in their minds, which means they can never do it again. They... suppress their sorcery. It becomes a mysterious miracle, or I'm sure you've heard of mysterious healings, or deaths, or catastrophes?"

Thea's eyes grew distant, her lower lip trembling, just a fraction. "I-I–"

"That's enough, Lucien," Ianthe murmured, taking the girl's hand. "She understands what can happen." Thea turned into her, and Ianthe squeezed her hand and drew her closer.

Of course she did. Most of them did, and now he'd unwittingly blundered into some dark scar of memory that the girl owned. "My apologies. I did not mean to touch a nerve." He cleared his throat. So many times these days he was missing social cues and blundering through human interactions. He'd never been so careless before his incarceration.

Lucien knelt on the rug at Thea's skirts, taking her hands in his. "Expression is incredibly powerful, more so than harnessing your will, but so dangerous, Thea. So uncontrollable. That is why we use ritual and meditation to teach ourselves to harness our will."

Thea looked eminently subdued. "What if I cannot learn to do so?"

Miss Martin kissed Thea's forehead and hugged her. "I remember a time when I was certain I would never learn to harness my will. The more I could not do it, the more frustrated and impatient I became. But it finally happened, and once learned, it became so much easier, Thea. That is why we set you such complicated tasks to study at first—to unknot a rope with your mind, or to use telekinesis to move a wooden puzzle piece from the bottom of a tower of them whilst holding the others in place—because whilst Expression is powerful, it cannot perform complicated tasks. It will come, Thea. Trust me in this."

Thea nodded.

"Finish your breakfast," Miss Martin pressed. "No more talk of Expression and dire disasters. I believe we have enough on our plate as it is." She glanced his way, finishing the last mouthful of her tea. "Have you quite finished, my lord? I believe we have an old acquaintance of Morgana's to question this morning about her potential whereabouts and a Relic Infernal to find?"

Lucien stood. "Actually, I was starting to wonder at your lack of enthusiasm this morning. You seem quite calm, considering someone—possibly a dangerous sorceress with a price on her head and a yearning for revenge—has stolen two infamous relics."

"One relic, Rathbourne. We're not quite certain she has the other in hand yet. As for lack of impatience, Drake sent out Sensitive's to comb the streets of London last night for hints of sorcery. If they'd found anything, we'd already know it." She flashed a warm smile at Thea. "I want you to continue trying to freeze and boil the tea. However, if you find yourself growing irritable, you are to set aside such a task and return to your meditation. Use your rituals to simply gather your power to the point where your skin is brimming with it, then disperse it and do it again. The more you use ritual, the more your mind will form that path, until *it* becomes instinct, not emotional channels. I shall see you tonight, hopefully."

They left her staring forlornly at the dining table.

Lucien leaned back in the carriage and tried not to stare at the woman bound to him. He could sense her emotions pricking at his skin like needles, and the color wash of it over her face was immense, despite her expressionless face.

She was staring, arrested, at a pair of young children playing in the park across the street. The girls couldn't have been more than nine or ten and were laughing as they deliberately splashed each other, stomping their boots into puddles. Ianthe fingered the locket at her throat and looked as though the world might not have existed around her.

Through the bond, it felt as though her heart was breaking.

Lucien looked again at the girls. Happy young lasses, wrapped up in bonnets with a plaid shawl thrown over their shoulders. One of them had shiny black hair knotted into a plaited chignon, and the other wore pigtails.

He couldn't for the life of him figure out why the sight of them ached within her so much. Pressing a hand to his chest, he squeezed, but it was merely a phantom emotion. The bond between them was strengthening. If he wasn't careful, he'd begin to hear her more outspoken thoughts—and she his.

"You are fond of Thea," he said, both out of curiosity and also to see if he could discover what had set her emotions roiling.

"You sound as if you're surprised."

"Perhaps I am. I would never have suspected you to own a maternal side."

Ianthe reacted as if he'd slapped her. "You do not know me at all. I know you hold me partly to blame for your incarceration, but that does not mean I am a cold, wicked woman, devoid of feelings."

"I know." Lucien cleared his throat. "My apologies. I didn't mean to offend you. I just... I was trying to understand you."

"What you must think of me." She gave a tight, pressed-lip smile. "All these words you throw my way: mistress, whore, unmotherly—"

"I never called you a whore," he said sharply.

A flash of violet eyes. He *had* hurt her. "And yet, what have you demanded of me?" At his own flinch, she smiled bitterly. "It's all right, Rathbourne. I'm used to it."

Then she turned to look out of the window again.

And he suddenly felt quite ill and ashamed of himself.

"I'm sorry that you feel that way. I did not think of our agreement as such, no more than I thought myself a lesser man for bending to your will during the day. I wanted you, and I feared the imbalance of submitting to your will with no recourse, which is why I demanded such a thing of you." His gaze lowered. "Perhaps it was wrong of me."

There was an echoing moment of silence. When he looked up, Ianthe's eyes were wide, and she looked surprisingly young. "Well. Look at the pair of us, treating each other kindly. That was something I did not expect."

"Perhaps we have both made assumptions about each other?"

More silence. It was awkward, and she looked flushed and somewhat sweet.

"What is your relationship with the Prime?" He was beginning to suspect that he'd been very, very wrong in regards to everything he knew about her.

"Why?"

"So I can stop making assumptions about you, and perhaps because last night was rather... intimate. I'm curious about you. You have the body of a courtesan, but in bed, you're somewhat... Not shy. That's not the word I'm looking for. Perhaps not quite certain of what I was doing to you at times or what my intentions were. You kept hesitating."

"Perhaps the word you're looking for is 'inexperienced'," Miss Martin said, puffing up like a peacock. "I do hope it wasn't boring to a man of your caliber."

"Certainly not boring. It was more than I'd ever hoped for," he replied, though he couldn't stop chewing over her words. "Inexperienced?"

She looked away. "Forget I said it."

"No. I want to know what you meant by it." A sudden thought struck him, a thought that made his stomach twist a little. "The Prime's not your lover, is he?"

"Well, I thought it might take you a little longer to discern the truth. There goes your revenge, my lord. No, I'm not his mistress. I never have been, and I never will be. That place is already taken. Why do you think I was so certain Mrs. Ross had not stolen the relic? Let us just say that her whereabouts that night were quite well-known and her alibi is foolproof."

"But you love him?"

"Of course I love him. He is terribly dear to me." She seemed to enjoy his discomfiture.

Lucien's eyes narrowed. Miss Martin actually laughed, a soft, husky sound that he liked very much.

"Come here," he said.

"But it's not nighttime, my lord." Miss Martin blinked her eyelashes at him flirtatiously. "I don't have to do anything that you say. Quite the opposite."

Reaching forward, he hauled her into his arms. Miss Martin gave a startled squeal that died as he settled her in his lap. Her skirts fell around his thighs, and the snug curve of her bottom settled against his groin. Miss Martin sucked in a sharp breath.

"Why do you hold him so dearly?" he asked, toying with the buttons on her dress. It was buttoned all the way to her throat, where a fringe of lace brushed against her neck. Red suited her. It was a color made for dangerous women, though her admission of inexperience threw him a little.

"Why does the precise nature of my relationship with Drake concern you so much?" As he drove forward to press his lips against the soft skin beneath her jaw, her fingers pressed against his mouth, stilling him.

Lucien looked up, then sucked one of them into his mouth, circling it with his tongue. Miss Martin's pupils were so very large, her lips parting breathily. She might be unused to such displays, but she didn't dislike them. White teeth sank into her lower lip. He wanted, very badly, to replace it with his own mouth.

And couldn't.

"It doesn't," he lied. Again those fingers denied him.

"Answer my question, and I'll answer yours."

That irritated him, for as much as he didn't particularly want to explore his own motivations in pursuing the answer, he did indeed want to know the truth.

Lucien nipped at her fingers. "Because *I* want you. Because I wanted to steal you away from him. Because I wanted to fuck him out of your mind. That's why I wanted to know what he is to you, especially now that you speak of him having another mistress."

"He was never in my mind."

"In your heart then." He started to undo the buttons at her throat.

"My lord," she protested in a whisper.

"It's not night. You have no obligation to let me please you, unless you wish to. And you owe me an answer."

Thick lashes dragged over her violet eyes. Miss Martin looked both helpless and fascinated. Her hand splayed flat over his heart, holding him at bay. "Drake was the father I never had," she blurted. "You don't have to do this. He's not your competition."

That satisfied something inside of him that Lucien hadn't even known was bothered. It also raised numerous questions about her. "Your own father chairs the Vigilance Against Sorcery Committee." Grant Martin was a thorn in all of their sides, and a bastard to boot. "Does that have anything to do with you?"

"Of course it does. My father thinks that I am filth. He threw me out onto the streets when I was seventeen. I had no one. Nothing. Only the clothes I wore and a future where I could earn my living on my back or as some rich man's mistress." Her laugh sounded brutal. "You will never understand what Drake did for me. He'd felt my sorcery— the way I expressed it—and he came looking for me. He offered me a life as my own woman and took me under his wing as his apprentice when nobody had ever given a damn about me, and when such a position was highly coveted. Of course everyone in the Order thought I was his lover. What other use could a man have for a young woman? Why else would he help her? I love him for that. I love him for showing me that men can be trusted. That someone wanted to be my father, without trying to ever take anything from me. You don't know what it is like to grow up knowing nothing but shame—"

A queer feeling twisted in his stomach, an echoing ache. *Yes, actually, I do...*

"—and then realizing that you *do* have worth. That everything that you had despised about your own nature was something to be celebrated and accepted. It was *encouraged*. Does that explain it all?" Tears pricked at her eyes, but they were fiercely determined and very, very protective. "I would do anything for Drake. Anything at all."

The cut of it went deep, that the Prime could be a father figure to her, when he had never given a damn about a son of his own blood. It was an ugly feeling, for Lucien hadn't known he'd even craved such a thing.

"Yes, it explains it." It also explained her anger at the way he'd assumed such a thing too. Taking Miss Martin's hand from his chest, he set it on his lapel, then took her chin in his hand, his thumb resting against those pretty lips. "Why did you agree to this?"

"Because I wanted you," she whispered, her fleshy lower lip teasing his thumb. "Perhaps I knew it would be like this between us? Perhaps I just wanted... something to take my mind off everything. When you touch me, sometimes it feels like I'm not alone. And I don't think I could stand to be alone, not right now." A tear slid down her porcelain cheek. Cupping his face in both hands, Ianthe leaned forward and licked at his jaw.

His cock leapt against his trousers. Lucien bared his teeth in a snarl and tilted his head back, granting her access as he shoved both hands under her skirts. He hadn't liked the thought that she'd done this with the idea of herself as his whore, or that she'd done this to protect the Prime, but desire... the idea of her wanting him made something primal rear inside him.

Such soft skin... Warm, plump thighs... He went straight for the heat of her, slipping two fingers between the slit in her drawers, and grasped her hip with the other hand. There was wetness there. Miss Martin gasped against his neck, her teeth sinking into his flesh as he rasped his thumb over her clit and buried his fingers to the hilt inside of her.

"Fuck my hand," he whispered, nuzzling his mouth against her throat.

There was a flash of uncertainty in her eyes; then she rocked her hips forward gently, filling herself with him.

"You were not a virgin," he said.

Miss Martin laughed her husky laugh, and her body tightened around his fingers in response. "Why are you so fascinated with me?"

I don't know. He met her gaze with a challenging one of his own. "Perhaps I just want to know how far I can push you."

Nipping at his fingers, she rocked forward again, a slow undulation, as though she was beginning to learn what he wanted and perhaps what she herself needed. "As far as you want to, my lord. I won't break."

It was an effective sidestep away from his question. "How many lovers have you had?"

Her dark gaze was oh, so knowing. "Two. The first was... unexpected, but not undesired. I was lonely and curious. I wanted to know what it felt like for someone to pretend to care for me for just one night, and then... Well, he far exceeded my expectations. The second was out of curiosity. It didn't last long, and it didn't end well. Quite soured my opinion on the subject for a few years."

Hardly innocent, but still untutored. "I shocked you last night." He began rubbing slow circles around her clit with his thumb. The scent of her desire was rich and heady. As she rode him, her eyelashes fluttered as if the sensation his thumb was wringing out of her was entirely too much.

"Yes," Ianthe gasped, her mouth parting and her nails digging into his shoulder. "Rathbourne."

"Yes?"

"I enjoyed every second of it," she whispered, her hips jerking with small, taut movements.

He could feel the press of her body, the way she clenched around his touch. The idea that she'd enjoyed his mastery made desire flush through him. He wanted her to find her pleasure with him. He needed her to, but he couldn't force it. "What part of it did you enjoy?" he murmured, pressing his cheek against hers so that his breath brushed her ear. "The fucking?" Her body clenched again. "Or the surrender?"

There. That was it. Ianthe moaned lightly, her nails digging into the sleeves of his coat. "All of it."

Cupping his free hand behind her nape, he dragged her closer, thrusting a little to give her what she could barely force herself to take at the moment. Her skin was soft as he brushed his face against her throat, then moved lower, unbuttoning buttons as he went, and licking his way down all of that pale, creamy flesh until he found the soft curve of her breast, still cupped carefully in her wealth of lace and the restriction of her stays. Lucien's tongue darted beneath her bodice, finding her nipple hard and swollen.

"Oh," she whispered, arching into the caress. "Yes."

"I think you like being under my command." This time teeth accompanied the words.

Miss Martin cried out, clutching his hair in her fist. Lucien surveyed her shocked face over the smooth expanse of bare skin, then softened the sharp pain of his bite with his tongue. What was it about her that drove him to such lack of composure? He wanted to ruck her skirts up, tumble her back on the seats, and fuck the sense out of her. She was madness-inducing. He'd never felt such lack of composure when it came to a woman.

Control it...

Turning and pressing her back against the seat, he knelt between her parted thighs and pressed them wide. Her drawers were soft silk and wet with her desire. Grabbing her by the bottom, Lucien dragged her hips to the edge of the seat and buried his face between her thighs, licking through the silk, his tongue tracing small circles around the hard nub there. His cock was hard. Aching. But this was purely for her.

It had nothing to do with controlling his own fierce need...

Miss Martin gasped. "Rathbourne."

"Not the time for questions, love." Spreading both thumbs against her draws, he parted them, leaving her at his mercy.

She shivered as his breath wet her sensitive skin. Anticipation locked her up harder as Lucien enjoyed the moment, letting it extend until she was practically quivering.

"Look at you," he whispered, "all pretty and pink."

Then his tongue found her clit.

Miss Martin's thighs clenched around his head. "Oh, God!"

She was both delicious and responsive. Lucien drowned himself in her, listening intently to her soft sounds, feeling her body's tension twist tighter and tighter, until...

She came with a shocked cry, her fingers gripping fists of his hair. Lucien panted on his knees, a smile of satisfaction crossing his face as he looked up at her flushed face.

This time, her pleasure was real.

Afterward, he drew her into his lap, letting her head rest against his chest. There was no help for it. Ianthe was going to look breathless and utterly ruined when they arrived. It made his chest clench a little. From her relaxed pose, it seemed she hadn't thought of it herself yet, but he didn't like the idea of her arriving at Balthazar's Labyrinth and having hard eyes notice the disheveled state of her hair or the flushed skin at her throat where his whiskers had grazed, of people assuming what she had called herself.

Whore. It was an ugly word, but one in which the men he knew cast too easily. And one which she knew, far too well, it seemed.

A finger traced the buttons on his waistcoat. "Do you want to...?"

God, yes. He wanted to tumble her to her knees and drive himself into her willing body. Instead, he shook his head. "Tonight. There's time for that later tonight."

Miss Martin's gaze dropped to his lap, sighting the evidence of his lack of composure. She looked dubious. And guilty.

"What's wrong?"

"Nothing," Miss Martin said. "I just feel... like I shouldn't have enjoyed myself. Not when everything's going wrong."

"And energy-wise, how do you feel?"

She frowned. "Wonderful."

"Your affinity lies with sexually charged sorceries. Consider what we just did a way to strengthen yourself. Not something to be ashamed of. Here, sit up. We're nearly there."

Miss Martin sat up quickly. Lucien busied himself with fixing the buttons at her throat, and then turned her in his lap, so he could smooth her hair back into place. It wasn't perfect; he was far more skilled at unraveling a woman, rather than putting her back together, but it might do to fool all but the most practiced eye.

When he had finished, she glanced at him from underneath those thick, dark lashes. There was a question there.

Lucien shifted her to the seat beside him. "I swore to protect you. That includes your reputation."

Ianthe considered his words, the moment drawing out. "You're a...complicated man."

Their eyes met and held for long moments.

"Yes," he replied, "I am."

CHAPTER EIGHT

THE GIRL was crying again.

Morgana set aside the letter she had been writing and glared at the door separating her sitting room from the room that Louisa was currently attempting to flood. She'd been trying to ignore it, but the exhausted half-sobs reminded her only a little too well of all the times she'd been locked away in small rooms as a child, after she'd been beaten by her uncle. The only difference was that she'd soon stopped crying. Tears earned you nothing, and this was hardly comparable. After all, the girl had an entire bedroom with a nice bed and soft blankets. Not a small closest tucked under the stairs, or even the box that her uncle liked to put her in for the day. *She* wasn't being starved. *She* wasn't being beaten for not being a boy, or for being another burden, another mouthful to feed when food was scarce. There could always be bloody worse things to cry about.

Morgana scraped back the chair, stood in a swish of dark aubergine skirts, and rapped sharply on the door. "Cease that noise at once, or you won't get any supper!"

It worked. Silence descended, golden, blessed silence. Thank goodness.

"Threatening children again, are we mother?"

Morgana stifled the leap of her heart. Visits from Sebastian always required a steeling of the nerves, but he'd taken to the habit of sneaking about on cat-quiet feet. Sometimes she wondered if he knew how much his presence unnerved her. "You're late."

He always was.

It was always fifteen minutes, or ten, here and there. She'd chided him for the small rebellions, but punishing him for each and every infraction would have gained her nothing. It was something her uncle had taught her. The more you punished someone, the more they seemed to be able to tolerate it. By doling out pain in rare increments, the tension built. You were always waiting for the fist to fall, always on the tip of your toes, watching your tormentor for the slightest hint of movement. Sometimes she'd just wished her uncle would get it over and done with, and perhaps that had been the worst part.

Her son stood staring through the windows at the park in the Square, the gray afternoon light washing over his features. There was a beaver hat in his hand, which he toyed with absently, and his coat and trousers were impeccable and richly furnished. He looked like some devastatingly handsome noble, but that was innate, not something she'd been able to provide with rich clothes, fine boots, and countless hours of tutoring. Sebastian had his father's air; arrogance lingered in the upright tilt of his chin and the firm press of his lips spoke for little tolerance for others and their foibles.

The only discrepancy in his appearance was the lack of tie and the way his shirt was unbuttoned just enough to show the glinting gold of the collar around his throat. Sometimes Morgana wondered if he flaunted it like that on purpose, whenever he was within the house she'd rented, as if to say: *You might be able to control me with this mother, but I will never forget what you have done to me, or forgive you for it.*

"I had something important to attend to," he replied.

No doubt that something important had been perusing the books in the library, or strolling through the gardens behind the house and tending to his precious bloody roses. "Matters are moving quite swiftly at the moment, Sebastian. We're beginning to set our act into play. If you keep me waiting one more time..."

He looked at her, giving her his full chill-inducing attention. The mercurial color of his eyes was Drake's, but the predatory intensity behind them were not. Her ex-husband had never been this dangerous. Drake had been warmth and heat; Sebastian was pure ice. "You'll what? Send me to my knees with this collar?" Tapping the hat against his leg, he took a step toward her, his lips curling into a smile that never reached his eyes. "How long do you think that ring you wear on your finger will protect you? How long can this collar keep me as your slave?"

It was something she'd thought about almost every day since his twelfth birthday, when his powers began to manifest, a strength of sorcery like the boiling clouds of a thunderstorm on the horizon. She'd never seen anything like it, though she'd long since known that this son of hers, this son she'd stolen from the Prime, would be dangerous and difficult to control indeed.

The previous Cassandra, Lady Rathbourne, had predicted it after all, with her belly thickening with Drake's bastard.

That day seemed burned into her memory. It had been a tea party, with all of the Order's malicious eyes watching as the two women circled each other around a table laden with small cucumber sandwiches, honey cakes, scones, jam, and clotted cream. They all knew that Morgana had been on the outs with her husband after the unfortunate poisoning of his nephew and heir. Begetting Sebastian had been a feat in itself—an explosive argument between them that she'd turned to her advantage—and the precious, precious little weapon growing inside of her had been her insurance policy against the divorce Drake had threatened her with.

If not for Drake's mistress, Lady Rathbourne, and the unfortunate fact that she too was swelling with child, Morgana might have been able to sway him.

It had been a small moment at the tea party, a matter of losing sight of her rival between the astrology games they'd all been playing and the setting up of the readings. There'd been a bump and a *'pardon mademoiselle'* in that syrupy French drawl, and then Lady Rathbourne had smiled at her insincerely, one lace-gloved hand brushing Morgana's middle, her eyes widening in shock as prophecy grabbed hold of her.

"*This son shall never be yours,*" the Order's Cassandra stated in a ringing voice, strangely stripped of her accent, her pupils narrowed to pinpricks and unseeing.

With a gasp, Lady Rathbourne had staggered away as the prophecy released her, felling a servant with a platter of lemon cakes and almost sending the sandwich table to a similar doom. Eyes everywhere had turned, locking on the spectacle, and whispers sprang up, hidden behind lacy fans.

Morgana hadn't been able to stay there. She'd fled instead, one hand on the ruffles used to camouflage her thickened state, the other almost wringing the starch from her handkerchief. In a quiet corner of the gardens, she'd found refuge, but there was no respite from her thoughts. *He'll never be mine.* She could fool herself all she wanted, tell herself that she'd finally found something, someone who would love her no matter what and never betray her, but she'd had her own doubts. A child had to love its mother, did it not? But that hope had been shattered by the foul-tasting tang of foretelling that lingered in her own mouth.

Even the baby moved within her restlessly at that moment, a spiteful kick, as if to say that he too agreed.

There was no time to think her way out of it. The divorce proceedings began a week later. Not even threatening to abort their son had stayed Drake's hand long enough. By law, the child would have been his. With the Order signing an Execution warrant for her for the poisoning of Drake's nephew, she wouldn't have even remained alive to see her son grow and have a chance at luring him to her side.

Fleeing Britain was her only hope, and it gave her a vicious pleasure to cross the Channel, knowing that by then Drake would have received her letter with the bloody remnants in the rag she'd sent him. *'Here is your son. Tell your mistress that her foretelling came true: I will never have him, but neither shall you.'*

A lie, of course, but imagining the pain Drake had felt had been the only thing to put a smile on her face in those early days. Nobody threw her away. She was tired of men ruining her life with their fists and their broken promises. She was never going to trust another man again.

Not even her son.

"If you ever tried to remove the collar, Sebastian, I think you'd find the pain quite beyond what I have been delivering when you disobey me. I'm told trying to remove it is almost... unendurable."

Only a faint flare of his nostrils betrayed any hint of emotion. "We shall see. Do you remember that tale you once told me about your uncle? About how he tried to lock you in that box one too many times? It was an interesting bedtime story for a boy of seven, and I never forgot it, but like other tales for children, it has an interesting moral to the story. I wonder when I will reach that moment when pain becomes nothing more than a minor annoyance, and the desire to remove... this" —he touched his throat— "becomes the overwhelming emotion. I wonder if you will be quite so sanguine then."

Morgana allowed herself a faint smile, though a trickle of sweat slithered down her spine. "Let this be another lesson then: one always keeps a trump card up their sleeve, Sebastian. If you think the collar is the only way I can control you, then you should think again."

"And how would you do that?" Sorcery began to build within him, the air suddenly growing cooler as he drew energy into him. "I am stronger than you."

Stronger yes, but with no finesse. "Oh, I won't stand against you, Sebastian. Not with sorcery. I know just what you can do with sorcery, how strong you are. Indeed, that small town in Provence knows exactly what you can do too, does it not?" She smiled at the faint flicker of doubt that crossed his brow and took a step toward him. It was the sort of thing that wouldn't have kept her awake. People died. Houses collapsed. The earth sometimes tore itself apart. Such was life, and she had little compassion for strangers when no one had ever showed compassion toward her. But this son of hers *was* his father. She had to remember that, and it gave her unique insight into his character. If Sebastian could lose himself to Expression and destroy so much at one little death—just an insignificant servant girl he should barely have noticed, let alone cared if she was crushed beneath the wheels of a powerful ally's carriage—then imagine what he would do if she threatened someone he cared about?

Morgana let out a steaming breath. The air was freezing now, so cold that her lungs caught, but she took another step and reached up to button his shirt collar. "If you ever break free, Sebastian, I won't fight you. I will let you destroy me without even raising a ward against you." She slipped the last button through its hole, hiding the wretched collar, and stepped back, giving him a gentle pat on the cheek. "But I shall take everyone else I can with me. That little girl crying in the room next door..." His gaze turned sharply toward the room, but she caught his chin and turned his face back to hers. "The butler, the maids, the footmen... That old harpy next door who you've taken quite a shine to... I won't fight your power, Sebastian, but I will amplify it. Imagine how much of London I can take with me if I ride your strength? Imagine how many people you'll kill? I'll make sure you survive though, my precious boy. You'll be standing in the circle of a pile of rubble, and all about you, you will hear the screams of crushed children and mothers crying for their babies. The scent of blood and death will be your legacy to the world."

It was the first time she'd ever seen such emotion in his eyes. He lived the horrors that she spoke of, seeing it in front of him, the memory made even sharper for the fact that he had lived through it once before, and still felt the whip of guilt.

The floor began to shift beneath her feet as she stared up at him, her fingertips resting against his cheek. This was the dangerous moment, for if he lost control of his emotions, then he might level the city regardless of his intentions, or hers. It was starting to hurt to breathe, the air so intensely frigid that she could almost feel icicles forming in the dew of her eyes.

"Think of that little girl crying on her bed. Use the fear of that, of what you could do to her, to fight the anger you're feeling. Control it, Sebastian."

He shut his eyes, his fists clenched firmly. A shockwave of raw power lashed out, making the table shudder and the chairs rattle and shake across the timber floors. Morgana caught his coat in a fist, trying to stay upright herself.

She could see the moment her words penetrated, and as his jaw locked hard, the trembling floor began to stabilize and the rattling of the shutters grew weaker.

Timing it perfectly, Morgana sent a lash of sorcery through the ring on her finger. The collar around his throat tightened just a fraction in response, and Sebastian turned white as his nerves lit on fire. Pain broke his hold on emotion and his concentration. By the time he was gasping at her feet, one knee pressed to the floor and both hands curled around the collar, the room had stopped shaking entirely.

"Now get up," she said, spilling hot, steamy breath into the cool air. "Let us not have this discussion again."

Circling the secretariat, Morgana sat again and examined the letter she'd been writing, signing her name with a flourish and trying to pretend that her hands weren't trembling. She let him take his time to gather himself after that little display. It was easier now. The first time had been the worst. There'd been a wide-eyed look on his thirteen-year-old face, as if he simply couldn't believe that she'd done it. Betrayal was the emotion she most disliked, for it reminded her too much of her own past, but she'd hardened her heart and turned away from him then, just as she did now.

If only he could have been hers... If he could have loved her right from the start, things would be so different. He'd bought this on himself. No mother cared to be despised by her own child.

"I assume," he said hoarsely, as he dragged himself to his feet, "that you have some service required of me."

Morgana sealed the letter. "Several tasks. As I mentioned, our plan is unfolding as we speak. Here." She extended the letter. "I want you to deliver this to Lord Tremayne. Tell him I've agreed to his terms."

"I thought you said that he asked too much."

"I've since reconciled the matter in my mind. His terms of agreement can be overcome." Morgana leaned back in the leather chair and pressed her fingers into a steeple. "In fact, perhaps I should warn you, his terms apply to you directly. I wouldn't want you losing your temper when I'm not there to control it, should the Earl happen to mention it."

"And *why* would I lose my temper?" This was the deadly soft voice she knew and recognized. He was recovering much more quickly from one of their little 'episodes' these days. "What task have you pledged me to now? Murdering some creditor? Fucking his wife or his mistress, perhaps both at the same time, so the old goat doesn't have to bestir himself to keep them from his throat?"

"No, Sebastian. I know you find such things distasteful."

And there had been that incident three months ago, when an ally of hers, Lady Wormwald, had wanted to see if he looked as pretty beneath his clothes as he did with them on. Sebastian had always been a potent attraction for such potential allies, and Morgana had never shirked at offering him up before, but after Lady Wormwald... Well, she'd never thought that men would be bothered by such duties, but perhaps it was best not to set him into another situation like that, where his emotions could potentially overwhelm him. She'd bribed Lady Wormwald's husband to keep quiet, and really, he was well rid of the bitch, but Sebastian was Morgana's most dangerous weapon. She couldn't afford for Drake to hear even the quietest whisper about him.

Sebastian's shoulders relaxed a hint. "Then what must I do?"

"You're to marry his daughter. An alliance to prove my trustworthiness to Tremayne this time aroun—"

"No." A hand slammed on the secretariat, disbursing papers everywhere. "No, I won't do it."

Morgana looked up, gauging the depth of his distress and finding not quite enough to warrant caution. "Yes. You will. It's not like you have to fuck the little bitch. Husbands and wives keep separate beds all of the time, and Tremayne wishes her to remain pure for some reason. I'd argue, but in fact, I'd much prefer it if our bloodlines *don't* mingle, as I have plans for Tremayne, but—"

"Do I not get to make one bloody decision in my life? Not even one?"

"If you interrupt me again, Sebastian..." She didn't bother with the rest of the warning.

He breathed out a laugh, his eyes wild. "Your uncle should have cut your throat. He should have realized what a little snake he had under his roof and just how poisonous you could be. It would have done the world a favor."

"And then you wouldn't exist!" It didn't sting. It *didn't.* She wouldn't let it.

"Would that be such a very bad thing?"

Another tremor shifted through the room, surprising her. She hadn't even felt him drawing in his power. The letter opener vibrated off her secretariat and disappeared into the shiver of papers on the floor. Morgana grabbed for the small writing desk, swallowing hard. This was stronger than before, almost enough to shatter the glass in the windows.

But this time, Morgana didn't have to do anything to stop it. Something shattered in the small bedroom next door and a frightened scream cut through the world.

The tremors stopped immediately.

The girl was crying again, curled up against the door from the sound of it, as if to escape whatever had happened inside the room. Morgana had never been so grateful to hear tears in her life.

She let them drag out, each sucked-in sob a knife into the heart of her son. She could see it in his eyes, in the hopeless way he shut them, his head bowing as if he'd finally given up.

There were shards of ice across her desk, like those found drawn on a window in crisp mornings, which was... a little concerning. The room was so cold and still. The whole house sounded empty of life and noise, as if he'd drawn heat and life from all of it in but a second.

Dangerous, something whispered in her mind. *He is more dangerous than you ever believed him.*

Not even Drake could gather so much power so quickly.

And just like that, her fear disappeared.

Not even Drake could stand against Sebastian's power, if she wielded it. The entire Triad of Councilors would wilt at the immensity of it. All she had to do was find a way to take it for herself.

Sebastian took the letter in hand with a blank, hopeless expression. "Is there anything else you desire of me?"

Yes. There was so much more, and yet she wasn't quite certain she dared at this moment. Had she been missing the signs of how close he was to the edge all along? Or had he learned to hide it? She would have to be so, so careful with this son of hers.

"Just... Just deliver the letter. And this one." She dug through the mess at her feet, finding a sealed envelope with a single lock of hair in it and an instruction on delivery. "Time to make Miss Martin pay her dues. See that our little *friend* drops it on her bed. Let us hope she's taken heed of my warnings and done as she was told."

"I won't let you hurt that child."

"I never intended it." Morgana managed a tight smile. "Murder is so messy." And final. If you destroyed your tools, then who knew when you would ever need them again? It was the same reason that Sebastian had been birthed into this world. "All I need to do is make sure the girl disappears quietly and is never seen again and nobody knows any better."

Sebastian slid the two envelopes inside the pocket of his waistcoat. There was no sign if he agreed or not, which bothered her a little.

"Then... take the afternoon off," Morgana said slowly. "Do something for yourself, whatever you would like, as long as it doesn't betray us. Your choice. I shall see you here by dinner, as we have a full evening planned." She tipped her head to him, noting the startled glance he shot her. Perhaps this would be a better, more careful way to manage him? "I can be kind, Sebastian. I would like to be kind. If you would only stop defying me, you would know more of it."

Black lashes darkened those beautiful, blank eyes. "The problem is: can I trust it?"

Drake slammed the book he'd been perusing shut and lifted his head, turning it uncannily toward the south. Sorcery thickened the air, on a scale the likes of which he'd never felt before. It welled like a furious storm, bits of it breaking off and earthing itself like lightning bolts of pure power. So imprecise and violent, an enormous tidal wave of power that hovered on the edge of the horizon with threatening intent. This was not the type of sorcery he'd encountered before, with its carefully manipulated threads. This just wanted to smash, to lash out, to bubble up, and spill all over the world like a volcano that was starting to tremble.

All of the blood started to run from his extremities, flooding in toward his heart. *Oh, hell.*

"What the devil was that?" Eleanor Ross looked up from the map she'd been dangling his pocket watch over, noting his sudden absorption. She knew him far too well, well enough to sift through the silent message he was sending her with his face and body. "What happened?"

"Someone is using Expression."

"Where? Can you stop it? Can you trace it back to them?"

Drake tasted the metallic bite of sorcery on his tongue as he closed his eyes. South. Not too far away, perhaps within three miles. He had to upgrade his original assessment of power. Anything that felt so strong this far away had to be enormous. No one person should ever be able to channel that much energy.

The loss of the relic had cost him sleep ever since he discovered it, but this... this terrified him. Finding sorcerer had to be his priority. Ianthe and Rathbourne could chase the relic, which he couldn't afford to forget, but if he didn't find who was bleeding that much power over the West End then there might not be a West End for much longer.

There might not even be a London.

CHAPTER NINE

'Not everyone sides with the Order of the Dawn Star. It might be the most legitimate group of practitioners in the Empire, but there are those who chafe against its rules, or who were cast out in exile... And then, of course, there are those occult beings who were never truly quite human in the first place...'

- Thoughts on Occult London, by Sir Geoffrey Mellors

THE PORTOBELLO ROAD markets were in full swing as Rathbourne escorted Ianthe along the busy thoroughfare. Barrow boys bellowed at the top of their lungs, and laughter and music filled the air.

With a sigh of relief, Ianthe saw what they were searching for and followed as Rathbourne pushed his way into the Black Horse Pub. They stood for a moment in the smoky confines, Rathbourne's nearness a welcome respite. One of his hands rested lightly on the small of her back, almost protectively, even as his gaze searched the room. Only three of the chairs were occupied, men nursing ale and staring contemplatively at their tables. The Black Horse wasn't a place that anyone came to in order to socialize. It was a haven of neutrality in their occult world, and the pall over the room stank heavily of black sorcery. A touch malevolent, like sour, old beer mixed with the air of a freshly opened grave.

Hardly a place that Ianthe enjoyed.

The bartender had been swiping down the filthy counter, but he paused as he saw them, his mouth thinning to a hyphen. Without a word, he spat on the floor, then tipped his chin up toward her challengingly.

He was a small man, standing on a stool behind the counter and peering over his half-spectacles at them. Some said there was imp blood in him. It was certainly true that he didn't quite feel human. Something about the Shadow Dimensions clung to him, or perhaps that was because he had a long-held fascination with planes of existence that nobody should dabble with. Cochrane's sorcery was as black as night.

"Mr. Cochrane," Rathbourne said smoothly. "Fancy seeing you here."

"Indeed," Magnus Cochrane replied, setting down the rag and leaning on the counter with his knuckles. "Thought you was in Bedlam."

"I was. Decided to take a turn about outside."

"Didn't think the Prime were that forgiving." Cochrane spat on the floor again, and the movement dislodged his sleeve, revealing the heavy brass manacle around his wrist with its burning, coppery charms. The manacle kept him chained within the tavern's physical limits, where he could do no more damage. Cochrane was very good at not-quite breaking the Order's Laws, but he'd come close one too many times. Certainly more than was in the public's interest. He turned his leering gaze toward

Ianthe. "Ah. Here's the Prime's pet puss. Startin' to make sense now. What you hunting?"

"Mr. Cochrane," she said, trying to ignore his stare and the way it settled on her bodice. It wasn't as if there was an inch of skin to see, but she suddenly felt naked. "I—"

Rathbourne reached past her and grabbed a fistful of the little man's necktie, yanking him facedown onto the bar and pressing his nose into a faint circle of beer that someone's tankard had left behind. "I would choose your words more carefully, Cochrane. The next time you make some vulgar remark toward Miss Martin, I will see to it that you spend the rest of your days sipping your dinner off a spoon."

With a pleasant smile, he let go of the man's necktie, and Cochrane swayed back, almost falling off his stool.

Silence fell throughout the tavern. One man's chair scraped back, as if the crowd were poised to flee.

Ianthe closed her mouth slowly.

That moment in the carriage returned full force, when Rathbourne had gently patted her hair into place, then matter-of-factly smoothed the wrinkles from her gown. She hadn't known what to make of it then, and she didn't know now.

He's protecting me, that's all. But it didn't feel like this newfound interest in her reputation stemmed from his oath to her. No, she'd seen it in his face when she'd taken the words that some of the Order's sorcerers called her— behind her back, of course—and used them on herself.

It had felt like... an olive branch. And she could not quite pretend to herself that a part of her didn't ache for more of that. The way Lucien looked at her, at times... She had spent so many years alone, trying to pretend that her study of sorcery fulfilled her life, but in the deepest quiet of night, when she was alone in her bed, she sometimes wished for someone of her own. A husband to wake up to. A family. The daughter that she had watched grow up from a distance, snuggled into her lap, where she could breathe in the sweet rose scent that always lingered about Louisa's hair...

But none of that was to be.

It was dangerous, this bond between them. It made her want things she shouldn't. She'd only be left alone and heartbroken at the end of this quest. Her focus must be on her daughter, nothing else.

Magnus Cochrane gave her another appraising look, but this one didn't feel quite so slimy. "I see," he said, and from the flinty look in his eyes, he did, but didn't dare comment more on the subject.

Several of their spectators let out loose breaths, and Ianthe's shoulders relaxed. If Cochrane had thrown down upon Rathbourne, she'd have been obliged to protect him. For, despite that surge of power he'd lashed out with yesterday, she wasn't entirely certain he was up to it himself.

"So what do you want?" Cochrane demanded.

"We want passage to Balthazar's Labyrinth," she said. "We're looking for Mr. Elijah Horroway. I have some questions for him."

"Ain't here," Cochrane replied with a blank face.

"The spirit of Mr. Horroway then," she shot back. "And I know that's in the Labyrinth, no doubt trying to find some way to fully resurrect itself. Come along, Cochrane. If you dilly-dally too long, my companion here might grow impatient. Believe me, you wouldn't want that. He's barely civilized as it is."

Cochrane grunted, then hopped down off his stool and disappeared behind the counter. Rathbourne exchanged a slightly amused look with her at the threat she'd used. Ianthe shrugged.

All they could see was the top of Cochrane's bald head. Then he waddled out toward a wall of curtains and reached up to tug on a bell pull there. The red velvet curtains slid back, exposing an enormous iron wheel embedded into the wall, like the door to a bank vault, which it had once been, of course.

A panel slid open in the door, revealing an inch or two of a cold stone face. It could have been a mask or rock carving. "Yes?" Came a harsh whisper, like the breath of air slipping from a newly opened tomb.

"Themselves want entrance to the Inn." Cochrane jerked his thumb back toward them.

"They paid the price?"

"Not yet." Cochrane gestured toward the small stone altar on the side of the door.

Unease ran through Ianthe. She'd heard tales from the Colonies about curses that could be applied using a person's hair, fingernails, or skin. Still, blood was blood, and the sorcerers to be found within the Labyrinth were those belonging to the Darker disciplines.

Taking out the little athame most sorcerers carried with them, she cut the fleshy, scarred pad of her thumb, then allowed a drop to fall into the silver bowl on the altar. "Let no harm be done by my will within. I grant the sorcerers of the Labyrinth safe passage and ask for it myself."

Almost an inch of blood lingered in the bottom, and as her droplet hit the crimson liquid, small circles spread outward, a shiver of sorcery trickling cold fingers up her spine. The oath was set and would backfire upon her should she break it. Wordlessly, she handed the blade to Rathbourne, who echoed her gesture.

"Done," she told Cochrane, tucking her athame back within her reticule. "Now let us pass."

"With pleasure." His evil little leer had returned. Reaching up, he hauled hard on the iron wheel, straining to put his weight into it. The wheel turned slowly at first, then moved with well-oiled glee until the circular door popped open.

Instant noise assaulted them; foul-mouthed curses spat into the street beyond as a tall woman in a cloak argued with a hunched old man over his barrow of goods. It was like stepping into another world, one hidden from the eyes of the normal people of London. A dark echo of the Portobello Markets, well-lit by tallow candles that wept fat globules of melted wax, instead of gaslights. Dozens of occult shops, herb gardens, apothecary's, laboratories, and even a museum lurked within. Some said there were even duels to the death held for entertainment value in the courtyard of the tavern down the end of Main Alley.

"Welcome to Balthazar's Labyrinth." Cochrane gestured them inside.

The gatekeeper on the other side of the door stepped aside with slow, heavy steps, and Ianthe hopped over the rim of the door, trying to look unconcerned. This wasn't her first time in the Labyrinth, but as always, she felt a shiver of nervousness. She wasn't protected here. The Prime had no control over what went on within this slick warren of alleys that was hidden from Null eyesight. Oh, some of its denizens were still wary enough of Drake's power to be careful with her, but others here had bones of contention to pick with the Prime. Destroying his envoy would make some of them into great names amongst those who dabbled on the edges of the Order.

The creature guarding the door slowly shut it behind them and swung the wheel with ease to latch it shut. Part-construct, it resembled an enormous stone golem. A charm had been painted on its forehead in blood, and its blank eyes were pits of gray.

Locked in. If only she didn't feel so nervous. No sense in portraying it, however, as the people leering at them would sense it and be upon them like vultures.

"Come along then," she said to Rathbourne. "Let's go corner that rat, Horroway, and see what he knows."

"Perhaps I'd best take the lead," Lucien murmured, eyeing the riffraff in the alley.

A hand to his sleeve stopped him. "And do what, precisely?" Miss Martin asked, her eyes serious as she looked up at him. "I'm well tutored in wards, courtesy of Drake. There's not much here that I cannot handle. Guard my back."

Then, with a purposeful swish of her bustle, she swept in front of him, striding over the cobbles as if she owned the place.

Bloody woman. Lucien growled under his breath and strode after her. If there was one place in all of London that made him hesitant to step into, this was it. The Labyrinth was a rambling set of streets that had been here for several hundred years. It looked like something straight out of Shakespeare's times. The eaves and rooves were crooked, some almost leaning against the opposite roof. Little shop faces opened into the alley, selling an assortment of goods: bat's feet and potions, all manner of oddments, rare astrology books, grimoires, dark pendants, and jewelry to deflect curses... Each shop had its own dark wares, and curious, invisible eyes watched them as they passed by the diamond-paned windows.

Dirty glass above kept the weather off the street and curious eyes out. If parliament ever realized it was here, it would send half the cabinet into conniptions. The Order had sworn itself to the monarchy years ago, and enough of them had done their part in certain wars or Colonial expansion, helping to leash other countries to Britannia's will, for the Queen and her cabinet to consider them allies, at least. Those war heroes and adventurers were considered servants of the empire, but as far as most of the Null world knew, they were but a source of parlor tricks and games and pretty sparkling lights. Not quite respectable, but certainly entertaining, and oh-so dashing in their uniforms.

If the cabinet knew the full extent of sorcery, of blood and death and poisonings, Miss Martin's father would finally be able to push through a law against them. This was London's dark secret, or one of them, a place belonging entirely to those of an occult nature. A place ungoverned by the Prime's long hand, with rules of its own and those of a mind to enforce them.

"This way," Miss Martin called over her shoulder and led him down an offshoot of an alley, which appeared even smaller and darker.

Steam billowed out of a grate in the cobbles, dashed aside by Miss Martin's skirts. Several barrow boys watched them pass, looking almost human until one of them blinked and a translucent eyelid slid shut over its eyes then vanished. Lucien let his hand fall to the pistol at his waist and stared them down as they passed by. Hell spawn, or their offspring. Miss Martin had charmed the bullets for him that morning, carving neat little runes of *strength*, *death*, and *invulnerability to magic* into them. He wasn't going to be as helpless as he had been yesterday.

"Horroway's most commonly found at Grimdark & Hastings. It's a bookshop owned by his friend Marius

Hastings. Don't trust either of them, and don't turn your back."

"Truly? And here I thought I'd passed my apprenticeship." Lucien guided her around a puddle of... something. Black and inky in the cobbled streets, it gave a strange gurgle as if something moved within the dark waters. "I have been here before, Miss Martin."

"You have?"

"How else do you think I bought the book containing a summoning spell for a demon? Or the focus objects for the ritual?"

"You were... different then." *Stronger,* she meant.

He had no time to reply, for the sign heralding Osiris Place appeared, and tucked just off it was the bookshop, Grimdark & Hastings.

Miss Martin paused on the threshold as if to make a dramatic entrance, and then speared the two occupants within with a hardened gaze. "Elijah Horroway. A word, if I may."

A man had been leaning against the counter, his battered top hat casting shade over his face and his coat collar tucked up. The coat looked dusty and there were several stab holes in it. On his hands was a motley pair of fingerless gloves. He didn't move, peering down into the book he'd been studying.

His friend, however, Mr. Hastings, backed into the wall, hands held up in surrender. "Miss M-Martin," he stuttered. Light flashed off his half-moon glasses, disguising his eyes. He was prematurely thinning on top, with a cascade of gingery curls around the side of his head. "What an unexpected delight." Wide eyes danced helplessly toward Horroway, who straightened and tucked something back within his coat.

"What d'you want?" Horroway ground out in a voice as dry as the grave. Those gloved hands rested flatly on the counter, and he tipped his head to the side.

Lucien still couldn't make out Horroway's features. He wasn't certain he wanted to. But he strode casually to the center of the room, hands resting lightly on his belt. He wouldn't put it past Horroway to break Guest Oath here. Though perhaps, considering his condition, he wasn't bound to it. There was no blood in *that* body, after all.

"Hastings. Out."

"Y-yes, ma'am." Marius Hastings skidded for the door and vanished.

Miss Martin took her time, tugging off her gloves one finger at a time as she surveyed the room. She had a flare for the theatrical, he suspected. "I'm after information, Horroway."

"Are you now?" Horroway gave a dry laugh, then tugged a flask from his pocket and poured some of its contents into the tumbler in front of him. His elixir, no doubt. "Brazen tart like you... What makes you think I'd be so obligin'? What you goin' to offer me? A run up cock alley?"

They both watched as he threw back his special potion, one that anchored his spirit to the flesh he inhabited, or so it was said.

"Language, Mr. Horroway," Miss Martin chided. "I suppose it's one of the first few civilized arts to leave a body, hmm?"

That earned her a slit-eyed side look. Lucien stepped closer.

Horroway turned around slowly, leaning back with both elbows resting on the counter. His face was straight out of a penny dreadful—or perhaps a grave—pockmarked and somewhat flaccid. His pallid mouth didn't quite look as though it worked properly, resembling a gasping, breeched fish. Only he wasn't gasping. He wasn't breathing at all. A brass chain was tucked inside his filthy waistcoat, and on it hung an hourglass. Once he had to flip the hourglass— every month it was rumored—he'd have to find a somewhat fresher body to claim.

"Looks like this one's growing somewhat haggard," Miss Martin said.

"You threatenin' me?" Horroway demanded. "That's the danger o' comin' in here, into me own turf. Guest Right might hold you, but it don't affect me none."

"The Guest Oath forbids me from harming you," Miss Martin replied sweetly. Power slid into her, like silk moving over sand. It brightened her complexion until she was almost vibrant. With a muttered Word, she flung one hand wide, and Horroway flew back over the counter and stuck to the wall, quivering like a dagger, with his boots almost two inches off the floor. "But it doesn't say anything about containing you. I wonder how long your grip on that foul-smelling body lasts? I wonder what would happen afterward, if you lost hold of it, or if you didn't get to your elixir in time, hmm? A containment ward causes no direct harm, does it?"

"Fuckin' Covent Garden Slut."

"That's enough," Lucien warned, crossing his arms over his chest and eyeing the... man. "If you speak to her like that again, I'll beat you bloody. Tell Miss Martin what she wants to know, and then we can leave, and you can go back to rotting."

That earned him a vicious glare. "What you want?"

"The truth. How long has Morgana been back in England?" Miss Martin showed not a hint of fear as she stepped closer.

Clever, how she didn't ask if the woman was here already. Horroway wouldn't quite know how much she knew.

"Don't know," Horroway said, licking his lips with a dry, cracked tongue. "Ain't seen her since the divorce."

"Oh, come now, Horroway. Presume I'm not an idiot. The two of you were bosom buddies, once upon a time... Wasn't there even talk of an engagement, before her betrothal to the Prime? You followed her around like a puppy at her heels, until she dismissed you for Drake, and then rumor has it you helped spirit her out of the country once Drake and the Order's Council put a price on her head. Has she contacted you?" Miss Martin asked.

"What for?" Horroway sneered.

"I don't know," Miss Martin shrugged, though there was a strange glitter to her eyes. "Perhaps she needed a place to hide? Perhaps she needed information about... certain relics."

"Ain't know nothin' about relics."

"Interesting how you answer that, but not the other question I asked."

This was the Miss Martin Lucien knew and recognized from the Grosvenor Hotel last year, when she'd arrested him. Capable, devious, fully in command of her wits, and confident of her strengths... Only in the privacy of her own rooms did she ever reveal a softer side with hints of vulnerability. It was a dangerous combination, for on one hand he admired her strength of will, whilst at the same time he found the woman who turned to him for comfort alluring. He wanted to know all of her secrets, wanted to understand what put that sadness in her eyes at times when she grew distracted and stared out of windows...

"Don't know where she is, don't know what she wants, don't know—"

"But you're not denying that she's in the country."

Horroway's mouth slammed shut. Then he bared his teeth at her. "You fuckin' bitch, you didn't know."

The faintest of smiles crossed Miss Martin's mouth. Slowly, with her skirts swishing, she paced in front of Horroway, looking for all the world like an academic contemplating a problem. "She's back in the country, back in London, but she's not come to you for help, has she? Oh, how the mighty have fallen. Poor Elijah. All of that loyalty you placed behind her, hoping that she'd come back to you one day... No hope of that though, now you're like this. Morgana wouldn't want a husk of a man. No, whom else would she turn to? Hmm." Miss Martin tapped her lips. "She never did have any female allies. Always men, strangely enough. Or perhaps not allies, perhaps we should call them what they were—puppets. So who is still alive out of all those who danced to her tune? Well, of course, there's Tremayne, but then they parted on bad terms after she and Drake conspired to steal the Relics Infernal from him, and Tremayne isn't the sort to dance to her tune for long. There's Roger Maddesley, but how much influence does he have these days? Chester Hemmingfield, perhaps? He's ambitious and no friend to the Prime..." She glanced toward Horroway. "What do you think?"

"I think you're fishin' for information, and I don't plan on givin' you any more of it."

Lucien tugged his pocket watch out of his coat. "How much time does he have on his timepiece?"

Plucking a handkerchief from her reticule, Miss Martin used it to tug the chain from Horroway's shirt. "Hmm, hard to say. A few days by the look of it."

Which was time they didn't have... "Perhaps we could take him back to your house and lock him in the cellar? Far away from any fresh bodies."

"Hmm."

"Fuck you!" Horroway snarled, twisting against the invisible hold that pinned him to the wall.

"Tremayne, Maddesley, or Hemmingfield?" Lucien demanded. "Who's helping her?"

"How in the seven hells should I know?" Horroway shot back. "Do I look like I keep track of her swains? Maybe you ought to widen your list? There's more sorcerers who grow tired of the Prime's yoke than is on that list!"

"He's lying," Lucian said, with some certainty. It was more difficult to read the faint, faint flicker of color over Horroway's face—more of a mottling than the iridescent glimmer of color that Ianthe sometimes wore—but he knew he wasn't wrong. "Something in that last mess was a lie."

Both sets of eyes locked on him. Miss Martin wore a considering look, but she turned and aimed that pointed brow at Horroway. "So it's someone who we've mentioned."

"Ain't fuckin'—"

Miss Martin spat one of her ritual words, her fingers clenching into claws. Horroway gasped as his flask flew from his pocket into her hand. Miss Martin unscrewed it and threatened to pour the elixir within all over the floor. "I've already warned you about your language, and I wouldn't toy with my sense of patience at the moment, Horroway. Morgana has something that belongs to me, and I want it back." A trickle of effervescent green liquid splashed and hissed, as it burned straight through the timber floorboards. "I find myself becoming quite vexed. Tell me the truth, and I'll leave you here to rot. I truly do not care about your fate. Not at all."

"Don't you dare—" Horroway writhed, a look of fury upon his face, as he watched her pour more of his precious elixir upon the floor. "You bitch! You fuckin' bitch! Fine! I know where she is! She's at the Windsor Hotel. Her and her lover." He sneered, spittle flying from his lips in his vehemence. "And good luck to you there, at getting past him!"

"Her lover?" Miss Martin's eyes narrowed.

"Some pretty fop she has chipping along at her heels. Wears a dissembling veil over his face, some kind of spell that hides his identity, but he's strong. Stronger than you, stronger'n your precious Prime! Ain't nobody I know."

"So you have seen her." Another droplet of fluorescent green splashed upon the floor. "But you're not working with her?"

Horroway looked aside, his filmy eyes lost. Despite his distaste, Lucien felt a flicker of sympathy, for the man looked like he'd been cast aside like a used toy, knowing that he was no longer man enough to please a woman it was rumored that he'd once loved.

Horroway was one step away from a monster, however. That was something he couldn't forget. Sometimes the bodies he came by weren't from a grave.

"Didn't she want you anymore?" Lucien asked, steeling himself. "What did she ask of you then?"

"You ought to know."

Lucien paused. "What do you mean by that?"

"Your lord father's diary," Horroway spat. "She wanted it. Don't know what for. Don't much care."

"Lord Rathbourne?" Lucien's mind raced. He'd never have suspected the man to be involved with Morgana. "Did you get it for her?"

"Couldn't find the blasted thing." Horroway saw the look they exchanged. "And that's the truth."

"I'm not sure you're acquainted with such a notion," Miss Martin murmured.

"Rot in hell. I don't know nuthin' about no diary."

"If you tell us who has replaced you as Morgana's ally, we shall walk out of here and leave you alone. Perhaps we'll go annoy him instead."

"Aye, and good luck to you." Horroway laughed, a dry bitter sound. "Don't know much, but I ain't stupid." Those hate-filled eyes locked on the pair of them. "They ain't friends, but they've got a similar cause: to cast the Prime down."

"Who?"

"Tremayne," Horroway sneered. "Who else wants to see the Relics Infernal back in hand and the Prime cast down as much as Morgana does?"

They exited the Labyrinth without further ado.

"Remind me never to set foot on your bad side," Lucian remarked, taking her arm. "You are positively ruthless."

Miss Martin looked distracted again, but at his words, her eyes saddened. "Not really," she whispered, and he might not have heard the words if he hadn't been listening for them. "But sometimes, we find ourselves pushed beyond our limits. There's not a great deal I wouldn't do at the moment..."

"To get the relic back?" he asked, handing her up into the hackney that they'd arrived in.

"Yes," she murmured, "to get the relic back."

And for the second time that day, someone lied to him. Lucien's gaze sharpened upon her.

"What about your father's diary?" she asked, a clear diversion.

"Hell if I know. The Lord Rathbourne I knew would never have lowered himself to consort with such people."

"He made you raise a demon," Miss Martin said. "Did you ever ask him why?"

That verged on a conversation he never, ever wanted to have. A cold sweat sprang up around his collar. "I presumed it was because he wanted me to unleash it upon Drake. If it killed the Prime..." He faltered. The demon would have been traced back to him, and hence Lord Rathbourne. It made no sense.

"Why you?"

Lucien frowned. "I don't know."

"Did you ever see his diary?"

"No." Lucien looked at her. "But I know where he would have kept it."

CHAPTER TEN

'Sometimes seeing the future is a gift; sometimes it is not.'

- Lady Rathbourne

MISS CLEO SINCLAIR, the Earl of Tremayne's daughter, became aware that she was being watched.

It started as a prickle down her spine. He was quiet, whoever he was, and trying not to let her sense him. That was vexing. She would have been frightened, but she was quite certain she wasn't going to be kidnapped today.

Or murdered.

Oh, she'd woken with the feeling that *something* was going to happen. Premonition kept itching along her skin at odd moments, and she kept getting this breathless sensation as though something enormous lurked on the horizon, but she was fairly certain it wasn't going to be dangerous. Those sorts of premonitions always hit her like a downpour, sweeping her out of the monotony of everyday life and into the current of foretelling, regardless of whether she wished it or not.

Could this be what she'd been sensing all day?

Not danger, but something *else*? She didn't think so. Nothing ever happened to her, nothing exciting anyway. She was her father's Golden Goose, more precious than a solid-gold statue of Buddha. Her purpose in life was to while away her time here at Tremayne Manor until she was called to come predict something for her father or do a foretelling for one of the lords and ladies who paid him a small fortune for them.

Four steps to the rose arch in her father's gardens, and then she'd be downwind. She let the gravel crunch beneath her feet, counting silently.

A curl of cologne drifted past, all bay rum and bergamot with a hint of rosewood and lemon. A gentleman then. One that was well in hand, for that was a special blend she'd only smelt rarely, and only on the richest of her father's acquaintances. Those who spoke with crisp Eton vowels and went *hur-hur-hur* when they laughed.

Cleo lifted her head, the ends of her blindfold brushing against her throat as she paused by the rose trellis. She chewed on her lip, then made a decision. "Are you following me, sir?"

There came a choked silence. He hadn't expected her to be aware of him.

"Unless, of course, it is mere coincidence that you are going to feed the ducks in my father's locked and walled garden too?" Her basket brushed against her skirts as she turned. There was nothing but stillness in front of her, though she could still scent his cologne. "Now you're making me feel a little silly. I know you're there." She touched her blindfold. Nothing like adding a little mysticism, a little drama. "You cannot sneak up upon the Cassandra, did you know?"

"My apologies." The voice was deep. Not very old, she thought, though older than she. He sounded slightly French, and a little out of his depth, as though he were searching for words to say. "I did not mean to disturb you."

"Well, clearly. You were sneaking so quietly behind me."

An awkward silence ensued. "I'm sorry."

"For being caught, or for creeping around after me in the first place?" She'd long since learned that blunt questions often startled truthful answers out of people, or she could pick up little truths out of their reactions, anyway.

"I did not know you were a diviner." This fact sounded rueful, as though, had he known, he might have stayed away.

"I'm not. I'm *the* diviner. The current one, anyway."

"Are they all blindfolded? I had thought..." He trailed off. *He* was aware of rude enquiries, even if she considered them minor inconveniences.

"It helps to make the visions clearer. My father blindfolded me when I was five. I had a foretelling, saying that if I ever saw the world again, I would lose the Gift." And so she'd never dared take the blindfold off. It was the only thing that made her valuable to her father. She didn't want to lose that.

"You haven't seen a single thing since you were five?"

"Oh, I've seen a lot of things, some of them not very nice. Sometimes it's quite interesting. If I had my vision what would I see but roses and grass and trees? Whereas, without it, I can see all manner of things, sometimes even the world." She didn't give him time to gain his balance; instead, she stretched out her hand, gesturing for his arm.

"Are you going to walk with me? Take a poor, blind girl safely to the water's edge?"

"I'm certain you were managing quite well enough without me." Movement whispered, as though he laced his hands behind his back. It was a subtle withdrawing, told in a gentle murmur of fabrics.

Cleo tilted her head on its side. "Don't you like touching people?"

"Not really, no. And something tells me that touching someone who can see the world might be a little dangerous. What if you could see all of the secrets inside me?"

She smiled. Touch often gave her insight into a person, sometimes even forcing a prediction or foretelling upon her. Oh, yes, he was very interesting. "Are there secrets to see?"

"We all have secrets." There were shadows in his voice.

"Well then, it seems you have set me a challenge."

The stranger took a step back, but she didn't reach out and grab him.

"Oh, don't be silly, that would be too easy." Cleo felt a wicked smile dawning. She didn't want to simply know his secrets. She wanted to unearth them. There was no fun in simply knowing them, and no guarantee that premonition would ignite at a single touch either. It took long hours of meditation for her to force a foretelling. Otherwise they came at will, and certainly not hers.

"That's what bothers me," he murmured.

"Are you going to stay awhile? I rarely receive visitors, and none of them interested in me."

"What makes you think I am?"

Cleo swung her basket. This was a truth she wasn't certain she wanted to give him, but then she didn't want him to go away either. "People don't talk to me very often.

They only ask me questions about themselves. They rarely answer mine. Thus, I suspect your interest lies in me, not in what I can give you."

There was a breathless moment of waiting. "I'll stay awhile," he said finally. He was watching her face when he said it, she could tell, and it made her heart lift a little.

"So what is your name? Am I allowed to know that?" Cleo asked, turning once again toward the pond. He was right. She didn't need his help. Sixteen years of traversing these paths blindly had ingrained them in her head.

He hesitated. "Sebastian."

Sebastian. She mouthed the word, liking it. She hadn't heard that name before, at least, not in connection to her father. "My name is Cleo."

"I know."

How unusual. Cleo had thought herself a well-kept secret, except for within certain circles, but the surety of his tone led her to a suspicion. He had known whom she was, and he had come looking for her in the gardens. This wasn't just some stumbled upon assignation.

His interest was definitely in her.

Not her father.

Truth, said her premonition, lancing through her like white fire.

Cleo hid her gasp in a muffled cough. "Well, what are you doing here? What is your purpose in trespassing?"

"Trespassing?" He sounded surprised. "I'm not trespassing. I was sent here to deliver a message."

"Oh, that." She'd heard the ruckus in the foyer and the cool masculine voice that had left her father sounding faintly subdued. It hadn't sounded at all like this quiet, gentle stranger who liked silences. An entirely fascinating situation, for the Earl of Tremayne was rarely subdued. He wore his anger like a coat, and the usual means of describing him were: blustery, pompous, loud, arrogant... a list that went all of the way to demanding. But something about this stranger made the earl cautious. "That was over an hour ago. Does my father usually allow messengers to linger on his grounds?"

There was nothing but silence.

"Cat got your tongue?" she asked.

"Are you usually so... outspoken? You should be more careful with strangers."

It wasn't a threat. He actually sounded somewhat taken aback. "Nothing's going to happen to me today. I'd have sensed it." She reached up and gestured to her blindfold. "I don't always see everything that's going to happen, but disasters, or catastrophes? Always. Alas, there are no major scandals in my future."

"Scandals?"

"Well, were you referring to a young lady being thrown over the back of a dashing young stranger's horse and carried away to be ravished, or were you referring to something else entirely when you warned me to be careful?"

"Someone reads those newspaper serials to you, don't they?"

"My companion," she replied cheerfully. "She particularly likes the ones where dukes do dastardly deeds. Nothing less than an earl will do." When he didn't answer, she tilted her head toward him. "Oh, I'm sorry. I've shocked you, haven't I?"

"I... was just wondering how to answer that." He sounded faintly amused. "After all, I'm not a duke. Or an earl."

"I won't hold that against you. After all, you look like an Adonis. Everything can be forgiven for that, apparently."

His coat rustled, as if he turned toward her sharply. "How did you—?"

"The maids are all aflutter. Even Cook commented about those pretty eyes, and the only thing I've ever heard Cook refer to men as is 'trouble,' or 'not worth it.' My companion seemed to prefer your thighs, though I'm not going to repeat any of that," she said firmly. "Mrs. Pendlebury should be ashamed of herself. She probably would be, if she'd known I was listening. There has never been a man like you at Tremayne Manor before, apparently, and considering the wealth of visitors streaming through the door inquiring after their futures, that is something to be said indeed." She tilted her head. "You're quiet again."

"I am actually wondering if there is some hole somewhere that I can crawl into and hide," he drawled. "You are... not at all what I was expecting."

"Were you anticipating a poor little blind girl, sitting in her attic, hoping nobody would pity her?" Cleo couldn't stop the tart hint to her tongue. Gravel stopped crunching beneath her feet, and she turned automatically, finding the path again. Another thirty or so steps to the lake and the folly.

"No, I—"

"And why would you be expecting anything at all?" she continued, hunting for truths. "I thought you were here to see my father. Why would you have even cast a thought my way? Most people generally don't. I think my father prefers it that way." Her voice roughened. "Then I can be his little secret, locked away in my secret garden."

All she could hear were the ducks, the buzzing of insects, and someone, perhaps one of the gardeners, yelling something in the orchard a mile away.

"Well, considering we're to marry, I did give you some thought."

Cleo dropped the basket. "*What?*" She couldn't have heard that correctly. Could she? And why on earth could her Divination not warn her that there was a handsome, taciturn stranger in her future, one who felt like danger?

Gravel shifted. He was picking up her basket and the items within it, kneeling at her feet she suspected. She couldn't move. She wasn't entirely certain what she was even thinking, or felt at this moment. She should have been angry. How dare her father do this to her? Not even a mention of it! Not even a by and by... Or at least an introduction.

She didn't know this stranger, this Sebastian. And now he was going to own her and make her decisions for her, and oh, my goodness, she hadn't thought it before, but he was probably going to expect heirs from her.

Mrs. Pendlebury's mutter about those thighs sprang to mind. She hadn't quite understood it at the time, though she had some idea, and now she was going to find out exactly what Mrs. Pendlebury had meant.

Knock me over with a feather...

"I'm sorry. My mother said a special license had been prepared, so I thought your father had told you that you were to marry, but you had no idea, did you?" Sebastian knelt at her feet, and she could feel his gaze on her face.

It was doing its best to rival a sunset, judging from the heat in her cheeks.

"I'm—I'm..."

"Speechless," he said. "Well, there's a first."

Cleo shut her mouth. Premonition had fallen willfully silent. There was not a single itch along her skin at all.

"I wanted to see what you were like," he murmured. "Might I enquire how old you are?"

That made the floodgates open. "What, you didn't ask? What kind of marriage is this?"

"This... wasn't entirely my choice. I discovered the fact only hours ago, when my mother sent me to deliver the letter agreeing to it. I forgot to ask about you. I was too furious, considering the wedding is set for tomorrow."

"*Tomorrow?* But— When... I don't—" She was speechless again. And livid with her father. Did he intend to simply inform her on the day and expect her to happily don her wedding gown before marrying a stranger?

There was nothing to say to that. Absolutely nothing. But her father was going to hear about it, oh yes. Taking a deep breath, she rubbed her temples. It wasn't Sebastian's fault. Nor hers. And he had asked her a question, hadn't he? "I am one-and-twenty. I've been here at Tremayne Manor all my life, so it may seem I'm more sheltered than most. No doubt I am." In some ways. In other ways, she had Seen quite enough of the world—of disaster and blood and torn bodies, of changing weather patterns, sorcery, maliciousness... visions that woke her up at night and left her with no rest.

The worst one was the one that seemed to recur, over and over again. London's Doom, she liked to think it. An enormous hovering cloud of roiling darkness that crept over the horizon of London, with flickers of lightning dancing within it. Only, she wasn't certain it was lightning, after all. She'd seen so many horrible things, and this was but a cloud, and yet it was the most frightening thing she'd ever predicted. There was... so much emptiness to it. So much pain. It made her heart bleed, even as she wanted to run screaming.

Cleo shook the thought away. If she dwelled on such things, she'd spend most of her life crying. Bad things happened. If she let them, they would make her life nothing but a nightmare, and she refused to live like that.

"Well, that is some relief," Sebastian said, standing and delivering her basket back into her hands.

"That I'm sheltered?"

"That you're not a child."

He was, no doubt, referring to her figure. With her blindfold obscuring most of her face, her age could be difficult to predict, and her form was somewhat insignificant. Plus, her father liked to dress her in white lace that drowned her. No doubt Tremayne liked the idea of some pure, virginal foreteller, and thought it played up to the image some people had. If unicorns existed, he'd have probably chained one to the lawn.

"So... You didn't ask what age I was," Cleo said slowly. "You evidently didn't ask much about me at all. Did you ask if I were pretty?"

"No."

That could be interpreted in two ways. Either he didn't care, or it didn't matter to the situation at all, for there was no changing it. Perhaps both.

"I told you, I was angry. I was thinking that I clearly didn't have very much choice in this and that I was going to be married to someone I didn't even know." He let out a slow breath. "And I knew your father. I wasn't... hopeful of much."

"You thought I was going to be an overbearing troll with a big nose and thick dark brows and piercing eyes that squint a little, didn't you?"

"Are you certain you cannot see a thing? That sounds very much like your father."

"I know his face," she admitted. "It's the only one I remember."

"I was thinking," he said slowly, as if chewing over the words, "that your father is not a very nice man at times. I couldn't imagine his daughter being... well, being you."

169

"What does that mean?"

"You are not at all like your father."

Cleo resumed her walk, taking slower steps. Sebastian, her fiancé, fell into step, which was possibly the strangest thought she'd ever had to encounter. *My fiancé.* What strange words. They didn't feel real. None of this felt real.

"*Do* you think I'm pretty?" she asked, tilting her head up at him.

This was a secretive silence, full of a sudden tension between them. She was beginning to like his silences. They told her so much.

"You are not... without your charms."

Cleo burst into laughter. "Do you know, I quite think you've never courted a young lady before, have you?"

"No." The word was bleak and a little cold. "What was required of me was never courtship. I could tell you that you were the most beautiful creature I'd ever seen, but none of it would matter. I have seen beautiful women before and thought them the ugliest monsters I've ever encountered."

What a strange way to refer to it—it *was never courtship...* She felt something akin to a chill run over her skin. "I'm sorry."

"For?" The shadows in his voice fell away.

"You sounded sad," she said. "I hate it when people are sad. There is too much of it in the world."

"It's not sadness, Miss Sinclair. I'm angry." This was a whisper. "I'm very, very angry, and it terrifies me. Sometimes I think it's going to eat me alive."

Cleo's skirts swished in the grass. "You shouldn't be afraid of yourself, Bastian."

"Bastian?"

Cleo hid a small smile. "I like the sound of it. We may as well be familiar. I know it's very fast, considering I only just met you, but then my father did barter me away in marriage to you. And you sound nice. I can trust you."

"Miss Sinclair—"

"Trust me." She deliberately bumped against his arm, swinging her basket happily. "I know these things."

"But you know me not at all. I have done... a great many things that I am not proud of. Indeed, I begin to wonder if there is *anything* to be proud of."

That stalled her. He felt so *right* to her, that it had to be her seer abilities. She'd never been wrong about a person before. "Did you mean to do any of these things?"

"No."

"Then why did you do them?"

"Miss Sinclair, it's not—"

"I won't tell anyone. I am very good at keeping secrets."

They walked along for a few moments.

"My mother, Morgana, is a sorceress. A long time ago, she felt she was wronged, and she has vowed to bring her vengeance upon those who wronged her. I–I—"

"She makes you do bad things, doesn't she?" Cleo whispered. "Why do you not tell her no?"

"I cannot. It's not as easy as making a choice." His voice hardened. "When she wants something, there is very little one can do to stop her. She finds ways to force your hand."

Of that, Cleo could understand a little. "She threatens those who surround you?"

He breathed out a bitter laugh. "Sometimes. When I was twelve, she gave me a gift. It was a Sclavus Collar. She told me to put it on, that it was a great present indeed. So I did."

Cleo sucked in a sharp breath. She'd only once heard of such a thing, a collar that could force incredible pain upon its bearer and turn them to the will of another who wore the matching ring. It made her feel sick. Twelve... Just twelve. A little boy betrayed by his own mother. She didn't even know what to say. "But that is forbidden."

"You do not know my mother. She fears my powers." He echoed that laugh again, a sound full of blood and hate that made her a little uneasy. "She should. If I had one chance, just one, I would cut her down where she stood. What does that make of me? Do you think I am a nice man now?" There was a darkness to his voice that threatened to suck her into prediction. "You would be better off never knowing me."

"Perhaps." Cleo considered her words. She still couldn't seem to reconcile him as a bad person in her mind. She had met bad people before, those who had hurt her, or demanded visions of her. Those who had blood all over their hands. He was nothing like them. And she had the tenuous feeling that he stood on the dark edge of a cliff. One step in the wrong direction, and he would fall into darkness and shadows he could never climb out of. But if he took a step backward, perhaps he could be saved. And if he could be saved, then she would do it, she vowed deep in her heart.

"If you had the choice to do such things, would you do them?"

"No."

"Then you cannot think yourself responsible for your actions," she told him simply. "If there is no choice available to you, then your ills fall on her shoulders, not yours. You mustn't blame yourself for her deeds. You are but a tool in her hands, Bastian. I–I understand how that feels. My father has used a great many of my visions for his own purposes, and I know that some of the things that I have seen, come to pass because of what he has learned from me. But the truth is, I cannot stop myself from predicting such things. It simply overwhelms me, no matter how much I try to withstand them. So I have decided that he makes the choices to take what he learns and twist it to his advantage. Not me. I won't bear his burdens."

"I don't even know why I'm telling you of this." Sebastian sighed. "I've never told a single person what she does to me. You have something that is beyond beauty, Miss Sinclair," he admitted, and there was a little hint of unease in his voice. "I am starting to think that of the two of you, you are far more dangerous than your father."

"Well, now." Again her cheeks heated. "You are starting to get the hang of it. Young ladies quite like it when devilishly handsome young men tell them they're the dangerous ones. May I ask you a question?"

"I'm not certain what would stop you."

"Well, this one's a little... more... confronting than usual."

"Good God. I'm almost afraid."

Cleo laughed, then let it fade. "Stop it. This is serious."

His silence seemed to acquiesce.

Cleo let out a steady breath. Her heart was galloping along in her chest. "Do you *want* to marry me?"

He was a long time in replying. "No."

Cleo sucked in a sharp breath. "Well, I don't want to marry you either. I've just met you, yet I can already tell that you are rather... grim. You should smile more often." With that she strode ahead of him, reaching into her basket for the small paper bag of breadcrumbs. Three more steps.

Footsteps followed her slowly. He was watching her again, she thought. "I don't have a lot to smile about."

"Neither do I," she replied, throwing a handful of breadcrumbs out in front of her. Ducks came squawking in from left and right, their feathery bodies jostling her skirts.

"I'm blind, I'm locked away at this estate like Rapunzel in her tower, I foretell horrible things every day, and sometimes I wake up screaming, because even in my sleep, I cannot escape my predictions." She tilted her head toward him. "I don't have a single thing to smile about some days, but that doesn't stop me. I find things to make myself smile. Like feeding ducks. You cannot remain glum when an entire horde of ducks are dueling to the death at your feet for a tiny morsel of stale bread. Can you hear that?"

The quacking was positively overwhelming.

"Hear what?"

"Their battle cries," she said, her lips softening. "I've even named them. That—" She pointed to her left, "is Sir Eiderdown. He is always particularly strident. I daresay he is assaulting Lord Featherbottom as we speak. It's a little bit Montague and Capulet, you see. They have a *history*."

"I think you're quite correct." His face was tilted away from her, distorting the words. "That is clearly attempted murder."

"Good work," she said. "That was quite amusing. You're getting into the spirit of things now."

More silence. It made her skin itch.

"What are you thinking?" she asked. "I dislike it when people are quiet. I cannot see them, you see, so it is quite rude when they do not let me know what they are thinking."

"I am thinking that I am actually smiling. Also, that you are quite a strange girl."

"Is that an insult, sir?" she asked with a teasing smile. "For I assure you, you are surrounded by my knights. I would hate to see them have to defend my honor. They worship me as the Lady of the Breadcrumbs, you see. They might peck you to death. In the least, they'll ruin your boots."

"I'm fairly certain that's already happened. I think you rather fortunate not to be able to see where we happen to be standing."

There was a distinct odor that one couldn't deny. "Well. Now you've made me worry about where to put my feet."

"Where do you want to go?" he asked, sounding suddenly closer.

She jumped. "You are very quiet, sir. And to the folly. I like to sit in the sunshine—well, what there is of it—and soak up the heat. Summer is my favorite season."

He cleared his throat. "Would you— Would you mind?"

"Would I mind what?"

He tugged at the edge of her basket, encouraging her to take a step forward. Cleo lost the breadcrumbs, grabbing hold of the basket handle with both hands. The ducks erupted in a flurry of battle as Sebastian steered her to safety.

"No, I don't mind," she admitted. It was a little bit of a whisper, if she were being honest.

"I shouldn't have said what I said earlier."

"Which part?" Her heart started to beat just a little faster.

"That I didn't wish to marry you."

There wasn't much to say to that, but she tried. "Oh."

"There could be worse things—"

"I bet you charm all of the ladies with that tongue."

Another thoughtful silence. "That wasn't really what I meant to say either."

"You mean to say that you didn't particularly intend to marry, and you're not very happy about the situation. But having met me, you think you're quite a lucky fellow now and you can barely contain yourself, and would like to ravish me, right here. Of course, that wouldn't be very gentlemanly, so you are restraining yourself."

"Something like that." There was that hint of warmth again, as if he were smiling. She ached to see it. His voice softened. "Do you ever feel as though you're not in control of your life?"

"All of the time. And why do you make such serious turns in conversation? I was actually attempting to see if I could pry a laugh out of you. I think I am this close to it." She held up her thumb and forefinger an inch apart.

"I think you *could* make me laugh." Sebastian sighed, and took two steps up into the folly.

Cleo followed him, feeling the cool shade plunge over her. She moved to her favorite spot, a sunny little space where she could sit on the stone rail. Tilting her head back, she let the sunlight drench her. Its warmth was delicious, and apart from Duck Waterloo, the afternoon was peaceful. "Do you know, I never understood the interest in men like Rochester or Heathcliff."

Sebastian leaned against the folly rail at her side, his weight shifting it. "You're trying to form some sort of correlation between them and me? Sorry, no mad wives in my attic. I don't own an attic."

"Actually, I was almost thinking that I understand it now. Brooding men are rather interesting." She turned her face. He was very close to her.

So close that she could touch him if she wanted to...

A breathless feeling caught hold of her. Did she dare? She had been unusually bold today, but this was taking a rather large step over the line drawn in the sand between them.

And if you don't take that step? Her life stretched out before her, full of its usual monotony. Cleo was so weary of being trapped in her glass tower, as if coming into contact with the rest of the world would destroy her. She was not some brittle, precious object. She was a young woman, one of flesh and blood, who yearned to be touched, to explore beyond these walls, to learn what the world out there held. She wanted to be kissed. Just once.

Very well, then.

Cleo took a step, finding the lip of the stone edging of the folly. She stepped up on it, grabbing a handful of her skirts, and pointed somewhere toward the lake. "Look!"

Instinct made him turn to look, the edge of his sleeve shifting beneath her hesitant glove. He hadn't even noticed she was touching him, until he realized she could not have possibly seen anything on the lake.

Cleo reached up and pressed her lips to his as he turned back, guided by the startled intake of his breath when he realized what she was doing. Too late. Their lips met, and she leaned forward, forcing him to catch her or let her fall on her face.

Her hands met the abrupt wall of his chest. His mouth was still beneath hers, his breath hot and uneven against her own lips. If not for the thundering beat of his heart beneath her palms, she would have thought him particularly unmoved.

He was not unmoved.

Not even close to it.

Good lord, he was tall. He was also quite warm, his gloved hands catching her sleeves, and holding her there. With an unsteady breath, he lowered his head until his forehead rested against hers. "Cleo," he whispered, "what are you doing?"

Tension suffused him, and he slowly drew back.

"I believe it's called kissing, though I've only come across partial fragments of such a thing in my novels, and Mrs. Pendlebury will never give me the more exciting details. She just harrumphs and clears her throat and says, 'Now that's enough of that.' I have to bribe one of the maids into reading those bits to me."

"We're not allowed to kiss," he said.

"It's all right. I didn't see any of your secrets, Bastian." She turned, stepped down off the stone, and gathered her basket. There was a slight sway to her step. After all this time, she'd finally had her first kiss, and it had been all that she'd dreamed of! Her heart was playing some kind of orchestral beat, perhaps opera. She certainly felt like she was soaring, and that had been but a chaste brush of her mouth against his... "Don't think that's going to stop me from learning them, however. I consider myself quite the archaeologist of human nature."

"No, I meant—"

She stopped and turned back toward him. A bad feeling was beginning to grow in her.

We have to keep your visions pure, her father whispered in her head.

"Do not tell me that he forbade... kissing." Her voice shook. Here was freedom, right in front of her, and yet so close to being snatched away. For a moment, she'd begun to hope for things she'd never dared dream about before: marriage, a home of her own, someone who gave a damn... children.

"It was one of the conditions of marriage," Sebastian replied. "This *is* a marriage of convenience, Miss Sinclair. It's an alliance between my mother and your father to prove that they can trust each other. We have nothing to do with it. That's all it can ever be."

"We shall just see about that." Cleo didn't need to be a diviner to predict that there was a very loud argument in her father's future.

"No, we won't." Sebastian took her arm. It wasn't painful, but it was very firm, and she noticed that he made sure his gloves settled over the silk of her gown. Two layers of fabric between them. "You don't want to cross my mother, and I cannot protect you from her." He let out a harsh breath. "I cannot protect you from me. I shouldn't be here. I'm sorry, Miss Sinclair. I should never have come to see what you were like."

"You *can* call me Cleo, you know?"

"I don't think that very wise at all." This was the voice she'd recognized earlier in the foyer. A firm, cold voice that had made its mind up and wouldn't be swayed. "Goodbye. I shall see you on the day we marry, and then rarely after that." And then he turned and walked away, his steps deliberately loud.

Cleo faced in his direction, her fists clenched. "I am going to teach you to smile, Bastian. And I am going to make you laugh and steal kisses and... and tell me your secrets. All of them! I will not let my father dictate the rest of my life. I will not let him take everything else away from me." Her hands lifted to the blindfold and swiftly untied it. Silk slithered down her face, but she shut her eyes, almost blinded by the light streaming through her thin eyelids.

That was where she paused. Her heart thundered through her veins. She couldn't hear him anymore. Only her racing heart.

Doubt flooded through her. What if this Sebastian truly didn't want her? He was a stranger, after all, and had declared his intent to maintain a marriage of minimal contact. What if she removed the blindfold and lost her Vision? Her father would not want her then: she would have no value to him, and perhaps then Sebastian's mother would not want them to marry either? His mother might desire this purely for the alliance, but she had to be greedy for the wealth of knowledge Cleo could give her.

There was no sound. She stood alone. Like always.

Cleo slowly tied her blindfold back in place.

The moment she did Vision locked hold of her, stretching her up tight onto her toes and arching her back. She had the vague sensation that she'd grabbed hold of something to stop herself from falling, but then heat seared her veins, and she was lost to the world.

Then, just as suddenly as it had come, it was gone again. Cleo found herself on her bruised knees, breathing heavily, her heart racing as fast as the horses at Epcot. Every part of her was warm and flushed, as if she could still feel the imprint of his skin on hers. She'd never been a part of a vision before, always she'd been a silent bystander, trying to interpret what she saw. But that... Cleo swallowed. That vision was very easy to interpret.

It also seemed that Mrs. Pendlebury had been right in all matters.

Well, now... Her mouth curled in a shaky smile. She still wasn't certain she could stand. "Try and run, Bastian," she whispered. "I think it quite inevitable that we meet again."

CHAPTER ELEVEN

CLEO COCKED her head and listened, before locking the door to her room. Her father was out on business, and she had overheard enough of his afternoon meetings to know that he was up to something. There had been mutterings about some form of relic, and she'd heard him pacing his study, chanting something under his breath. It wasn't in her realm of study, but she'd heard the words once, and spent the afternoon meditating until she could unearth the memory.

He was trying to perfect a ritual chant that would summon a demon.

Cleo knew the laws. She also knew her father. She had never thought him a bad man—a bitter one, perhaps, who had found himself exiled to this estate outside of London for the whole of her life—but this... this unnerved her. A demon was a dangerous creature to toy with, a supernatural creature from another plane who *could* be contained for information or some service, and yet often managed to trick their way out of such protective measures. Every story that she'd ever heard about demons had ended badly.

She had vowed to help Sebastian somehow, and yet now she was facing another decision that made her stomach twist itself in knots.

For years she'd wondered what could destroy an entire city in her London's Doom vision. She'd never been able to answer it before, but now... A demon, unleashed, could destroy London. It could do it in a heartbeat.

She had to stop her father, but going to him wasn't the answer. Indeed, she'd decided that even mentioning that she'd met Sebastian would not be a very good idea either. Thus, she had to take care of matters herself.

The advantage to being blind, wearing white lace, and looking like a doll was that people thought you were stupid, or helpless. Her father thought her nothing more than his puppet. He said things when she was nearby, as if he thought she wouldn't understand them and certainly couldn't act upon them. He had taught her how to harness her will, but never allowed her to learn areas outside her talent of divination. Cleo had been a very good student. She had spent many, many hours practicing her foretelling and predictions.

Taking out a set of crystals that she used to help clear her mind, she crossed her legs and sat on the floor beside her bed with her back propped against it, just in case a vision hit her. Once her mind was clear and open to probability, she started whispering names of people who might be able to help her.

She went through a whole list of names she knew, and none of them seemed to spark any potential prediction, or if it did, then it wasn't a very helpful one. Some of the images that hit her were downright bloody, so she discarded them immediately.

Finally she said the one name she'd been avoiding. "My father."

That name obliterated her in darkness and the sound of screams. She shook off the premonition with a hard swallow. Telling her father she knew anything was not going to end well.

Cleo bit her lip. Who was powerful enough to deal with Sebastian, her father, and this shadowy mother Sebastian spoke of? Who was powerful enough to deal with a demon?

The Prime.

It was a dangerous thought. The Prime had betrayed her father once. His name wasn't even allowed to be spoken of within these walls. Her father hated him, but there was a little tingle along her skin, as if she had made a right choice.

"The Prime," Cleo whispered, and let her mind open to possibility.

Vision clamped down hard on her and her body went rigid.

A man turned to his lover—the woman whose eyes Cleo was looking out of—grief etched on his face. *"Is there no other way?"* he whispered.

"If you see them, you'll set into motion a chain of events which will only end in disaster," Cleo found herself saying, only it wasn't her voice.

Then she was looking at a man who stared in the mirror. She couldn't see his face, only his back and the finely tailored fit of his coat, but his reflection was far older than he was. Wings of gray gleamed at his temples in the reflection, and there were faint lines around those mercurial eyes; eyes that seemed to look right at her, as if the reflection saw her standing over his shoulder. The young man reached out and touched the mirror and it exploded, shattering his older reflection.

Vision flashed, again and again and again. She saw the same older man divided into three, and each of the pieces were pulling in different directions. Then he was standing in a room, and a shadow slipped up behind him and stabbed him in the back. Blood splashed across her sight, and when it dripped away, there were three gleaming relics sitting around a pentagram that had been carved within a circle. Over a dozen robed figures knelt around it, chanting, and the older man was tied within the circle and bound to the floor with his bloody ribs spread open in supplication.

The vision shifted, becoming something she knew far too well: her recurring nightmare. Cleo saw what she had called London's Doom, only this time she wasn't dreaming. It began with its usual sense of dread, with clouds boiling over London and people screaming as they fled. Lightning flickered within the darkness, building up to something...something that shouldn't be unleashed, something that would destroy the entire city. Cleo stood alone in the city streets, helpless to do anything as the darkness approached. Houses were smashed by wind, and bodies crushed all about her.

She was in the vision, like she always was, and she couldn't escape.

"No," Cleo whispered, though the word disappeared into the winds that were whipping past her as the cloud rolled inexorably toward her. She'd never seen the end of this nightmare. She didn't want to. It was always the same. Always terrifying and merciless, sucking the hope out of the world.

"Stop it, Cleo!" she told herself, unable to turn away. "Wake yourself out of it."

The edges of the vision began to grow hazy, as if her physical body were snapping out of her meditation. And then something caught her eye, something that was different.

This time, there was a tiny spark of golden light floating upward in the air, as if it were standing up against the darkness. It was so small, it should have meant nothing, yet it seemed like the darkness couldn't swallow it whole.

When she woke out of her meditation, it was with a gasp. She was no more aware of what any of it meant, but at least she wasn't screaming.

Cleo spent long minutes with her knees huddled up against her chest and sweat dripping down her face. She felt like she'd run for miles, her entire body wrung out in exhaustion.

What was she going to do? She hadn't missed the signs. This was it. Sebastian had something to do with her most vivid nightmare. So did the Prime and her father. It was finally here, and she didn't want it to be.

Just because you don't want it, doesn't mean it's not going to happen. Do something about it.

But what? I'm just a young woman trapped in my dollhouse.

Cleo curled her fingernails into her palms. She hadn't been given this vision for no reason. She alone knew it was coming; she alone could help stop it. That was the price of knowing the future.

Dragging herself to her feet, Cleo spent long minutes pacing. What was she going to do? It wasn't as if contacting the Prime would set this disaster in motion. She was vividly aware that the storm clouds were building on the horizon regardless and she was the only one who could sense it coming.

Denying it wasn't going to help.

Pacing in her room wasn't going to help.

And there had been that one golden spark standing up to the impending doom. That was a good sign, and the first time she'd ever seen some sort of answer to impending disaster. Was that spark herself? Or did it mean that if she contacted the Prime, she somehow set a new player into the game who represented the spark? She wasn't certain, but it gave her some small hope.

The Prime was her answer. Clearing away her crystals, she found her way to her bed and knelt to withdraw her letter writing set from beneath it. Most of the time, she dictated her correspondence to Mrs. Pendlebury, but it had occurred to her, at the age of thirteen, that there would come a time in her life where she might not wish to rely on others seeing what she had to write. And so, using a ruler to keep her letters straight and a small device that held it pressed flat over her sheet of paper, she had taught herself how to carefully feel out letters. One of the maids, Ellie, was literate, and for a few pounds slipped into her pocket, she had become Cleo's eyes. It wasn't perfectly legible, but Ellie had always been able to make sense of what she wrote.

Cleo thought about what she wanted to say for a long time. Then she set her pen to her paper and set about crafting a note that she would pay Ellie to give to her younger brother, who would deliver it.

CHAPTER TWELVE

'Thou shalt not suffer a sorcerer to live...'
 - Grant Martin, Head of the Anti-Sorcery Vigilance Committee

THERE WAS NO sign of Morgana at the Windsor Hotel, not that Ianthe had expected it. No, she'd have moved on as soon as they took Louisa. After all, one could hardly hide a kidnapped child in a public venue without someone commenting.

Sorcerer's appetites being what they were, they stayed at the Windsor to dine for a late luncheon. She had to force herself to be practical. In the first four days after Louisa went missing, she'd barely eaten and her weight had stripped from her figure dramatically, until she'd almost fainted. A weakened sorcerer was no match for the Prime's ex-wife.

So Ianthe put away a white soup, two beefsteaks—much to the waiter's surprise—and a crème brûlée. It all tasted like ash in her mouth, but she forced it down as a means to an end. Lucien managed the soup and a mouthful of her dessert before pushing it aside.

"Not hungry?" she asked, watching him carefully.

"Not used to rich food."

The tired circles under his eyes were slowly vanishing, but the hollow slash beneath his cheekbones indicated his straitened circumstances for the past few months. At least he'd managed to eat more than previously. That had to be a good sign. "Well, why don't we go seek out Lord Rathbourne's grimoire and find out what Morgana might have wanted with it? That should be a pleasant diversion."

"You never met the man, did you?" Lucien actually smiled, though it held a touch of bitterness. "I'm not surprised to find he had some connection to Morgana. I just wish this connection didn't involve me."

"Do you have any idea what it might be?"

A fragile sense of tension ran through him, his shoulders hunched slightly, as he stepped out into the street. "No. No idea."

It bothered him more than he'd admit, she suspected. Ianthe glanced sidelong at him from beneath her lashes. "Well, let us go and find out. Lay at least one ghost to rest."

"Let's."

Perhaps it was her distraction with him, or perhaps too little sleep, stretched over too many nights, but Ianthe was halfway across the street before an ebony lacquered carriage caught her eye. The breath went out of her when she saw the gold sigil on the door, and she jerked to a sudden stop as it disbursed its occupants. A man stepped out, tall and lean and dressed in impeccable tweed, then reached up to hand down a thin young woman in pale pastel blue. Ianthe barely saw the woman. All she saw was the man—barely touched with age, curse him, his stride long, his dark wavy hair neatly pomaded, and that stern mouth still a hyphen, as if nothing about the world pleased him... and never would.

Lucien walked into her, catching her by the upper arms. "What are you doing?"

Some distant part of her mind kept working, even when her body was frozen in shock and fear. She'd heard that he'd taken a second wife. Poor woman.

"N-nothing." Ianthe turned away, blindly heading in the opposite direction. Anywhere. She didn't care. Just not here.

Lucien's footsteps hounded her. "Someone you know?"

No. Not really. Not ever, in fact. "Did you not recognize the crest on the carriage?"

His brows drew together. "*Ad servium veritatum?*"

"To serve the truth," she translated. "It's the crest for the Vigilance Against Sorcery Committee."

Recognition dawned in those amber eyes. "Your father."

"In the flesh. I'm sorry. It took me by surprise. I wasn't expecting to see him."

Lucien caught her hand, his eyes searching. "Ianthe—"

"It's all right. I don't think he saw me." The words spilled out, fast and hard.

"Ianthe, your heart is pounding. My heart is pounding. I feel like it's going to thump its way right out of my chest."

The bond. They stared at each other.

Lucien gently turned her toward a small park. "Come and sit down. You look like you've seen a ghost."

"Well, it's a fairly accurate summation." Only one man haunted her like this. She'd thought she'd escaped that vengeful specter, but just one glimpse of her father had sent her fleeing into memories. Ianthe felt like a young girl again. It had taken all of her courage to confront him years ago, and weeks of preparation. Afterward, her sense of elation had been vivid. She'd felt powerful for the first time in all of their encounters, but walking into him so unexpectedly revealed the truth.

Grant Martin would always hold the power between them.

Somehow.

Lucien guided her to a seat beside a small fountain. Ianthe dragged her cape jacket tighter around her. Of all the people to run into today. Here. Now. With Lucien by her side. She didn't want him to see her like this.

"We should be on our way," Ianthe said, noting the curious look he sent her. "We need to find Lord Rathbourne's grimoire and work out what Horroway meant."

A hand on her shoulder stopped her. Lucien looked stern. "I think we have time to catch our breath." Dragging off his coat, he settled it over her shoulders and knelt in front of her. The warmth of his body heat was instantly reassuring. "Tell me about your father."

"You should already know him."

"I think every sorcerer in the Order knows your father. The man is what I imagine a demon made flesh would be like."

As head of the Anti-Sorcery Committee, Sir Grant Martin had made it his duty to drive them from the city. If not for their loyalty to the Queen, and the fact that Drake had singlehandedly saved the Queen from a demon attack in his youth, her father might have made headway into seeing them cast out of the staunchly religious country. Occultism, however, was at a fever pitch. The Queen herself had once had her fortune predicted by a diviner.

"Why does your father hate you so much? Has he always held such an opinion?"

Ianthe looked away. Hate. The truth was an arrow straight to the heart; she didn't even know why it bothered her. Whenever she thought of Grant Martin, all she felt was anger and disappointment. So why did something within her desperately long for his approval still? "We all have that first time where our sorcery expresses itself for whatever reason. Mine was... it was shadow constructs. My mother had died when I was four, and my father believed that sparing the rod spoils the child. He used to lock me away in the attic for days on end, with only a tray shoved through the door for company, whenever I made some sort of transgression against his never-ending rules.

"I was lonely and afraid of the dark, but my governess used to leave me with a candle to stay the darkness. And one night, I made the shadows dance. They became my friends. The only ones I had for such a long time."

Lucien's head lowered toward hers, his hand resting on her shoulder. This gentleness of his confused her. "And he found out?"

"I was running in the gardens one day when I was twelve. I tripped and ruined my pretty skirts, right in front of one of his guests. Father was furious, and he started to drag me toward the attic. I couldn't bear it anymore; I just... I just couldn't go back to that attic. Not alone. And so I lashed out. My shadows became constructs with weight and form. They caught his arms and pushed him away from me." Ianthe picked at the hem of her skirt, seeing it all over again. "You should have seen his face. I thought he was going to kill me. The next day, he packed me off to my aunt's in the country and set about destroying every sorcerer in the country."

In the distance, a clock tower chimed four o'clock in the afternoon. Ianthe looked at it. The day was wasted, and they were only just making headway. A burst of thought came upon her: Louisa was out there somewhere, all alone, without a single shadow to comfort her. Ianthe sobered. "Come. We've much to do and little daylight left in which to do it."

She pushed herself to her feet, offering his coat back to him, but Lucien didn't move to accept it. He stared down at it, as though he'd never seen it before.

"What are you thinking?" she asked, tilting her head toward him. "You have this look about your face..."

"I was thinking that I thought my childhood was terrible."

It struck her right to the heart. He had no idea. Not truly. But she pushed aside the memories as maudlin. She was well free of Grant Martin. Well free of those memories. "Don't you pity me. I rarely think of him," she admitted, laying his coat over his arm and heading for their own carriage, parked behind the Cotswold Mews. "He cannot hurt me anymore. I made certain of that."

"Did you?" Lucien was watching her face far too closely as he fell into step beside her. The stark white of his shirtsleeves gleamed in the afternoon sunlight, and his gray waistcoat clung to the hard musculature of his chest. "Or are you just telling yourself such a thing?"

Ianthe flushed. "Do you pretend to read my mind now?"

"Not your mind, no. Your emotions, however, are painted across your face. Your father troubles you."

"Your father troubles you," she shot back.

They shared a long, steady look.

"Which one?" Lucien asked, with a faint, mocking lift to his brow.

"Both of them, I believe. Tell me about Lord Rathbourne, for I know your grievances with Drake. Did he beat you? Lock you away? Force you to give up all the lessons you loved, and instead turn to meaningless hours of prayer?"

Lucien cut her a cold look. "No. He didn't care enough to bother."

Then he turned and strode away from her, across the grassy lawn of the park. Ianthe stared after him. That was it? After all she'd revealed? "Wait!" she called, grabbing a handful of her skirts and scurrying after him. "You cannot simply leave it at that." Catching his sleeve, Ianthe added, "Please."

Lucien looked bleakly across the park. She didn't think he was going to answer her; every inch of his body was a stiff line. Then his lashes lowered, covering those amber eyes. "Do you know the one time that Lord Rathbourne gave a damn about me?"

Ianthe shook her head.

"It was right before he forced me to summon the demon. After years of neglect—or no, not even that, but indifference—he finally began to pay attention to me. He invited me into his workshop to show me the mysteries he was studying: time, space, planes of existence behind my knowledge. Then he offered me a gift, Ianthe. A collar. I didn't recognize it for what it was. I'd never seen a Sclavus Collar, for such things are forbidden. He told me it would increase my powers, so that I could act as a wellspring for him. He needed the additional strength of my power, for he had a difficult undertaking to pursue."

Lucien blew out a breath. "It was stupid to believe him, but... I never thought his intentions toward me were malicious. I never had cause to doubt him, and I was proud that he'd asked me. I wanted to please him. He'd always preferred my cousin Robert to me. This was the one thing that Robert couldn't give him, for he has the magical ability of a turnip."

Picking up a small rock, he toyed with it, still looking down. "Do you know the worst thing about what happened a year ago?"

Ianthe couldn't contain her sudden surge of pity. She slid a gloved hand over his, stroking his knuckle with her thumb. She didn't like seeing him like this. "What?"

"It made sense," he said, looking up and meeting her eyes. "Why Rathbourne never cared for me. In a way, it was almost a relief to discover the truth. He wasn't my father. No wonder he barely tolerated me."

"But what was so bad about that—?" And then she realized.

Lucien's smile was thin-lipped. "Precisely. I trade one father who doesn't care for me, for another who I'd never even met. And now *this* father of mine needs my help. Can you wonder why I don't fully trust the offer?"

For the first time, she didn't have the words to defend Drake.

CHAPTER THIRTEEN

IT TOOK precisely five minutes to break into Rathbourne Manor on the outskirts of Kensington.

Lucien strode into Lord Rathbourne's study, raking the room with a hard gaze as he set the candle he carried on the mantel. Little had changed. Over the mantel hung Lord Rathbourne himself, sneering down at the room, forever caught in his favorite expression. The artist had done a brilliant rendition, all the way down to the thin moustache that flagged Lord Rathbourne's lip and the pinpoint glare of his pupils.

Lucien turned his back on at least one of his ghosts. Rathbourne held no sway over him anymore.

White sheets draped the furnishings, heavy with dust. Until his case was heard later this summer, the courts would hold the property in trust. How Robert would hate that. It gave him some grim amusement, until he realized that this grim mausoleum and the old, ancestral estate were the only things he truly owned in this world, if the courts ruled him sane.

What kind of future was that?

To allay the answer, Lucien paced to the window and flung the heavy velvet draperies back. Within seconds, he was overwhelmed by a miniature dust storm. "Damnation." He coughed, turning away and waving his hand in front of his face to clear the air.

"What did you expect?"

Ianthe stepped inside the study, lifting her pale, oval face to survey the heavy bookshelves. Her creamy skin held no watercolors right now. Her emotions were muted, bearing only a faint, radiant shimmer of amusement. A beautiful woman of ivory tones and faint rosy blushes, wearing a red gown. His gaze slowed as it traced the pale curve of her shoulders. It was difficult to think of her as he once had—as the enemy.

Something hard and tight within him softened as he looked at her.

This was not the mad villainess he'd spent the past year picturing in his revenge-fueled fantasies. She was warm flesh and blood, with her own demons, her own secrets. He wasn't certain he particularly liked this slow-building camaraderie between them, or perhaps he didn't fully trust it, but a part of him was intrigued to discover more about her.

Kindred spirits, in some ways. She alone understood what it felt like to be betrayed by your flesh and blood, or the man you thought was such.

"Here," she said, stepping forward and brushing dust off his coat. "Dust looks like it's going to be the greatest danger here."

He'd been cautious as they entered, however. Lord Rathbourne liked his privacy and had once employed a host of wards and hidden tripwires to all manners of magical mayhem. Nothing of them seemed to remain. They'd faded into dust and air, along with their master. "Hopefully."

"Where would he hide the grimoire?"

"Not here." Lucien crossed to the bookshelf, tugging on some ancient play of Euripides. With a groan, the fireplace began to move.

"Hidden staircases?"

"It gets better. Lord Rathbourne was the sort of sorcerer who liked the darker practices. Anything that gave him power."

"Please tell me we're not going to find bodies down there."

"No. A skull or two, perhaps."

The grinding in the walls slowed. Lucien lifted the candle and waved it into the darkened tunnel.

"Suitably gothic." His proud, invulnerable Miss Martin looked like she was going to faint.

"Are you all right?" Lucien asked her.

Miss Martin let out a slow breath, her eyes darting around. "I'm fine. I'm just not... fond of small dark spaces."

Like attics. His heart actually clenched in his chest. He'd never have realized the cause behind such a weakness before their earlier conversation.

Hell, he actually wanted to draw her into his arms and curl her against his chest. "I have a candle," he promised, voice softening, "and I'll be here too."

Those dark eyes surveyed him, as if to gauge whether he was mocking her or not, and then she looked back down the narrow stone passage. A chill breeze whispered over his skin, and he knew what she was thinking.

"It won't blow out."

"I'm not entirely certain I won't make an embarrassing scene if it does," she said dryly, trying for humor and failing. "It's possible I might try to climb you. Like a tree."

"Miss Martin, the devil incarnate, scared of a little darkness?"

"I could thrash you sometimes, Rathbourne," she mock-growled, but faint glimmers of indigo-gray crossed her face.

Fear.

Without thinking, Lucien summoned a mage globe, gleaming with iridescent white light. It came to hand immediately, and Lucien looked down in shock. It hadn't hurt him to summon it. Mage globes of white were virtually powerless, but still... Was the problem his sorcery, or some part of his mind?

"Oh. Thank you."

Lucien gestured, and the faint globe rose from the palm of his hand, hovering in front of them. The strain came immediately, cold sweat springing up against the back of his neck, but he didn't dismiss it. Ianthe stepped into the tunnel, her skirts pressing against his trousers, and one hand on his sleeve, as though his presence gave her some peace of mind.

He couldn't have dismissed it if he'd tried.

"Rathbourne's occult study is not far. There should be a staircase at the end, which will wind down to the cellars." Lucien held his hand out as she stepped forward, as if to prove she wasn't afraid of the dark. *Stubborn woman.* "Let me go first, Ianthe. There might have been something he left behind to guard his private domain."

"Very well," she murmured as he strode forward, "but only because the view is more enticing from back here."

Lucien glanced back, noting her impish smile, and couldn't stop his own from forming. "One would think you enjoy your nights."

"Whatever gave you that idea?"

The sound of her gasps, her body arching up beneath him as he traced her skin with his tongue...

The mage globe dimmed a little. *Concentrate*, he told himself harshly. Her teasing manner intrigued him, however. There'd been little humor between them thus far.

"Tell me about Cross," Lucien said, shouldering through the small passage. It ended, just as a gaping yawn opened up beneath his feet. The staircase.

"*Remy?*"

Remy. His fingers actually curled into a fist. Ridiculous, really. It wasn't as though he'd sensed anything between her and the magician, but then, she'd said the Prime had never been her lover... Which left at least two men, somewhere out there.

"What about Remy?"

"How did the two of you meet?"

"He'd advertised in the newspaper for an assistant," Ianthe replied. "We suited each other. He provided me with an income and a way to thumb my nose at my father, and I wasn't frightened of him, unlike the other applicants. Once you've grown up in Grant Martin's household, there's no stare you cannot meet. It had Remy quite perplexed at the start. I think he quite likes people to either be in awe of him or terrified. I was neither." Ianthe considered something. "I'm certain Drake had a hand in my gaining the position too. He wanted to provide me with pin money, once I'd finished my apprenticeship, but I refused."

Lucien glanced back over his shoulder as they reached the lower floor, and held a hand out to help her down the last few stairs. "Why?"

Those fingers were warm. Ianthe stepped past, examining the darkened chamber before them, but she didn't let go of his hand. "When my father threw me out, I had nothing, Lucien. It was an eye-opening experience. By the time Drake set me on my feet, I had vowed that I would never be beholden to another person again. When I finished my apprenticeship, I trusted Drake, but I didn't want to be supported by him. I wanted to be my own person."

"Cross pays so well?" He didn't forget the luxury of her house, or her eminently fashionable wardrobe.

"My aunt left me a small inheritance a few years ago," Ianthe admitted. "It was time to begin thinking of the future, so I bought the house and channeled the remaining funds into investments."

"So you didn't need to work as Cross's assistant anymore? Why continue then, until three months ago?"

"Lucien." Her smile was gentle. "I enjoyed the work. It gave my life some purpose."

"When you're not hunting miscreants for the Prime?"

"Yes, well, there's that."

It seemed somewhat lonely. "You've never considered marriage and children?"

Those pale features froze in a polite expression. "What man would have me? I'm a sorcerer's whore, according to popular opinion, and if I'm honest, why surrender my authority to a man? I am in the unique position of living my life according to my own whims."

"You don't want children?"

She turned away, examining the small cellar room they'd entered. "I don't know whether I would be a good mother."

Something about the softness of her tone drew his eyes. Not the entire truth then. "And your father? How did becoming a magician's assistant help 'thumb your nose at him'?"

"He'd been making noises about taking Drake to court and suing him for destroying my character. The words he painted Drake with were ghastly; a sorcerer preying upon innocent young maids and seducing them to Satan's side. It was ridiculous considering he was the one who threw me out, but a few of my father's friends were muttering about it. So I wanted to put a stop to his plans to paint me as some innocent young girl and Drake as a vile seducer. I sent him front row tickets to my first show from an anonymous source.

"I knew my father would show up. He could never resist a chance to mince around with his social class. So I put on my spangled outfit and stepped on stage, and showed my father what I'd become. He stormed out after the first act, but he was waiting for me in my dressing room." Shadows darkened her eyes. "It's the only time I've seen him since I left his house. It was terrible and confronting, but a part of me exulted. I finally had power over him. I told him that if he continued to make his threats against Drake, then I would tell the world who 'Sabine' was. I threatened to take a lover and flaunt myself to the world as some rich man's mistress. I would ruin him, if I could." Ianthe sighed. "I was younger then, of course."

"You wouldn't do the same now?"

"No. I think I'm weary of making decisions for the sole purpose of striking at my father." A faint Gallic shrug. "Other things seem more important these days. The people in my life who truly care for me, not the ones I was cursed to have the misfortune to belong to originally."

That stung, because whilst she had those people in her life, he had no one. He'd never realized what was missing from his life before she walked into it, but although she was part of the problem, she was not the whole of it. Lucien gazed around the darkened cellar they'd stumbled upon, a bleak scowl upon his face.

"Call it age bringing about a certain amount of wisdom." Ianthe's smile seemed wistful, but then her attention turned to the room below. "Well, this looks... friendly." Ianthe stepped forward, beneath the heavy gothic arches that supported the ceiling, her fingers trailing over one of the massive stone gargoyles that stood watch.

Lucien barely heard what she said. His entire body was still vibrating with the truth that had struck him: he was alone. Not one person gave a damn about him these days. The ache of it struck him right through the heart.

He tried for nonchalance, however, as he didn't want her to notice that aught was amiss. "You cannot be so old as that."

"How old do you think I am?"

Lucien leaned one hand against the arched doorway, considering her from the top of her elegantly coiffed chignon to the tips of her toes. "If you think I'm going to answer that, then you think me a fool. A gentleman never comments on a lady's age."

"I though you weren't a gentleman. Isn't that what you said before?"

"It has nothing to do with etiquette. It's an act of pure preservation. Nothing more."

Ianthe's smile softened, the shadows of the room limning her features and highlighting those dangerous eyes. They were like darkened clouds—endlessly changing, as restless and dramatic as an approaching storm. She was beautiful. He could never forget that. Nor could he stop his gaze from seeking her out as she turned to the books on the desk.

Perhaps it's because you haven't been with a woman for so long?

Perhaps... Or perhaps not. The thought discomforted him a little. She reminded him of himself. Both of them had been effectively orphaned by cold, distant parents, but whereas she seemed to have found herself and thrived, he was still trying to find his feet. That showed a strength of will he both admired and respected.

And envied, if he were being honest with himself.

"Here, I think I found something," Ianthe said, flicking through the pages of a book. Every inch of her face lit up in animation, and he felt something clench inside his chest. "It's not a diary. Oh." Her expression fell as she flicked through the pages. "Rather monotonous, truly. A study on theosophy, though Lord Rathbourne seemed hardly the enlightened sort." Her nose wrinkled up as her eyes traversed the page. "Good gods, what a bore."

"One could say that you have his measure already."

She moved on, examining the bookshelves and the smattering of leather-bound books on the desk. "A translation of the *Epic of Gilgamesh*," she murmured, casting aside books. "*The Parabola Allegory, The Sixth and Seventh Book of Moses*. Interesting collection. Lord Rathbourne seems to have been a dabbler, rather than one allied to a particular field of study..." He sensed the moment that she realized his quietness. Those dark lashes swept up, a faint frown furrowing her brow. "What is it? What's wrong?"

Nothing. Lucien panicked.

"You can tell me, you know. After all, you know some of my worst secrets. In a way..." Ianthe took a deep breath. "I know we're not friends, but I feel this odd sort of kinship with you. Neither of us were wanted, not truly. And I would never share what you told me with others."

Not alone. Not if he gave in to this. But the hesitation remained. How long had it been since he'd placed his trust in another?

The answer to that lay all around him. A year. A year since he'd been shown the value of another's trust. Bitterness and cynicism had swallowed him up in that time.

He had the sudden shocking realization that he didn't know himself anymore. He had become someone who watched the world through wary eyes.

"It's difficult, isn't it? To place one's trust in another's hands. Or your body perhaps, hoping that you won't be hurt," she said.

That jerked his head up. She'd feared his intentions when she'd given herself to him? "You weren't afraid of me."

"Of course I was frightened, Lucien. I barely knew you, and you yourself admitted you wanted revenge. Or want revenge," she corrected. "But you didn't hurt me. My trust was not misplaced, and now you know some of my secrets..."

The offer lay between them, tremulous as a truce between warring armies. He had the feeling that it wouldn't come again if he refused her this one time.

Take it, or don't...

"It gets to me." Something unfurled within him, something he'd been holding onto for a long time. "Being here, under the shadow of *him*."

Ianthe glanced around, but he knew she saw only the bookcases and the heavy desk. This room wasn't weighted in memory for her, the way it was for him.

The desk where Lord Rathbourne had spent most of his life behind, scratching out his notes in the bloody grimoire that Ianthe held in her hands right now. Ignoring him as a child, but lavishing attention on his chubby, spoiled cousin, Robert. Robert who always pleased Lord Rathbourne. Robert, who, for some inexplicable reason, was better than Lucien. More. No matter how hard he tried.

Everything held a ghost of memory: the heavy skull that sat atop the desk; the hourglass; the scarred bench surface where Lord Rathbourne had worked his alchemies; the drawer where the Earl kept the strap he'd used to punish Lucien whenever he'd caused some minor indiscretion; the silver circle set into the floor, where Luc had stood when he called for the demon...

His chest tightened, nostrils flaring, and he clenched his eyes shut, turning his face away. "I was here... When I called the demon forth." An eerie prickling stirred over the back of his neck. This was where his life had changed, and not for the better. The last time he'd been here, pieces of Lord Rathbourne had been splashed all over the walls. Lucien had broken free of his collar, as the ring controlling it had been destroyed in the blast, and found himself covered in blood, and filthy with the oily stain of the demon upon his soul, knowing that he could not stay. Anywhere. Anywhere, but here...

That was when she'd found him, three days later, at the Grosvenor Hotel.

"It's just a room, Lucien," Ianthe said softly. "Just memories." He looked up and those gorgeous eyes shuttered. "We all have them. No doubt yours are as pleasant as mine."

Closing the book she'd been perusing, she set it aside, moving toward him with a faint swish of her skirts. It was as if she could see right through him. "You're not alone, Rathbourne. Not this time."

It helped ease the jagged edges within him. Lucien bowed his head, hungry for her to touch him, but unable to ask for it. "It feels like I've always been alone. I've never belonged to anybody." *And I want to, damn it.*

"Forget those memories," she whispered, her hand sliding over his cheek, "and look again. It's just a room."

Lucien let out the breath he'd been holding. She was right. He cupped his hand over hers, holding it to his cheek. Not enough. He wanted the crush of her body against his. Curling his arms around her, he dragged her close, burying his face into the side of her neck.

Ianthe wrapped hesitant arms around him. There was tension within her, something that eased as soon as his arms came around her, as if she too needed this. Lucien's buttocks hit the scarred desk. He was trapped in a cage of skirts and the scent of lilacs. A pleasant prison, indeed.

And he felt like he didn't want to let go of her.

Ever.

They stood for long moments. As her breast rose, his fell. Against the chill of the room, the warmth of her body was a welcome respite. His cock stirred, far too aware of the press of flesh against him, but Lucien forced himself to think of other things. This comfort that she gave him was just as precious as a tumble into bed. For the first time in months, he felt some sense of peace steal through him. This was only pretend, but it was... something he hadn't realized he'd been searching for.

"Well," Ianthe said, letting out a breath and easing away from him. Those fingers fussed with his lapels. "Aren't we a pair?"

Too soon. He was tempted to drag her back, but that was madness, wasn't it?

Instead, he brushed his fingertips over that full, luscious mouth, feeling his own tingle with suppressed need. He wanted to kiss her, but could not. And perhaps that was the problem? Denied by his own pride, his desire only swelled at the thought of what he could not have. Could not touch. Or taste.

And she knew it.

Ianthe's breath hitched. Her fingers tugged his tie from where it was tucked within his waistcoat. She looked up, a sultry glance from beneath her lashes. Apparently he was not the only one thinking lustful thoughts. "Why not create some new memories? For the both of us?"

"It's not night."

"True." Those fingers slid down his waistcoat, flexing against the fabric, as if she enjoyed the sensation beneath her fingertips. She turned her hand, brushing lower against his erection.

Violet eyes lifted to meet his.

"To disapproving fathers," she murmured, a faint smile playing about her lips as she went to the floor in front of him, her skirts spilling about her. A supplicant on her knees, but it was not forgiveness she asked.

"Christ." Lucien's breath exploded out of him, but he certainly wasn't protesting. "You don't have to do this."

"I don't do anything unless I wish to do so."

"Really?" He captured her chin, lifting her face so that he could see everything it revealed. "Then you wanted to be in my bed?"

Ianthe hesitated, and a pretty rose flush spread through her cheeks. That was not what caught his interest, however. Colors danced over her skin, a wash of yellowy-green guilt, and something... blue. A blue so bright and vibrant that it reminded him of a summer sky with not a cloud in it. He hesitated before making his guess. Longing? Yet there was nothing sexual about the flash of color. It was pure, chased away by the dark indigo of doubt.

Lucien froze. He couldn't quite decipher what that look had been about...

They stayed like that until Ianthe's dark lashes slowly lowered, shuttering her pretty eyes. Her gaze fell, her hands sliding up his thighs. "I wanted you in my bed," she admitted in a soft voice. "I wanted you under my hands, under my mouth... I wanted permission, in a way, to take what I wanted. Permission to surrender to your needs, and in doing so, to exploit my own."

"Nobody was stopping you," he murmured, brushing a strand of hair off her face.

"Only myself."

He understood that in a way. She'd been raised in a strict environment, and though she had rebelled, echoes of society's restraint still lingered within her. By demanding her nights, he had, in effect, given her guilt-free permission to accept his deal and explore her budding sensuality.

"It was easy to give into your demands, Lucien, for then I could pretend I had no choice in the matter."

Lucien stroked his thumb across her cheek. "And then you could enjoy this without feeling the shame."

Those dark lashes lowered. "Yes."

"Look at me, darling." As she slowly complied, he felt a nervous flutter along his skin, knowing how important this moment was. "There will never be shame, not between us. No, this is but desire, Ianthe, and it is pure and clean and whole. I don't care which of your father's lies you still hear, no matter how much you claim otherwise; he is wrong. I don't care what society will say about us; they know nothing. You and I, we are all that matter here, now, between us. All you need know is this: do as you please."

"We're in the middle of an important investigation," she whispered, and he saw the guilt in her eyes. "It's easier at night, when there's nothing else I should be doing."

"Is not giving in to desire going to help us find Morgana faster?"

"No."

"Is this going to strengthen the both of us, considering the sexual aspect of our power?"

"Yes."

Lucien leaned closer. "I think this is important. For us. For our bond. For you. You've been carrying a weight around on your shoulders. It's not good for you."

Her hands quivered on his thighs. "Thank you."

"It's my pleasure." At the flash of budding emotion on her face, he forestalled her. "No, really. It is. Use me to please yourself. Do as you please. I will not utter one word of protest."

That earned a smile, followed closely by a look of determination that took his breath away. "Then I shall."

His cock strained behind the fabric of his breeches as her breath whispered soft entreaty there. His skin heated as her hands slid higher, so lightly that they almost trembled over the buckskin of his breeches. Every muscle in his abdomen tightened in sensual anticipation.

And she was barely even *touching* him.

"Tell me what you want," he whispered.

"I want to be under *your* hands." Another sensual whisper from those rosy lips. "Under your mouth. Under your command. I want. That's the truth. I wanted *this*. It's very simple, really, and yet, not at all."

One delicate finger traced the firm bulge of his erection, like a lit spark set to flesh. A button parted under her careful ministrations, then another... She was seducing him in slow measures, wrapping him around her little finger, stealing the very breath in his lungs and taking command of the rapid thump of his heart.

And all the while, she watched him with those dangerous, dangerous eyes.

Lucien was fairly certain, in that instant, that he wasn't going to survive Miss Martin. Not intact. Not whole.

"Do you know what I want?" he whispered, curling his finger around that one strand of hair that always refused to obey her careful ministrations and rubbing his fingers down its black length. Soft. So soft.

"What?"

The devil knew it. He could see it in her eyes as she leaned closer and rubbed her cheek against the engorged length of his cock.

Lucien sucked in a sharp breath and thrust his hand back for support, knocking a pair of books off the desk. "I want that pretty little mouth—"

Something shifted in the air in the room. It stole his attention.

"Yes?" she asked in a taunting whisper as her tongue darted out, caressing his molten skin. Lucien froze, one hand clenched in her curls, as she pressed forward and bestowed a chaste kiss against the buckskin barely covering his cock. Breathing seemed dangerous in this moment. Not now. Not *bloody* now. But he looked up, alerted by some instinct, some *tremble* along his skin, that something wasn't right.

"Do you feel that?"

"Is that supposed to be some sort of innuendo?" Ianthe teased, and her hand brushed against his cock.

Lucien caught her wrist. In the darkness, something red gleamed.

Eyes. A set of glowing, red eyes.

"Ianthe," he whispered. His cock flagged.

Some sense of his concern must have betrayed him. She looked up, her voice as quiet as his. "What?"

"I think we just tripped one of the wards in the room," he told her, not daring to take his eyes off the creature shuddering free of its stone trappings with a cracking sound. "Lord Rathbourne must have put it over one of the books on his desk."

Ianthe froze, her back to the threat, and her pale face tilted up to his. Her previous languidness melted off her. "What is it?"

"A stone construct. The gargoyle, I think."

Another low groan tore itself through the room, and he had the sudden realization that there'd been two of them guarding the entrance. "Fuck."

"Good thing we weren't caught with your breeches entirely down."

Lucien stepped slowly to the side. His flagging erection couldn't have felt more vulnerable as he swiftly rebuttoned himself. "Not the time for a jest, Miss Martin. I'm fairly certain I'm never going to have you on your knees without the hairs on the back of my neck rising."

"Yes, this wasn't entirely what I meant when I said 'let's create new memories'."

Bizarrely, he couldn't stop himself from smiling. "Don't you ever show fear, woman?"

"I'm not very fond of small spaces, remember?"

Yes, but far from running from such things, she was the type of woman who braced herself, stiffened her upper lip, and then waded into battle. A warmth spread through him: admiration.

"Constructs," Ianthe muttered, turning to face the doorway with her hands flexed at her sides. "It had to be constructs."

"At least they're only stone."

"Not bodies?" She gave him a tight, thin-lipped smile. "Small mercies, my lord."

Lucien looked for a weapon. Something. Anything. Nothing on hand, except for the fire poker. Good lord, he was reduced to this. He did, however, snatch it up.

Ianthe shot the poker a look, then turned that look upon him. It spoke volumes.

"Later," he said.

"Would you like me to take point?"

He gave a gruff nod. "If you would."

"Can you keep them off my back?" Ianthe's fingers flexed, a pair of mage globes forming an inch from her palms and flickering with blue lightning.

"I'm not entirely certain. I'll try."

"We need to discuss this at some point," she murmured. "You cannot continue like this, Rathbourne."

"*Later.*"

Saved by the gargoyle. It skittered toward them, its stone claws clicking on the cobbled floors, and its eyes gleaming with a vacant, demonic light. Buoyed by latent magic, color flooded its body until its hide was no longer stone but an iridescent ripple of oil on water. A slick pink tongue darted out, tasting the air, and then it danced back into the shadows behind a column.

"It's quicker than I imagined." Ianthe raised her hands.

Her mage globes rose into the air, throwing back the shadows. They hummed neutrally, pale globes of light with the odd static crackle of lightning dancing over their surfaces.

Quick as a hunting cat, one of the gargoyles darted forward. Lightning lashed out, but it dodged away, leaving a smoking pit in the floor where it had been. Burnt stone flavored the air. The second gargoyle feinted, and Ianthe flicked her fingers, casting lightning toward it. It too, twisted in midair, muscle rippling down its flank.

The pair of them took turns, as though testing her weaknesses. Ianthe took a step back, toward him.

"Without Lord Rathbourne, they have no wits," he said, "though they seem to act with animal intelligence."

No, they were just stone. Keyed to attack anything within their perimeter, until either they or the intruders were down. Anything short of complete annihilation wouldn't stop them.

Bully for us.

His gaze darted to the doorway. "If we escaped this room, they might not follow."

Both of them looked at the pair of gargoyles prowling the floor between them and the door.

"Any more brilliant ideas?" Ianthe asked.

"Run? One of us has to be faster than the other."

"Very amusing. How do you know it's not me?"

The first gargoyle launched itself on top of one of the bookshelves, running along it as nimble as a cat, its demonic tail lashing random books of the shelves.

"Watch out!" Lucien yelled, brandishing the poker. He spun to face it, but the gargoyle suddenly curled its back claws around the shelf, and then shoved itself away from the wall with one arm.

Shit. The enormous bookcase launched itself toward them, the gargoyle riding it. Lucien grabbed Ianthe by the waist, trying to swing her out of the way. A whip-like tail lashed around his boot from behind, yanking him off-balance just as the bookcase careened down across the desk, vomiting books like some tidal wave. The mage globes imploded with a small, thunderous crash.

Lucien hit the floor and kicked up with his boot, hitting the gargoyle in the face. It felt like kicking a wall, pointless and jarring. The creature snapped its fangs, teeth sinking into his boot. Sharp, wretched teeth sunk through the boot into his skin. Lucien yelled, but by some miracle, the boot came free, leaving the blasted thing with it. The gargoyle shook its head like a dog, worrying at the leather.

Heart in his throat, Lucien looked for her. "Ianthe?" Where was she? Lucien shoved aside the table. A mess of red skirts lay toppled beneath a mountain of books and the leaning bookshelf. She wasn't moving. "Ianthe!"

Get up! Lucien leaned his back beneath the bookshelf, where it had caught on the desk, and put all of his weight into it. The enormous thing shifted, and he ground his teeth together. "Can you move?"

Ianthe gasped, rolling onto her hands and knees. "Behind you!"

Shoving a hand out, she triggered the power stored in one of her rings. Lucien's coat hem flapped as the weight of pure force flung past him. One of the gargoyles had been mid-pounce. It hit the wall with a boom, powdered stone exploding onto the floor. The face slid free like a mask, tumbling onto the ground, the red eerie light of its eyes slowly fading like an ember and then dying. All that remained was the snarling nose, its leering teeth, and one eye.

"One down."

"One to go." Lucien twisted his head as he dragged her out from under the bookshelf and then let it fall onto the desk again. "Where did it go?"

Claws skittered over stone, almost sounding like hushed laughter. Lucien spun, but there was nothing in the shadows.

"I begin to suspect this is what a doe feels like when hunters are converging upon it," Ianthe said.

There was a flash of movement to the side, but when he turned, there was nothing there.

"It feels like it's mocking us." Lucien retreated a step and felt her do the same. They stood back to back, she with her hands raised and her power gathered, and he with his pathetic poker.

"Maybe we'd best take away its shadows," Ianthe said, and spat a power word. Light flashed into the room as a pair of mage globes formed as brightly shining as an electric bulb.

The gargoyle froze as it crept toward them, hissing at them.

"Lord Rathbourne obviously liked his constructs." Ianthe pushed her sleeves up, staring the remaining gargoyle down. "Two can play at that game."

The mage globes spun. Faint shadows sprung up on the walls as they whirled like a child's jack-o'-lantern, growing into humanoid shapes. The shadows stretched, and he realized that they were moving.

A shadowbinder in all of her glory.

Three of the shadows launched forward as the gargoyle attacked, grabbing hold of it. Its momentum slowed, its powerful haunches straining, but they could not stop it entirely. It gained an inch.

"I can give them presence," she gasped, "but not a great deal of weight. The gargoyle will outweigh them."

"Can you add force to the tip of the poker?" He brandished it.

Ianthe nodded, a trail of perspiration working down the side of her face. Handling several complex weaves was providing a strain that only frustrated him. He should have been able to help her.

The poker suddenly dipped as the end flared white-hot. Lucien grabbed it with two hands, straining to lift it. He staggered forward. A pair of red eyes locked on him, and suddenly the gargoyle stopped straining. Instead, it crouched low, as if to pounce.

Everything happened too quickly. The gargoyle launched itself at him, slipping free of the shadowy constructs, and Lucien brought the poker down in a resounding sweep that would have done his fencing tutor proud. It smashed into the side of the gargoyle, jarring all the way up his arm. Power flared, the gargoyle's eyes widened, and then...

The detonation threw them both backward. Lucien staggered into Miss Martin and another bookshelf fell. They both went down. Lucien cracked his knee hard on the cobbles, a pair of books bouncing off his shoulders as he curled himself over her. One hit him right in the spine, its edges sharp. Lucien winced.

And then it was done.

Silence. *Stillness*. Peace?

Pain flared through his knees. Skin scraped off, he presumed. Lucien looked up, but nothing moved.

Miss Martin blew a strand of hair out of her face, then tucked it behind her ear as she sat up. The chignon was beyond repair, and her skirts were torn. A streak of dirt marred her pale cheek, and it was that that suddenly enraged him.

It was his duty to protect her. From all things. And so far he was failing. What good was he? He might as well hide behind her fucking skirts!

"Bloody, *fucking* hell!" He turned and threw the bent poker he somehow miraculously still held. It made a rattling, tinny sound as it bashed into the wall and tumbled to the ground.

"Rathbourne?"

Lucien stood with his head down, his chest straining within his waistcoat. "It's nothing." Swallowing hard, he fought the violent surge of anger within him. Power trickled along his skin, igniting the hairs on his arms. How easy it would be to punch a hole through the wall right now, but that was Expression tempting him, taunting him. Not sorcery. Not skill. Not everything he'd fought so hard to learn, only to have it vanish from his grasp right when he needed it the most.

A gentle hand brushed against the small of his back. Lucien flinched, his fists curling, but contained it.

"Are we going to discuss that?"

"No, we are not." He let out a shuddering breath and turned around. Violence rode him, tightly reined in but practically vibrating through his muscles. He wanted to kick something, but was thwarted by her presence. One didn't go around tromping through a room in a violent whirlwind, unless one wanted to be considered fit for...

...Bedlam.

His nostrils flared. Strangely enough, that thought jarred him out of his fury. It was done. Neither of them was injured, and he was not some bedlamite, raging against his circumstances. He was better than that.

He would be better than that.

As Lucien turned to face her, his gaze fell on a book on the floor in front of him. It had tumbled from the cutout hollow of another book.

Rathbourne's grimoire, full of all of his occult writings, including the mysterious link to Morgana, one hoped.

"There it is."

Ianthe's hand paused in the air, halfway between them, as if she'd been reaching for him. It fell. "What?"

"The grimoire! I knew it was here somewhere."

Hidden in plain sight within another book.

Grabbing it, Lucien flicked through the pages of spidery scrawl. Every sorcerer had their own grimoire. They were both a diary and a spell book, showcasing the design of each sorcerer's individual chants, wards, and ritualistic runes. There was enough reading here to keep him entertained for all of the sleepless nights he was sure lay ahead of him.

He shook it at her. "We've found it."

That pillow-lipped mouth curved in a broad smile, as if they both shared the victory. Or perhaps they had. Her blood had to be up - his was. "Time to discover some of Lord Rathbourne's secrets."

"Stimulating reading, I'm sure." He tucked the grimoire under his arm. "Come on. At this rate, it will be dark before we know it." He stepped over a pile of rubble, shooting it a dark look. "That's going to give me nightmares for weeks."

"They were just constructs, Rathbourne."

"You try unbuttoning your breeches with a cockstand, while having a willing young woman on her knees in front of you, and try not to think about what's watching you in the darkness."

Ianthe laughed. A throaty, luxurious sound that made all of the light within her suddenly glow. She lost all sense of decorum, holding her glee within her by means of a clapped hand over her mouth. The sounds she made... Hardly seductive, but it felt like she'd shoved a fist straight into his chest and curled that small hand directly around his beating heart.

I made her laugh. It was the first time he could recall seeing her so abandoned, and the odd flush of pleasure he felt, at knowing he'd brought this about, made him both happy and irritable. She didn't laugh enough. In fact, he'd barely heard that sound at all since they'd met.

Lucien rubbed his chest. *Gods, what was wrong with him?*

"You'll never enjoy fellatio again without thinking about it!" A strand of dark hair had come free, and she tucked it breathlessly behind her ear, looking both girlish and playful.

"Thank you for the reminder," he drawled.

"Or perhaps," Ianthe's sharp-eyed gaze cut toward him, filled with humor, "we'll just have to see what we can do about that."

Everything in him fluttered. Lucien could do nothing more than stare at her as she gathered her skirts and stepped past him.

Hell.

CHAPTER FOURTEEN

'Music is so very much like sorcery. One starts slowly, learning a series of notes, the same as one begins to form conscious pathways to ritual, in order to force the will to manifest. The more one practices sorcery, the swifter those pathways form, until one merely gathers his will together and the will changes the structure of the world around you. The steps in between become invisible, but they are still important.'

— *Of Music And Magic*, by Johann de Villiers

NIGHT FELL. Outside, a storm shook the building. Blackened clouds brewed overhead, the occasional scythe of lightning highlighting half of London.

And despite knowing there'd be little sleep for him tonight, Lucien sent Ianthe away. He knew what she'd want to discuss: his weaknesses, his lack of sorcery. He was not in the mood. He just wanted to be alone tonight, regardless of that look in Ianthe's eyes.

Upending the bottle of brandy, Lucien trailed his fingertips across the ivory keys of the piano he'd found in the library. It was far enough away from her chambers that it wouldn't interrupt her. The song was familiar, his mother's favorite. Instantly, it took his thoughts to another place.

Lucien closed his eyes. He could see his mother now, all husky voice and laughter, her hair hanging in dark curls over her shoulders as she guided a younger version of him through the notes. His memories of her were few: her soft voice, her perfume—jasmine, always jasmine—and the impeccable style with which she dressed. He could never quite imagine her face properly. Those eyes had been the same dark amber as his own, but when he tried to put all of the components of her face together, his mind threw up a half-finished canvas, dulled by time.

As if tainted by his emotions, the tune changed, becoming a little slower, a little darker. He knew this song. Knew it, because she had played it frequently. Lady Rathbourne might have been all that was elegance and grace, but her passions ran a little darker, or so it was said. Music and opera stirred her. She liked tragedies, rather than comedy, and she was frequently sad. A bitter sweetness lingered about her, but she had always loved him. He was the one person who could light up her world and fill it with her smiles.

Lucien played the song through, hesitant, relearning the chords, stumbling sometimes, and then dabbling with the notes until he would hit the right one which stirred his memory anew. Then he played it again, stronger, slower, striking the right sort of haunting melancholy, which was underscored by the storm outside. They worked in perfect counterpoint.

Music was something he'd forgotten his love for over the years. How long since he'd played? Ten years? Eight?

Yet it rose within him, as if it had never truly faded away. Gone, but not forgotten.

Using the passion of the piece, the *longing* within it, he let the power of his will build until he felt fit to burst out of his skin.

He was almost there, almost on the verge of levitating the bottle of brandy, when the first ache began in his temple. Instantly, his nostrils flared, sweat sprang into being down the back of his neck, and the small working of sorcery that he'd been forming undid itself. The bottle hadn't quite shifted, but it vibrated a little as the force of his will vanished.

Lucien brought his hands down in a jarring display upon the piano, his head bowing.

Curse it.

So close...

What was wrong with him? Why could he not manipulate sorcery without feeling this discordant ache? It had worked before, when he'd produced the mage globe, but he'd been distracted by Ianthe's nervousness, not really thinking about it at all.

There were no answers. Not here.

Lucien grabbed the bottle of brandy again.

The spirits burned down his throat, leaving him with a heated knot in his gut that felt nice. Oblivion. Numbness. That was what he sought tonight. His body ached with need; he could have slaked it. Ianthe had been more than willing, but as much as he would have liked to have drowned himself in flesh and heat and sex, that was beginning to become part of the problem itself.

The truth was, he was starting to like Ianthe. The problem being that he didn't quite know how he felt about that.

"I still want revenge," he'd told her—his parting words to her tonight—but they had sounded desperate, even to him.

Putting his hands back on the keys, Lucien turned to a tune that haunted him. The first few bars played out in quivering, aching loneliness. Could he trust her? He wasn't certain. Did he want to trust her? Yes. And heaven help him, he wanted to do a hell of a lot more than that. He wanted to bury himself in her, to shut out the world for the next three days, and simply lock them both in the bedroom together, as if they had no cares in the world. As if they could pretend that all of the weight of the past meant nothing.

Worst of all?

He wanted to kiss her.

That maddening mouth. It taunted his memory. Lucien's hands moved faster over the keys, stealing notes of growing passion from the pianoforte. Far easier to throw himself into this, where he stopped thinking and simply let it all spill out of him in the throes of emotion. Blood danced through his veins as he poured his heart and soul into the music.

To want such a thing was insane. He himself had set the terms of their bet, and now he wanted to break them.

Dangerous woman.

What was he to her? He knew she was keeping secrets. They haunted those violet eyes, her breath catching the entire ride home from Rathbourne Manor, as if words died on the tip of her tongue, each time he looked at her.

You can't have her.

You shouldn't want her.

No matter how many times he told himself that, it didn't matter.

The windows rattled in their casement. Lucien took another drink, then set the bottle on the top of the piano where a sticky ring had formed. Running a hand through his disheveled hair, he sighed. A prickling sensation rose along his spine.

That was when he began to realize he was not alone.

"Für Elise. It was beautiful," Ianthe said wistfully, from the doorway. "I didn't know you could play."

Lucien kept his head bowed. He couldn't look at her. Not in this moment. It felt like an intrusion into a private moment he'd been having, and yet he couldn't resent her for it, not when a part of him was also hungry for company.

Lightning lashed through the curtains.

Don't ask her... Don't...

"Join me?" The words sounded rough.

"Is that a question or a demand? It is night, after all, and you still want revenge, after all." The words were both a dark jest, and a challenge.

Lucien slowly turned. Rose silk draped her form, the robe tied just beneath her breasts. Those feet were bare, and somehow the sight was more intimate than anything else between them. This might have been a normal night between husband and wife.

But it wasn't.

"What do you want to do?"

Ianthe looked troubled. She padded across the parquetry floor, her gaze sliding to the storm through the window, then back to him. "That's a dangerous question."

"Is it?"

Their eyes met. He kept waiting for her to say something, some question about what had happened today between them, but her gaze dropped to his hands, and then she reached out and touched him. One languid stroke, her fingertips trailing over his. Wistful, perhaps.

"You have beautiful hands. I see now why you're so skillful in bed. You play the piano with the lightest touch, almost a caress. It's the same way you touch me."

Lucien cleared his throat. "Can't sleep?"

Ianthe shook her head ruefully, her hair bunched into a lazy chignon, as if she'd merely stuffed pins into it any old way. Reaching out, he caught her fingers in his and drew her into his lap. The silk of her rose-colored robe slithered over his trousers, her firm bottom nestling snugly against his cock. He was aware of it. He was always aware of it— that slow burn beneath his skin whenever she was around—but he ignored the ache, rested his chin on her shoulder, and leaned around her to position his hands again.

The first notes rang out. Something lighter of tone: Beethoven's the *Waldstein*. He managed the first and second movements, but couldn't quite manage the rapid left hand runs of the rondo with Ianthe in his lap. The notes jarred and he fell still, leaning his chin upon her shoulder and drawing in a deep breath.

"I can't sleep either," he admitted, turning his face into the curve of her throat and breathing her in. Faint traces of her perfume lingered, but he could scent the base notes of her skin.

"Did you read Lord Rathbourne's grimoire?" she asked.

"Most of it. It makes little sense. It keeps saying that he's preparing me for the ultimate sacrifice. Then he spends entire passages gloating about revenge and how this will finally earn him back his honor."

"Sacrifice?"

Lucien shrugged. It had made all of the hairs on his arm stand on end, coinciding with what Lady Eberhardt had said, but he refused to dwell on it.

"I don't like that word, Lucien." Ianthe tilted her head toward him, fear painting icy blues across her skin.

His thumb stroked over her silk robe, absorbing the sensations. "Don't you? Why? Concerned for me?"

"Of course I am."

His heart twisted in his chest. "Don't be."

She tried to turn around. "Lucien—"

Hands curling around her waist, he held her in place. The easiest way to hide the fear in his heart was to keep his face turned away. "Perhaps that's why he used me to summon the demon? Maybe I was to be the blood sacrifice to appease it? If so, more fool he. The plan backfired."

"If it backfired, then why would Morgana have been so keen to get her hands on the grimoire now?"

"Perhaps she was tying up loose ends, or thought Lord Rathbourne had written something more? Perhaps he knew something he didn't write down? Who will ever know? That's just one more dead end for us to overcome."

Almost petulantly, Ianthe stabbed the A minor. It rang through the room, clear as a bell. "Perhaps, perhaps, perhaps. I'm tired of chasing my tail. I *need* to find her. What does she want, damn it?"

"Drake's heart on a platter?" It was said nonchalantly, but he knew it was a mistake as soon as she stiffened.

"Don't say that." Those soft words tore him apart. "Please don't say that."

A hard lump formed in his throat. Lucien stroked her hip, pressing a kiss to her exposed nape, gentle touches designed to soothe. He couldn't believe he was about to say this. "He's safe, love. The Prime's the strongest sorcerer in all of England, and he's protected by a handful of Sicarii. After all, he tore that demon's physical form to shreds last year, before he sent it back to me. Nobody else has ever managed such a thing. Morgana would want to get up early in the morning to pull the wool over his eyes."

"But what if she *does* somehow manage it?"

There was something about the way she said it that tore his heart to pieces. Not for the Prime. For her. Lucien grimaced. Things were becoming entirely unpredictable between them. He couldn't explain this softening toward her, but at the same time, he no longer wished vengeance upon her. The very thought made him feel somewhat ill. "She won't," he promised. "You have my word that I will do everything within my power to stop that from happening."

This time, he couldn't stop her from turning to the side on his lap. Violet eyes searched his face. "You would protect him?"

"Not for his sake." It was a confession that shook the both of them, judging by the look in her eyes.

Something changed in the air between them. Ianthe looked away, as though she couldn't bear to see it.

"Oh," she said softly, and plucked at a key. "*Oh.*"

Lucien cleared his throat. "What are you doing down here?"

Ianthe's head fell forward. She struck the C key. "I think you know why I'm here." It was the faintest whisper, as though she barely dared admit it. She tugged something from the pocket of her robe and placed it on the top of the piano.

A small packeted sheath.

Hell. Lucien pressed another kiss to her silk-clad shoulder. She wouldn't have dared before, but this was an affirmation of her desires. Ianthe was slowly spreading her wings, learning to take what *she* wanted.

Turning her, he set her on the keys with a discordant jar of noise.

Their eyes met. A sad smile touched her mouth. "Mrs. Hastings won't know what to think about all of this noise."

"I daresay."

One hand inside each of her knees, he pushed them open, the robe slithering over her skin and revealing a hint of her plain cotton nightgown beneath, as he dragged his chair closer. Ianthe hesitated, then reached up and brushed a loose strand of hair behind her ear. A faint blush stirred her cheeks.

"Perhaps we can help each other to sleep?"

"I don't think what you have planned has anything to do with sleep."

"True." Lucien pressed a kiss to the inside of her wrist and looked up. "But it's not what I want that matters. Not here. Not tonight."

Ianthe's breath caught. There was sadness there in her eyes. He realized it had been lingering there for some time now. It arrested him, but then she blinked and the expression was gone, dust in the wind.

"Why did you come down?"

"I... I couldn't sleep, but I could hear the music. There was something so hungry about it. A longing. It drew me down here."

Had she come searching specifically for him? Ianthe's hand cupped his face, sliding down his cheek until her thumb caught his lip.

Lucien turned his face into her palm, biting at the fleshy mound at the base of her thumb. A shiver ran through the both of them. Lightning flashed in the distance. "And what did you long for, Ianthe?"

"You."

How well he knew that feeling. "This is growing dangerous."

And she understood. Every touch, every moment between them, only intensified the bond. It wasn't just the sex, but the intimacy—and he hadn't expected that when he'd agreed to this. If they continued in this vein, one day soon, the bond would be unbreakable.

"Would it be so very bad?" Her eyes were enormous pools of shadow as she gently asked the question. "It's only been a few days, and yet the very thought of losing you, or our bond, sends a shiver down my spine. It's become... a part of me."

Lucien bowed his head, pressing it into her palm as she stroked his face. "I don't know anymore. I want you."

She swallowed. "I want you."

"I know," he told her, shutting his eyes. "I can feel it." He felt the certainty along the bond they shared, but with that certainty came another. "You're keeping secrets from me."

Ianthe froze.

"You don't have to tell me. I know you are."

"Do you not have any secrets from me?" Her voice was roughened honey.

Lucien looked up. Of course he did. "I keep wondering how far I can trust you."

Those dark lashes covered her eyes. "So do I. But you must know: I would never seek to harm you, Lucien."

"No?"

"No." She wet her lips. "You have become... important to me. I don't know if it's the bond, or if it's simply because of what we've shared. Sometimes it feels inevitable." Her voice dropped to a whisper. "You. Me. Sometimes it feels like fate. No matter what I do, I somehow always keep coming back to you."

"You mean the way you were the one who brought me in a year ago?"

"Yes," she said, dropping her gaze, and yet it was not the complete truth. "I ache," Ianthe told him, her eyes sad. "And it's all you. Always you."

"An ache? Here?" His palm spread flatly over her middle.

Those brilliant eyes flashed as she looked up.

"Or here?" he whispered, sliding his hand lower until his palm cupped her between her thighs.

Licking her lower lip, she closed her eyes and nodded. The aching sense of yearning in her expression made his heart beat a little faster. Perhaps they were both still too wary to meet each other in the middle, yet here, only here, was it easy. This was easy. To want. To take.

"You want me," he said. "Say it."

A roll of her hips brought her heated flesh closer to him. "I want you."

"And what part of me did you want?"

But she slid her hand behind his nape and drew him closer. Lucien leaned his knuckles on the piano keys, obeying her with another discordant wash of noise. Their faces were but an inch apart, her breath caressing his mouth. His gaze lowered to those sweet lips. How he wanted to taste them... It ached within him, like a hard fist curling around his cock. His hands slid over her thighs, dragging silk and cotton with them, until he could feel heated flesh.

Kiss me, he dared.

Kiss me, came the reply.

But he was not yet ready to lose.

And neither was she.

Thwarted need flashed across that pretty face, and then she turned it into his neck, her small teeth sinking into his flesh with a faint, teasing nip that spoke of her frustration. Lucien's mouth parted, and he tilted his face up, allowing her access as she soothed that slight pain with a heated lash of her tongue. A trembling psychic touch brushed along the back of his thighs, making him flinch. It came again, higher, stronger, more sure of itself, until it felt like a feather dragged over his balls.

Lucien caught her wrists. They stared at each other. Her psychic touch vanished as he slowly set both her hands behind her on the piano, a silent admonition in his gaze. This was not her moment to command. It was his.

One finger traced the smooth skin between her clavicles and headed south to her full breasts. Ianthe swallowed.

"You were made for a man's touch," he whispered.

Haunting vulnerability flashed across her face, and she turned it aside. "That's what my father said to me once."

And not kindly, he guessed. Lucien examined her half-turned away expression. "I did not mean it as an insult, but a compliment. You are beautiful. Passionate. Like a storm on the horizon, not quite unleashed. There's an untamed sensuality brewing within you." He traced her throat. "It is nothing to be ashamed of."

Ianthe's lashes fluttered closed. "I know I should not feel the sting of shame, but I still hear his words even now. Especially now."

"Why now of all times?"

Ianthe inhaled slowly and looked away, a hint of red dawning like a sunrise in her cheeks. "Because of you." The words were barely a whisper, but they struck him right through the heart. "Because I did not dare, before you. Because I did not... *want*... before you. Not like this." She looked up helplessly. "It was easy to accept your challenge to own my nights. Easy because then I did not have to put it into words that I wanted you, that I wanted to be in your bed, beneath you..." She turned her face away again with a harsh exhale. "I missed you tonight. I wanted you to come. That's the truth of it. I couldn't sleep because you weren't there. I could hear you down here, and that's where I wanted to be."

Every muscle in his body tensed. This was as close to a declaration as either of them had come—an admittance that there was something between them, something dark and thrilling, something dangerous, something... more. That she was the one who voiced it did not surprise him. She had always been braver than he in so many ways.

Thunder rumbled, vibrating the casements. Lucien hovered, torn by indecision.

"I'm scared," she whispered, "and I'm alone, and I don't want to be alone, not anymore. Not tonight."

It shook him. His own thoughts reflected back at him. He'd have never guessed that she felt this way. His demons were vast, but she hid hers so well. With a shudder, he pressed a kiss to her forehead, breathing in the scent of her hair. "I don't want to be alone either. I wasn't supposed to like you." He brushed his thumbs lightly back and forth between her thighs. Then again. Each stroke lighter than the last. Brushing higher up her thigh, then away, as she shivered.

"Are you saying that you do?" It was said breathlessly, and there was a faint tremor there that belied the ease with which she asked.

He could have said: *Sometimes. When I'm not fit to throttle you.* Or, *Especially when you're like this, molten beneath me.* But Lucien bowed his head beneath the weight of the feeling. "Yes, Ianthe. Yes, I find myself liking you."

"*Oh.*"

Just that. But he saw the arrow hit its target, saw the faint bewilderment within her give way to a vicious joy that was swiftly muted by something else, something that scared her.

He understood it, because it scared him too. The ground beneath his feet was rapidly giving way, leaving him in a foreign land, a land he'd never been in before.

"And here we are," he mocked, "at an impasse which neither of us expected."

"Where do we go from here?" Ianthe whispered.

"Anywhere. I don't— I'm as at sea as you are."

A hush fell between them.

"I... don't think I can."

A brutal blush speared her cheeks.

Lucien absorbed the impact and graced her with a smile. It was not rejection, but a safeguard, a means of mitigating the risk. *That* he understood. His thumbs resumed their heated stroking. "Then let this just remain this. Uncomplicated."

"This was never uncomplicated." Ianthe said it with a faint laugh, but there was no humor there.

"Then we make it uncomplicated." Lucien leaned closer, his mouth hovering but a half-inch from her ear. "What do *you* want? Right now?"

"You," she whispered against the corner of his mouth, lips almost pressing to his, but not quite tasting them, "inside me." A decision had been made. She was brave now with his confession. Her face turned toward his, breath caressing his sensitive lips. "No more talk."

"Very well." Reaching past her, Lucien gently closed the lid on the grand piano. That dark curl sprang from behind her ear, and suddenly he could not bear to see it controlled anymore. Reaching behind her, he plucked first one pin, then another from her hair, and another... Until it cascaded down her back in a series of loose waves. Curling his fingers through her hair, he slowly fanned it out across her shoulders. A wave of midnight silk, gleaming in the candlelight. "There. That's better. Not perfect, but better."

"What would be perfect?"

"This." Sliding his hands up inside her robe, he pushed it off her shoulders, uncovering the thin-capped sleeves of her nightgown. The curve of her shoulder slipped loose from one sleeve, revealing the sharp etching of her collarbone. Lucien tugged at the ties on her robe, and Ianthe sucked in a sharp breath, but she surrendered it to him, leaning back on the piano.

"This," he said, drawing the tie free of its loops and discarding it behind him. Her robe sagged, falling open to reveal the hem of her nightgown riding up around her hips. Those thighs, like white satin... He slid his palm up one, absorbing every inch of soft skin, wanting it to be his mouth on her skin, not his hand...

"This?" With trembling hands, Ianthe watched his face as she began to undo the string that held her nightgown together. Rosy nipples darkened the fabric, and the cotton draped over them, caressing every one of her curves like a lover.

Lucien's breathing raced as she gave a willful shrug of her shoulders. Each sleeve slipped free, captured on her upper arms, as Ianthe stared at him with a dare in her eyes.

"Yes," he said, reaching out with one finger to brush the cotton from where it caught on the upper slope of her breast. Heat pulsed in his cock. Every touch of her skin sent electric shocks to his brain, which seemed to communicate themselves everywhere. He was heat and need and the fierce clench of anticipation.

But a part of him wanted this to be good for her, better than it had ever been before, which was incendiary. Before had always been about control, about slating his desire and she hers. It had been nothing more than physical want. This... This was different.

Lucien kissed her throat, her cheek, her ear... Everything but her mouth, that sweet, treacherous mouth that consumed his thoughts. Curling his fists in her hair, he dragged her head back and bit her chin. Every thought he owned was broken down to its base equation.

I need...

I want...

Her...

I want her...

"Lucien." His name was raw on her sweet tongue.

"What do you want?"

"This." Hands caught his, dragging them lower until they filled with soft flesh.

Her magnificent breasts. So lush and full... as if they'd been made for a man's attention. Cotton rumpled under his touch as he stroked her nightgown out of the way. Ianthe shuddered, and something that sounded almost animalistic burst from her throat. "Yes. *Please*, yes."

Lucien's mouth dipped, his deft hands parting the cotton. A darkened nipple sprang into view, taut and quivering with her hastened breath. His hot mouth closed over it.

Delicious.

It was his turn to make that rough, raw sound in his throat. Tongue swirling in teasing little circles, he looked up at her flushed, abandoned expression. The sight of it made him bold. Grabbing hold of her nightgown, he tore it in two, halfway to her thighs.

Ianthe gasped, capturing his upper arms in surprise. Then her gaze softened, growing heavy-lidded, as she arched back, offering him her body. Passion filled her gaze as he ripped again with slow, heated jerks, until she lay revealed, the flush of candlelight painting her skin with a golden glow. A Botticelli in all its glory. Soft curves, ebony hair, and the faint shell-pink flush of sweetness gleaming wetly between her thighs.

Lucien traced trembling fingers down between her breasts and lower, trailing off as he reached the thatch of dark curls between her thighs. "You are... breathtakingly beautiful." On the return, his hands slid up her sides, parting the cotton, even as her faint, quivering breaths made her breasts lift and fall. "You feel like silk beneath my touch."

He lowered his face, tracing his tongue around her navel. "Like a feast for a starving man."

One that he ached to partake of. But first... her. Her pleasure. His ruin.

A tremor ran over her skin as he slowly tipped her backward until she lay on top of the piano. The leash of his control slipped away from him, his fingers sinking into her hips with slightly less care than he should have owned when touching something so precious.

Dragging her to the edge, he hooked her bare feet up on his shoulders and leaned over her. Glistening pink flesh teased him from behind those dark curls. He drank her in, breath teasing her.

"*Lucien.*" It obviously unnerved her to be so on display before him.

"No shyness, love. Not between us." Thumbs spreading those tender pink folds, he took his time, licking her from end to end. A slow taunting movement. One to drive her out of her mind.

Ianthe arched her back, her heels digging into his shoulders. "Lucien!"

She tasted divine. Lucien nuzzled in again, tasting her and teasing her. Hands cupping her rounded bottom, he laid waste to her, drowning himself in that heated flesh until she was crying out softly, her fingers curling through his hair.

A strangled sound burst from her throat as he slid a finger deep inside her, curling it up to stroke her *there*. Then she was tensing around him, her head thrown back with a gasp, as sweet tension exploded within her.

"Yes. *Yes*, oh please, Lucien..." Ianthe writhed on the piano through her release. "Please. More."

Biting at the soft flesh of her breast, he fumbled with his trousers. His erection sprang to hand, hard and aching, and Lucien tore the packet of the sheath open with his teeth. Ianthe reached between them, tugging the oiled sheath from his hands and sliding it over his engorged length. That invisible tickle of touch explored the length of his hard shaft, earning a hiss from his throat. God. He groaned, his balls drawn up tight. It wasn't going to take much tonight.

"Now," she whispered, as he dragged his cock over her lush, wet opening. "Take me now."

"As you wish." Lucien sank forward, into her tight, wet, satiny heat. "Oh God." He made a strangled sound in his throat. This was bliss. Heaven on earth. Everything.

The first thrust spilled noise from the piano, but the storm drowned it out. Slow and steady, a soft sinking into of flesh. Ianthe was having none of that however.

"Faster," she whispered, her fingers closing in his hair and her legs wrapping around his hips. "More."

Lucien bit his lip as he thrust home. The room vanished as his attention turned inward. The storm, the noise of the piano, all gone as he fucked his way into her... All he could feel was her. This. Pressure danced its way up the base of his spine, and he curled his face into her throat as he lost himself to the sweet pleasure-pain of release.

"*Yes,*" he hissed.

It was an eternity of bliss. No more concerns, no more fears. Just her hands slowly stroking up his back as he came back to himself. Every inch of his body felt more alive than it had ever felt; the intense rush of his blood through his veins, his racing heartbeat, the sweat slick on his skin, and his cock softening as he slid from her body...

But more than that, he could somehow sense her. It felt as though he existed in two skins. His ears rang with the beat of two hearts, both achingly in sync. Their bond. He would never be the same after this night, and it filled him with both dread and hope, which was something he hadn't thought he would ever find again.

Ianthe lifted her face, her hand pressing over his heart in wonder, as if she could feel the same thing he could. "The bond strengthens."

"Faster than expected." He nuzzled her forehead, kissing her there. Perspiration clung to them as he curled her into his arms. Uncomplicated, he had promised, and he knew the words now for a lie.

For, out of all the problems he faced, this was the greatest complication he knew.

But neither of them could admit it out loud.

CHAPTER FIFTEEN

IF IANTHE had her time as a young girl again, she thought she'd have enjoyed growing up in a place like Cherry Tree Cottage.

Located in the small village of Tupnel Green, barely forty miles from London, it seemed like another world entirely. There was a pond in the center of the walled garden, with dozens of primroses surrounding it, rows of lavender, and herbs like rosemary and basil. Fuzzy bees hovered over the droopy heads of sunflowers, and shadows dappled the green lawn as oak trees swayed overhead. Within the secret garden, a blanket spread on the lawn with little cups and saucers set neatly there; several dolls and teddy bears were scattered around. It was perfect. Ianthe had thought that the first time she'd seen it, when she'd been wan and listless following the birth, cradling the tiny baby in her arms as Drake helped her down from the carriage.

A flash of dark curls glinted in the sunlight and a little girl raced across the grass in the garden.

"Tubby, give it back!" Louisa cried out in exasperation. "You know you're not allowed to have mama's slippers!"

Despite the brief pang in her chest, Ianthe stared hungrily as the girl scrambled under a hedge, careless of her skirts. They had that in common, a reckless yearning for adventure as a little girl. But where she would have earned the edge of her father's cane for such a romp, Louisa merely burrowed through the leaves without care nor fear of condemnation.

"Louisa! Come! You have a visitor!" Elsa called, catching sight of Ianthe at the garden gate. She waved her in and limped out onto the cobbled stones at the back of the house, her gout obviously having flared again.

"Aunt Ianthe!" There was genuine joy on Louisa's face, and she ran toward them, her bare feet slapping the grass and her pinafore stained. There was a ragged slipper in her hand.

Elsa sighed. "Louisa, where are your shoes?"

"Oh, I left them in the vegetable patch! I'll put them on in a moment, mama. I didn't realize we had visitors." She proffered a neat curtsy toward Ianthe, then seemed to realize she had the mangled slipper still in her hand and shoved it behind her back, smiling shyly. The fat puppy wandered after her, saw the slipper dangling, and launched itself up, teeth closing around the ruined shoe.

A game of tug-o-war ensued.

Elsa gasped. "Is that my—?"

The slipper tore, and both puppy and daughter spilled onto the grass at their feet. "Oh, no! Tubby, you naughty beast!" Louisa cried. "You've ruined it."

Elsa gave her *the look*, her hands on her ample hips. "What did I say about that dog?"

"He didn't mean it," Louisa said, dragging the offending puppy into her arms. "I'm sorry, mama. I know I have to keep him out of the house, but I was searching for Russell, and he must have gotten in, and—"

"You can do the dishes tonight then," Elsa said, "to help you remember to keep him out of the house in future, and Tubby is banished to the stables to sleep tonight."

"Yes, mama. I'm sorry, I truly am."

Elsa ruffled her hair. "I know. Now run along and show your aunt your tea party. I'm sure she would like to meet Russell, Sir Egmont, and Hilary. I'll bring out something for you to nibble upon." She aimed a critical eye at Ianthe's figure. "Your aunt looks far too thin. All that thick London air interfering with your diet, no doubt."

"Don't go to too much trouble." Ianthe hid her smile. Elsa had a great deal of opinions on London.

Following her daughter into the garden, she left Elsa to fetch them afternoon tea. She could hear Louisa giggling ahead of her and caught a flash of a white pinafore as she entered the hedgerow, but there was no sign of the little girl, just an abandoned tea party with three teddy bears, a doll, and a tin soldier.

"Louisa?" Ianthe spun in a slow circle. Sometimes they played hide and seek.

The garden was still. Lifeless. Even the wind dropped until only the drone of the honeybees broke the silence. Ianthe's smile faltered. Something was wrong. She could feel it. The buzz of the bees seemed to grow louder until it was almost vibrating in her ears.

Her stomach fell, just as clouds slid over the sun. "Louisa?"

A nearby shrub rustled, but there was no sign of the little girl. Ianthe hurried into the garden as the secret little glade darkened with shadow. "Louisa, where are you?"

That was when she glanced at the picnic rug again. The teacups were all knocked over and the rug had draped itself over a forlorn teddy bear, as if something had been dragged kicking and screaming away from it.

Ianthe's heart leaped into her throat. "Louisa?" she yelled, grabbing hold of her skirts and hurrying forward.

How had this happened? How had she lost her daughter in but the blink of an eye? Where was Louisa? What would Elsa say? She should never have come here. Elsa would have protected Louisa; Elsa wouldn't have lost her. What kind of mother could she call herself?

"Louisa!"

Please, no. Not my child.

"Miss Martin." Strong hands cupped her forearms, and Ianthe fought them for a moment, until warm breath kissed her face. "Ianthe," Lucien said, his voice low and gentle. "Ianthe, wake up."

Ianthe woke with a gasp, into a warm, dark room masked with golden candlelight. Her heartbeat thundered through her veins and that lingering sense of loss was almost unquenchable. Lucien knelt on the bed over her, his expression stern and searching, his knees straddling her and pressing the blankets down tightly over her legs. He wore a burgundy robe that he'd evidently thrown on in a hurry, and one heavily muscled thigh speared out from beneath it, covered in dark hair.

"You were having a bad dream," he said, his fingers curling around her upper arms, as if he was afraid she'd vanish if he let her go.

The memory washed over her. Only, it was but a bad dream. This, her waking life, was the true nightmare, and no matter how she tried, it seemed she couldn't escape it.

She must have made some kind of choked noise, a tear sliding wetly down her cheek. Ianthe didn't even know if it was she who reached for him first, or the other way around, but she found herself in his arms, her wet face pressed against the soft wool of his robe, and his arms curling around her. Strong hands cupped the back of her head as he held her there, rocking gently.

"It's all right. You're safe now. You're awake."

Ianthe sobbed harder. Safe?

She clung to him, her chest heaving with the effort involved in containing her tears. Those hands slid slowly down her spine, then back up, and he made shushing noises. It felt nice to be held. Nice to know that someone else might be able to hold all of her broken pieces together.

But then reality began to intrude. That was only another wistful thought, was it not? She'd thought something important had changed between them in that moment in the library, but then Lucien had left her here alone, in her own bed, gently shutting the door in her face as he turned to seek his own. She didn't know what to make of it. He confused her.

Ianthe pushed away, wiping at her cheeks. Her entire face felt like a storm of bees had attacked it; hot, flushed, and swollen. She was a mess, and she couldn't afford to be. Louisa needed a mother, but the sad truth was that all she had was Ianthe herself.

It would have to be enough.

"Was I c-crying out?"

Those heavy lashes had half shuttered over his golden eyes. "Are you all right?"

"Of course. Just a nightmare—"

Lucien cupped her chin in his hands and tilted her face toward his, as though searching for the truth in her words. "I felt your fear through the bond. Fear and anger and a loss so profound it tore me from my own dreams. Something frightened you. Something—"

243

"No, I'm fine." That was panic now, locking hard claws through her belly.

The intimacy of the moment had her off balance. It was worse than being naked before him, for that was only skin. She could feel their tentative bond, feel him sorting through the emotions that travelled along it and echoed within him. Just as she could feel the ache of his curiosity and the stern, somewhat gentle worry inside him. Their bond was strengthening. It was both comforting and a concern, for what if he became so finely attuned to her moods that she betrayed herself and her secrets?

"Is there anything I can do?"

"Yes. *Fuck me*," Ianthe whispered, leaning forward and brushing her mouth against his jaw. Stubble rasped against her lips, and his thumbs were a question mark in the indentation of her chin before his grip weakened. *Hold me. Make me forget.* Closing her eyes, she licked at his throat, her own hands tearing free and sliding up within his robe, feeling the smooth silk of his skin.

And then something wet-slick brushed beneath her fingers... rough scars along his chest.

Ianthe looked down in surprise, but Lucien's face had hardened, and he caught her wrists again, so she couldn't touch him. Dragging his robe shut with his other hand, he took each wrist in hand, controlling her as easily as one did a marionette.

"As you wish," he murmured, pressing her back down onto the mattress in a tumble of sprawled limbs. He held her wrists pinned above her head, and she knew it was so that she wouldn't be able to touch him again.

"What happened to your chest?" He'd never once stripped himself naked before her, even as they... made love.

Dark lashes shuttered those eyes. "Nothing."

Her heart stuttered to a halt. So that was to be the way of it. One mad step toward her, then two steps back. Ianthe tilted her face away, suddenly angry with him, even if she did not truly have the right. After all, was she not keeping her own secrets?

She had forgotten herself. It was all too easy to find herself falling for her own act. Far too easy to believe his. His reluctance only reminded her of the precise nature of this assignation.

Lucien wanted revenge. She wanted her daughter back. As soon as Louisa was safe, Lucien would be free of her. Today might have felt like an odd softening between them, but the truce was questionable. Ianthe could not afford to make any mistakes, not now.

So be it.

Ianthe lifted her eyes to his. Lucien's hot amber gaze asked a question, one she didn't think she could answer. There were no easy answers here. "Fuck me," she whispered again, instead of asking about his scars.

There was a long moment of hesitation, as though Lucien fought his way through the same doubts. Then he turned his face toward her breasts, his gentle onslaught overwhelming. The press of his body between her thighs only reminded her of what had happened in the library.

No place for doubt here, nor for the heart-burning truths she fought her way through. Passion flared between them as Lucien set her body alight with his hands and mouth—slow, gentle licks, stoking the flames between them. Soft gasps sprang from her lips, and a low groan of need came from his. For this one moment, she could pretend this man was her lover, in both heart and mind, and not just body.

When he claimed her, it was a sweet joining. Lucien moved slowly, as though afraid to let the moment go, but she wanted more. She wanted mindless, passionate oblivion. Body clenching around him, she dug her nails into his upper arms and drove him to a breathless release. This time she couldn't share in it, no matter how hard she tried.

Afterward, they lay still for long moments, her body quivering as she lay curled in the hollow of his body and his arms. Occasionally he'd stroke his fingers against her hair, twisting a strand of it around his finger contemplatively. This intimacy was one she was unaccustomed to. Just pretend, she told herself as her eyes grew heavier and sleep finally, finally began to beckon.

"Who is Louisa?" Lucien whispered in the darkness.

Stillness leached through her body. She must have called the name in her sleep. Finding no way of answering that, Ianthe shut her eyes and pretended, despite her stiffening limbs, to be asleep.

CHAPTER SIXTEEN

'The first use of a Sclavus Collar came about in 1789, between two occult colleagues—John Davis, and Genevieve Huston—who were working to combine their wills. The idea was to meld their power and thus create greater works of sorcery requiring strength beyond what either of them had, however, when Mrs. Huston set the collar on Mr. Davis, she discovered that she could also bend his will to hers through the ring controlling it.'

— Origins of the Order of the Dawn Star, by Thaddeus O'Rourke

DRAKE SLIPPED out of his muddy coat and slid into a new one. He was exhausted and had spent half the night hunting London, trying to locate the sorcerer who had used Expression.

His lover, Eleanor Ross, waved his mail at him. "I think you need to read this."

"Not now," he replied tersely and pressed a kiss to her temple. "I need to find our young sorcerer before he demolishes London."

"This is important." Eleanor held up one envelope in particular. "A young man was paid a large amount to deliver this personally. Drake, my psychometry is picking up all kinds of readings on it. It makes me feel urgent, as if something bad is going to happen. I'm practically itching. The rest can wait, but I don't think this one can."

Taking the letter, he examined her face. Eleanor wasn't prone to dramatics, and she had a minor talent in premonition. She'd never been wrong before.

Drake slit the seal. The writing was almost childlike, but very careful, as if someone had taken their time with it.

There is a young male sorcerer I was introduced to this morning, who is wearing a Sclavus Collar. His name is Sebastian Montcalm, though I have not heard his name listed in my copy of the Order's registry, which I searched this afternoon. His mother holds the ring to his collar, and he has admitted that she makes him do bad things. He is a good man, who wishes to escape his slavery. I have no one else to tell, though I trust—and hope—that you can help him.

Please help him.

Yours in confidence,
A concerned friend.

Drake rubbed the piece of parchment. A Sclavus Collar was bad news. An unregistered sorcerer added to the danger, for he should know all of the sorcerers who lived in Britain. There was only one reason to keep it from him, and that didn't bode well at all.

Plots, everywhere he looked. Damn it.

"Well?" Eleanor's eyes softened with concern. "Is it important?"

"It is." He passed her the letter and kept the envelope. "Can you tell me where this came from? Anything you might pick up from it?"

Eleanor sat on the middle of their bed and crossed her legs, her breathing soothing into slow and steady meditation. Drake paced for long minutes, aware of time ticking away on the clock on the mantle.

"A young woman writes it," Eleanor intoned, her eyes moving behind her eyelids, as if she was seeing something. "I feel like... I can't see anything. I'm trying to write with my eyes closed? I don't know. I'm using my fingers to feel out the letters. I don't want to be caught. I'm worried about... about someone else? I can't see anything else, but I keep getting feelings about my father. Is she worried about her father?"

"No, the person I'm looking for is a young man."

"A young man..." Eleanor muttered under her breath, her fingers rubbing the letter. "It's getting hard to pick up anything now. A young man, yes. A dangerous young man. I... I feel sorry for him. I want to help him." Her eyes fluttered open, shock catching her breath. She dropped the letter. "There was a demon, Drake. I didn't catch a lot of it, but she's worried about a demon."

"Bloody hell." Summoning a demon was strictly forbidden now, though ancient members of the Order had originally dabbled with them out of curiosity. He'd sent his own son to Bedlam for summoning one, and he himself had... dabbled... as a youth. What was he going to do? He needed to find this dangerously out-of-control sorcerer, but a demon was on par with that, as far as risk went. Had they managed to summon one? Or were they about to?

"Montcalm... Montcalm... I've never heard that name before. Not in our circles. How am I going to find out more?" he mused, more to himself than anyone. "I could ask D'Arcy how to find this girl..."

"Do you trust D'Arcy?" Eleanor's voice was quiet. "He's your clairvoyant, yet he's mentioned none of this, not even anything about the relic's theft. He should have seen *something* coming. And would he be strong enough to pick up anything more about the letter than I could?"

"No." Which was truth.

"There's one person you could ask," Eleanor suggested.

"Why do I get the feeling I'm not going to like this?"

"Because you're not." She cleared her throat and folded the letter in her lap. "Tremayne's daughter is the current Cassandra. She's terribly accurate, and her talents far exceed my own. She could trace where this letter originated."

Drake shot her an incredulous look. "He won't let me anywhere near her."

"No, he won't. He might let someone else though, if they pay him enough. He doesn't have to know what the request is for. I know he doesn't sit in on most readings. I'm sure he has a chaperone in place, but that can be dealt with."

"Eleanor," he said, starting to see where her mind was going. "No. Tremayne's dangerous. If I were to list five sorcerers who might be involved in summoning a demon, his name would be on it." Taking her hands, he drew her to the edge of the bed. "You are too precious for me to lose. You don't know..." He let out a deep breath. "You don't know how long I've searched for a woman who cares more for me as a man than what I can do for her as Prime."

"Which is why I offer this." Eleanor squeezed his hands. "I love you. I don't want to lose you, and right now, I am seeing the odds stacking up against you. The comet is in the sky, Drake, someone has stolen a dangerous relic, there's a sorcerer on the verge of exploding with Expression, and now someone is toying with demons. It might even be the same person who stole the relic."

"Which is why *I* should go."

"And yet you won't get near her." Eleanor slid off the bed. "You cannot do this. I can. I'm a big girl, Drake, and more than capable of handling Tremayne, if need be, and the simple question is: Who else can you trust? Ianthe is already occupied, and we know there is an enemy within your closest ranks. You don't have anyone else to do this, and you need to find this unbalanced sorcerer, or there might not even be a city to protect from a demon. I could find this sorcerer using Expression, but would I be able to handle him? We both know the answer to that. Both these quests are important."

She was right, damn it all. He was stretched too thin as it was, but he couldn't say it. Sending Ellie into danger was like cutting out his own heart. Instead, he dragged her into his arms and pressed a kiss to her lips. "Be careful." He drew back, cupping her cheeks firmly in both hands. "Don't get yourself killed. That's my heart you're carrying. Be careful of it."

Eleanor smiled. "I always am."

Lucien woke before dawn and blinked several times, surprised to find himself nestled snugly around a warm, soft weight with the covers thrown over him. He had barely slept since Bedlam, his body unaccustomed to the soft mattresses and the excruciating sensitivity to the world around him. The only sleep he'd managed to snatch so far had come with him stretched out on the rug on his bedroom floor with a blanket and no pillow.

This... This was unexpected.

Lifting his head, he peered down at the black-haired beauty in his arms. Her silky hair was all awry, and her pale cheeks were still puffy from last night's tears, but she didn't move. Only her back rose and fell, her head neatly pillowed on his bicep, trapping him there.

Or not, perhaps, trapping at all. The truth was he quite liked the way her bottom nestled snugly into his hips, pressing against his dawning erection, and the way she had curled her fingers around his. Lowering his face, he buried it against the nape of her neck, breathing in her scent.

If he didn't have a thief to find, then he'd be quite content to spend the day here. Judging from the patter of rain against the window, it would be the best place to stay.

"Miss Martin?" he whispered, sliding his fingertips down the curve of her side, over her hips, then back up again. "Ianthe?"

She was difficult to wake. Lucien closed his eyes, enjoying the glide of her skin. With a murmur, she half turned, her hips flexing a little as he traced small circles there. Lucien's cock became steel. Pressing a kiss against the back of her neck and licking the hard indentation of her spine, he let his fingers trace lower, slowly tangling through the soft thatch of hair between her thighs and delving between slick folds.

Ianthe gasped. He felt her wake, that moment of *'where am I?'* palpable along the bond they shared, and then her body relaxed as she realized where she was and sleepy eyes turned his way.

"Good morning," he murmured, curving his palm around her thigh and opening them. Then his fingers delved back into her wetness.

"It certainly is," Ianthe gasped.

He lost himself in her body, in pushing her to pleasure. Within seconds, her soft moans and wicked writhing had distracted both of them. It didn't take long. Ianthe came with a soft gasp, her fingers curling in her pillow as she collapsed. He knew she hadn't reached release last night, and this assuaged the sense of debt he felt.

Panting, she slowly came back to herself. "You stayed the night."

"I must have fallen asleep."

Lying on her back, she circled her finger through his chest hair, but Lucien caught her wrist and subtly disengaged. The sheet covered him, but he'd not expected to wake here. All he could remember was coming to her bed last night when he realized how frightened she was.

A hand lifted to the sheet. "Show me," she said.

Lucien knew what she was asking. Every muscle in his body locked up hard. "No."

His body was a mess, and it was light enough in here for her to see the marks that the demon had left carved all across his chest and hip. Sitting up, he slid his legs over the side of the bed, but she came too. Her breasts pressed into his naked back, her arms locking around his throat and shoulders to hold him there.

"I could demand it," she said. "It's daytime now."

"You could." He tensed. With such a demand came the obliteration of their truce.

Ianthe kissed his neck. "Please, Lucien. It was the demon, wasn't it? Let me see what the creature did to you."

Nostrils flaring, he turned his face away, but those breasts brushed against his back again, dragging his attention elsewhere.

"You've seen mine," she whispered. "Let me see yours."

Hers? Lucien frowned, but her wicked mouth was gliding over the muscle of his trapezius, her teeth biting him neatly there. The sensation streaked through him, tearing a gasp from his lips.

"Hell, woman."

Slowly those arms were dragging him backward. And he went. He actually went. Hitting the mattress, Lucien stared up at her as she draped a thigh over his hips and straddled him.

Both of them were naked. The light in here was meager, just the gray tint of dawn peaking from beneath the curtains, but his eyes had adjusted and he could see every inch of her. Those lush, round breasts and that narrow waist that flared to wide hips... The strip of dark hair between her thighs.

As she could see him.

It was more difficult than he'd imagined. Lucien looked away as her hands traced one mark, then another.

"I'm sorry," Ianthe said, and sadness lurked between them.

"For what?"

"For the pain you went through. For this." A finger dragged over the worst one, the fire-slick burn that still seemed to ache sometimes.

Except now. Her touch felt like a brush of silk against an exposed nerve. Not quite painful, not quite pleasant, but intense. His hips shifted.

Ianthe leaned over him, her tongue darting out to lick one of his scars. Her eyes never left his, however. Slowly, she moved lower and lower, taking care to caress and kiss each one... Lucien swallowed hard. He couldn't help himself from sinking his hands into the mess of black hair and guiding her lower.

"So demanding," she whispered, but she went. Pressing a kiss against the hollow of his hip, she let her hair drag over the sensitive tip of his cock.

Fuck. His hips jerked.

"I believe I owe you a cock sucking."

Her pink tongue rasped over the head of his erection, and Lucien shuddered. *Jesus.* He couldn't stop himself from thrusting up into her mouth, his hands stroking her hair, curling in the thick, silky mass of it, and bringing her lower.

Ianthe hummed in her throat as she swallowed him deep, and the sensation streaked all the way through him. Hell. He was totally undone. Couldn't think. Could barely breathe. Just needed... Needed everything.

Teeth rasped over his sensitive cock as she paid homage to him with her wet mouth. Lucien groaned. "Devil take it, woman. Stop teasing me."

As if to torture him, her tongue curled around the very head of his cock, and then she followed it with her hot mouth. Swallowing him down and then sliding back up his length, her fist curled around the base of him and squeezing.

Hot pleasure spilled through his abdomen. "Ianthe," he breathed. "I'm going to come."

The sucking intensified. Clearly this was just what she intended. Lucien's eyes rolled back in his head, his spine bowing as he lifted half off the bed. The sheets were gone, but he didn't care anymore what she thought of his scars. How could you care—*how could you think*—when a woman was doing this to you? And suddenly it didn't matter, because *she* didn't care about the scars. He felt unveiled for the first time in years, completely given over to her. And then pleasure roared in a hot rush through his veins as he came.

Everything became blinding heat and pressure. The world narrowed down to the feel of her devilish mouth working him as though she wanted to drink him down. Every. Last. Drop.

Lucien collapsed back on the bed, panting and sated. "Bloody hell," he breathed. "You can see my scars anytime you like."

Soft laughter chased him. A warm, lush weight came into his arms, and then she rested her head on his shoulder, her hair tickling his face, but not annoying him. No, it was a sweet feeling indeed. Fully sated, sleepy again, with his arms full of warm woman, he felt like he could spend days here. Just like this. Not a worry in the world.

"You have nothing to be ashamed about..."

His good mood evaporated. "I hate them," he admitted roughly. "I feel nothing but pain when I think about them."

A pair of bright blue eyes came into view as Ianthe propped her chin on his chest and examined him. "And when you use sorcery? Do you feel nothing but pain then too?"

An explosive breath left his chest. There was nowhere to hide, however. "Ianthe."

"You don't use your sorcery. I'm only trying to get to the bottom of why."

"It's nothing," he growled, sitting up. Ianthe tumbled onto the pillows beside him as he threw his legs over the edge of the bed, intent on getting out. This discussion was over.

He was halfway to the edge of the bed when a hand locked around his wrist.

"Can I tell you something?" Ianthe whispered.

Lucien paused and looked down at her fingers. "Of course."

She opened her mouth, then suddenly pressed her hands to her eyes and groaned. "This is almost embarrassing."

"I'm fairly certain we've shared enough of our pasts to be beyond such things."

"No, but... I *am* embarrassed. I remember everything, and yet I'm fairly certain you have no idea."

"Now you're intriguing me," he admitted, turning and lying down beside her. "You have to tell me now. I've spilled my secrets."

"Some of them."

He gave her a steady look. "Are you the pot or the kettle?"

Ianthe let out a huff of air. "That's fair." Her gaze sharpened. "I think we both have enough secrets, do we not?"

And it was only now that they had begun to trust each other that such secrets were being revealed. Lucien stroked his fingers lightly down over her shoulder and the curve of her hip. "True, but it seems to me that you owe me one if I'm doing my math correctly."

She covered her face with her hands. "Do you remember when I told you that I'd had two lovers before you?"

"Ye-es." He maneuvered like a man traversing a field strewn with mines. "I'm the third."

"Technically, that's not entirely correct." Ianthe took a peek at him from between her fingers.

"I—" His mouth shut. "No. I actually have no idea how to answer that."

"You're going to make me say it, aren't you?"

"Absolutely," he told her, resting his head on the same pillow she shared. "I'm not walking into that heavily baited statement unarmed, especially considering that you could tie me in knots right now, and there's not a damned thing I could do to stop you."

"Oh, ha," she said drolly, then her amusement faded. "You were the first man that I lay with," Ianthe whispered. "Almost ten years ago now."

For a second, he thought he'd heard her wrong.

"*What?* I'm fairly certain that we've never..." *Are you?* asked a rather pertinent part of his brain, and a half dozen faces sprang to mind, none of them hers...

Ianthe cleared her throat. "I was seventeen. I don't know how old you were. It was the Summer Solstice of 1884, and the Rites were being held at Lady Haringay's Brighton home..."

Instantly, Lucien was assailed by memories; a sultry summer breeze, a garden party with pretty lights strung all through the trees, and *her*. Gowned in gossamer white with a filigreed gold mask and an aura of nervousness. He'd been drawn to her like a magnet. They'd danced, smiled, kissed... all with barely a word between them. Until Lucien had taken her by the hand and led her from the grove, just as the solstice rites began.

"*You* were my mystery lady?"

"I'm glad those are the precise terms you used."

A smile caught him by surprise. "I drank rather a lot that night. I didn't realize your hair was so dark." His gaze lowered. "And forgive me for being indelicate, but I'm fairly certain you didn't have those back then..."

Ianthe tucked the sheet closer around her breasts primly. "I wasn't finished growing. I was only seventeen."

"Hmm." Lucien tugged at the sheet. "I might have to refresh my memory."

"Lucien!"

The word was muffled by the sheets, which he'd burrowed his face into. Ianthe shoved him aside, and he went, with a laugh, which quickly turned into a frown.

"Is that why you barely gave me the time of day when I was formally introduced to you?"

"It was a shock to see you again," she admitted, "and it was quite clear that whilst I knew who you were, you had no recollection... of what lay between us."

Kneeling over her, he looked down. "All this time, I've wondered what the bloody hell I ever did to you. You hated me."

"It wasn't hate." She scowled back at him, then swallowed. "You've always been woven into my life, Lucien," she whispered. "It feels like I can never escape you, like we were... destined to find each other again."

"You sound as though that's a bad thing." His heart skipped a beat. "Is it?"

"No." Her eyes were pools of shadow as all of the humor vanished from this moment, leaving behind those sad watercolors that danced over her skin.

Secrets. They lay between them, and he knew it.

He finally understood that yellow-green emotion that flashed over her face sometimes, for he could feel it within him now as their bond strengthened. There had always been sadness and pain and fear... But he had never understood the other emotion, the one he couldn't quite place. Until now.

Guilt.

It had been there on her face when he first tried to scry for the Blade in Drake's home; it was there every time she said the Prime's name, and now, when she told him they'd been lovers before...

The thought struck him like a cascade, unleashing others—her unnatural patience regarding the relic, as if she

259

was waiting for something, her nightmares, her lack of action regarding this hunt...

Only someone whom Drake trusted could have stolen the Relic. Someone who knew Drake's wards, such as... an apprentice.

Someone whom no one would ever suspect.

Shock lanced through him. No. No, it couldn't be.

But it all made sense.

That was when he knew who the thief was.

CHAPTER SEVENTEEN

CLEO THREW her breadcrumbs to the ducks. She was alone, and for the first time in years, she wasn't content with the situation.

Sebastian hadn't returned. He hadn't contacted her. She was beginning to think his threat to stay away from her until the wedding, scheduled for later this afternoon, was a real one. There was also no indication that the Prime had received her letter. She didn't know what else to do. She couldn't just sit here and play damsel-in-distress for the rest of her life.

"Do you know," she told her ducks, "I am beginning to grow very tired of people who think they know what is best for me."

The ducks did what ducks do best, and clamored for more crumbs. There were no allies here. Cleo gave them what they wanted, the greedy beasts, then turned toward the folly.

She couldn't help but feel haunted by what happened there, though she stubbornly refused to touch her lips. It hadn't even been much of a kiss, after all, for she'd given it a lot of thought since it had happened, and had come to the conclusion that his kisses were all well and good, but a little more enthusiasm would have been appreciated. The next time he kissed her, Sebastian had better give it a damn good shot, or else she was not going to marry him.

Cleo sighed. That was a farce. She was going to marry him, no matter what. Firstly, she wanted out from under her father's overprotective wing, and secondly, she had to do something to help Sebastian remove this collar and escape his mother. Murdering his mother was not going to help Sebastian's troubled mind.

Cleo took one step up into the folly, then froze at the rustle of fabric. She wasn't alone. He'd come back. Hope soared through her chest, and just as she was about to call out his name, she caught a hint of perfume.

It was a woman, one who liked spicier scents, which led her to think the woman was older. Most debutantes wore floral perfumes, something that hinted at innocence.

"Hello? I know there's someone there."

Silk shifted. It had a particularly sleek rustle, which meant her visitor was most likely upper class, possibly nobility or a rich merchant's wife. "Apologies," the voice was smoky and richly toned. "I did not mean to startle you."

Well, that was twice in as many days.

Cleo couldn't sense any harm coming her way. Indeed, the day had been rather prediction-free, but she certainly wasn't going to take risks.

"I am here on official Order business," the woman said. "I was sent by the Prime, with orders that you are to keep quiet, even from your father." And for the first time the other woman faltered. "I-I have an official document requesting your help, but I wasn't aware that you wouldn't be able to see it."

A directive from the Prime. Cleo's pulse leapt. "Can you give it to me?"

The letter was pressed into her hand. The woman tried to help direct her toward the seat, and Cleo let her, just to add to the impression that she was helpless. People underestimated blind girls, and she was quite content to allow that.

Psychometry was not a particular talent of hers, but she had learned how to do it somewhat crudely. The document had been written by a man. She sensed that he was full of thoughts when he wrote it and that a great deal of trouble rode on his shoulders, but nothing else.

Could she trust this woman, this directive? Cleo opened herself up to the inner world and received a brief flash of Vision; a golden spark rising to defeat a roiling cloud of darkness, only this time, it was joined by another.

Well, that settled it.

"Who are you?" Cleo asked. "Be aware that I will be able to sense the truth in your words."

The woman hesitated.

"I don't have to help you," Cleo reminded her. "Indeed, perhaps I need assurances that I can trust *you*."

"My name is Eleanor Ross, and if your father knew I was here, he would have me killed. He denied my earlier request of visiting you. I had to sneak over the wall."

That troubled her, for Cleo had thought her father a great many things, but not a murderer. Yet the woman was speaking the truth—as she believed it. "I won't tell him. You mentioned the Prime. What does he want?"

"He received a warning that there was a young sorcerer collared and bound to another's will. His name is Sebastian Montcalm."

"What are his intentions toward the young man?"

"He wants to help him," Eleanor replied. "No sorcerer should have his will enslaved."

Cleo tilted her head, as if listening. "That's not the entire truth. Though it is part of it, I think."

"I have a small talent for psychometry. I used it to divine where the letter had come from and received some disturbing suggestions of a plot against the Prime."

"I see. May I ask you something?"

"Yes?"

"Why would you think that my father would kill you if he knew you were here? I had not thought him a violent man. A bitter man, yes, but not murderous."

"Your father..." Eleanor chose her words carefully, "has been responsible for at least one death. That's why he was exiled here, never to leave the grounds of his manor. It is thought that he is responsible for several others, however, there has never been enough proof to persecute him."

"He used sorcery to kill?" It shocked her.

"Yes."

"Then why was he not executed? That is a capital crime among our Order."

"He gave crucial information against an uprising against the Prime, on the grounds that he would be spared. In return, his sorcery was bound by the Order, until he is severely limited in what he can do. He can practice certain feats, but only those which an adept of the Second Tier can practice."

That would not sit well with him.

Cleo pressed her lips together. She was not a traitor, and though she didn't love her father, she wanted to. Or perhaps she wanted him to love her. But she had a duty to do what was right, and if her father was playing with another plane of existence and she knew about it, then she would be somewhat responsible for the deaths to come. "My father is going to summon a demon, I think. I overheard him perfecting his Words of Power. A demon would be able to remove his limitations, would it not?"

"It would do a great deal more than that. Could you see if your father *will* do this ritual? Could you see if—"

"He wears a warded crystal around his neck, which prevents me from seeing his future." Something that had always made her wonder. What did her father have to hide? "But I know that he's formed an alliance with a woman named Morgana. She—"

"*Morgana?*"

Cleo paused. "Yes. Do you know her?"

"Unfortunately, I've had the pleasure." Eleanor's voice was clipped. "I need to tell Drake what I've learned. This gives us even less time to prepare. Thank you. I will come again."

Cleo hesitated. "I wrote the letter."

"I know."

"If the Prime holds true, then I will work with him. I will help him stop my father, but there are several conditions I must place. He must help Sebastian free of his collar and his mother. No matter what happens or what he does under her influence, Sebastian is not to be harmed and neither am I."

"And your father?"

It hurt to say this: "If my father summons a Greater Demon, then he breaks the law. He becomes... dangerous and unpredictable, for if he does it once, then what would he not stoop to the next time? If he summons a demon, then it is upon the Prime to do what must be done, as according to our laws. I would... I would mourn my father, but he makes his choices, therefore he earns their consequences."

"You are a brave young woman."

"I don't know if I'm doing the right thing." Cleo bowed her head. "I hope that I am doing the right thing."

"If it feels like a hard choice," Eleanor replied, "then you probably are. Let that guide you, no matter what happens in the future. I'll return, when I have more information. Is this the safest place to see you?"

"It's the only time I'm not watched, however I'm supposed to be getting married this afternoon. There's been no mention of where I am to live."

"May I take a hair?"

Cleo nodded, and something sharp plucked at her head.

"With this I'll find you. If I'm not back within two days, then be very, very careful of what you do next. I wouldn't mention this visit to those who guard you; they are your father's employees, not yours."

"Oh, I worked that out when I was nine."

Eleanor hurried through the trees that surrounded the walled garden at the back of Tremayne's estate. Demons. Good God, it was true. She needed to warn Drake.

"Hello there, Eleanor," a male voice called.

Eleanor froze briefly before turning around. Dark figures slipped out from behind trees, all of them hooded. One, two, three, four... A branch crackled beneath a booted heel behind her, and she spun, finding another man, a taller man whose face she knew.

"Tremayne." She swallowed the hard lump in her throat. "You look well."

Lord Tremayne slipped off his gloves, one finger at a time. He'd aged since the last time she'd seen him, but those dark eyes were just as hard, and the smile on his fleshy lips was still unattractive. "Did you truly think that I would not have the estate warded? Granted, I cannot produce a ward these days strong enough to protect it or keep my enemies out, but I can certainly conjure one that tells me when little birds are slipping about, trying to go unnoticed."

Her gaze flickered to the men stalking nearer, then back to him. "You never used to own so much finesse."

"Yes, well. I have strong friends these days. They've been teaching me how to master myself."

"So I hear. I wouldn't have thought to call them 'friends,' however... After all, didn't the former duchess steal the Relics Infernal out from beneath your nose years ago when you thought yourself allies?" Eleanor began to slowly siphon little bits of energy, drawing in her will. Her heart pounded faster. *Foolish to have come here alone...*

Tremayne grunted. "Let us just say, the enemy of my enemy is my friend."

"And you want what Drake has, more than you want vengeance against Morgana."

"I want what that bastard *stole* from me."

"And then...?" She had to keep stalling him until she had enough power.

"Then?"

"Oh, please. Let us not pretend that you have any altruistic or forgiving qualities, Tremayne. Does the former duchess know that she must watch her back once you've defeated Drake?"

His gaze flickered to the left, which was unusual. "Nonsense. My alliance with Morgana will never be at risk."

Nobody was fooling anybody here. Eleanor raised a hand, flaming balls of energy erupting to life within her palms at a single word and searing her eyes as her mage globes formed. "Well, let us not waste time. I've learned a few things too, Tremayne."

Hurling one of them, she cast wards into place with her other, and—

An enormous wave of energy sent her tumbling, head over heels, her forehead smashing into a tree. Her sorcery flickered out, and for a moment, the world was black. Then she blinked through it, seeing a pair of men step toward her... No, it was only one, but her vision... What had just happened? Surely Tremayne wasn't strong enough to evaporate her wards like that and fling a solid burst of power at her?

"Very good, Sebastian." Tremayne sounded like a proud tutor.

Sebastian? Her skin grew cold. This was the collared one, the man who Cleo had asked her to save, a man who had just used Expression.

The man in front of her slipped his dark hood back from his face, and Eleanor's jaw dropped.

"*Drake*?" She was seeing things. He looked too young, though the dark hair was the same, and his eyes too, and... No, no, his skin was darker than Drake's, and there was a faint cleft in his chin. The resemblance was uncanny, it was...

And then she knew.

All those years of grieving, the pain she saw in Drake's eyes every June when the anniversary of his son's death grew near... The blood drained out of her face. That lying bitch.

"Afraid not, Eleanor." Tremayne stepped forward and dug a boot between her ribs.

She cried out, tumbling into the leaves. Movement swung out of the corner of her vision, and she wrenched her arms up to protect her face, but the next blow didn't land. Instead Tremayne gave a muffled '*umph.*'

Eleanor looked up.

"She's down," the cold, hard voice sounded nothing like Drake. The stranger who wore his youthful face had a hand pressed flat against Tremayne's chest. "You don't need to kick her."

"Oh, boy, you know nothing." That dark smile turned toward her, and the gloating look in Tremayne's face turned her stomach. "She's already dead. But first... we need to find out exactly what she thinks she's doing here and how much the Prime knows."

CHAPTER EIGHTEEN

'Trust is an ambiguous matter.'

– Old proverb

"TELL ME about the servants again." Lucien sank into the banked seat at the restaurant. He still didn't quite know what to make of his revelation that he was possibly sharing a table with the thief, only that he needed to know more.

Or more particularly, why.

Logic said he ought to betray her to the Prime. The relic was far too dangerous to have in the wrong hands, but the other part of him, the part that knew the sensation of love whenever Ianthe spoke of the Prime, told him to wait. This game wasn't played out yet. None of this made any sense, least of all why Ianthe would betray a man she adored. He'd merely uncovered a trick hand.

Besides, he had no sense of loyalty to the Prime. If he owed anyone his loyalty, it *might* possibly be her. With a scowl, Lucien broke off one of the small lilac flowers that sat on the vase on their table, toying with the wooden stem. The color reminded him of her eyes, but the petals were far too delicate and easy to crush. That was not Ianthe. Or at least, he prayed it was not.

"The servants?" Ianthe paused with a forkful of roast squab by her mouth. So far, she'd been eating mechanically, her mind a million miles away. "What servants?"

"The Prime's servants," he replied, reaching across the table to cup her hand beneath his as her gaze drifted to the window again. "I know you can't name any of them who might be our thief, but we're making no progress here." A full morning of fruitless searching stretched behind them, in which they'd traversed half the hotels in this part of the city. Morgana might have been staying at the Windsor at one stage, but she was long gone now.

"I don't think it's the servants. What about what Horroway said about Tremayne?"

"Certainly something to look into, but I want to establish a link between he and the Prime's house. So far all we've done is chase our tail. We know Morgana is in London and she's possibly working with Tremayne, but there's no evidence that either of them stole the relic. We need to start at the beginning, rather than look at a list of people who might, or might not, be suspects, and we need to move faster than we have been." He decided to push her a little. "One would think we were taking a scenic tour of London from the pace we've held in the last couple of days, rather than verging on the edge of certain disaster."

"I see." Ianthe's color had faded, but she sipped at her tea, thoughts racing behind her eyes as she took her hand back from him. A flare of icy gray tinged her expression: nervousness.

Come on. Tell me the truth. Tell me where you've hidden it. Or what you plan to do with it.

"Among the servants, who might have wished Drake ill or been persuaded it would be in their best interests to steal the relic?"

"None who had the opportunity or the means," she replied. "Lucien, Drake and I have been over this."

"Humor me."

Ianthe put her teacup down. "I just... I cannot think of any one of them who might have done it."

"Drake can't be so widely loved that one of them wouldn't have stabbed him in the back. After all, someone did. Just because you care for him, it doesn't mean they all do. We should draw them all in and interrogate them."

"He's a good master," she retorted. "A good *man*. They might not have meant to do it—"

"That's a rather generous assessment. There's a half dozen reasons that a loyal servant could betray his master: greed, fear... blackmail." The second he said it, his heart skipped a beat. He'd been looking at this wrong, trying to test her allegiances, but it was clear that her loyalty toward the Prime was not in any doubt.

No, but loyalty, whilst a strength, could also be a weakness.

Bloody hell. Lucien sat frozen as every instinct in his mind detonated with certainty. Ianthe's loyalty had never been in any doubt. Even now she argued as assiduously for the man as she ever had, but what if someone was holding something over her head?

"Well, we cannot interrogate them," Ianthe stammered. "Drake doesn't want the rest of the Order to know. With the comet in the sky, if the Order even suspects he has a weakness..."

Oh yes, he'd been looking at this wrong. "Very well. We'll keep looking for the person who would most desire the relic." Because that was who was blackmailing her, he was certain.

Morgana. And Tremayne.

"Why don't we separate for the afternoon?" she suggested. "You can continue covering the hotels, while I go see an old friend of mine. He used to know Tremayne. I should stress that neither of us should engage, should we discover where they're hiding."

He didn't like to think of her out there on her own. "I don't—"

"I can handle myself, Lucien."

Ianthe never liked to be considered vulnerable, but then perhaps she did not realize that it wasn't her vulnerability that concerned him, so much as the thought of her being harmed. Right now, she was far stronger than he, but still mortal. *If something happened to her*... His fingers curled into a ball at the thought, but the piece of lilac bit into his palm. He eased his fingers, so as not to destroy it. His fingers were too big, but he tried to soothe out one crushed petal.

Well, wasn't that a bloody revelation. Lucien sank back into his seat, fingering the flower. He wasn't about to enlighten her with it. "Where shall we meet?"

"At home? For dinner at six?"

Her home. Not his. But it was starting to feel like a place that had meaning to him.

"I shall see you there," Lucien said, then stood and tucked the bloody flower in his pocket before taking himself off to go hunt for mad sorcerers. "Be careful."

"I always am."

The idea didn't occur to Lucien until he was striding past Covent Garden. He'd promised to meet up with Ianthe again in an hour, but as he turned down a familiar street, he caught a glimpse of the Phoenix Theatre in the distance, and his footsteps stalled.

Within two minutes, he was pushing his way into the auditorium. The room was silent, the stage barren. Lucien stalked halfway down the aisle, then paused, a prickling sensation tickling over the back of his neck.

He turned sharply.

Remington Cross watched him from the entrance with those dark, enigmatic eyes, his hands in his pockets. He was stripped to his waistcoat and his shirt collar lay undone, as if the man had been at repose. Lucien hadn't felt a single ward set about the place, but his presence had obviously been detected.

"Fancy seeing you here." Cross's eyes narrowed suspiciously.

"A warm welcome." Lucien's lips thinned. "I'd stay to play, but I've got heavy matters weighing upon my mind. I don't have time to fence with you."

Cross's expression flattened, and for a second, it felt like he faced a tiger, lashing its tail as it considered whether to pounce, or whether to hear him out. "Ianthe?"

"At the heart of my concern. I need to ask you some questions, and I don't think I can tell you why."

"Come," the man told him, and strode toward his chambers backstage. Once there, Cross poured them both a whiskey, then nursed his own. "Is she safe?"

"I'm not certain. She's currently visiting a friend, searching for news of Morgana de Wynter and the Earl of Tremayne."

"Morgana? She's back in England?" That arched a brow. "And you left Ianthe there alone?"

"I don't think we're going to find Morgana. And... I don't think Morgana is a danger to her." Not yet, anyway. If

Ianthe had delivered the relic, then Morgana might have disposed of her. That she was still alive and hunting her blackmailer meant that the deed hadn't been done yet.

He hoped.

"What is going on? I don't like the sound of any of this. Morgana's involvement in anything is bad news."

"I don't know if I trust you," Lucien replied bluntly.

"Well, that's the first sensible thing you've ever said, but then you wouldn't be here if you had anywhere else to go, would you?"

They shared a look.

"I'm not a fool," Cross murmured. "Something's stirring in the Order, and there are potent signs that something big is about to happen in London. Now you bring up the name Morgana. That doesn't ease my mind one whit. Ianthe is dear to me. I should not care to see her in over her head."

"That's the reason I'm here, actually," Lucien replied. "I don't trust the Prime, not entirely, and I have a horrible suspicion about something. If I'm right, then so are you. Miss Martin is well and truly in over her head."

"Tell me."

"Answer this question for me first: Who is Louisa?"

If anything, Cross actually paled, despite his olive skin. "Tell me." He put the whiskey glass down with a flat, ringing sound.

"*Who* is Louisa?" Lucien repeated in a softer, firmer tone. There was a feeling of inevitability hanging around him, a faint ringing in his ears. Ianthe's revelation that morning about their past dalliance had rocked him, but in the wake of realizing she was his thief, he hadn't followed that thought through to its natural conclusion.

And now it was starting to make itself known. A cold sweat sprang down his spine.

"You know her history. Tell me, did you never wonder why her father threw her out?"

Lucien scraped a shaking hand over his face. "Her sorcery, I presumed." He'd *hoped*.

Cross examined a penny, flicking it over and under his fingers until it seemed like it vanished between each flick of his hand. "Ianthe's first act of Expression came when she was twelve. Her father suffered her to live under his roof for another five hellish years."

Which meant that something had happened to force Grant Martin's hand. Something beyond Expression. Louisa was the key to it, he felt.

And why did most fathers cast their daughters out at that age? What secret shame drove such an act?

"She has a daughter," Lucien blurted, and the instant the words formed, they felt like truth. The faint silvery lines about her hips and breasts had drawn his attention, but he'd barely seen her in enough light to notice if she wore stronger marks of childbirth or not. A lot of women bore faint marks gained when their weight fluctuated, or when their courses first arrived and their bodies changed. Not all of them were mothers.

Whore. That made him flinch. Ianthe had heard that word before. Her insistence on using a sheath, her lack of experience in the bedchamber... Perhaps a pregnancy had made her wary of such consequences.

"I've never heard her speak of a daughter." The careful way Cross said it wasn't a no.

"You suspect it though?"

Cross vanished the penny with a snap of his fist. "She buys dolls sometimes, and books. She likes children's books, especially fairy tales and frivolous stories featuring princesses, castles, and knights in shining armor. That kind of drivel. Once a month, she used to take two days off to visit someone, somewhere outside of London's outskirts. I've never asked about it."

That blasted bear beside her bed. That was why she kept it.

A daughter. A daughter conceived when she was seventeen. All of the pieces of the puzzle were slowly fitting together. *You were the first man that I lay with...*

No. No, this couldn't be happening. Lucien's nerves felt raw, and he pressed his face to his palms, breathing through his fingers. Jesus Christ. Did he have a child that he'd never known about?

If so, then where was she? What had happened? Had someone—Morgana—threatened to tell the world about the child? Or had she taken her?

"Are you all right?" Cross asked.

No. No, I'm not. After all, five and twelve equaled seventeen, which was when she'd admitted that she'd lain with him. Lucien gave a swift nod, however. There were limits to what he would share, and he needed to find Ianthe to hear it confirmed from her own mouth before he would let himself believe this.

"Well, I've shared mine," Cross reminded him.

Time to share his. Lucien barely managed to pull himself back together. "You know that we were searching for something that was stolen from the Prime's manor?"

A nod.

"I think I know who the thief is. What I didn't know was why." Their eyes met. "I think you just answered the 'why' for me. None of it made any sense, but if someone had taken her daughter—"

The color drained out of Cross's face. "You need to speak to the Prime about your concerns."

Like hell. "And betray her?"

"If this is true, boy, then she's in more danger than either of us would like to consider."

"I'll consider it." A strange ringing sensation echoed in his ears, a certain dizziness, as if the floor had been swept out from under him by this realization. He'd thought himself alone in the world. What if he was not?

And *why* hadn't she told him?

That one, at least, was easy to answer: *You did promise her vengeance after all...*

"At least think about it. Let me know how matters advance. Ianthe is dear to me. I should not care to see her hurt, so if you need help..."

"I'll let you know. I just need to confirm my suspicions." And work out if there truly was a little girl out there somewhere who bore his blood.

The door opened.

Eleanor barely had the strength to roll onto her side. Her hair tugged, so matted with dried blood that it had adhered to the pillow. She winced.

"If you want... another turn at me," she whispered, her lips cracked and her tongue clinging to the roof of her dry mouth, "then I'm afraid... I might not be able to oblige."

She didn't think she owned the fortitude to survive another questioning. The last time, she'd blacked out before she gave in, so focused on protecting the man she loved, that she'd bitten clean through her lip.

Light burned her sensitive eyes as someone set a lantern down in front of her. Eleanor moaned and tilted her face into the faded pillow to protect them.

"Water?" a male voice asked.

Water. Eleanor's eyes sprung open and she reached out, her entire body trembling. The stranger had to help hold her upright as he set the glass to her lips. Her arms were still red and bloody from the barbwire lash of sorcery that they'd inflicted upon her.

Then she realized who was kneeling in front of her. "Sebastian." Eleanor's gaze darted to the locked door, then back. Surely Morgana wouldn't have dared let her son in to see Eleanor?

"How did you know who I was?" Sebastian asked. "You recognized me."

Did he not know? Eleanor searched his eyes, but there was nothing but deadness there. "You are your father's mirror."

That made him stir. Sebastian poured her another glass of water, as if his actions could hide the flash of curiosity and uncertainty she saw in his eyes. "And you are his lover?"

Eleanor managed a weak smile that split her lip again. "Yes." It was the easiest answer. How did one explain that one man could be the other half of you? "You do not know how pleased he would be to know of you. He thought... we all thought you were dead."

Sebastian handed her the glass. "Why would he think me dead?"

"Your mother left a note for him, claiming that she'd used poison to remove you from her body. There was no reason not to believe her, as there were remains, as well."

"And why would he be pleased to know otherwise?"

"W-what do you mean? Drake's your father. You do not know how much he grieved for what he thought your mother had done. He's always born the guilt of it—that if he hadn't pushed through the divorce, Morgana might have stayed her hand."

Sebastian considered her for a long moment. "They're very pretty words. Were you practicing them?"

Eleanor sat up and regretted it. Her ribs were still tender. "I know why you feel such a thing. After all, I knew your mother; we did our apprenticeships together. Not everyone sees the world the way Morgana does—as if people are an enemy to be suppressed before they can cause her harm. I know she was most likely not a kindly woman. Your father, however... all he has ever wanted is to be a father, and yet he's never had the chance. You would be a gift to him."

There was nothing in his face to indicate her words had struck a nerve. It bothered her.

"You have two half-brothers, did you know that?" A bold move, but Eleanor wanted him to feel something; she needed to see if there was any part of his father inside him, or if he was merely his mother's puppet.

Sebastian's chin lifted in surprise, but that emotion was short-lived. "Do I?"

"Though you are the only one who was born within the grounds of marriage."

"Bastards then. Who?"

"The youngest is Adrian Bishop, a talented sorcerer, and the eldest is Lucien Devereaux, Lord Rathbourne—"

"Rathbourne? If you seek to turn me to my father's arms, then you've made a grave mistake. I know he put that bastard into Bedlam. You think my father sounds any better than my mother?"

"Rathbourne summoned a demon," Eleanor said. "He's lucky he wasn't executed. Bedlam was the only alternative the Order's Council would accept." Setting the water down, she rested her arms on her knees. "And now he's out. Rathbourne's trying to help your father find the Blade of Altarrh."

Sebastian glanced sideways. Reaching out, Eleanor extended her fingers toward the collar that gleamed at his throat. Before she could reach it, hard fingers locked around her wrist.

"Don't," Sebastian said.

"Do you want to know why I was visiting Tremayne's estate?" she asked.

"You'd tell *me*, when you deny that information to my mother or Tremayne, even when they're flogging you?"

"I think I can trust you. I don't think you'll want your mother to know the answer to that question any more than I do."

"And I think you like to gamble, Mrs. Ross."

Eleanor smiled. "I'm very good at it. I'm also very good at understanding who a person is."

"Then you know me better than my own mother does." It was said with a faint sneer. "Or think you do."

"Possibly." She pulled at his grip, and he let her go. "Your father received a poorly written letter from a young woman asking for his help. She'd recently met a young male sorcerer who was collared. She offered to help the Prime with a certain conspiracy, if Drake pledged to locate and emancipate this young man. There was no way that Drake could get to her on Tremayne's estate, so I came instead."

There was his emotion, quickly suppressed in a flash of dark eyes. Sebastian stood, turning away from her and lacing his hands behind his back. All those years apart, and yet he echoed his father's posture, a sign of severe emotional turmoil. It gave her some sign of hope that there was more of his father in him than his mother.

Eleanor's voice fell to a whisper. "I think you know who that young lady is."

"Tremayne will kill her if he knows she betrayed him." His nostrils flared as he turned back to her. "And she doesn't even know what manner of man she lives with! Bloody hell, what was she thinking?"

"I presume Miss Sinclair was thinking about you and how your situation was more dire than hers."

For the first time, Sebastian looked startled, and younger than he seemed. That alone told her more than anything he'd said.

Nobody had ever cared more for him than for their own selves.

Eleanor's heart ached. This wouldn't be easy for either father or son. This son was scarred so deeply she could only see the surface of it, and he would not give his trust lightly. If only she could do something to help them, but right now, her predicament was worse than either. She was helpless. All Eleanor had was this one conversation to make a difference. "I won't say anything to your mother or to Tremayne, however I cannot say that they won't figure it out."

"I'm to marry Miss Sinclair within the hour. Tremayne wished for her to remain at his estate, but perhaps... I could make my mother see that it would suit her more to have Miss Sinclair here, beneath her nose. Morgana might push the matter."

"If you could do so, then perhaps Miss Sinclair might not be at risk."

"My mother is involved; there is still a chance she might be harmed, but at least here, I can keep an eye on her."

"Can you stop your mother from hurting her?" Eleanor didn't like the idea of giving that woman any chance at the innocent young girl.

"No, I cannot." Sebastian's lips twisted wryly. "And I do not dare. The only chance I have of protecting Miss Sinclair is to ensure that my mother believes she means nothing to me. I am very good at being cruel." He hesitated though, as if the very idea of it seemed to destroy some hope he'd owned. "My mother plans to kill you. She means it."

Eleanor drew back with a gasp.

"If you will not tell them what they want, then she sees no reason to keep her rival alive."

"Rival?"

"You have what she's always wanted."

Eleanor looked down. "Your father's heart."

"His respect, his trust... She cannot even understand how you could have done it."

"The problem is, Morgana always thought that respect and love can be manipulated or bought. She does not realize that love itself means that one cares just as much for the object of your heart as one does for oneself. If not more so."

Sebastian stayed silent for a long moment. "Perhaps you understand her better than I thought. I cannot get you out. I cannot help you."

Eleanor nodded, though the shock of it was twisting through her veins and wreaking havoc on her heart. It was not unexpected, but she couldn't stop thinking of Drake. Of how she'd never see him again... That was the true regret, right there. He'd be devastated, blaming himself for letting her go on this mission in the first place. Tears pricked at Eleanor's eyes, but as Sebastian turned to leave, she knew there was one last gift she could give to the man she loved. "Sebastian?"

"Yes?"

"I know there's no hope for me, but if something ever happens to you, and you have no other chance of escape, then go to your father. I know Drake would risk his own life to rescue you, no matter what the odds against him were."

"He's got you wrapped around his little finger, doesn't he?" That smile was bitter. "Why would I do that? After all, raising a demon would be the least of *my* sins. There is no saving me, Mrs. Ross. I've known that for a very long time. The only thing I can do is hope to take that bitch with me when my ship starts to sink."

And then Sebastian was gone, with a faintly respectful nod in her direction.

CHAPTER NINETEEN

ANOTHER FRUITLESS day of searching. Ianthe was so frustrated that she wanted to scream. No luck, no matter where she turned. Now that she knew whom she faced, if she could find Morgana...

Then what?

Kill her, whispered a deep, dark instinct. *Get my daughter back.*

But finding her wasn't as easy as it seemed. Nobody on the dark side of sorcerous society knew anything about Morgana's whereabouts, and Ianthe had spent countless hours casting small location spells. It wasn't her forte, but at least she had Louisa's hair to use as a focus, much good it had done her.

Cursing under her breath, she turned to pace, and that was when she saw the letter propped on her pillow.

Her breath felt like it had been punched out of her. *No.*

It was the same piece of parchment as those that had previously been delivered, and she knew what this one would say. It was finally time to deliver the Blade. Finally time to get her daughter back.

If she could trust the kidnappers.

Night was falling and Lucien had vowed to be along in a minute, after he'd refreshed himself. She'd barely have a moment to herself to read it. She had to act quickly.

Snatching it up, Ianthe tore the seam with her fingernail, then hesitated. She felt ill. "Please," she whispered to herself. "Please let my daughter be safe." And then she steeled her nerves and opened it.

Tonight at 12pm. Highgate Cemetery. Look for Roslyn Hayes's grave. Come alone and bring the Blade. I need not emphasize the importance of the alone directive. If you betray us, the girl dies.

By the time she lowered the letter, a hot tear was sliding down her cheek. Emotion welled, threatening to consume her, but Ianthe crumpled the letter in her fist and threw it in the fire. She needed to act, to keep moving, or else she feared she'd fall apart.

Damn it. How was she going to get rid of Lucien? How was she going to get Louisa back without giving over the Blade? What would happen if Morgana did get her hands on it?

For she knew, deep in her heart that there were some risks she would not take. Louisa was the most precious thing in the world to her. There was not even a question about what she'd do if her choice came down to her daughter or the relic.

Think, damn it.

If only she had more time. If only she had an ally, one she could trust. Three days wasn't enough to know Lucien's intent. Sometimes when he looked at her, she saw something soften in his eyes, but could she trust that? Or did she simply *want* to trust it? He was the one who'd professed his intended revenge upon her only yesterday. It might have been a jest to him, but could she be certain?

I don't know. I'm so tired, and I can't think...

He would be here at any moment. That spurred her into action. Ianthe uncapped the brandy decanter in the corner, knowing Lucien's fondness for the spirit. It was only a matter of a moment to pour them both a glass and then take a small vial from the case under her bed. A few drops added to Lucien's drink would bring sweet oblivion to its drinker. The second she did it, she hesitated, staring at the amber liquid. Good God, what was she doing?

As if she'd summoned the devil by thinking of him, a sharp rap sounded at her door.

Her heart a lead weight in her chest, Ianthe shoved the brandy back in its place. "Come in."

The door opened, and there he was.

Tall, handsome, devastatingly dangerous... Hard edges rode Lucien's expression as though he was distracted, but when he saw her, heat flared in his eyes. He turned his body toward hers, as though drawn to her. Ianthe's heart started to race. Everything within her wanted to stride into his arms and drown herself in the nearness of him, to throw herself upon his mercy.

Please, please, can you help me?

Lucien frowned, almost as if he'd heard her. "No luck today?"

"N-none." Could she trust him? He'd told her of his scars that morning, opening himself up to her and revealing something that haunted him. But they both admitted there were secrets between them.

Lucien studied her. "We need to talk."

A hard lump formed in her throat. "I agree."

Tugging his collar open with a sigh, he made short work of his cravat. For the first time, Ianthe had the sensation he was hesitating, which was a rather unsettling feeling. Rathbourne had always been emphatically confident in his manner. It was only recently that she'd seen any hints of vulnerability. Even when facing down a barrage of imps with nothing more than his own physicality, he'd not flinched.

Her. He was nervous about her. Or more particularly, the forthcoming conversation.

That made two of them.

"We have been dancing around each other for days," Lucien said, discarding the cravat. "Yet I have felt as though we were growing closer."

"As have I." It was barely a whisper.

"I had hoped you would open yourself up to me."

"Lucien—"

He held up a hand. "I understand why you haven't. We did not commence this agreement on very good terms. Hell, I practically threatened to destroy you." With a sigh, he stepped closer. Every inch of his expression hardened with intensity. "I need to know the truth, Ianthe. I need you to trust me. I promise I won't betray that trust."

Heart in her throat, she stared at him. What was he saying?

"And perhaps, the best way to go about that is to give you my trust." Their palms met by his design. Lucien's gaze dropped as his fingers splayed against hers, holding them spread, and then he shifted, those long, elegant fingers slipping between hers.

Ianthe could not look away from him, from the beautiful golden halo of his eyes. So haunted. So hungry. Not for sex, but for intimacy. He opened to her in that moment, the bond itching beneath her skin, daring her to open up to him in response.

"You were right." Every line of his body spoke its reluctance. "My aura was savaged by either the demon or Lord Rathbourne when I attempted to break free of the bond he'd forced on me. I don't know if I can access my sorcery properly. It... hurts. It's like a knife straight to the brain, and my first instinct is to shy away from such pain."

"Oh, Lucien—" But he was not done, not yet.

"It scares the hell out of me. Will I ever wield my sorcery again? I don't know. But that's not the only thing that terrifies me. I have nothing, Ianthe. No friends, no family, not even my own house... I've never belonged to anybody. Except for you." His gaze dropped to their clenched hands. "I kept telling myself that this wasn't happening."

Us. That we weren't happening. Her heart broke a little as his loneliness scorched her.

Lucien lifted his other hand and paused with it but an inch from her mouth. Dark lashes framed his beautiful eyes as his gaze dropped to her lips. "But there's a limit to how much I can lie to myself. You scare me. Because I want you more than I've ever wanted anything in my life." He leaned closer, eyelashes growing heavier.

Ianthe's heart erupted in a flurry.

Is he going to...? Does he want to...?

But it was not his mouth that brushed against her trembling lips, but something even softer. She felt the soft, languid stroke of it all across her skin, drawing a shiver from somewhere deep within her.

Ianthe drew back. "What is—?" A flower. A lilac, somewhat bedraggled, but still soft with scent.

"I need to know," Lucien whispered hoarsely, "whether I am alone in this situation. Do you care for me? Do you want me too?"

A blatant understatement. Ianthe swayed toward him, her heart aching. "Of course I do. More than breath itself." She brushed the flower aside, looking up into his eyes. "I thought myself a fool for daring to, but—"

"Do you trust me?"

"Yes." Her hand curled in the collar of his coat. She wanted the kiss that he was promising, but he wouldn't stop talking.

"I've been patient, Ianthe. Please tell me what the devil is going—"

To hell with it.

Leaning forward, Ianthe reached up and grabbed the back of his nape, dragging his face down to hers, which was something she'd been wanting to do for days. The second she kissed him, Lucien's breath broke on a harsh exhale, and then he was clutching at her, dragging her against his chest, his arms forceful and his mouth aggressive.

It was everything she'd ever hoped for. Hungry, passionate, and fierce. It was full of longing, as though they'd each dreamed of his moment, burned for it. Breathless and aching, she let his demanding mouth sweep her away. On and on, showing each other what they felt with their bodies, their mouths. Their tongues clashed, and Lucien muscled Ianthe backward until her back met the wall. Pinned there, Ianthe looked up. As he forced her wrists against the wallpaper, dark shadows haunted his eyes. He was breathing hard.

"Why?" Lucien searched her expression.

She had broken their rules. Lost their bet.

And she didn't give a damn.

"Because I don't care about our bet," Ianthe whispered. "All I want is *you*."

And then she kissed him again.

That first kiss hadn't felt like surrender. No, it had felt like a demand, like a fervent plea. Like two halves of a soul finally coming together with an almost audible clash. His mouth was imprinted with the feel of hers, and Lucien liked it.

Had he ever thought it would be like this? To find someone who both fascinated and matched him on almost every level? It eased the ache within him. For Ianthe was more to him than kisses and sex; she was the future. His future. Here, in her, he saw more than the cold, empty halls of Rathbourne Manor. He saw laughter and an endless battle of wits. He could picture children running through the house, wearing his eyes and her smile. Warm bodies curled around each other in bed with endless rainy mornings, just listening to the patter of rain on the roof and losing themselves in kisses.

If only they could sort out this bloody mess with Morgana.

Lucien broke the kiss, breathing hard. He pressed his forehead to hers, capturing her wrists, stopping her from reaching for him again. He wanted her to. He wanted to lose himself in this sweet oblivion, but there was more at stake than this.

"I would have kissed you," he whispered. "If you had not kissed me first. God help me, I've wanted to do that for days."

"Then don't stop." Somehow, Ianthe broke his hold, her hands cupping his face. Desperation limned her features. "Kiss me, Lucien. Kiss me like you mean it."

"I do mean it." He stole her mouth again, as if he couldn't help himself. Lightly, he traced Ianthe's mouth with his lips, as though she was far, far too precious, and then he forced himself to let her go. "But we need to talk." He could hear the regret in his own voice. "I'll make this up to you. Kisses for days. Weeks. Now tell me the truth..."

"The truth?" Dazed eyes met his; then they sharpened, as if Ianthe sensed the guillotine blade about to fall. All sense of desire vanished from her face.

Time to throw the dice. This needed to be said. "I know you took the Blade."

Panic. That was panic he recognized on her face. Ianthe staggered back, clutching at the table, the shimmer-shine of tears dancing along her lower lashes.

"I'm not going to hurt you," Lucien told her, holding his hands up. *Trust me, damn you.* "I'm not going to betray you to the Prime, but I need to know exactly what is going on."

"Oh, God." Pressing her hand to her mouth, Ianthe turned away, stumbling toward the mantle and holding on for dear life with her back to him. "How did you—?"

"How did I know?"

Ianthe nodded, but she wouldn't look at him.

"I began to suspect you were involved this morning," Lucien said, reaching for the brandy to steel his nerves. The first sip was a fiery release. "You've been upset, but somehow restrained, and you weren't rushing. Oh, you made movements toward trying to 'find' this thief, but then you were quite content to pay your dues to me at night, as if there was no hurry. You were waiting for something, and ever since the demon attack, I've been able to see people's emotions as colors that mottle their skin. I recognized the fear in you and the terror, but it was only this morning that

I began to perceive the yellow-gray color as guilt. As soon as I saw it, I knew."

Say something, damn it.

Ianthe's shoulders slumped. "I need help," she whispered. "I never wanted to do this, to betray Drake, but I didn't have a choice."

Relief flooded through him. Lucien drained the brandy, then set it aside with a glassy thump. "Tell me," he prompted.

Wrapping her arms around her, she slowly turned. "It began a week ago. There was a note in my room—" Her gaze sharpened as she saw the empty glass, her pupils flaring. "Oh, no."

"Oh, no?" Heat spiraled through him, bringing with it a wave of lassitude. Lucien forced a blink. His eyelids were growing heavy.

Then there were hands capturing his wrists, holding him steady. "You drank the brandy!"

"Was I... not 'sposed to...?" Damn this buzzing in his head. Lucien staggered, and a warm weight curled into his arms, holding him up.

"No." Ianthe's face looked stricken. "I don't know! I was going to drug you, but then... Then you kissed me, and—"

Drug him? A flare of alarm went through him. Her face swam into focus. "Ianthe. What the hell did you give me?"

"A little concoction. It will make you sleep." A tear slid down her cheek. "I changed my mind... I wasn't going to..." Then she looked up, guilt written all over her face. "They want the blade. Tonight. I have to give them the blade!"

The world swam. They both staggered sideways, and Ianthe nearly fell atop him as his back hit the bed. "Jesus," he whispered. The room was spinning mightily now.

Somehow he had a fist in her skirts though. "You cannot go."

He couldn't help her if he was like this. He couldn't help her, and from the splash of emotions painted all across her face, she was going to do something rash.

"I'm so sorry." Ianthe dashed away her tears with a lace-gloved hand, as though she was trying to hold herself together. "I didn't know if I could t-trust you."

"Don't cry." Lucien's head slumped back onto the bed.

"And I should have known. I should have trusted you."

There was one last question to ask, and from the crushing weight of the heaviness seeping through him, he wouldn't have long to say it. "The girl... Lou...isa. Is she mine?"

"*What?*" Ianthe's voice sharpened, and suddenly her face swam into view, serious and pale. "What did you say?"

The room was spinning. "Is she...my...daughter?"

Ianthe's mouth dropped open. "*Yes.*" It was a whisper.

And then there was no more thought as oblivion overtook him.

CHAPTER TWENTY

IANTHE SAT upright with a gasp. She couldn't believe her ears. Lucien *knew*. He'd guessed, and he had not condemned her. Sucking in a sharp gasp, she pressed her hands to her mouth, but there were no answers from his slack form. A few drops of her sleeping potion had taken him deep into oblivion and would keep him there until her purpose was served.

What a mess.

"Lucien?" Ianthe whispered, then reached out and gave him a hesitant shake. "Luc?"

Nothing. He simply snored.

What did this mean? Had he told anyone? Had this been the ally she so desperately needed? But how on earth could she have known that when he'd made it clear that his main purpose had been revenge against her?

You don't have time to answer that, a little voice inside her said.

And it was the truth. She had an hour to dress, get to the cemetery, and then hand over the Blade in exchange for her daughter. Purpose steeled her. Reaching out, Ianthe drew a pillow beneath his head, wet tears streaking down her cheeks. "I'm so sorry." Leaning down, she pressed a kiss against his unresisting forehead.

If only he'd spoken up sooner, for she had not dared. Wiping the tears from her eyes, Ianthe drew herself up and stumbled toward the travelling chest where the Blade was hidden. Trembling hands unsnapped the hidden compartment, and there lay the Blade. Taking it out, Ianthe had another moment of hesitation, but it was swiftly drowned in resolve.

No tears for spilt milk. Lucien would not wake anytime soon, not with several mouthfuls of drugged brandy in him, and the ruthless, practical part of her didn't have time to change her plans. Not now.

For if she did not show up in time, then who knew what Morgana would do to Louisa?

Some sorcerers dabbled with poisons and potions. Some did not. Lucien had been one of the few who did, and knew exactly how to burn it out of his blood.

Seconds swam past him, and the next time he'd blinked back to consciousness, Ianthe was flinging open the travelling box she'd brought with her on the first day. Then he lost track of time again, and the next thing he knew, he was alone.

The trunk now lay split apart, revealing the hidden compartment in the bottom, which looked like it was lined with lead. Of course. So bloody close to him all this time. The lead would have hidden all trace of the Blade's presence.

Lucien staggered to his feet, shaking his arms to try and elude the effects of the sleeping potion. How many minutes since she'd left? He couldn't quite remember. She'd evidently had time to dress, which meant she had a good head start on him.

But where?

Snatching up her hairbrush, Lucien sank into the armchair before the flickering fire, trying to still his mind. It took long minutes to open himself to his psychometric abilities. Ianthe had forgotten one thing: Lucien could scry her whereabouts.

Wrapping her black hair around his finger, Lucien turned his gaze inward, toward that glittering star in the corner of his mind's eye, and a corona of gold exploded around him as his prescience snagged against the bond that bound them together. For one second, just one, he was staring out through Ianthe's eyes, no doubt through the link their bond created. Strands of ivy clung to their boots, and they stumbled, catching at a headstone to right themselves. A graveyard. Trees. A dark avenue bounded on both sides by stone arches. It looked familiar. *Damn it, where had he seen that before?* Think! Then the light was closing in on him, as Ianthe realized what was happening, and pushed him out of her mind.

Lucien fell out of the trance with a gasp. Highgate Cemetery. He had a muffled memory of attending his mother's funeral there, so many years before. The path was the Egyptian Avenue, a proud promenade where he'd once retreated to as a boy to hide his tears and escape the man he'd still thought of as his father.

What on earth was Ianthe doing in Highgate?

It must be where she was due to meet with Morgana, but when? How long did he have? He had no idea, but if he didn't act quickly, then he knew that all might be lost, for he'd felt the eerily cold handle of the Blade of Altarrh in their hand.

CHAPTER TWENTY-ONE

'White battle globes packed no more than a wallop. Electric blue could stop your heart, if but briefly. But red? Red was the color of death.'
— *The Inner Workings of Sorcery*, by Grainne O'Neill

IANTHE DREW her cloak around her as she stopped in front of Roslyn Hayes's grave, her eyes searching the darkness. It was almost midnight, she suspected, and her nerves were stretched so tightly, she felt like she was going to fly out of her skin.

A branch crunched under foot nearby. Ianthe spun, snatching power into herself so rapidly the air almost felt thin. "H–hello? Is anybody there?"

Fog curled across the ground like a translucent blanket. Out of it stepped three figures, all of them cloaked. The lead figure lifted their hands to their hood, revealing a beautiful older woman with dangerous green eyes. "Miss Martin," the woman said. "I trust you came alone."

Ianthe steeled herself. "Of course I did, Morgana. Where is Louisa?"

"Somewhere safe. Where is the Blade?"

"Somewhere hidden," she shot back. After all, she wasn't such a fool as to simply hand it over. This woman was as trustworthy as a snake, and she'd never deal fairly. "The moment Louisa is safely before me, I shall give you the directions to it."

"This is not following the instructions I gave—"

"You said, *Come alone, and bring the Blade.* Well, I have come alone, and I brought the Blade, though it is hidden for the moment. If you want it, then you have to meet my terms. I'm tired of hiding and lying. I'm tired of looking over my shoulder every second, trying to gauge who in my household I can trust. So you either take my terms, or leave here with nothing."

"What's to stop you from betraying us?"

"I'm not the one with untrustworthy credentials," Ianthe retorted.

A long moment of silence stretched out. "Do step forward, Sebastian," Morgana called over her shoulder with a dry note of annoyance in her voice. "Show Miss Martin that my word can be trusted."

A man stepped out of the darkness, as if he'd been using it as a veil, a small gloved hand tucked in his. The little girl at his side saw her and panicked. "Aunt Ianthe!"

Louisa! Ianthe stepped forward, her heart thundering in her chest, then drew up when both hooded sorcerers at Morgana's side tensed. Everything in her screamed at her to leap forward and wrap her arms around her daughter, but she had to play this correctly.

"The Blade," Morgana purred.

Ianthe tugged a small scroll of paper out of her pocket and held it up. Perspiration dripped down her forehead, a consequence from holding onto so much power for so long without using it. "The directions are written here. I buried it beside a tombstone in the cemetery, but you'll never find it in time without this note." She stretched out her hand in desperation, not daring to make a move. "Come, Louisa. Come to me!"

Louisa shifted forward, clinging to the stranger's hand and eyeing Morgana as one would a snake. Gone was Ianthe's carefree, light-hearted daughter whose only trouble came from her puppy Tubby and the mischief he caused for her at Elsa's. No. This Louisa knew that there was darkness in the world. She had changed in the space of a week, and Ianthe's heart ached for her. Every emotion within her welled up, almost snatching that rush of power out of her control. She wanted to destroy this woman for what she'd done to her daughter, but that was instinct. Expression... Not control. Not sorcery. And it was dangerous.

"Go to your mother, child." Morgana's voice dripped with venom. "Now give me the note. It had best hold the precise location of the relic."

The man, this Sebastian, cocked his head suddenly, as if hearing something no one else could. And the strangest thing was, Ianthe couldn't quite make out his face. An eye-twisting Veil still disguised him, she realized, but why? It had to have come from Morgana, whose talents for deception were unparalleled.

"There's something wrong," he said, his gloved hand curling tightly around Louisa's as the little girl took a step forward. "Something..." He frowned, or at least, Ianthe had the sensation he frowned. "It feels like the temperature of the air just changed."

Both Morgana and Ianthe exchanged a wary look.

"It's not me," Ianthe said, darting a glance at her daughter. She shifted her weight forward. Louisa was barely three yards in front of her.

"I warned you..."

The tension in the air grew tighter. Even Ianthe felt it brushing over her skin. It felt like... lightning. Gathering itself in the distance, felt, but not yet seen. "What on earth?" Was this a trick? A trap?

And then she knew. She'd felt like this before in the foyer of Lady Eberhardt's home when Adrian Bishop had stepped foot over the lintel of the house and come face-to-face with his brother, Lucien.

Lucien. Oh no. For she felt his presence then through the bond. Something her distracted mind hadn't yet discerned until this moment. But why was—?

And then she looked up at the man holding onto Louisa's hand. Knowledge pierced the Veil disguising him. It fell away from her sight, revealing a dangerously handsome man who wore Drake's face. No, not Drake's face. A younger, more perfect version of it, though this Sebastian lacked the warmth that she saw in Drake's eyes. His own were empty, merciless pits, and a shiver trailed down her spine at the sight.

A third son.

The son that Morgana had allegedly aborted, and the very same child that Drake mourned year after year.

A pistol cocked with an audible click, breaking the stalemate, and then Lucien stepped out of the darkness, aiming it directly between Sebastian's eyes. "Release the child," he said in a dark, smoky voice.

"Lucien?" she whispered. "What are you doing here?"

He seemed *wrong*, somehow. Thin and hazy.

"You treacherous bitch," Morgana snarled, and then everything happened in the space of an instant. Morgana flung her arms out, a trio of battle globes springing into fluorescent green life in front of her, the men at her side began chanting, and Lucien's pistol fired with a sharp crack that somehow sounded on the other edge of the clearing.

The first battle globe struck Lucien, and a shower of sparks detonated in the clearing, bright enough to sear the eyes. He vanished.

"Lucien!" Ianthe screamed, flinging a wave of pure force at Morgana.

No time to think about the consequences. Everybody was off balance. Ianthe seized her chance and launched herself forward, unleashing another torrent of crude power in the woman's direction. The copper bracelet on her wrist flared white-hot as her wards activated and deflected something that Morgana had flung at her. Then she was crashing into Sebastian, carrying him to the ground in a flurry of skirts.

"Run!" she screamed at Louisa.

Her little girl hesitated for a moment, then took off into the darkness. The flash of her white petticoats was the last thing Ianthe saw before the woodlands swallowed her up. Lucien? Where was Lucien? What had happened to him? He'd simply vanished.

The warm body beneath hers jerked, and Ianthe pushed herself upright, her corset straining and her hands covered in blood. Blood from his shirt, where the bullet had struck. Sebastian looked shocked, gasping a little, and it was difficult to steel herself against the pain in his eyes when he looked so much like Drake.

But she had other matters to worry about. Her daughter. Her Shield, who had followed her here, completely unprotected except for the wards in his matching copper bracelet, and weakened by the drug. Hell, what had Lucien been thinking?

Her mind blanked for a second, but then cleared as an image of Louisa sprang to mind. Nothing else mattered.

Nothing. Not Lucien. Not Drake. Not herself. Not even the consequences of her actions. She had to find her daughter before it was too late.

Rolling to her feet, Ianthe ran into the woods. There was no sign of Luc in the clearing, which could mean anything. Morgana and her trio of sorcerers were gaining their feet after some assault and sorcery flashed like the Northern Aurora over their Wards. It couldn't be Lucien. This was delicate, dangerous magic that tasted somewhat like burned cinnamon and was wielded with the expertise of a whiplash. Which meant that someone else was here.

Had to be an ally, but who?

"Louisa?" she whispered.

An owl cooed. Behind her, someone yelled, "Spread out! They have to be here somewhere!"

"Louisa?" She stumbled blindly forward.

A crack sounded nearby, someone crashing through the undergrowth. A little girl cried out, causing a stab straight through Ianthe's heart. She grabbed her skirts and darted in that direction. The moon was a thin sliver through the trees, casting just enough light to see by.

A flash of white. Lou. She turned in that direction, but a shadow jolted out of the trees and picked Louisa up. Sebastian.

By gods, she would—

A man stepped out of the shadows between her and Sebastian, his white teeth flashing in a smile. "Well, now. Miss Martin, I presume." White mage globes sprang to life in the cup of his hands. "I've been dying to meet you."

"And you are?" Ianthe took a step toward him, calling forth her own mage globes. They crackled with brilliant red, reminding him that she wasn't messing around. It was the most difficult globe to control, and required the most power. Ianthe peered over his shoulder, seeing her daughter kicking and yelling at Sebastian.

"Easy now, luv." The stranger darted a look at her globes. "We don't have to be enemies."

"Unfortunately, you're standing between me and my daughter. That means you chose your side long ago."

"Lorenzo, wait," someone barked, and then a second man caged her in. He wasn't mucking about. His globes burned the same fiery red as her own, lighting up the clearing. Stronger than this Lorenzo, perhaps, but his control wasn't complete. His globes wobbled on their axis as they spun, hinting at power, but not finesse.

"Oh, good," Ianthe spat. "I should hate to slaughter an apprentice, but you..."

With a single word, she sent her globes spinning toward each man. Eyes widening, Lorenzo threw himself aside, and she plucked her globe back toward her with a delicate flex of her hand. It spun in circles around her, spitting sparks of red lightning.

"Shit." Lorenzo's white globes evaporated, and he scrambled behind a tree.

One down... These idiots knew not whom they were facing. Morgana might give her pause—Sebastian certainly did—but she was both an adept of the sixth level *and* the Prime's right hand. She'd been facing adversaries like this for the past five years, and coming out on top.

She sent her globe spinning toward the stronger sorcerer, and his remaining globe turned to match it. With barely a sneer, Ianthe flung a wave of force at him. Both mage globes rippled as it passed, his eyes widened, and then he was flung backward into a tree, his head cracking sharply. Distraction always was the greatest weapon.

Slumping onto the ground, he croaked something at her, and his mage globes exploded with a faint *popping* sound.

"Amateurs," she muttered, striding after Sebastian. He was the real threat.

"Ianthe!" Lucien yelled.

"Over here!" She lashed out with her remaining mage globe, and sent it crashing at Lorenzo's feet as he made another brief appearance.

Cursing, Lorenzo scrambled backward on his hands, then rolled out of the way, his coattails fluttering as he dashed behind a tombstone. Ianthe flung another globe and marble shattered as it struck. Another popped into being and hit the next gravestone as the sorcerer darted behind them. Fine dust powdered the air.

"If I see you again," she called, "I'll have you delivered to the Prime in chains!"

Turning, she strode right into a wave of force that knocked her off her feet. Ianthe cracked her head as she went down, landing on the grass on someone's grave. Bloody hell. She pressed her fingertips to her temple, and they came away bloody.

"Mama!"

"*Louisa*," she breathed, and grabbed hold of the headstone to haul herself to her feet.

Louisa reached for her over Sebastian's shoulder, as if she could somehow grasp Ianthe's hand.

Mama. The first time she'd ever heard the words from her daughter's mouth. White-hot rage quivered within her, an inferno of fury, fear, and need.

Staggering, with blood dripping down her face, Ianthe went after him. Power lashed within her, and the air turned cold as she drew in as much energy as she could hold.

There was a hot numbness in her head, just behind her right eye, as if a needle had slid straight into her brain. A warning sign. Ianthe hesitated. She had no clear shot at Sebastian. There was nothing she could do to him without hurting her daughter.

An explosion of gold sparks went up to her left. Remy? What on earth was he doing here? That was one of his stage tricks.

Shouts arose, someone rampaging through the cemetery in that direction. Remy's laughter sounded like a gleeful cackle as he led some sort of diversion. Heart in her throat, Ianthe threw one last mage globe, shattering the right wing off an angel just in front of Sebastian.

He froze.

"Don't move," she snapped.

Sebastian faced her slowly, backlit by the moon. He held Louisa carefully in his arms. "You don't want to do this, Miss Martin."

"Try me." She advanced a step, another pair of mage globes springing to life and circling her head. *I have been blackmailed, threatened, and assaulted. I've had barely any sleep in the past week. And you bastards took my daughter and killed her parents. I have had* enough.

"Give me back my daughter," she said, stepping forward with her hands raised warily, fingers crooked just so as she wove strands of sorcery through the air.

"Can't," Sebastian gasped, "even if I wanted to."

He sank to his knees, teeth ground together, his hands quivering in the air as he let go of Louisa. One hand curled in the little girl's skirt, as if to hold her there, until, one by one, his fingers unclenched.

What the hell was wrong with him? Heart in her throat, Ianthe took a step closer, watching him warily. "Lou, come to me, please."

"Run," Sebastian whispered to Louisa as his eyes bled to black.

With a squeal, Louisa darted toward her, hitting Ianthe around the waist. Ianthe dragged the little girl into her arms, straining under the weight. "Oh, God," she whispered, sliding a shaking hand through Louisa's hair. "You're here. You're really here."

"Don't hurt him," Louisa replied, looking over her shoulder at the stranger on his knees. "He's the nice one."

Can't promise that. "Don't make a move, and I won't retaliate," she called.

Sebastian sucked air into his lungs, his nostrils flaring with pain. "Run, you stupid bitch. She's coming, and then I might not have a choice."

Morgana. Ianthe went cold.

There was that pressure system lurking on the edge of her awareness. She was not the only one drawing in huge amounts of power right now. It sucked at her skirts, at her skin, and she could see the heat shimmer in the air as energy leeched off her, spiraling toward the man on his knees. Cold pricked at her, gooseflesh springing into being all down her arms. "What on earth—?"

Her breath fogged in the air in front of her.

Sebastian shuddered.

"Destroy them," Morgana commanded, stepping forward out of the mists, emerald light gleaming from the jeweled ring at her finger. Her face looked skeletal in the eerie light, but intensely focused on her son.

Sebastian sank his head into his hands, his teeth a gleaming rictus of pain. He screamed, body flinching, as if something moved beneath his skin.

"Do it!" Morgana howled.

Sebastian screamed again, slumping forward onto his hands as if giving up.

"I'm sorry," he whispered, looking up at her.

The world grew still. A silent bubble surrounded Ianthe, leaving her frozen in time, curling her arms around her daughter. Louisa's heart thumped once against her chest, *thud-thump*... Silent seconds ticked by. She couldn't move, couldn't breathe... The world was a vacuum...

Thud-thump. That was her heart this time. And then time rushed back in upon her, sending her lurching forward as a ringing sound screeched in her ears.

A body hit her.

Hard.

Ianthe tumbled onto her back, cracking her head on something sharp as Lucien took her to the ground, covering both her and Louisa with his body. The power she'd been holding bled out of her, like water leaking from a bladder, and then the world flared white. Blinding her. Obliterating her senses as an enormous outburst of Expression punched outwards from a central point, like the rippled aftermath of a stone plunging into water. The surge of it washed overhead, slicing straight through tombstones and shearing them in half. Her hair tore itself free and whipped in the wind of the explosion, only the hard, male body pressing over her protecting her from the backlash.

Clothes smoked and burned. Lucien screamed in her ear, and her own hands blistered from magic-burn where they gripped his shoulders. The ground shook beneath them like a bucking horse, and it was all she could do to hold onto him and Louisa through the maelstrom.

"Open up to me." That was Drake's voice in her mind, and a familiar trickle of sensation burned in thin gold streamers along her skin.

Ianthe opened herself to him. The bond between Master and Apprentice soared to life within her, a bond that would lie dormant until needed.

Without thinking, Ianthe gave herself over to it, and a new conscience winked into her overcrowded head. Drake would be able to see through her eyes and help her direct her power as best needed.

Energy danced through her effortlessly, and somehow she wove her sorcery into a shining shield that sprung into being around the three of them. The tear of power stopped ripping at her skin, her clothes, her hair... Lucien collapsed over the top of them, panting as if he'd run a race.

Then Drake used her to wield her sorcery in ways she'd never imagined. She could feel him dispersing the blaze of raw matter that had erupted from Sebastian. Not confronting it, but letting it flow through her as he grounded it. Ianthe became nothing but a conduit, an observer, marveling at the delicacy of the weaves Drake wove.

Morgana launched forward, grabbing her son and dragging him to his feet, as if sensing the Prime's presence. She pushed Sebastian toward the trees, and they vanished, his power cutting off so abruptly that Ianthe's skin tingled.

It was over.

It was finally, blessedly over.

"*Who was he?*" Drake asked.

"*He's your son,*" she sent back, slumping onto the ground beneath her lover and her daughter. "*He's the child that Morgana claimed to have destroyed.*"

Shock severed the connection. Ianthe could suddenly feel her body again, heavy as a stone. Then her eyes rolled back in her head, and she fell into blessed, peaceful darkness.

"Is she alive?" Remington demanded.

Lucien swallowed hard, lowering his fingers to the pulse beneath Ianthe's jaw. *Please, please...* There it was. He nodded with relief, kneeling in the grass beside her. His back was blistered where sorcery had burned directly through his coat, and the scent of burned hair made him gag. "Yes. Something happened. I could feel some other presence in her mind."

"Drake," Remington replied. "There's not many people who could do what she just did."

"I'll get her home." Leaning down, Lucien curled his arms gently beneath her and drew her carefully into his arms. Ianthe seemed so small, so light. There was more weight in her skirts than her body it seemed, and it shocked him, for she was such a powerful, confident woman when awake. It didn't seem right.

"Hello there, Louisa," Remington said, kneeling in front of the little girl who clung to Ianthe's skirts. "I'm your aunt's employer, Remington, and this is—"

"Lucien Rathbourne. A... friend of your aunt's," Lucien interrupted. Louisa. His child. Jesus. Their eyes met—hers the same peculiar shade as his own—and Louisa turned into Remington's arms almost bashfully. She slid another long sideways glance at him, as if she sensed something strange about him.

"I'll take Louisa," Remington told him, and their eyes met. Remington saw her eyes too.

Watching Ianthe crumple beneath that blow had struck Lucien like an icy dagger to the heart. He hadn't been able to protect them, nor was he close enough to divert the blow or ward them. The only thing he could do was knock her beneath the flood of raw power and hope that they survived.

Too late. Too slow. Too weak. There was nothing he could have done in that moment, not the way he was, and frustration seared through his veins.

A year ago, he could have protected her. A year ago, his own power could have matched Morgana's, and he might have been able to defeat her. But he was not that man. And as much as he tried to pretend to himself that he would regain his strength, he didn't have the time.

If you hadn't been so arrogant, you could have seen her Healer yesterday. He could have helped you heal yourself. You might have been able to do something, anything, if you had your power.

Lifting her close against his chest, Lucien breathed in Ianthe's light perfume, reassuring himself that she was whole. He could feel her consciousness beginning to come to the surface through their bond. She would be all right, hopefully. No. He would make certain she was.

There's a reason most sorcerers choose not to bond, my lad. An old friend had once told him that.

What a bloody mess.

CHAPTER
TWENTY-TWO

CLEO HAD thought that the marriage would change things.

She was wrong.

A horribly unforgivable state for someone with the ability to see glimpses of the future, but there it was.

The ceremony in itself was quite nice, though brief, and had more of the air of a transaction than a joining of two people forever. Indeed, Cleo thought her new husband might even be a stranger, someone she'd never met before, for the coldness of his voice and the amount of attention Sebastian gave her. She tried to take his arm in the nave, for she was well outside of her usual boundaries in the church, but Sebastian passed her off to her father without breaking his stride and said he'd join her later that afternoon.

He was off to see if his new boots had arrived.

Her trunks were removed to the house he leased with his mother, and without further ado, Cleo was handed up into the hackney that would take her there.

Alone.

She hadn't left Tremayne Manor since her father had first put the blindfold on her.

When Cleo arrived, the housekeeper, Mrs. Gibbons, gave her a brief tour of the house, then escorted her to her room. "Dinner will be sent up in an hour or two, ma'am."

"Do you think I could take a turn in the garden?" Cleo asked.

There was a slight hesitation. "I think it wise if you rest this afternoon and stay in your room. I'll send a maid up to help you with your gown."

The door closed, and Cleo turned, frustration lancing through her. Curious about her new circumstances, she explored the room, a task that took her all of five minutes. Only the door on the far side of her chambers refused to budge when she tried it: locked, apparently.

"*Where the master stays*," Mrs. Gibbons had said earlier and coughed discreetly.

It took Cleo all of a minute to pick the lock with a hairpin.

Sebastian's chambers were cooler than her own, but there was nothing personal in the room, beyond piles of books, stacked haphazardly, to tell her about the kind of man she was married to. Cleo touched the old leather-bound spines, but she couldn't even see what type of books he read.

Not a single thing owned any hint of personality. Doubt was an unfamiliar emotion. She'd met Sebastian but once, after all... Who was her husband? The man who dwelt in silences and tried not to smile as he escorted her out of the carnage of heavy duck artillery? Or was he the cold man who hadn't hesitated in making a casual threat to her father that morning, as if he was discussing the weather.

Afternoon slowly slid into evening. Cleo dined in her chambers, listening as people came and went. Something was happening. Though her premonition had been willfully silent today—nerves, she suspected, tore her concentration—a sense of heaviness and tension stained the very house. Cleo cracked open the window, only to hear Sebastian reprimand his mother, somewhere below her window.

"I don't care what you do," Morgana snapped. "Just keep her bloody quiet until we get to the cemetery." A horse neighed, and wheels crunched over gravel. "This cannot go wrong, Sebastian. We must retrieve the relic from Miss Martin at all costs. She had best not think to cheat me, or I swear that girl will bear the brunt of it."

"It's all right," Sebastian murmured, and he sounded like *her* Sebastian again. "You'll get to see your mother again very shortly. I promise. Then you'll be safe. You just have to remain silent for a little longer. Can you do that?"

"I'll try," a little girl whispered.

"That's the spirit, Lou."

The sniffling of tears stopped and the din of voices cut off dramatically as the carriage door was closed. It wheeled away as the chill of evening fell, and Cleo was forced to shut the windows.

Well, now. What on earth was going on?

She paced for at least an hour, but there was no sign of her husband's return. Nobody had been up to see to the fire, and supper had been quite forgotten. Much like herself. She was still in her bloody wedding gown, with its stiffened skirts and the lace that dug into her throat.

You thought it would be better, she told herself, blinking sleepily. *You little fool.* She was cold now and curled up on Sebastian's bed, dragging the cover over herself. Her eyes closed, her breath softening...

Something alerted her to the fact that she wasn't going to be alone for very long—footsteps in the hallway outside.

Cleo had a moment where she didn't know where she was and realized she must have fallen asleep at some stage. She sat up with a jerk, the covers tumbling loose around her.

The door opened and Sebastian strode in, easily identified by his brisk stride. The scent of his cologne swept around her as Cleo froze. Definitely her husband. Something light hit the floor, possibly his cravat. A button popped, and he paused in front of the liquor cabinet and poured himself something to drink. "*Fuck.*"

"Long night?" Cleo asked.

A choked cough sounded; then he cleared his throat and turned. "Miss Sinclair. I... didn't expect you."

How awkward.

"I was just... I couldn't get out of my wedding dress." Swallowing her nerves, Cleo tipped her chin up. "And I believe it is Mrs. Montcalm now, is it not? Or perhaps, Madame? Which would you prefer?"

"I don't particularly give a damn. I suspect it will make little difference."

Well, two could play at that game. She was starting to regain her mettle. She might not know this house or what was expected of her, but she could learn it. And it had been bloody hours since anyone had paid her the least amount of attention. "Then I shall be Mrs. Montcalm. It suits me. Do you need help undressing?" She slid off the bed and crossed slowly toward him, running through a map of the room in her mind.

Sebastian sidestepped her and went straight to the liquor cabinet. "No, I don't."

That felt uncomfortably like dismissal. "I'm only trying to do my wifely duties."

"Your wifely duties are not required," he replied, though his voice roughened toward the end there. Fabric rustled. He sounded as though he was wrestling with his coat. "Nor will they be."

"None of them?" she replied innocently. "But, sir, I'm quite willing to perform—"

"None of them." The coat hit the floor, and he slammed the crystal stopper back into the liquor decanter.

"Well, unfortunately, I *do* require help undressing." She turned around, presenting her back to him, and dragged the soft curls that tumbled down her back over her shoulder. "I cannot reach all of the buttons."

Silence. Sebastian swallowed, then set the glass tumbler aside. "You should have rang for the maid."

"I did. They must have been busy," she lied. "What's wrong?"

"Nothing."

The distance between them remained the same. Cleo waited, her head tilted to the side, so that she could hear him better. Every hair along her skin lifted. Her bodice felt too tight.

With a muttered curse, Sebastian stalked toward her. "Here," he said, and gave a roughened tug to the top two buttons, clearly intending to get this over and done with as swiftly as possible. The buttons were soft pearl and tightly hooked. One scattered to the floor and clattered away. Sebastian cursed again. He had to slow down. Had to work them more gently. Breath whispered across the back of her shoulders, and his roughened fingers danced occasionally against her bare skin, igniting her senses.

Perhaps this had not been a good idea. She felt like she stood on the precipice of a cliff, preparing to leap into water when she didn't know the depth... even as a part of her desperately wanted to make that leap. Every brush of his fingers felt like lightning, striking through her veins.

Heart hammering, Cleo bit her lip and tilted her head forward. Agitation made her skin feel flushed, her body restless. She had to say something. "Had your boots arrived?"

"What?" He was remarkably stiff on his right side, almost as if he favored that hand.

"Your boots. The ones you were so set on acquiring after the ceremony. I thought they must be quite grand indeed to send you chasing after them at such a time."

Sebastian's hands set to work again. He was fumbling quite badly now, wrestling with her buttons. "Yes."

Liar. Her lips pressed together.

"There," he said.

The gown slipped forward, clinging to the edges of her shoulders. Cleo hesitated. "My corset?"

If anything, the silence grew even more strained. "Cleo." His breathing was heavier now.

"I cannot remove it myself," Cleo admitted quietly.

Once again Sebastian came to her aid. He tugged her laces undone roughly with his left hand, his right pressed lightly against her spine.

It was torture. And she had done it to herself.

With a sigh, he stepped away from her. "There." Her silken robe was pressed into her hands, and then he turned and shuffled back toward the liquor.

Cleo stared blindly after him, want kindling along her nerves. It was clear that she'd been dismissed. Her entire body trembled. She didn't quite know what to do. Well, at least she could remove her dress now. She set about undoing her tapes and loosened her corset until everything collapsed around her feet, leaving her in only her thin chemise. Heat scalded her cheeks. He had his back to her, she knew it.

Was she so insignificant?

Cleo dressed swiftly in her nightgown, using her robe for discretion. Not that she needed it, she thought. Afterward, she stood there with her chemise fisted in her hands. Sebastian had stoked the fire. It crackled behind her, and he turned to the decanter again, judging by his footsteps. "You should return to your own room."

"I can't."

"I'm tired, Cleo. I don't want you in here."

Well, that was blunt. Cleo's cheeks burned. "I stumbled into the maid when she was bringing me dinner. She dropped the teapot all over my bed. She thought I'd best sleep here, and they'll try and air it in the morning."

She was met with another one of his precious silences, as if he was fighting to sort her words out in his head. "You cannot stay here."

"We are married, are we not? I know you don't wish to consummate the marriage, but I'm certain you'll be able to restrain yourself, and it's a large bed. You'll barely know I'm in it."

"I'll sleep on the trundle," he growled. A muttered curse caught her ear. Then he upended the liquor decanter, the scent of brandy flavoring the air.

"Seven hours married, and you've already turned to drink," she murmured. "This bodes well."

Fabric shifted and she almost suspected that Sebastian hissed under his breath. "Cleo, I'm hellish tired. I cannot argue with you tonight."

"Were we arguing?"

"Please. Just...don't. Don't push me tonight." For the first time, he sounded exactly as he claimed. Exhausted.

She could smell something now too. Spirits mixed with... Blood? Desire washed away from her as her mind replayed the past few minutes in her head. His stiffness, the muttered curses, the wince as he tugged at her laces... "Are you hurt?"

"I'm fine." It sounded like he had something in his mouth, and as glass clinked, she realized it was the top of the decanter. With a grunt, he tore a piece of fabric, and something slithered over his skin.

"You *are* hurt. Why didn't you say something?"

"It's nothing."

"Nothing, my foot!" Cleo hurried toward him, hands outstretched. "Here, let me help—"

Her hands met his half-opened shirt. Hard muscle flinched beneath her fingers. His stomach. Then her wrists were captured, and Sebastian held her politely away from his body. "I can manage."

Now that she was thinking again, and not sidetracked by the feel of his hands on her buttons, she could scent a faint burning scent. "You only have two hands. Let me help you, Sebastian. I feel terrible for forcing you to assist with my gown when you're injured."

If he'd been in the right frame of mind, she thought that he might have kept arguing. Instead he sighed and sank down onto the stool by the vanity. That's when she knew he was exhausted. "I was shot."

"*Shot?*"

The bottle upended. He swallowed. "The bullet went right through me. It's fine. Most of the bleeding's stopped."

"Where?"

Sebastian caught her hands and directed them to his shoulder. "Right through here."

Her hands slid over the bulk of a bandage. He'd been trying to wrap it around his neck and shoulder, without much success. Cleo pushed his shirt collar out of the way, inspecting the job with her fingers. "Has someone seen to it?"

"I cleaned it with alcohol and cauterized it earlier." His head slumped forward.

"That's hardly proper treatment. I'll send for a doctor—"

Sebastian caught her wrist as she turned for the door. "No."

"But—"

"No," he said again with force. "No doctors, no surgeons. Just help me put this bloody bandage on, and all I'll need is sleep."

"What about infection?" she whispered.

"It will be fine."

Cleo swallowed. "I could cast a small healing ward over it. It might not seal the skin, now you've cauterized it, but it might help with the degree of healing."

"Thought your talents ran to Divination?"

"They do. I've reached the Fourth Level, however. I know the minor Healing Arts, though I'm certainly no adept."

The offer sat there as he considered it.

"Don't you trust me?"

"I trust you." Sebastian barked a laugh, which swiftly fell silent. "I'm just not used to such offers. I keep searching to find your angle, but then I remind myself who I'm dealing with. You're not like my mother, or any of her acquaintances."

"I should certainly hope I'm not. Why didn't she heal you?"

"Because I disobeyed her."

What kind of woman let her son hurt like this? "Hold still. I have to touch you." She lifted her hands and pressed them over his wound as she pushed the bandage aside. Sebastian tensed, the skin flushed with heat.

Power welled through her as Cleo opened herself up, drawing heat from the fire, from his skin, from deep inside her... From everything that surrounded her. It felt like she was a flower, finally blooming. The world fell away, all of the cold, harsh realities of it, and her senses grew stronger.

Suddenly his heartbeat thumped through his chest like a drum. Cleo could sense the tension within him, as if he watched her blindfolded face, and smell the faint burnt tang of sorcery that clung to his clothes. He'd expended a great deal of power today.

"You should be careful. You have the scent of overexertion all over you. If you use too much sorcery, Bastian, you might burn yourself out."

At that, she released the ward with a soft power word, and Sebastian gasped as a cool tingle slid across his skin. Beneath her touch, the wound burned like menthol, a strange hot-cold beneath her hand, as her magic sank itself into that fevered skin. She was left touching smooth skin, newly reknit, and only faintly throbbing with heat now. By morning, he should have healed completely.

"Thank you," Sebastian said gruffly.

"You should have told me sooner. How did this happen?"

Silence again, broken only by the sound of him swallowing. Liquid swished as he lowered the bottle. "Don't ask, Cleo. One of Morgana's schemes."

"And the girl?"

His head shifted as she felt him look up. "How did you—?" Then he grunted. "Did you See it?"

"No. I'm not myself today. I can't seem to grasp my precognition through the distraction. I overheard Morgana speaking in the courtyard, however." She pressed her hands to her thighs as she knelt in front of him. "There. We're all done. You should come to bed."

"Cleo."

"I promise I won't ravish you."

"I should stay on the trundle in my dressing closet."

That wouldn't do. She couldn't chase him from his own bed in such a condition, and she'd been telling the truth: Hers *was* drenched, a ridiculous ploy she hadn't thought through all the way. "Will your mother not think that unusual? She might... wonder if my presence bothered you."

Sebastian stayed stubbornly silent.

"I promise I will stay on my side of the bed. I won't bite. Unless you snore. Do you snore?"

"Not that I'm aware of." He heaved himself to his feet. "Do you honestly think you're fooling me?"

"No, not at all." Sebastian shifted, so she added quietly, "Do you honestly think you're fooling me?"

This earned her a long minute of silence. She counted, letting her heart beat out the seconds.

"Very well then. We wouldn't want my mother to think there was anything unusual between us." A glass clinked against the dresser beside the bed. Then he began to undo his shirt.

The pop of each button made her chest tighten with nerves. She didn't know why. Cleo crossed to the bed, feeling somewhat flustered. It was one thing to think of wifely duties, quite another to listen to the stealthy glide of linen and cotton as her husband undressed himself. Her imagination was a vivid thing, after all, and she had seen enough in her visions to have some idea of what husbands did to their wives. She'd always thought the idea a somewhat gruesome one. It had been like watching a duel—the heavy thrust and pull of flesh, the subjugation of the female, the grimace of emotion on their faces.

Her cheeks were burning. She'd always thought she would force herself to endure such a thing, if she ever married, but she'd never thought she'd feel like this: all nerves, all breathy anticipation, her body almost leaping out of her skin.

And, if she were honest, there was a lush heaviness between her thighs that made her feel rather uncertain.

"Ah," Sebastian murmured with a hint of heat to his voice. Some manner of clothing hit the floor, making her throat tighten. "Now I realize what will finally subdue my wife. You're very quiet, my dear."

"I don't like that word," Cleo whispered with a blush.

She could hear him thinking his words through. "Subdue?" The word sounded somewhat muffled, as if he dragged something over his head. Then he moved to his belt.

Cleo swallowed. Hard. Her nightgown felt like a thin barrier. Even now her nipples strained the fabric.

"I don't like that word very much either." He sighed, and then his trousers hit the floor. More material rustled. His nightshirt, perhaps. The bed dipped as he sat on the edge of it. Silence brewed again between them.

"I'm not going to touch you, Cleo." It was a hushed confession, as if he felt her nerves.

"It would be all right, if you wished to." She thought he'd be gentle with her.

"Perhaps I do not wish to?" And then he dragged the covers over himself, leaving her feeling very much alone again.

Cleo lay down, dragging the covers over herself. *Perhaps I do not wish to.* Her mind could conjure a thousand reasons why he might not want her. Moving slowly, she swallowed the lump in her throat. That was enough of that. She was not going to give into any of those horrid thoughts. She'd had enough of them when her father couldn't be bothered dining with her, or gave her but a brusque kiss on the forehead as he came and went, always on some business that was more important than she.

It felt strange to have another person in the bed with her, especially one so much heavier. The mattress dipped, and she was fighting not to roll into him. That would probably send him straight out of bed. Crossing some lines required a careful military campaign, not a full-on assault, and after what he'd said, she wasn't certain she wanted to wage such a campaign anymore. All of the day's hopes were dying a small death in the middle of her chest.

"That wasn't a very nice thing to say," Cleo whispered.

Sebastian rolled over, his breath whispering against her face. "I—"

"But then, I think that's exactly how you want me to feel. After all, I'm very used to not being wanted."

Sebastian sucked in a sharp breath.

Cleo rolled away, curling her hands into the blankets, her abdomen locking tight with a great deal of suppressed emotion. None of this was going the way she'd thought it would. Her eyes pricked with tears. "Do you know, I was so happy this morning? I thought my life was going to change. I don't expect you to love me. I don't expect you to even wish to be around me all the time, but please, do not be cruel. I know I am just an insignificant blind girl who you never wished to marry, but I didn't particularly want to marry you either. You were nice to me the other day, but I just wanted to escape. The worst thing you could ever do to me would be to lock me away here and not give a damn. So I won't hope for love, I won't, but if you could just care, just a little, that would be enough for me."

Pressing her blindfolded face into the pillow, she breathed in the hot air of her own breath in an attempt to suppress the boiling emotion within her. What a fool she'd been, thinking this but a game, and now she was trapped by her own cleverness, for her mattress truly was a sopping mess, and her husband didn't want her in his bed.

Something brushed against her hair. She usually braided it, but she'd left it out, hoping he might think it pretty. Cleo stilled, her breath catching, as she lay there in agony, letting him stroke her soft curls.

The whole feeling of the encounter changed. Her tears dried up, her heart becoming a hollow thump in her ears, but he said nothing. Or perhaps what he meant to say was lost in this somewhat gentle touch, which seemed to only emphasize the distance between them.

"I'm sorry," he said. "I've lived so long in cruelty that I forget the damage careless words can wreak." He breathed out a helpless, saddened laugh. "Or perhaps I never expected such a barb to so easily wound you. Perhaps I'm too used to dealing with those who do not own a heart, and then here you are, wearing yours on your sleeve." His fingertips rippled down the lawn nightgown that covered her spine. Then they disappeared, yet she felt as if regret flavored the air between them.

"I cannot touch you, Cleo, for a thousand reasons. Least of all is your father and my mother. The irony of this situation is that in trying to protect you from them, I have brought you into the realm of a far more dangerous predator."

Trying to protect you... Her heart began to race. She was so confused. One moment she didn't seem to know him at all, and the next he became her Sebastian again. "Who?"

"Myself." Another faint touch brushed her hair, as if he couldn't seem to help himself. "I'm dangerous, Cleo."

"I don't believe that."

"Yes, but you've only seen one side to me."

The nightmare flashed into her mind, London's Doom roiling in the distance. Cleo stopped the words she'd been about to say. She couldn't pretend that Sebastian wasn't dangerous, but it was difficult to reconcile such destruction with this man, who stroked her hair as if it were spun gold.

"I don't like to be touched," he said, and this time his voice was a hollow echo, as if he lived some memory that stained him. "It... almost hurts. It makes me feel physically ill, and I become nothing more than rage. The only reason I'm telling you this is so that you don't touch me during the night. I wouldn't know you, Cleo, and I do not care to hurt you. I see *her* face in my mind, and I lose myself. I don't know where I am or what I'm doing. I cannot stop thinking of others. Of what they've done to me."

"Who? Your mother?"

"No." He laughed bitterly. "A woman I knew, not so long ago. Her name doesn't matter, though she's the only one whose face I recall."

Had he loved this woman? Instantly, her mind shied away from such a thought. This wasn't love that he spoke of. In his voice, only hatred lingered. She didn't understand any of it, or perhaps she didn't want to understand.

Cleo's mind raced. "Your mother makes you... entertain them, doesn't she?"

"I fuck them for her," he said in a hard voice. "At first, they liked hurting me. It's easy to do when she gives them the ring for the night, and I used to just submit to it, after I ran out of the strength to fight them. You would think a man could stop himself from... from reacting, but there are ways..."

"Then what happened?" she asked in a tortured whisper. "Why do you remember one face among many?"

He shifted on the sheets. "Cleo—"

"I have seen a great many things," she warned. "Horrible things you couldn't even imagine. I can bear this."

"Perhaps I could imagine," he said roughly. Then he added in a broken voice, "What if I *were* one of those horrible things?"

"I wouldn't believe it," Cleo said, sliding her hand across the sheets before remembering what he'd said about being touched. She curled her fingers into a helpless fist that trembled.

"Then you do not know me at all. The reason I remember that bitch's face is because she was the first one I turned upon. I made her hurt until she begged at my feet. I used everything they'd ever done to me against her until she was sobbing. And I didn't care. I wanted to destroy her."

It was ugly. Cleo dug her nails into her palms, feeling a little uncertain. "You are a victim of your own circumstances. This wasn't your fault—"

"You still don't understand, do you? She liked it. There she was, lying at my feet, begging me for more, and I wanted to hurt her so badly, that I did it to her again. It was the first time I've ever held any power. I liked it, Cleo. I liked hurting her, and I have done it again and again, to all of them."

There was nothing to say to that. She couldn't even breathe. Inside, she was choking.

"You are in bed with a monster," he whispered. "There is no hope for me. I cannot bear for you to touch me. I shouldn't have lain down with you." He shoved the covers back. "It was a stupid hope, but if you touched me, and I forgot where I was... All I can think about is what would happen to you. What if I hurt you? Could you ever smile at me again after such a betrayal? Could you ever again think of me as the man who met you in your gardens? Or would you only see the truth?" Sebastian slipped out of the bed. "Stay there. You're safe from me. I won't touch you."

"Bastian," Cleo whispered, sitting up and clutching the covers to her chest.

And he waited. He stood there in the dark intimacy of the room, with his secrets spilling all around him, and waited for her to make him a promise that she couldn't utter.

"You cannot stay in here again," he said, after too long a silence. "I'm sorry, you didn't realize what you had married. You won't have to see me again. I'll sleep on the trundle."

And then he was gone, and for the second time since she had met him, she was speechless.

CHAPTER TWENTY-THREE

THE WORLD lurched. Ianthe curled sleepily into strong arms, dreaming of endless gardens where she could never quite find what she was looking for. There was a moment of uncertainty as she blinked, then opened her eyes. Candlelight greeted her, along with a glimpse of the hallway in her home. She was in Lucien's arms, her cheek resting on the velvet lapel of his coat.

"Awake?" he murmured.

"Yes."

Lucien set her down gently, and Ianthe wobbled like a newborn lamb, her strength weakened by the toll of the night's exertions.

"Where is Louisa?" she asked.

"Safe," he replied in a hushed tone. "Upstairs in bed."

"I need to see her." Panic flared. She couldn't believe her daughter was truly *there* until she saw it with her own eyes.

"Ianthe—"

"Please," she whispered.

He seemed to read her mind with one glance. "This way," he said, without another word and led her upstairs.

"I have to fetch something first," she told him, swiftly disappearing into her own rooms and coming out moments later with something in her hand.

Lucien hesitated at the door to Louisa's room.

"Are you coming in?" she asked.

"Would I be welcome here?"

"Of course you'd be welcome—"

"I'm not her father, not to her. All she knows is another man. My own daughter doesn't know me, and whose..." Lucien broke off with a curse.

"Whose fault is that?" Ianthe whispered, the words tasting dry in her throat.

Lucien searched for the right words. "That's not what I meant to say."

"No?"

Lucien's eyes flashed with grief. "We're both tired. This isn't a conversation we should be having in these circumstances. We'll discuss it in the morning," he murmured, then turned and strode away. "I need to have a bath."

Ianthe clung to the teddy bear in her hands, watching him go. She wouldn't cry. She would *not*. But those words had crushed a small piece of her.

You have earned his scorn, something whispered in her mind.

"Well, what do you think?" Louisa's voice drew her attention, from inside the room.

"I think the bad lady and her friends had best consider fleeing for the Continent before your aunt decides to finish matters" –that was Remy– "as she's very angry with them."

"The bad lady said that Aunt Ianthe's not my aunt," Louisa whispered, and there she was, tucked up in bed, as

Ianthe peered through the narrow crack. "They said she's my mother. That she didn't want me and gave me away to Elsa and Jacob to raise me."

"What do you think?"

Louisa's voice grew small. "I know she's my mother. Elsa told me a year ago, but I don't think she didn't want me. She wouldn't have come for me if she didn't, would she?"

God bless Remington, but he leaned down, his elbows resting on the bed, and cupped Louisa's hands within his. "Your mother would have moved Heaven and Hell to get you back, because she loves you. I think she loved you enough to find some wonderful parents for you when she realized she couldn't look after you as well as they could, not when she was so young."

Ianthe had to clear her throat. That bitch. Of all the things that Morgana could have done, making Louisa feel that she was unloved was at the top of the list.

Remington's dark eyes raked over Ianthe as he heard the noise she made. "And now, if you'll excuse me, princess, I believe someone else wants a word with you."

Louisa's pale face turned toward her. Ianthe's heart both bloomed and sank within her chest. Remington patted Ianthe on the shoulder as he went out, but she barely saw him. Louisa filled her world.

"Hello," she whispered, taking one step toward the bed.

And then Louisa bolted out of the covers and threw herself at Ianthe, her thin arms wrapping around Ianthe's waist.

"I'm so sorry," she whispered. "So sorry, Lou."

Louisa wiped away her tears. "I knew you'd come and save me. I waited every night for you."

A rush of heat crawled up her throat, and she dragged the little girl in tight, rocking her faintly. "I'll always come for you. If you believe nothing else, then believe that. I love you with all of my heart, Lou."

Louisa lifted her worried face. "What happened to mama? And papa? Mr. Cross wouldn't tell me."

"I'm so sorry," she whispered, brushing the hair off her daughter's forehead. "There was nothing I could do for them when I found them. They had gone to Heaven, to live with the angels. I paid some men to have them both buried in the churchyard of St. Mary's—you know, the one with the roses that Elsa liked so much? And then I came looking for you."

The little girl rested her head on Ianthe's shoulder, looking like she was fresh out of tears. Those big blue eyes were red and swollen and brokenhearted. "What about Tubby?" she whispered.

Ianthe lay them both down on the bed, curling up beside her daughter. "He's safe. The O'Brien's are looking after him. Once this is all done, I'll take you home to fetch him." Reaching down, she pulled the gift from her pocket. "I do have something I've been keeping safe for you, however."

Louisa's eyes grew wide as she sighted the teddy bear. "Hilary!" she cried, and dragged the ragged bear to her chest as if it were the lifeline she so badly needed.

For the first time, Ianthe felt like she might not be so hopeless at this after all.

After Louisa fell asleep, Ianthe went looking for Lucien. Matters might be able to keep until morning, according to him, but she was certain she wouldn't sleep a wink. Not until she'd apologized.

She found him in the bathing chamber off his room and knocked lightly at the door. Lucien was shaving his jaw by the mirror, his hair wet and a towel wrapped around his lean waist. Burns marked his back from the blast of sorcery earlier.

He paused.

"I know you don't want to speak to me just now," Ianthe said, shutting the door behind her, with a lump in her throat. "Just hear me out. I need to apologize.... for everything. For not telling you that you had a daughter, for not telling you... about the trouble I was in. I'm so sorry," she whispered, unable to look him in the eye anymore. "I didn't know what to do. I didn't know—"

"If I were ally or enemy."

She nodded, her shoulders slumping. Lou was safe. But there were consequences to pay now. Tears made her vision blur. What was she going to tell Drake? How could she ever atone for this?

"I don't blame you for drugging me, or for not trusting me. All of the foolish things I've been saying these past few days... Why would you not believe them—that I meant to take my revenge upon you?" With a sigh, he stared down into the basin of water, his hands resting on the vanity. "I never meant any of them, you realize?" Finally, he looked up, the lance of his amber gaze burning through her. "That was my pride speaking. I was angry at you for your part in my incarceration—" he held up his hand as she moved to speak "—an incarceration which was duly earned. You were only doing what you were asked to do by your superior, and I was a danger to society at that stage. But my recent anger was merely a shield, an attempt to protect myself. Every day, every hour, I find myself yearning toward you. And I didn't like it one bit."

There was simply nothing to say to that. Nothing at all.

Lucien dragged a towel over his face, patting his cheeks dry. "I also owe you an apology. I spoke rashly before in the hallway." His tone softened. "You did not deserve those words."

"I— What?" Of all the things she'd expected, this was not one of them. "I don't quite follow you."

Lucien raked his hands through his hair as he turned to survey the room. Each movement was brusque, like a caged bull suddenly released, aware of its close confines and trying desperately not to destroy all of the dainty furniture. "Yes, I'm angry. I won't deny that, but I have been thinking of what it would have been like for a young, unmarried woman of seventeen to find herself with child. From the little you've spoken of your father, I can't imagine he would have been pleased, and..." Lucien let out a deep breath. "I'm sorry, Ianthe. You dealt as best you could with circumstances no young woman should ever have to deal with. I cannot judge you. I have no right to judge you. Please accept my humble apologies for my earlier words. I allowed my own feelings of abandonment, perhaps, to speak. It was wrong of me."

The entire world seemed to tilt on its axis.

"Thank you." The words were but a whisper. The truth of it, however, blazed across her heart, pouring pure sunshine through her veins.

If she dared believe it...

"I keep thinking of my father," he admitted, sinking down onto the edge of the bath and folding his hands in his lap. He looked down, dark hair falling forward across his face. "Of how I have hated him for what he did to me. I blamed him for not being there, and I told myself he could have tried harder. If he'd wanted me, he could have used his power to take me from Lord Rathbourne and raise me as his own. The entire time I was in Bedlam, I felt like an animal, poked and prodded by its keepers, and shunned as mad. And he put me there! He put me there, Ianthe. What other proof did I need? I hated him. Or maybe... Maybe I hated myself. Because I felt, deep in my heart, that I wasn't good enough for him." His head bowed. "All I could think of was Louisa looking at me and feeling exactly how I felt—that her father didn't want her."

"No, no it's not like that. She would never feel like that." Ianthe stepped forward, into the vee of his thighs, one hand sinking into his hair. He pressed his face against her middle, clasping her roughly around the hips as he dragged her closer to him. "Drake tried to visit you once. In Bedlam. It was toward the start, but you... reacted poorly. It was decided that it would be best if he didn't visit again. At least, not until you were lucid."

The look in his eyes... as if she'd cut out his heart. And then realization began to dawn. "I remember."

"He wanted to explain to you why this was the best course of action. The Council—they had decided that you had already raised a demon once, which made you a risk. They wanted you executed. You will never know how hard he fought for you, Luc. And Louisa... She has a heart the size of the world. She will know the truth, because I will tell her. It was my fault, not yours."

Lucien linked fingers with her. "That doesn't sit quite right either."

Ianthe tipped her chin up. "I made my choices. This is my price to pay."

"Was she happy there?" he asked gruffly.

At least she could grant him that. "She was happy. She was loved. They were wonderful people."

"Were?"

"Morgana killed them." That was all she could manage with the way her throat locked up. Ianthe closed her eyes. "I found their bodies a couple of hours after the first letter arrived. It was the first place I went."

Delicate butterfly kisses danced over her closed eyes as he stood. Ianthe blinked them open when Lucien drew back from her, his hands cupping her cheeks so carefully.

"What do you plan to do? About her?" Dread turned her insides again, but she had to ask. Legally, Louisa belonged to him if he chose to pursue the matter.

Lucien's expression grew grim. "I believe that's something we'll discuss when all of this is over. I'm not going to make any more rash decisions, Ianthe, and it's our decision to make, not yours, not mine. I intend only for my daughter's future happiness. She will need a mother." His gaze dropped, as if to hide the regret she saw there. "And she barely knows her father."

Hers. Louisa was hers. A thrill of elation and dread ran through her. *What type of mother could I ever*— She stopped the thought there. This time she had options. She was financially secure, and though her reputation was tarnished, she had a place in the Order, if not society. All Ianthe had ever dreamed of was a garden of her own and a little girl, playing hide-and-seek in the hedges with her, squealing with laughter. She wanted that more than anything. "I intend to be her mother," she stated, and Lucien paused, as if digesting this fact, then nodded.

That was a relief. It gave her resolve strength. If he believed she could do it, then so could she. "And I want her to know her father."

"There will be questions," he stated, "if you choose to adopt her. She looks too much like you, and I fear the resemblance will strengthen as she ages." Something wistful filled his expression. "She's beautiful."

"I shall deal with those questions as they arise."

Again that hesitation. "There is another solution to consider."

"You wish to adopt her as your ward?"

"Yes, however, not in the way you imagine."

"Oh?" He could read her mind now?

Lucien took a step toward her, the backs of his fingers trailing over the smooth slope of her upper arms. Ianthe shivered. He seemed absorbed in the process, and then the sharp glint of his gaze met hers. "We could marry."

That pronouncement took all of the air out of the room. "We could *what*?"

"Marry," he repeated. "I could adopt her as my own. Everybody will know the truth anyway–she has my eyes. This way Louisa would have the benefits of both parents, as well as a certain type of legitimacy. She would have the backing of my name and position. Nobody would dare call her a bastard, and if they did, I would crush them."

"Yes, but..." Her mind was reeling. "I thought you wished free of this... this bond?" *Of me.*

"I did. Once. And then I realized there is not a single person I may lay claim upon in this world. Nobody but you. You have stood at my back when I have fought, and guarded me when I was not strong enough to face our enemies. I want to know you in every sense, Ianthe. I want you to trust me. I want..." And here he faltered. "I want to give you my trust. Marry me. Show me that I'm not alone, not anymore. Teach me to love my father. Teach me to know my daughter."

It was the best thing to do for Louisa, but Ianthe couldn't help wondering if it were the best thing for *her*? For Lucien owned a piece of her heart, her soul, but did she have any of the same claims upon him?

"I'm afraid," she whispered.

337

"Of?"

"Daring to trust..." That it would all be all right.

He understood. It gleamed in those dangerous eyes. Lucien took her hand and turned it, exposing the intimate bareness of her wrist. "Ours has not been the easiest relationship," he admitted, lowering his mouth to the base of her hand. Soft lips brushed over her skin.

"I think... I'm not sure how you see me. I was so convinced you still craved vengeance."

"Perhaps that's because I'm not the one who has trouble seeing you for what you are. You doubt my intentions because you doubt your own worth."

Ianthe stood arrested. Was it doubt about her own worthiness that challenged her, rather than his? She'd always considered herself fearless and determined, but when it came to this, to a place where she was laid bare, all of her old vulnerabilities rose to the fore.

"Oh, my goodness," she whispered. It was true. All of it was true.

"Do you wish to see yourself through my eyes?"

Coldness shivered through her heart, but that was fear. Doubt. Unworthiness. Those old demons that haunted her. Ianthe inhaled sharply, heat rising through her cheeks. "I'm not sure."

"Be brave," he whispered, stroking her hips with those talented hands. "You have a lover's soul, a healer's soul. Passionate, affectionate—when you can give yourself over to trust—and nurturing." His hands stroked her hair out of her face. "Every time I have faced doubt in the past week, your first instinct has been to protect me from it, or to help me see past it. You kiss my scars, as if they are precious, and constantly tell me I was not at fault, when you will not set aside your own guilt. You see my mental scars as something to be overcome, not something to be ashamed of, and with you by my side, it makes me feel as though I *can* overcome my vulnerabilities. I heal, because of you, Ianthe. I see a future unfold, because of you. I hope, and it is all you. You are my first champion, but when it comes to yourself, your courage falters." Anger lit in his eyes. "Your father deserves to be hung, drawn, and quartered for what he has done to you."

Heat flooded her eyes, and then wetness. "I know what he told me was always lies designed to trap me in a cage of doubt, but no matter how much I tell myself that, it's difficult... difficult to believe."

"It's terrifying to admit that I might never wield my power again."

Ianthe stroked his hand. "Perhaps... we can both work on our weaknesses. Together."

"Together," he whispered. "Marry me, Ianthe. Not for Louisa. Not for me. For yourself. Trust me."

Ianthe closed her eyes. She would do it for Louisa *and* for herself—for that trembling, well-guarded scrap of her heart that barely dared. She would make herself vulnerable to him. If he wanted to cut out her heart, then she was serving it up to him on a platter. *I love you.* For a moment, she was frightened that she'd said it aloud, but Lucien gave no sign of hearing it. His hands stroked the silk that covered her hips as his hungry gaze roved over her. Patiently, he waited for her answer.

"Very well."

"Very well," he grumbled, but his hands tightened on her hips, as if he'd feared that she'd say no. "I offer her an earldom, and she says 'very well'."

"What would you have me say?" Her heart felt curiously light, unfettered for the first time in years.

"I would have you overwrought with pleasure, my dear." A faint smile touched his mouth, a teasing light in his eyes. "But perhaps I know just how to take you there."

"Or perhaps," she responded, sliding her hands up over his bare shoulders, "I will take *you* there."

His eyes lit with curiosity. "You're going to dump me in the bath if you're not careful."

"Well, we can't be having that." She slid her hands down the chiseled muscle of his torso and abdominals, tugging a finger into the knot of his towel. "It would be a shame to get you all wet."

Slowly, she pushed him back toward the bath. He went down, one hand gripping the bath rim, his legs still hanging over the edge. The towel was sopping wet, unraveling to reveal the hard length of his cock. Water slopped everywhere as his long body folded into the bath.

"I can see that you like getting your own way," he said, with an interested gleam in his eye.

Ianthe bit her lip, trying to suppress her laughter. "I'm so terribly sorry. But look... Now you're all wet. Whatever shall we do?"

Those amber eyes narrowed. "Well, you can start by getting rid of this." He tossed the drenched towel at her, and it splatted against her chest. "Then you can climb in here yourself, madam."

Ianthe dropped the towel. "So impatient," she admonished, grabbing a fistful of her skirts and stepping into the bath.

He dragged her down into his lap. Hot water wet her thighs and waist. The crepe of her skirts floated around them.

One hand cupped her nape, dragging her down for his kiss.

Here she was confident. He wanted her. The truth of that could not be more apparent. At least, no matter what happened, they would always have this. A way to communicate without words... A means to bridge the gap between them. And she trusted this, if nothing else.

Afterward, they lay in the still darkness of his room, limbs entwined, and naked flesh pressed against each other. Lucien stroked her back with trailing fingertips, as though lost deep in thought.

"Having regrets?" Ianthe teased, tiptoeing her fingers up the hard plane of his stomach.

Lucien shifted, turning so that they were face-to-face, their palms linked. "About?"

"The thought of being leg-shackled?"

Heat darkened his eyes, and his palm curled over her hip, sliding down to cup her bare bottom. "There are other compensations, I'm finding." He leaned forward to tongue her breast. "Like having you at my beck and call, day and night."

Ianthe moaned, submitting to his skilled mouth. They weren't the words she'd hoped for, but then, she was the one who'd begun in a teasing manner. Cupping his cheek, she forced his mouth from her skin. If he started this again, she'd never get any sleep. "Lucien."

"I like that." A rumble sounded from deep within his chest, like a cat's purr. Lucien tucked his head beneath her jaw, nibbling at her throat. "My name on your lips."

"I like it too." Unbidden, she tilted her face up, allowing him access to her exposed throat. Soft lips traced her collarbone. It was a slower seduction than any he'd undertaken before.

But then, it had never meant anything before beyond sex.

Ianthe bit her lip. She could feel the change between them, tenuous and delicate. He touched her with reverent hands, curious and explorative, as though he had all the time in the world to learn her. Or as though he was intricately interested in each inch of skin beneath his touch. She didn't know what to make of it. All she knew was that she liked it. Immensely. It felt like she was a precious, precious thing, held in his protective hands.

It felt like he cared, like she was the only woman he wanted. Ever.

With a sigh, her thighs parted, and Lucien came over her, the tip of his cock breaching her soft core. One hand cupped under her bottom, he thrust hard, filling her to the core. Ianthe gasped.

"Gods, woman, I can never get enough of you." Lucien nipped her chin, then soothed the small ache with a kiss. "You feel so fucking good."

And so did he. Every inch of him burned within her, his weight a welcome... *Every inch.* Her eyes went wide.

"Stop!" Ianthe's hand pressed against his chest, staying him.

Faint light from the fire warmed the sharp line of his cheek and lit those devilish eyes. "What's wrong?"

"It feels too good," she whispered, "because we forgot the sheath!"

Lucien groaned and buried his face in the pillow beside her ear. "I forgot." His hips gave one last tiny, yearning thrust. "Not that I would regret it. Lady's choice, however." Resting on his forearms, he began to withdraw.

"Wait," she whispered.

Their eyes met.

Ianthe couldn't quite find the words.

"Are you going to torture me all night?" Suppressed emotion strained within his muscles as he sighed. "Ianthe? Do you want me to get the sheath?"

Every little move rocked him within her. Ianthe swallowed, her fingers curling over his shoulders. "Did you mean it?"

"Mean what?"

"That you would not regret it?"

Their eyes met again. Something seemed to shift in Lucien's expression. *Yes.* With a soft shudder of his hips, he thrust within her again. Slow. Steady. Taunting. His decision, at least, had been made. Ianthe shifted beneath him, her inner muscles locking tight around him. Her palms softened on his shoulders. Her heart was full to bursting; this decision had consequences.

But he had asked for her trust. He had asked for marriage. If there were to be consequences from this, then a little part of her welcomed them.

A baby. The thought both terrified her and exhilarated her. The phantom ache in her heart, the part of her that had never nursed her daughter, desperately wanted a second chance to prove herself.

"If it happened, I would welcome it," Lucien whispered, his breath warm against her ear.

"What will be, will be." This time, she would not be alone. This time, she was not so frightened. She could do this, if it happened. She felt closer to Lucien than she'd ever felt before.

Tucking her knee over his elbow, he shifted her position, so that his next thrust took her by surprise.

"Oh, my goodness!"

Lucien smiled his devil's smile. "Like that, do you?" He fucked her again, nice and slow, a hint of strain tightening his jaw.

His cock rasped over something deep within her. Ianthe shifted restlessly. "Yes. Yes!"

"More?"

"More!" she gasped. "Oh, Lucien! Lucien!"

The kiss took her by surprise, his mouth seeking hers in the warm dark, his tongue plunging within to tangle with her own. Hips pistoning within her, he shifted the angle until his cock rasped over something deep within her. Ianthe came apart with a gentle cry, her fingers clenching in his sweaty hair, her face screwed up in ecstasy.

Lucien came with a soft grunt, the muscles beside his spine trembling beneath her hand as he flexed within her. The spill of his seed wet her, and then with a gasp, he collapsed on top of her. Hot breath burned her throat, and the press of his weight left her breathless before he rolled to one hip.

One thing became clear in the quiet room as they caught their breaths together.

Their heartbeats were echoing as one.

The bond was intensifying.

Lucien caught her eye as he bowed to kiss her lips. *So it does.*

Ianthe paused, brushing her fingertips against his cheek. *I heard that.*

Lucien merely smiled. Rolling onto his side, his cock slid from her damp body as he tucked her against his hip. His large hand splayed over her midriff, tracing the faint silvery lines that speared out like a corona from her navel. "It makes sense now, why you could never allow yourself pleasure before."

Ianthe curled into him. "It's not the same for a woman as it is for a man. It doesn't always happen for me."

"Especially when your daughter is missing."

"Especially then," she whispered. "That time on the piano... I felt so guilty. How could I possibly enjoy myself when she was out there alone? But I needed you so badly then, for I was so close to breaking."

They stared at each other, perfectly in tune with each other.

Ianthe swallowed. Intimacy still unnerved her a little. "When do you wish to get married?"

"Not yet. There are other considerations right now. Morgana is a threat, and she dared put her hands on Louisa once to get at you. I fear she will do it again." Hard lines bracketed Lucien's mouth; this was a man who would not be crossed. "I intend to make certain Louisa is never harmed again, even if I have to destroy that bitch myself."

"How do we find her?" Ianthe's voice was small in the dark. This was her fault, because she had not trusted Lucien to help her with Louisa.

"We begin here," Lucien replied, spreading her hair out across their pillow and stroking his hands through it. A casual gesture, but one not lost on her. It was intimate, this moment between them.

"Here?" He was distracting her. She couldn't quite fathom why they should start here.

"Someone left the letters on your bed," Lucien said. "Someone inside this house knows where Morgana is. We simply have to find out who."

A chill ran through her. She'd never thought to look for the traitor on the inside, because when she had no allies, she'd had no power. She had not dared, because one small misstep could have cost her Louisa. That was not the case now.

"But in the morning, Ianthe. In the morning. We both need sleep, or we're more likely to trip over Morgana's wards and hand her our lives on a platter. I don't know about you, but I'm exhausted. Some insatiable wench keeps demanding that I tup her."

"Wench," she objected, pinching him lightly.

Lucien laughed. And as she curled into the arc of his arms, she couldn't help thinking that, for the first time, his smile looked genuine.

CHAPTER TWENTY-FOUR

'Expression is dangerous because it is tied to emotion, and what is emotion, but a weakness?'

– Morgana

THE BUTLER knew nothing, nor the downstairs maid. Ianthe paced in front of the fireplace, her nerves a mess, as Lucien questioned the florid cook. He glanced up from his last question and shook his head ever so slightly at her, over the head of the weeping Mrs. Mayhue. With his newfound abilities, he was finding it easier to see who was lying and who was not. Now they had three people on their list that knew nothing about the letters and blackmail.

That left Mrs. Hastings and Thea.

A horrible, yawning pit began to gnaw inside Ianthe's stomach as Lucien saw Mrs. Mayhue out. *Not Thea. Please, not Thea.* But who in her household would be vulnerable to outside influence or deception? A young girl newly apprenticed to the mistress of the household, with her own

347

dark past? Or the extremely efficient housekeeper who ran the place like a tight ship?

"Come in," Lucien directed, and Thea walked hesitantly into the light, her face pale and her eyes huge in her young face. A young girl, trying so hard to be an adult. Trying so hard not to—

Thea took one look at Ianthe, and then her face screwed up and she burst into tears.

"Oh, hell," Ianthe muttered, and drew the poor girl into her arms. "You little fool. You should have come to me."

Hypocrisy at its worst, for had she herself not been in this very situation? It was difficult to find yourself alone in the world, not knowing who to trust or where to turn to. She could never blame Thea for what she'd done. No, her anger was aimed at Morgana, that manipulative, vicious bitch who knew just how to alienate her victims.

I am going to wipe that smug little smile right off Morgana's face. With my fist.

"Talk to us, Thea. Tell us what happened," Ianthe murmured.

"I d-didn't w-want to do it," Thea murmured, lifting her head just enough for her words to escape. "B-but they said that... that if I didn't, they'd t-tell you about... about what I'd done and you'd throw me into the streets, and... You know I cannot go back home. Not to my mother. You know!"

Ianthe clutched her closer, her eyes closing in despair. How well she knew that feeling. Thea was only eighteen, after all, not so very much older than Ianthe herself had been when she'd found herself facing similar circumstances. "Shush," she whispered, pressing a kiss to her ward's temples. "I would never throw you out, Thea. You should know that."

"I d-didn't know what to do, and all they wanted was for me to leave the letters on your bed. I didn't see the harm in it." Thea's eyes glimmered as she looked up sharply. "You know I'd never have done anything more. I promise. I—"

"I know."

Ianthe let the girl sob against her shoulder until her tears were finally worn out. Lucien poured a small snifter of brandy for the girl, watching silently as Ianthe settled her on the sofa.

"Here," he murmured, offering the glass to Thea. "This might help settle your nerves."

"Tell us about it, please," Ianthe said, offering her a handkerchief.

"He said if I didn't do as he asked, then he'd—"

"Who said?" Lucien asked sharply.

"There's a... a group of young sorcerers. We were all approached, usually out shopping or visiting or on our rare half days off."

"Approached by who?" Lucien demanded.

Thea's reddened eyes lifted to his. "H-his name is Noah Guthrie. He said he'd help me learn my magic faster. Said that the Order just wanted to shackle it, to tie me to their leg and turn me into a good little p-puppet. At first I said no, but then... I couldn't make the rope knot." She turned to Ianthe. "You kept telling me to keep trying, but... I just... I just wanted to know how to be a sorcerer. I didn't want to fail anymore. So I went to his meeting. I thought it couldn't hurt to attend just one... And there were others there like me; apprentices, those thrown out of the Order, those who'd never been found. And Noah said there was n-nothing to be afraid of, that you were just repeating your propaganda against..."

"Against?" Ianthe whispered.

"Expression." The word was a dry whisper.

"So he encouraged you to use Expression repeatedly," Lucien said, then sighed and scraped a hand over his face.

"There w-was to be an initiation." The girl's face paled. "We all swore by our blood that we would never betray our circle, and Noah said that Eliza, one of my friends, had betrayed her oaths and told her Master. He said she h-had to b-be... punished..." The girl dissolved in tears again. "He said we had to do it. It was only supposed to be a demonstration, but something... something happened. Eliza stopped breathing. I don't know why. I don't know how—"

"I should have guessed." Bloody hell. "You've been distracted and out of sorts for nearly a month, when you were doing so well beforehand. I didn't understand why you'd slid backward with your control, but guilt would do it. Fear. All of those emotions eating away at you." Ianthe shook her head, then dragged the girl into her arms. "You didn't hurt Eliza. There is no magic in this world that could make her die from breaking a blood oath. You were tricked. Most likely it was poison, or some expert sorcery you couldn't detect. I know the Sicarii can wield a stiletto-sharp whip of magic that can kill at a distance and leave you none the wiser. He probably did it himself, so he'd get what he wanted. A group of young, inexperienced sorcerers that he could blackmail."

Thea sobbed.

"Thea, sweetie." Ianthe leaned back to brush the girl's hair out of her wet face. "Can you tell me where this Noah Guthrie met with you?"

Thea wiped her face. "I can do better than that. I followed him one day. We—he and I... We were..." Her gaze dropped, as if she were ashamed. "And I thought he might have been out walking with someone else, so I followed him back to a house, and there was an older lady there. He called her Morgana, and she asked about me, asked if I was doing what she wanted me to do. I'm so sorry, Miss Martin. I knew in that moment that he never cared about me. I knew I was in trouble."

"I see." She wanted to get her hands on Noah Guthrie and wring his bloody neck. Toying with a young girl's emotions like this was both cowardly and cruel. "The address Thea?"

"I don't know where it is precisely, I can't remember, but it was in the eastern end of Knightsbridge. A pretty stone house with rose gardens all around it. I didn't think to note the precise address."

Ianthe released the breath she'd been holding. "Thank you, Thea. It's a start."

CHAPTER TWENTY-FIVE

DRAKE ARRIVED barely ten minutes later. Ianthe had gone to check on Louisa, so Lucien stalled his father's words and led him to the conservatory where he'd first taken tea with Ianthe. It seemed a lifetime since that meeting. How much things had changed.

"How is she?" Drake demanded the second the door had shut. He looked like he'd aged a decade overnight.

"Preparing herself for battle," Lucien replied. "Upset, of course, but holding herself together. I would not care to be Morgana when she gets her hands upon her."

"And she has... her daughter with her?"

"Our daughter," Lucien said softly. There was no surprise in his father's eyes.

"You knew."

Drake sighed. "Not at first. Several years ago, Ianthe saw you in the street and turned white as a ghost. She pointed you out to me as Louisa's father, and I realized then that the girl was of my blood."

Lucien strolled toward the orange tree, examining it, but seeing none of it. "Ianthe told me you were the one who insisted that she work with me to recover the blade."

"Yes."

"She thinks you did it to free me from Bedlam and help restore me to the Order's good graces, plus of course, there's the fact that you could be certain I wasn't involved, incarcerated as I was. And if you're that good at pulling strings, one can imagine that you might possibly have meant to set us on a collision course with each other." This time he looked up.

Drake eyed him steadily. "Ianthe needed to confront her past."

"One could say the same for me."

"One could."

"I dislike being pushed and pulled about."

With a sigh, Drake dragged out one of the wrought iron chairs and sank into it. "I know you think the very worst of me, but the truth is the decision killed three birds with one stone. It wasn't as though I was sitting there rubbing my hands together like some Machiavellian villain in some penny dreadful. I had few resources, and it seemed like a good idea at the time. I haven't particularly given it a great deal more thought, considering events, but sometimes you take a gamble."

"With people's lives?"

"Yes," Drake snapped, "with people's lives. That's what a position of power means. It's not a privilege; it's a responsibility. If you want to take this up with me at a later time, pray do so, but to be honest, Lucien, I've got a great deal on my mind."

"Considering your ex-wife wants you dead and now has the means to do so."

A flash of something—pain?—shadowed his father's brow. Then the man wiped his face free of expression. "If Morgana wanted to cut my heart out with that Blade, then I would offer myself up willingly, if I could trust her to make a deal and uphold her end of it." He swallowed. "She has Eleanor, Lucien. I know that means nothing to you, but to me, Eleanor is everything. If I could trade myself for her, I would without a second's doubt."

That dark head bowed with weariness. "I am what this position has forced me to become, but don't think for one second that it's easy to make these decisions. I made a choice to let Eleanor do something risky, and now she is paying for it. I don't even know if she's still alive... I feel the weight of that decision, as I do all of the others. It will haunt me until the day I die, but I am Prime. Either I make those decisions, or I sit and twiddle my thumbs while my enemies cut my feet out from under me, including all of those allied with me."

Damn it. How could he hate this man in this moment, when Lucien knew exactly how he'd feel if Morgana had her hands on Ianthe?

Drake lifted a weary head. "May I ask, did my gamble pay off?"

"Yes," Lucien said tightly, "it did. I'm going to marry her."

"And restore some of Louisa's respectability and Ianthe's good name? That's very noble of you."

They stared at each other.

"Ah," Drake said, his eyes softening. "So it's like that, is it?"

"I don't know what you mean."

"I think you do." Drake pushed to his feet, as though he could see straight through him. He leaned heavily on his cane. "I knew you wouldn't hurt her, Lucien. You always owned a soft spot for those who had need and those in dire circumstances."

As if he had any inkling of the son he'd seeded or his personality. Lucien snorted and looked away.

"Do you think that I didn't care? Do you think I just turned my back on you for all those years? I always had someone watching over you. Your governess, then your tutor, and finally, your sorcery Master. Rathbourne either didn't care or he didn't know. All of them delivered frequent reports on how you were as a boy and the type of man you were growing to be. Through their words, I watched as you scored your first run at cricket, or that time you broke your arm protecting your friend from those bullies at Eton. I was there when your powers finally came in, and it gave me great pleasure to know that you had a talent for both of your parent's gifts, wards and divination—"

Lucien cut him off with a sharp slash of his hand. He couldn't hear this. He wouldn't. "The truth is, you might have watched over me, or you might not have, who knows? But the fact is, you *weren't* there. All you were to me was a stranger. Now I hear tales of prophecies explaining why you couldn't be in my life, and I find I have two brothers, two more men who mean nothing to me. They, and you, feel like a memory I can't quite grasp, some detail right on the tip of my tongue... But ultimately, it doesn't matter."

"Then why are you here?" Drake asked in a tired voice. Hurt shone in his eyes, but Lucien turned away, refusing to see it.

Hell, he knew what it felt like. There was a gaping chasm in his chest, as if his heart had been ripped out years ago. He didn't want to see the echo of it in his sire's eyes, or he feared the carefully leashed emotions inside him would come bubbling out in a spew of vile words and anger. Would his own daughter think the same when she discovered he was her father? For that's where Ianthe was right now, breaking the news to her. He would have been there himself, but a part of him was outright terrified that Louisa would hate him.

"I am here because a dangerous relic has been placed in the hands of a madwoman," Lucien replied, nostrils flaring as he fought to contain harsher words. "I am here because at the moment, I am nothing more than a burden to Ianthe, rather than an ally." Pausing by the windows, he stared out over the city sprawl. Reticence loomed in his chest, but the truth had struck him last night, and though he'd fought with this decision all morning, he had found no other answer to his dilemma. Pride was only costing him—and Ianthe. "Last night exacerbated a problem I've been dealing with. Ever since the demon's assault, I've been... highly sensitized." Lucien swallowed hard, looking down at his curled fists. Exposing such a weakness felt like cutting out his heart all over again. "I cannot utilize my power. I cannot protect Ianthe against her enemies, and I can't do anything to protect my own child if I am like this. I–I don't know if I will ever be able to use my power again. Not fully."

His words fell into a chasm of silence.

"Then why ask me for help?"

"Ianthe said you might be able to help me. Your talent lies within wards, but it's rumored that you understand sorcery and the barriers a mind can put up against it."

Something brushed against his trouser leg, the same cat who'd been toying with Ianthe's skirts the first morning. Luc picked it up, feeling the warm purr against his chest. He still couldn't look at his father.

"The question isn't: can I help you? The question is more along the lines of: will you let me? I need to explore your aura, and that requires a great deal of trust. You need to open yourself up to a psychic probe."

Ash couldn't have tasted dryer in his mouth, but he didn't feel the Prime would ask this of him if it weren't necessary. "I'll try." He had Louisa and Ianthe to think of.

"You'll also need to describe the assault in full. I need to understand what happened so I can perhaps treat the barriers your unconscious mind has put in place. From the sounds of it, there was trauma involved, and perhaps your mind associates your power with pain. Now, every time you try to channel your power, some part of you remembers what happens. It's like forcing yourself to touch a hot frying pan after you've already burnt yourself badly. You could be subconsciously stopping yourself from performing sorcerous works. The mind is a powerful tool, and when sorcery comes from your will, your conscious mind, then it is like fighting yourself every time you try to wield it.

"It's also not the sort of thing that can be dealt with in a single afternoon either, Lucien. This will require frequent visits and meditation to reroute the way your mind thinks when it comes to sorcery. If you've subconsciously allied sorcery with pain, then it's going to take a great deal of effort to retrain yourself."

These were words he understood. It was far easier to deal with fact, rather than emotion. Emotion had beaten him bloody over the past twelve hours. "Then I'm going to be of no use this afternoon?"

"It is unlikely that you will regain your abilities within the space of a day," Drake said carefully.

There it was. The truth. "I can't sit by and watch her walk into danger."

"Then don't," Drake replied. "Let me examine you. There's a possibility you could act as someone else's wellspring, if you're not mentally scarred too badly."

"Wellspring?" A cold trickle traced his spine. Lord Rathbourne had wanted him to act as wellspring to him a year ago—to give his own power up to the man, to use as Lord Rathbourne desired. Look how well that had gone.

"I'm sure you trust Ianthe," Drake replied. "She could do it, if you allow it."

Lucien licked dry lips. Every muscle in his abdomen tightened, as though anticipating a blow. Bloody hell. Anything but this... But then, how else could he be of use?

Squeezing his eyes shut, he didn't want to accept that fact. But he trusted her, didn't he?

After all, had she not placed her own trust in his hands by giving him the truth? How easy it was, when you were the one asking for trust, not the one giving it. "How do we do this then?"

The Prime turned the weight of those silver eyes upon him. "You will need your Anchor."

It started with a faint tracing probe that lit along his nerves like ants marching a hot trail over his skin. Lucien's muscles locked tight, but he forced himself to remain still on the daybed, trying not to instinctively shove against that tentative touch.

"It cannot hurt you," Drake murmured, the words sounding as though they came from a distance.

A warm hand slid into his, and a familiar perfume caused him to turn his head slightly to the side. "I'm here," Ianthe murmured. "You're safe. Your father and I are both here."

Confusion reigned. He danced between both memory and the present. The words 'Your father' brought to mind Lord Rathbourne's face. Lucien shook his head. "No. No." That was the day he'd learned the truth and his entire world had split apart.

"Take me back to that day, Lucien," Drake murmured. "It cannot hurt you, not now. Take me back to that moment when I sent the demon back to its master."

Fire. Pain. Betrayal. They all lashed through him, leaving him twisting on the daybed. He relived it. Fought against the demon, throwing all of his power at it and feeling it burn him up from within...

"Begone!" he screamed, and the demon flinched as he turned his will upon it.

Then a smile stretched over its lips. "For the moment, perhapsss... But one day soon we shall have a reckoning."

Seconds later, it vanished, and he was left lying on the floor of Rathbourne's house, panting, with his skin on fire.

Lucien sat up with a scream, pain lancing through his skull as he jolted free of the memory. There were warm hands on him, two sets of them, and the pain instantly lessened as Drake's power washed over him.

Gasping, he held onto Ianthe's shoulders. "I didn't remember it saying such a thing. It told me that one day it would be back to take its revenge upon me."

Both of them were silent.

"What's wrong?" he demanded, turning his gaze upon the Prime, who looked just as troubled.

The Prime shook his head, "Nothing's—"

"*Don't* lie to me!"

Lucien could feel the truth through the bond he shared with Ianthe. He may not know the man, but *she* did, and she knew when something was bothering the Prime.

"You said you banished the demon, but..."

"But?" His voice was tight.

"I don't think you did."

The words were a blow. *No.* No. It couldn't be free. It would have come after him, surely. No demon had ever submitted freely to the yokes of servitude. Only dark rituals and immense sacrifices could raise one, but in every story he'd ever heard, they'd all turned on their Master's the second they had a chance.

And this demon... it had had its chances.

"It's moving freely about on our plane?" Ianthe demanded, horror in her voice. "Surely we would know. We'd have heard news, or there would have been massacres, or... something. A demon cannot hide its presence for long. It would need to fuel itself with blood."

Drake hesitated. "I think you managed to force it to retreat to its plane, but I don't think you entirely shut the gates to it. There's something in your head, and it's not me or Ianthe. There's a bond there, as if *something* is tied to you. Plunging you into a trance awoke it. I could feel an alien presence, a strong, alien presence, staring back at me."

Like the day he'd been at Lady Eberhardt's and peered into her Shadows of Night. Lucien's blood went cold.

"That's not all you meant to say," Ianthe whispered. "I can see it in your face."

Fear pounded in his chest. Lucien couldn't deal with the demon again. He just couldn't. He'd barely survived the first time, and he was but a *shell* of that man.

"You're not a shell," Ianthe whispered absently, patting his hand. Her eyes never left the Prime's face, as if she didn't even realize what she'd just said, but both he and Drake shot her a hard gaze each.

Then they turned that look on each other.

"Can it hurt me? Can it... return?" Lucien demanded. "You owe me the answer to that, if nothing else."

"I don't know." Drake raked a hand through his hair. "Lucien, I think you *are* a gateway for the demon now. It hasn't quite worked out how to get back, but I fear, given enough time, that it will. I've managed to repair some of the damage its psychic assault caused, and I've warded your mind against it, so it cannot see through your eyes, or whatever it's doing in there, but there's no guarantee it cannot break free."

"Then what should I do?" he choked out. "Kill myself? Or—"

"Don't be ridiculous," his father snapped. "Who knows what your death would bring about? A summoning ritual needs some sort of sacrifice to even bring a demon through; perhaps your death would be the sacrifice it requires to manifest again? Maybe that's what it's waiting for? Then it has a nice, freshly delivered body to inhabit, already flush with power."

Lucien shoved to his feet. "I cannot live with this in my head!"

"Lucien." Ianthe stood, in a swirl of violet skirts, and caught his sleeve. He could feel her reaching out to him through the bond they shared, and that small hand stroking his sleeve was enough to settle his racing heartbeat a fraction. "You're not alone."

It all unfurled in his mind. Ianthe, standing hand in hand with him against the demon, trying to win a battle that would never be won. Ianthe, motionless on the floor in a pool of blood, cut down as easily as a child. By his own hand. The demon's hand. *Yess*, something whispered inside him, and he flinched.

This couldn't happen. He took a step away from her, even as Drake slowly rose to his feet behind her.

Make it swift. Do it. "I release you from your bond," he told her, forcing the words through stiff lips.

Ianthe flinched back, as if struck. "What?"

"Our deal is done. I will serve out my part of it, but I release you from yours." He couldn't stand it any longer. Catching the Prime's gaze, he turned away from the flash of grief he saw there.

Long strides carried him to the door, then a swish of skirts hurried after him. "Lucien!" she called.

He ignored her. Emotion seethed within him, throbbing in his right temple. It felt like his skull was going to split open.

He knew what that feeling was now. The demon, lurking malevolently inside him.

"Lucien! Wait!"

"There's no point. I need to fetch my coat. We still have Morgana to roust. Unfortunately, I don't think I'm going to be much help." Bitterness flavored his words.

"Don't be a coward," she yelled. "Do you think I'm an idiot? You're afraid the demon will take you over and then you'll hurt either myself or Louisa."

"Yes!" he hissed, turning on his heel back toward her and bearing down on her. He flung one arm out wide. "I swore to protect you, and my daughter. I cannot do that when I'm the danger!"

"It can be managed," she began, in a more reasonable tone. "Drake knows a great deal—"

"You weren't there!" His lungs heaved with emotion, and Lucien raked a hand through his disheveled hair. Everything he'd fought so hard for in the past year... His sanity, his freedom, now this. Now her. The last sacrifice was almost too much to bear. "It nearly tore me apart, Ianthe! I couldn't stop it! I couldn't force its will to mine! And I tried." His voice broke. "I tried to stop it from killing those people, but I couldn't." He forced himself to harden.

"I know better this time. I can't fight it if it chooses to try and take me."

"Then what are you going to do? Tuck tail and run? How far can you go, Lucien? Is there any place that's safe? A mountain top in the Andes? The Arctic? Where can you go that it cannot reach you?"

"I don't know, but I guess I can find out. I'll do this for you. I'll help you take down Morgana, but then we're finished."

Ianthe searched his eyes, shaking her head. "No." She reached for him, but he took a step away, and her hand curled into a fist, then dropped. "You said you would marry me."

"I'm sorry." This was the way it had to be.

They stared at each other, the clock in the hallway ticking out the seconds. A single tear slid down Ianthe's porcelain cheek, but her mouth had that defiant cast to it that he knew too well.

He couldn't stand it any longer. Taking a step back, he shoved his hands into his pockets. "I'll fetch my pistols. Send for—"

"No! I won't give in so easily! What I know is that you stood by me, regardless of my actions. You believed in me," she cried out, scurrying after him in a swish of skirts, "when I didn't even believe in myself. I cannot offer you any less, and now you know how it feels... to be afraid of yourself, to doubt yourself, and yet have someone stand here and challenge you to prevail." She stabbed a finger into his chest. "I took that step. I believed you, even when I doubted myself, because I couldn't live in fear anymore. This is your moment, Lucien. *Your* fear to conquer. And maybe it will happen, maybe we'll lose this fight. But maybe we won't..."

Maybe we won't... The dream of it ached, bitter and sharp, for that was all it was. A dream. He shook his head, turning away from her. "This is different. This threatens you all." His boot heels rang out on the marble tiles, but not hers. She wasn't following him. It ached, like a fist around his heart, but better that it end this way.

He wouldn't forgive himself if it ended with Ianthe hurt.

"I love you!"

Shock welled up through him. His feet wouldn't move, but his head turned, drawn inexorably toward her. "*What?*" The words felt like they were torn from him.

And there she was, standing at the end of the hallway, with her fists clenched and her pulse pounding in her throat. Stubborn, passionate Ianthe, with her heart on her sleeve. He could shatter it, for it was as fragile as glass, and then she'd let him go, and she'd be safe... But his own chest ached with longing. Something there would break along with hers.

Ianthe's expression turned stubborn. "I love you, you fool, and I will not let you go. I will not release you from this bond! If you won't fight with me, then I will fight *for* you. You need me." Her voice cracked. "And I need you."

"I can't." This was the only thing he couldn't fight against. For how long had he ached to hear those words?

"You don't know that," she shot back, taking a step toward him. "This is a knee-jerk reaction because you're scared, and I understand that." Stepping closer now, she reached up to cup his cheek. "Don't throw away everything we have, because of fear. We don't know that the demon *can* overtake you. It's been a year, Lucien. Why hasn't it tried? What is it waiting for? Don't you think it would have taken its shot while you were starved and tormented in

Bedlam? Weak? And now you have me, and I am *not* going to share you with some creature from a hell dimension."

He turned his face away, but she didn't back down. Cupping his face in both hands, she forced him to meet her gaze. "I love you, you fool. And it scares the hell out of me, but I believe that together we can face just about anything this world can throw at us."

"Ianthe—"

Reaching up, she slid his arms around his neck. That warm body pressed against his, her cheek brushing against his jaw. He was smothered in a cloud of lilac perfume. Drenched in her heat and her touch, he had the feeling that he was no longer alone in this.

"We will do whatever needs to be done," she whispered as his arms hesitantly curled around her waist. "Of all of us, Drake knows the most about Greater Demons and their reach. He can look into whether this has ever happened before, but for now, you are safe. It cannot reach you, or touch you here, and if it does, then I'm your Anchor. I won't let it drag you under."

How insane, to think that but a few days ago they'd been at war. Lucien shut his eyes and buried his face in her hair. "You're a fool," he whispered gruffly. "You should be running from me and this bond. I–I will release you—"

"I don't wish it, and neither do you, if you would only stop and be honest with yourself for once."

Lucien buried his face in her hair and squeezed her tight, because, if he *was* being honest with himself, he did want her. And Louisa. Forever.

"Of course, you do," she retorted, and for some insane reason, he couldn't stop himself from laughing.

"You're insane," he rasped.

"Trust me. We can defeat this."

Lucien caught her face in his hands and drew her mouth up to his in a punishing kiss. *Brave, stubborn Ianthe.* What would he do without her?

"You have something to say," Ianthe said, pouring herself a cup of tea and trying to stop her hands from shaking after that little revelation. Lucien had just left to arm himself, and they needed to get moving, but she could feel Drake watching her. "Spit it out. Do you think I'm wrong to hold him to our bond?"

"No." Drake leaned back in his chair, looking tired. "I think you're possibly the only thing that could hold him together through this."

She took a mouthful of tepid tea and frowned. "What do you mean by that?"

"Demons cannot force a human to do anything; it has something to do with that inner strength of will that shields us at our very core. We naturally resist intrusions to our very sense of self. So they toy with emotions, Ianthe. Fear, loneliness, and lack of hope all give the creature a path to slowly chisel away at. Once a man gives up hope, he hasn't the means to fight the creature, but Lucien's feelings for you are powerful. That gives him strength."

"Will it be enough?" she whispered.

"I don't know."

Ianthe set the cup down. Silence weighed heavy in the room. "You do know that I'm sorry." And now she wasn't speaking about Lucien.

"There is nothing to forgive."

"I gave them the Blade, Drake! It could bring you down, and you know it, and—"

A hand pressed gently over hers. "There is nothing to forgive," he repeated in a quiet, firm voice and squeezed her fingers.

Tears sprang into her eyes, her throat thickening. "You have always been too good to me."

"Your greatest problem, Ianthe, is the fact that you don't believe yourself worthy of kindness. You are more than worthy. In fact, you should demand it. Sometimes I should like to take your father by the throat and beat him bloody for what he's done to you."

"He's not my father," she whispered, feeling it for the first time in her veins. "You are. You always have been. If you'll have me."

With a choked sound, Drake drew her into his arms and kissed the top of her forehead. "I could not be prouder to call myself thus."

Ianthe rested her forehead against his shoulder. All her life she'd felt like she was an abomination. No matter what she did, she was always wrong, and the guilt of all of her choices had been a silent condemnation of her own making. It was Grant Martin's voice that she heard in her head still, telling her she had lost the blade and cost poor Eleanor whatever torment she was suffering at the moment.

She could listen to Grant Martin's voice forever, if she let herself, but it was Drake's words, Drake's love for her that pushed her to see that to do so would only be a lie. She was tired of lies. She was tired of guilt.

She deserved better for herself.

"I will help you get Eleanor back." A weight had lifted from her shoulders. Purpose descended, cool, crystal, and decisive. "I promise you, we will get both her and the Blade back. Then we shall make Morgana rue the day she stepped foot in our lives. But first," she said, standing and brushing the wrinkles from her skirts, "I must make sure my daughter is well, and then I will check on my Shield."

Drake's lips curled in a faint smile. "That's the first time you've called her that." He was happy for her, despite his own problems. "It's about time you realized you are the best thing that ever happened to Louisa. Now go and be her mother."

"I will," she promised, looking him directly in the eye, "on one condition."

"Oh?"

"The next time you look your stubborn son in the eye, you need to promise that you'll set aside your own sense of guilt too."

CHAPTER
TWENTY-SIX

CLEO HAD never thought herself a violent woman, but she was considering poison as she sat and sipped her tea the following morning with Morgana. *You are in bed with a monster.* The words kept repeating in her mind. Poison would be too kind.

"You look... tired, my dear. Sebastian's been kind to you?" Morgana seemed exuberant this morning. She kept humming under her breath.

"Quite." Until she knew the full extent of the situation she had found herself in, Cleo didn't dare be too rude.

"You know," Morgana stirred her tea, then tapped her teaspoon on the top of it before setting it aside with a clink, "you and I could become friends."

That did it. Cleo couldn't contain her bitter laugh. "Friends?"

"It is better to be friends than to be enemies," her mother-in-law said.

"You mean, I would live longer if I professed to be your ally." It was one thing to be polite to a viper, quite another to listen to this drivel.

The following silence was pointed. Morgana set her teacup down, judging by the rattle of the saucer. "I have no such intentions toward you, my dear. Indeed, you are a very valuable little—"

"And now you sound like my father."

"I wonder what he'd think of this little display of viciousness from his precious daughter, hmm?"

"He'd probably mouth something meaningful to you, pat you on the hand, and then come to ask me precisely how to bring you down." Cleo bit into a biscuit. She was through with being helpless. "You are two of a kind, after all."

Morgana actually laughed. "Well, perhaps you aren't the little fool I mistook you for after all. He doesn't see it, does he?"

"Who?"

"Your father. He thinks you his obedient little pet. Do you know what I think?"

"I'm sure you'll tell me."

"I think... that there's a reason Eleanor Ross was creeping about your father's estate," Morgana's voice dripped with satisfaction. "I'm fairly certain I know what that reason was, but your poor, dear father doesn't have a clue."

"Eleanor Ross?" Cleo repeated in a horrified voice. Then added quickly, "Who is Eleanor Ross?"

"Oh, nobody of importance. Not for much longer anyway. Would you like another cup of tea?"

What had happened to Mrs. Ross? How had Morgana gotten her hands on her? No doubt that was precisely what she was meant to ask. The question had been baited. "No, thank you," Cleo said quietly. "I find I've had quite enough."

Silverware clinked. "Clever *and* careful. I'll have to watch you very closely. Indeed, it's a shame we cannot be friends. I admire clever young women."

"I find that difficult to believe."

"Oh, now you're making me wonder what my son's been whispering over the pillow—"

"It wasn't... He didn't..." And then Cleo stopped, realizing that she'd walked into Morgana's trap. Very well. It wasn't as if the woman wouldn't have checked the sheets. Still, she had to recover somehow. "He's... a monster." It made her feel ill to say it, but she had no doubt Morgana would believe this lie—for Sebastian did.

"Most men are," Morgana replied with little sympathy. "That's why you cannot trust them. They believe it their right to control the world and do as they wish with their womenfolk. Even when they make you believe them to be kind, there is always that ugly beast within that can turn on you at any moment. Don't ever trust a man, my dear. Learn to use them instead."

Cleo didn't know what to say. There'd been bitterness there toward the end. "You speak of your divorce?"

"Ah, my noble husband Drake." Definitely bitterness. "A thousand promises that he made me, all of them broken."

"I thought you were involved in the poisoning of his nephew?"

"Do you know it's the one time in my life that I haven't actually been guilty of what was accused? There is irony for you." Morgana set her teacup down. "Of everything else, yes, I did it all. But... I believed Drake when he told me he would love me forever. I actually forgot, for a moment, what men were like. Let's put it down to the misguided hope of youth." Her voice roughened. "I never made that mistake again. And would you think me so foolish as to kill Drake's heir? The trail led back to me as neatly as a line of breadcrumbs. I am many things, but not a fool."

"Then who do you think did it?"

"Lady Rathbourne, I'd probably guess. She wanted my husband, but he wouldn't stray, not unless he had cause."

Cleo tilted her head. Did she dare believe the woman? "Last night I felt the collar that you have put on your son."

"He's a man," Morgana replied. "He even looks so very much like his father. How could I trust him?"

"So you leashed him instead. A self-fulfilling prophecy by the sound of it, and I would know."

There was a long moment of silence. "What did Eleanor Ross tell you?"

"I thought we were speaking of your son, and I still do not know who this Eleanor Ross is."

Morgana's smile echoed in her voice. "Well, let's play along then. Eleanor Ross is my ex-husband's mistress. Goodness, perhaps *she* murdered Drake's nephew and blamed it on me? She always did tag along at Drake's heels like a puppy. What did you tell them?"

"Them?"

"The Prime and Mrs. Ross."

"How would I know the Prime?" Cleo asked. "My father's kept me locked away at his estate for all these years. I cannot see. It's not as though I've been making secret assignations with someone. How could I have even contacted the Prime or Mrs. Ross?"

"How indeed? Do you know it's always the innocent-seeming ones you have to watch? Or so I've always believed. So be it. Perhaps I'll ask Mrs. Ross?" The older woman patted Cleo's cheek. "You would be wise to—"

The second Morgana touched her, a vision sunk its hooks deep into her. Cleo dropped her teacup, distantly registering the sensation as it burned its way across her lap. She cried out, but her eyes were wide open behind her blindfold.

A dark-haired woman lay in a small dark room, her face dirty and her clothes ragged. She looked up as the barred cell door opened and then dragged herself up into a sitting position, wincing as she did. Another woman entered, her skirts swishing around her ankles. She knelt, just out of reach of Mrs. Ross's shackles, her green eyes slightly tilted and still beautiful, despite the signs of age weathering her pale skin. Her smile, however, was vicious. "So be it then. If Drake wants your bloody heart, then he can have it. In a box."

Then the vision shifted. A guillotine descended. Blood splashed against stone walls, and crows took off into stormy skies. The storm clouds swirled and swirled, circling Morgana as she tilted her face toward the sky. They were so thick and threatening, and they swallowed her whole.

Cleo sucked in a sharp lungful of air, clutching at the tablecloth as the vision left her. Porcelain smashed and cutlery chimed on the flagstones. Her heart was thundering in her chest.

"What did you see?" asked a sharp voice near her ear.

She couldn't breathe. She hadn't even felt the vision coming. Cleo shook her head and tried to regain her decorum.

Morgana fussed around her, fetching her a cup of water. It was almost laughable.

"Your own actions will destroy you," Cleo whispered, dragging the napkin off the table and patting at her scalded lap. "This is the beginning of the end for you. So perhaps *you* would be wise to be careful of just precisely who you threaten. If you kill Mrs. Ross, I will let you walk your path. I will let you fall. Indeed, you will never know if I steer you clear of it or give you a push in the wrong direction. You have been warned."

"It is never wise to make an enemy of me." Morgana sounded less certain than she had been though.

Cleo reached for the teapot and poured herself a fresh cup in the midst of the carnage. Her hands were still shaking, but her voice was measured. "I have never had an enemy," she mused. "I wonder who will win, the one who sees the future, or the one who clings to the past?"

Cleo found Sebastian in the garden. She still didn't know what to think about his confession last night, but she had no one else to help her. "Your mother is going to kill Eleanor Ross."

A pair of clippers snicked together neatly. "I know."

"Well, are you not going to do something about it?"

"What should I do?" he asked, snipping at another stem. Roses, she thought, from the heady scent of them. "Storm Mrs. Ross's prison? Murder my mother? I'd like to, but there's the unfortunate matter of the collar..."

"Well, we have to do something!"

"There is no 'we'."

"You're the only one I have," she shot back, her voice thick with emotion, "and I'm the only one you have. If we're not in this together, then what's the point?"

Bees buzzed as he hesitated before saying, "Careful. My mother's watching from the window. She looks vexed." He moved on, snipping at something else. "What did you say to her?"

"We had a lovely little conversation over tea, full of threats and bloodied promises. This is a pit of vipers, is it not?" Cleo rubbed her fingers together in thought, then ripped her chin up when she heard his swift intake of breath. "Oh, goodness. I didn't mean you."

"It's the truth," Sebastian replied, his voice muffled as he turned away from her.

"No, it's not." She followed the sound of his footsteps across the lawn hesitantly. "Would you stop pacing, please? I'm afraid I'm going to fall face first into the roses."

He stopped and Cleo almost walked into him before realizing.

"You cannot pretend this isn't going to happen. You cannot run away from it. We have to do something. This is *my* fault, Bastian. I sent a letter to the Prime—"

"I know. You bloody little fool. You should have stayed out of this mess."

"I wanted to help you," she cried. "And I didn't stay out of it, and now an innocent woman is going to die because of me!" Then her mind registered what he'd said. "How did you know I contacted the Prime?"

Sebastian swore under his breath. "Listen, this is not your fault. Mrs. Ross told me about—"

"She told you? You've seen her?"

"Yes." His answer was abrupt.

"She's here, isn't she?" Cleo's heart started pounding, jacking into her throat. Premonition tingled *yes* along her arms.

A hand grabbed her wrist and warm breath washed over her face. The scent of him was lush with earth, roses, and sweat, all things she'd never thought to associate with her elegant husband. "You are *not* going to do a thing about it. Morgana will kill you, Cleo. If you know nothing else, then know this: My mother is dangerous. She has the Blade of Altarrh in hand as of last night, and she won't hesitate to use it."

It was the first time he'd touched her voluntarily. The physical impact of it stole her breath. "The Blade of Altarrh?" Why did that name sound familiar? She couldn't quite place it. "A part of me will die if they kill Mrs. Ross. A little part of me will never forgive myself. Please. Please help me."

He turned away, blowing out a breath in frustration. "Fucking roses." The clipper's hit the lawn and clattered.

"You say you're a monster," Cleo said. "I know you're not a monster, but if you pretend this isn't happening, then what do you become? Every little shadow darkens your soul. You'll become something I don't think you want to be."

"And what do you suggest I do?" Sebastian snarled. "I cannot break the wards on the cellar. It's too complicated for my magic, and my mother will know I did it. She'll take me down with sorcery before I can even lift a finger."

"I don't want you to be hurt."

"That's the problem." Fabric rustled as he paced. "She won't hurt *me*, Cleo. She'll come after someone I care about, and she'll do it while I watch and cannot react."

Her heart became an odd pitter-patter in her chest. "And who do you care about?" She was met with another one of his silences. It told her everything she was afraid to hope for. "Oh," she said. "*Oh*. I'm not afraid."

"You should be." Bleak, hopeless words. "And now that she's seen this entire little encounter, I'm going to have to tell some pretty convincing lies."

Cleo caught his wrist. "Wait." Her mind raced. "Knock me over."

"What?"

"And look angry."

"I'm not going to—"

"Yes, you are," she whispered. "Or I will."

"Bloody hell." He shook her off. "I'll do something for Mrs. Ross. I promise. Don't you attempt anything. Now, there's a rake behind you. I'm sorry." Then his shoulder hit hers in a heavy thud of heated flesh, and he pushed past her as if toward the house.

Cleo's foot caught on the rake and she went down, tumbling to her bottom on the grass. She stayed there, in her puddle of skirts, hot emotion lodging in her chest. What a horrible mess she'd found herself in, but the oddest sensation was that of relief. Sebastian was going to help her. She had an ally in this mess, and he had a chance at redemption, if he dared to do this.

When tears flushed through her eyes, she let them soak her blindfold as she buried her face in her hands.

He couldn't get near the Prime; his mother had eyes watching the Duke far too closely. And he couldn't rescue Mrs. Ross himself. Such an act would only earn him untold punishment, and if Morgana realized how much his wife had gotten beneath his skin, then she'd know exactly how to cut at him.

There was only one hope.

So Sebastian wrote a letter, using a scrap of Louisa's hair that he'd kept, to prove who it came from, and then waited for his chance to deliver it.

CHAPTER
TWENTY-SEVEN

"IT'S GOT TO be a trap," Lucien said.

"I know," Ianthe replied, her skirts swishing around her ankles as she paced. They'd been halfway to the door when the letter arrived, care of some young street urchin. "I know! But Eleanor... If she's hurt, then Drake will be devastated. And the address leads to Knightsbridge, which is where Thea said she tracked Noah Guthrie to."

Lucien rubbed at his face. "Why would someone tell us just how many sorcerers Morgana has at her beck and call? Or give us her address? You don't find that conveniently suspicious?"

"I do, but then I think perhaps Thea and I aren't the only ones who were unwilling to help her. What if she has her claws in someone else?"

True. "Where's the Prime?"

"He's fetching the carriage and reinforcements." Ianthe rubbed the lock of Louisa's hair that had fallen from the envelope. "We're going to need them if Morgana has this many sorcerers on her side."

"You want me to do what?" Remington asked, crossing his arms over his chest and looking down at Ianthe.

"There's no one else I would trust more to guard my daughter and my ward," Ianthe told him, slipping the warded metal gauntlet over her wrist and wriggling her fingers. Magic tingled across her skin from the charms laid into the cold steel. She would need every advantage she would get, and she wouldn't need to concentrate very much in order to activate the gauntlet's inset wards. Only direct a trickle of sorcery through it.

"I'm not quite certain what that says of me, that you see me more as nursemaid than a warrior."

"I see you as someone I trust with something more important than my own heart," Ianthe replied, leaning up on her toes to kiss Remington's cheek. "I have to go. Drake has few enough allies as it is, and someone needs to guard Lucien's back. Be kind to Thea, please. She's had a rough week."

"Haven't we all?" Remington drawled, but he looked quietly pleased with her statement.

That said, Ianthe turned to the armchair in the corner. Louisa held Thea's hand, her pretty amber eyes troubled.

"I shall be back as soon as I can," Ianthe promised. "Thea is going to take care of you, and so is Remington. Nobody shall get past the two of them, I promise. You'll be safe as houses."

"I don't want you to go." Louisa lowered her head, her eyes shining.

Ianthe hesitated. She knelt down, taking Louisa's hands in hers. Her heart felt like it was going to tear in two. "Louisa—"

"I'll go," Thea blurted instead.

"What?"

"This is partly my fault," Thea insisted, hurt flashing in those hazel eyes. "I should never have delivered those letters! I should make amends."

"You can barely unknot a rope with your mind!" Ianthe protested. "No, you're not going. It's too dangerous for you!"

"But—"

"She's right," Lucien said softly, stepping forward into the room. All eyes turned to him, but he went to Louisa, kneeling down so that he could take her small hands in his. "I know you've been through an ordeal, Louisa, and you're scared that if your mother goes away, she won't come back. Is that true?"

Louisa nodded.

"Ianthe has to go," he said, squeezing her little fingers. "Morgana is very dangerous, more so now she has the Blade, and there are not enough of us to stop her if Ianthe stays. If I could, I would shoulder her burden and do her duty as well as mine." His eyes darkened. "But I cannot. I am not strong enough, not at this time, to stop Morgana before she comes after us. I will promise you this though: I will bring your mother back to you."

Louisa bit her lip and whispered, "Okay."

"Good girl." He stroked her cheek, then caught Thea's gaze. "You have amends to make, you say? Then this is your task. Look after Louisa and help her wait for us. We should be back before sunset. Once this is done, your penance is over. You have no more debt to Ianthe, do you understand?"

Thea nodded too, slipping her hand inside Louisa's.

"She hurt my mama and papa," Louisa said.

"Yes." Ianthe stroked her face and the smooth baby-fine cheek. "Yes, she did. And I will make her pay for that."

"Are you going to hurt her?"

"I am going to make Morgana wish she'd never set eyes on either of us."

Louisa took a long time to think it over. "Good." A single tear slid down her cheek, but Ianthe kissed it away.

"When I get back, you are going to come and live with me and your father. We can show him how to take tea with Hilary and Sir Egmont. Would you like that?" She held her breath for a moment.

A mixture of happiness and nervousness lit over the little girl's face, as though she did not dare dream it would happen. "Yes. Yes, please."

A little girl, so like herself. A little girl who feared to believe in her dreams. Ianthe pressed their foreheads together, cupping Louisa's nape with her hand. If Lucien had only just begun to teach her to hope that the dream could come true, then she would in turn teach Louisa the truth too. "I'll be back for you. I'll read you your favorite story tonight, before you go to bed."

Louisa smiled shyly. "Goodbye, Mama."

It was the second time Louisa had called her that. Ianthe's heart broke in her chest, and it took every ounce of her willpower to walk toward the door. It felt wrong to leave her daughter behind when she was walking into danger, but there was no choice. Not only did she have amends to make, but if they did not remove Morgana as a threat now, before the other woman grew too powerful, then the danger only escalated. Morgana had two of the Relics Infernal. She only needed one more to topple Drake, and there was no way Ianthe could protect Louisa from the other woman if Drake fell and Morgana came to power. No doubt the other woman would demand a reckoning from her, as Ianthe had not exactly obeyed the letter of Morgana's demands last night.

The world would not be a safe place for any of them if they did not act now.

Still, she paused by the door and waved back, blowing Thea and Louisa a kiss each. Lucien's hand was steady at her back as he guided her through the door, shutting it behind them.

"You're a very brave woman," he murmured.

"Don't. Please," she choked out. "Or I think I may cry."

CHAPTER TWENTY-EIGHT

"WELL, WELL," Morgana said, swinging a lantern into the small cell and pushing back her hood with a pale, slender hand. Her smile was dangerous. "You should see the sunset, Eleanor. It's beautiful and full of portent." Setting the lantern on the table, she turned and drew a slim, elegant knife from her sleeve. "Today is going to be a very good day."

Eleanor gasped, her barely-healed lip splitting open again. The Blade of Altarrh. She could almost feel the malevolent haze emanating from it. "How did you get that?" What had happened to Drake? Was he injured?

No. She forced herself to calm. No. Morgana's smile was only that of a gloating Madonna. The woman wouldn't have been able to contain herself if Drake was hurt or cast down. She would have been crowing from the rooftops.

"I have my means," Morgana taunted. "It is always simply about finding the right point to apply pressure. Everyone has something they won't risk, whether it's a secret or someone important to them."

"Even you?"

Morgana's smile faded. "People are weaknesses you cannot afford, and there is no secret I feel shame in keeping. No, Eleanor, I'm the exception to the rule."

Gathering her dignity, Eleanor dragged herself to her feet, the chains rattling across the floor. "I think you're lying to yourself."

"Oh? Do tell."

"I think you've always wanted someone to belong to you, but you cannot fathom how to keep them loyal, because you don't understand loyalty. All you know is betrayal."

Those green eyes narrowed. "Learned from the day I began walking, I assure you, and nobody has ever dealt me otherwise. That's not a weakness, Eleanor."

"Isn't it? Then why do you still crave it? Look at you." She let her pity show. "Your own son despises you. Drake turned from you. No man will have you. And you want them to belong to you so desperately that the misery of losing them has turned you into this. A bitter old woman with no true power, no true friends, or allies, or—"

"Stop!" Morgana hissed, lunging forward with the blade drawn. "Don't you *dare* pity me!"

The blade stopped an inch from Eleanor's throat. She stared into the other woman's eyes, refusing to be cowed. *Go ahead.* Eleanor tipped her chin up. She was no longer that pale young girl who stammered and apologized to the other young female apprentices, as if her poor birth was her own fault. Drake had taught her the value of her worth, and if this bitch was going to kill her, then Eleanor would meet her death with grace and dignity.

Morgana's lip curled back from her teeth, and she pulled the knife away.

"You," Morgana spat, "pathetic Eleanor Whitby, a girl taken directly from the orphanage, with a minor talent in psychometry, if at all... You always looked beyond your station, Eleanor, nosing around the tutors as if that could make up for your lack of breeding and talent. Gods, it makes me ill to even think of you in his bed. Why would he choose you? You're nothing. You've always been nothing."

A spark of rage unfurled in her breast, but Eleanor held her head high. "It doesn't matter what you say or do to me, Morgana, you will never win. Even in death, Drake's heart belongs to me, and mine to him."

A dangerous glitter filled the other woman's eyes. "So be it then. If Drake wants your bloody heart, then he can have it. In a box. Henri! Phillippe!"

Two heavy-set men shouldered inside the cell. Morgana gestured them into place with a swift cut of her hand. "Take her wrists and pin her down."

They moved to grab her, and Eleanor fought. It was no use. Without access to her power—carefully blocked by the warded bracelet around her wrist—she was as weak as anyone else.

Morgana grabbed her by the throat, pinning her to the stone wall. "How dare you think you could replace me? How dare you think that you"—the knife dug into Eleanor's breastbone—"pathetic, little bitch that you are, could ever be half the woman that I am."

Power gathered along the Blade. Eleanor felt it growing, even as the point cut into her skin. She cried out, twisting her face away, but there was no hope. No relief from the slow, inexorable push of hot iron into her flesh. Eleanor screamed.

"What are you doing?"

The room was suddenly freezing. Sebastian stood in the doorway, his eyes raking over the scene. Power gleamed over his skin, giving him such vitality that he almost glowed. Eleanor slumped, breathing hard, as Morgana turned to face him.

"This is none of your business. Go back to your roses." There was a faint sneer to Morgana's voice, and she turned back to her task, as if dismissing him.

"No."

Morgana shoved away from Eleanor, leaving her gasping as blood trickled from the cut beneath her breastbone. The woman turned to face her son, power lashing along the Blade as she pointed it at him. "Don't you *dare* defy me, especially not after that debacle last night, where you almost cost me this!" Morgana held up the relic. "Now get out of here. I've had enough of you for the day!"

His cold gray gaze flickered toward Eleanor, then back to his mother. "No," he said again, slowly, as if making up his mind. "I cannot let you do this. I will not."

As if to emphasize the words, Sebastian straightened, his fingers curled faintly at his sides with flickers of lightning-coated power dancing over them. Just a hint of a threat, but one made dangerous by the weight of power that could be felt within him.

It felt like everyone in the room held their breath.

Eleanor didn't hope to escape this, but in saving her, was he risking himself?

Morgana seemed shocked. "What do you mean, 'you cannot let me do this'? Who are you to tell me what I may or may not do?"

"Unfortunately, I'm the only one with the power to stop you. That's who I am, Mother."

"Power?" Morgana took a step toward him, and Eleanor could feel Morgana gathering her own sorcery. "Have I taught you nothing? Power is not strength, not when one is inept in wielding it with finesse." She lashed out, the ring on her finger sparking as some type of sorcery was channeled through it. "Just a taste, my dear."

Sebastian winced and went down on his hands and knees. His hair lifted, almost as if with static, and when he looked up, the expression on his face was murderous. "I will *not* let you do this."

"This is a sudden change in demeanor. I thought we had discussed what would happen if you ever went up against me again. What has brought about this change?" And then Morgana's eyes widened. "Ah. Of course. How did I miss that? Oh, Miss Sinclair, well played."

"Leave Miss Sinclair out of this." Sebastian straightened.

"I should have seen that coming." Morgana *tsked* under her breath. "I thought it odd that you knocked her over in the garden. You've always had a weakness for those pathetic, innocent little creatures. Your poor blind wife... Of course she'd appeal. I just didn't think you'd already formed an attachment."

"Leave... her out of this." Sebastian's power crackled around him.

The attack was instant.

Sparks flared into being around his body, forming thin golden lines between them that suddenly tightened, and sank through his clothes, into his flesh. Sebastian screamed, his fingers curling into whitened claws. He raged against the invisible net, fine white pressure lines forming all over his skin.

"Stop fighting it!" Eleanor screamed, recognizing the effects of a Bathingway hex. "It intensifies if you fight it!"

A flash of gray eyes, and then Sebastian forced himself to relax. The pain would remain, but at least now he had a chance. Looking up, he flung everything he had at his mother.

Morgana staggered back, a deft flick of her hands deflecting the pure wave of force away from her. Eleanor's back slammed against the wall, her ears ringing as her head hit the stone. For a moment, she blinked, and it felt like time had slipped away from her. Then she found herself on her hands and knees amongst the rubble that was all that remained of the wall, with Henri and Philippe sprawled beside her. Blood trickled from both men's ears, the force crushing their brains instantly. The only reason she was still alive was because Morgana's wards stood directly between them.

Eleanor barely had time to grasp what had happened before horror filled her. There was a terrible silence in her head, almost a ringing, as if she'd been standing inside a bell when Sebastian's power had struck it.

Expression. And not just on the base level of the spectrum, but a wash of power so intense that she knew nothing would be able to stand in its way. Not even Drake. The type of power could bring London to its knees, if channeled correctly.

"Sebastian," she gasped, or thought she did. It didn't sound right. *Don't. Please don't!* Her mouth wasn't working properly, one side of her face felt like it was drooping, and her head was throbbing now. Throbbing like her brains wanted to spill out of her ears. Gods. What was happening to her?

"Aisle stop oo." Sebastian's voice sounded so far away. So distant. So strange. "No matter whar-muss do."

Eleanor tasted blood.

Energy welled into a crescendo. It spiraled around the room, drawn from every living thing within the nearby vicinity. It radiated toward him in ripples that worked in reverse, flooding him with power. No one human should be able to do this. No one man could contain all of that power.

Eleanor realized what he was going to do. "Stop!" she screamed, or tried to. Somehow her chains were broken, the iron links seared away halfway down and dripping slag onto the floor. Her left hand wouldn't work. Numbness tingled through it, and she fell onto her face as the left side of her body gave way. It was like watching her own actions from outside her body.

Sebastian. Drake. Had to... stop this.

And then someone grabbed her by the hair and plunged the Blade into Eleanor's back in a hiss of burning pain that lit all her nerves on fire.

And all she could do was scream.

CHAPTER TWENTY-NINE

POWER EXPLODED out through the walls of the house, flattening the rose bushes someone had lovingly tended. Ianthe threw herself at Lucien, flinging her gauntleted fist up in front of them. Her wards invoked themselves a split second before a wave of force smashed into the pair of them, sending them cartwheeling across the manicured lawns.

When she came to, she was breathing heavily into Lucien's coat with his arms curled around her. Her entire body ached, like some enormous hand had just reached out and swatted her. All along the street, porches tumbled from their frames and tiles slid from rooves. Startled heads popped out of door and windows to see what was going on.

"Are you all right?" Lucien demanded. She could feel his concern along the bond between them.

"Ouch." She winced in reply. "What on earth was that?"

Lucien helped her to sit up. "Expression."

Of the group, only Drake was on his feet, staggering with his hands outspread as he dispersed the ripples of pure power and grounded them back into the earth. The ground stopped shaking and silence fell, as if everything nearby had felt it. A squirrel shot past, fleeing for the undergrowth.

Adrian Bishop helped Lady Eberhardt to her feet, and the woman looked spitting mad as she pulled her skirts down over her stockinged legs. The stone lion she'd brought with her butted his head against her.

"This," said Lady Eberhardt, throwing Drake a concerned look, "this is not good. Who could draw so much power? If Morgana has that on her side, then she might be well-nigh undefeatable."

If Lady Eberhardt sounded worried... Ianthe looked to Lucien.

"It's Morgana's son," Lucien said, helping her to her feet. He nodded toward Drake. "It's my brother, this Sebastian."

"Three brothers," Lady Eberhardt muttered. "Three relics. This isn't going to end well."

Drake gasped, lowering his hands as the last of the sorcery melted away.

"Brother?" Bishop asked, shooting Lucien a hard look.

"Surprise. There are three of us." Lucien shrugged. "It's always the youngest of the family who throws the biggest tantrums. Or so I've heard." Then he paused. "Or are you the youngest? I never did quite work out where you fit in the family."

"Bishop's the youngest," Lady Eberhardt said. "His mother helped console Drake following the divorce."

Bishop ignored the pair of them. "That was not a tantrum." One of his Sicarii blades formed in his hands.

"Oh, he can get louder if he wants," Lucien replied. "Nearly buried us beneath half of Highgrove Cemetery last night."

"Stop it," Ianthe said, seeing the flash of pain on Drake's face. "And put that away," she told Bishop. "You are *not* killing your brother."

Bishop and Lucien traded glances that seemed to echo each other. Despite the physical differences between them, the resemblance was almost uncanny in that instant.

"How do you plan to stop him?" Bishop asked. With a flick of his fingers, the knife vanished into thin air.

Ianthe crossed to Drake's side, seeing the worry in his eyes. "Can you deflect Sebastian's power? Can you stop him from tearing the city apart?"

"Maybe," he said.

"If you had help?"

Drake considered it, then looked toward Lucien. "If someone offered up their well of power, I might be able to contain him, or disperse his sorcery if it flares again."

"It's going to flare," Lady Eberhardt said. "I can feel it building again."

"You're potentially the strongest here," Drake said, looking directly at Lucien.

Ianthe held her breath.

"And I can barely manage to tie my own shoelaces with sorcery at the moment," Lucien said bitterly. He looked down at his feet with a frown, then sighed and slowly stretched out his hand. "Take what you need. Use me as your wellspring."

A flood of heat and pride filled her. The man she'd first encountered—the bitter, vengeful duke—was slowly vanishing, leaving behind a man who weighed his sense of duty against his feelings of hate and did the right thing.

Ianthe's heart clenched in her chest and her lungs seized. This was a man she could both admire and respect.

As if sensing it, Lucien looked toward her sharply.

"Thank you," she mouthed.

"I would not be careless with such an offer," Drake said, crossing to take his son's hand. As their palms clasped, a shudder went through Lucien and through their bond; Ianthe felt something settle over him and take hold.

"We have company," Lady Eberhardt called, turning to face the back garden. A barrage of rampaging imps spilled out of the greenery like a flock of howling monkeys. They were followed by a tall figure in a black velvet coat with a froth of white lace at his throat. Two other sorcerers made their presence known, settling in behind him.

"Tremayne," Lady Eberhardt spat.

"Eberhardt," Tremayne replied. His eyes narrowed as he settled his hands around the hilt of an ebony cane, but he was smiling. "Fancy seeing all of you here."

"Told you it was a trap," Lucien murmured.

But Ianthe wasn't so certain.

"Well, it looks like someone's been dabbling in areas he shouldn't have been," Lady Eberhardt said, stepping forward. "I was fairly certain you couldn't so much as ignite a fart in a teakettle with your sorcery restricted, Tremayne. What did it cost you to overcome the Council's restrictions? Your soul?"

"Oh, Agatha, I always thought you said I didn't have one." Tremayne traced a circle on the lawn with the tip of his cane, pouring power through it. "But let's just say... I have friends in high places these days."

"Low places, Tremayne. Not high. And I wouldn't trust a demon as far as I could throw him. He'll eat you alive. Eventually."

"You never did have the guts to reach for power."

"I prefer good, decent common sense." Lady Eberhardt grunted and used her finger to chisel a line in the turf with a lance of pure fire. "I must admit that hearing rumors about the Relics Infernal and then finding you involved is rather disappointing. I grow weary of always being right about people."

Ianthe took a few steps backward. Nobody wanted to be caught between the conflagration of whatever was about to be thrown in this vicinity. "Do you need help?" she called, eyeing the imps. Lady Eberhardt's lion was pacing in front of her, keeping them at bay, but they were starting to grow bolder.

"I've got this," Lady Eberhardt called, pushing up the black chiffon of her sleeves and facing the horde of imps. "Bishop, you can stay right here, you can. Drake, perhaps you'd better go see to that raging storm that's about to erupt inside. I can feel all of my neck hairs rising again. Quite gives an old woman the chills."

"Stay here with Lady Eberhardt," Lucien insisted.

Ianthe frowned, catching at his sleeve. "I don't think that wise."

Lucien clasped her cheek, pressing a swift kiss to her forehead. "I need to stay with my father." His thumb stroked her cheek, his eyes intense. "And I cannot protect you, not with my attention split."

"I'm not quite certain when it was that I needed protection," she replied tartly.

"You're Louisa's mother," he replied. "You should take care of yourself for that reason alone, if not for the fact that you're also my Anchor."

Anchor.

Her heart twisted. He would not say anymore. She knew it. Clenching her pride tightly in hand, she nodded, then took hold of his lapels. "And you're her father. Be

394

careful." And then she reached up on her tiptoes, before her courage failed, and pressed a kiss to his mouth. "You're also the man I love. Be careful of my heart, Lucien Devereaux. I've only just given it to you, and it's quite precious to me."

His eyes were wide, startled, as though he couldn't get used to such confessions. "Ianthe."

Biting her lip, Ianthe stepped back. A violent explosion rocked the garden as Bishop flung a wall of shadow toward Tremayne in retaliation for the explosion. "*Go,*" she mouthed, then turned her attention back to the fight. It didn't matter if he didn't feel the same way. He had given her enough of herself back. She felt more certain of herself than she ever had.

The lion roared as it leapt toward an imp, its marble teeth crunching into the creature's bronze throat and slamming it to the ground. Lady Eberhardt's hands were moving in eerie patterns, scarlet battle globes circling her as Tremayne flung a set of his own.

Ianthe snatched power into her body, fairly humming with it. The gauntlet tightened around her wrist as she activated it, and she flung a punch of pure power from its metal knuckles toward Tremayne's blue battle globes. The force as they met rocked her back, her skirts streaming behind her in the wind. Blue lightning spewed over the garden, earthing itself in sizzling spots on the lawn.

Lady Eberhardt turned black eyes directly upon Ianthe, as Lucien and Drake strode toward the front door, snatching at her sleeve. "You'd better watch your young lad's back, my dear. I did a reading this morning."

"What did it say?" Ianthe demanded, flinging another wave of power toward a pair of imps. It knocked them into the roses, and one hissed at her, crouching low behind a shrub.

"Staying behind's all very noble, but you're not the one in danger, my dear."

"Lucien?"

Lady Eberhardt's eyes flickered to Lucien, then back again. "Just watch his back. You need to be by his side. I'll keep an eye on this brother, and Drake can handle the last." Her voice softened for Ianthe's ears alone. "The brothers are the key. Three relics, three brothers, three sacrifices."

"What the hell do you mean by that?"

"I saw two brothers enter that building," Lady Eberhardt replied. "Only one of them comes out whole."

"Why didn't you tell him? Why didn't you say something?"

"What's meant to be, is meant to be. One doesn't mess with fate, besides..."

An enormous whoosh of fire burned over their wards as Bishop and Tremayne faced off.

"Besides?" Ianthe called.

Lady Eberhardt hesitated. "I think this needs to happen, if we're to have any chance at defeating Morgana."

Ianthe tore her arm free, leaving Tremayne and his pet sorcerers to Lady Eberhardt and Bishop, whom Lady Eberhardt had been quite intent upon seeing remain behind. Maybe she'd seen more in her cup of tea leaves than she'd mentioned?

"Lucien!" Ianthe called, slamming the front door open. The house was immaculate. A bunch of the most beautiful roses filled a vase on a table in the hall, and black and white tiles stretched out into the distance. There was no sign of Drake or Lucien.

She could feel them however, that tiny golden itch in the back of her mind causing her to lift her head. Upstairs. He was upstairs. And so too was the source of the hurricane brewing on the edges of her mind.

Ianthe put a hand on the rail and took the first step. A faint tremble ran through her, the walls shaking. The pressure began to make her ears ring.

"Lucien! Drake!" She hurried up the stairs.

No guards. That was odd. Not even a ward or a whisper of a broken one...

Ianthe's heart gave a dull thud in her chest as Drake's words played through her memory again. *Lucien, I think you are a gateway for the demon now...* And what was Morgana trying to do through the Relics Infernal? Raise a demon... No. No, it couldn't be. Could it?

But the thought played out in eerie determination in her head. Lucien and his brothers were meant to be sacrifices; Lady Eberhardt kept saying it. And somewhere within her lover was the path to the Shadow Dimensions and the demon within. Lord Rathbourne had been Morgana's ally, after all. Perhaps, by forcing Lucien to summon the demon last year, he'd been trying to create a link for the demon to follow. That was what he'd meant in his diary!

If Morgana played her cards right, she wouldn't need all three relics. She would only need one. The Blade. And a human vessel for the demon to occupy.

A sacrifice. Lady Eberhardt was right. Ianthe wasn't in any danger, but Lucien was.

Ianthe's blood ran cold. "Lucien!" she screamed, grabbing a fistful of her skirts as she began to run.

You need to get out of here, right now!

You need to get out of here, right now!

Lucien swayed as the force of the thought hit him. Ianthe. Her psychic touch felt like silk and roses, brushing against his senses through their bond. It had been strengthening every day as they grew physically and intimately more involved, but this almost knocked him off his feet.

Ahead of him, a door splintered out into the hallway as a pulse of power lashed out through the walls, splintering plaster and cracking the cornice. He pushed her out of his mind. *Can't. Rather busy at the moment.*

The connection between them softened until he could only sense her remotely, the same way he always did.

The Prime absorbed the impact, grounding it with a delicacy Lucien could only admire. Drake hadn't bothered to draw on the temporary wellspring bond between them, using his own power in deft weaves to divert whatever was happening in that room. Lucien was an adept of the seventh Order, but he couldn't even compare to this. His father was the composer of an entire symphony, whilst he himself was but a single cellist.

"Are you ready?" Drake demanded.

Sweat dripped down Lucien's throat, but there was no pain in his head. Only a feeling of intensity, as if something was watching him—something that felt like a predator. He nodded, ignoring it.

Together, they linked hands. Lucien opened himself psychically, and his father's presence swept into his mind, usurping his power.

Instinct wanted to cast Drake out. It felt alien to surrender to someone else's will, and though he'd been taught how, during his apprenticeship, no sorcerer truly enjoyed being used as a wellspring.

Drake let go of his hand, now that the mental link was forged, and stepped through the door. Lucien followed and found himself in the remains of a cell. Part of the wall was blown out, revealing a terrace and glasshouse.

An elegant woman in red stood within the whirlwind, her raven-dark hair whipping around her throat and her skirts lashing behind her. Threads of shimmering sorcery laced the air in front of her, faintly malevolent, as she bore down upon a man in the center of the devastation, a man on his hands and knees, screaming in pain...

"Morgana," Drake called.

She looked up, an expression of malicious delight fading swiftly, as she noticed the Prime. Then her gaze slid past Drake, toward Lucien. And she smiled. It was an expression that turned his blood to ice, for she was truly pleased to see him there, and he couldn't think why.

"Hello, Drake. It seems you've brought me a present." As Morgana turned, something moved behind her, sagging against the wall—a mess of blue skirts and dark hair with blood spattered all down her.

"Eleanor!" Drake cried out.

Lucien hauled him back as his father took a step forward. He alone seemed to recognize the danger in the room. Cracks slithered up the plaster as a brutal pressure choked the air, but it seemed like no one else saw them. Morgana and Drake were both too busy with each other.

"Drake," he warned.

Sebastian had lifted his head as Morgana's attention changed focus. His eyes were pure black with power, and for one eerie moment, it felt like Lucien could read his mind. Sebastian's face calmed, as if he'd been wrestling with his own conscience, but now a decision was made. It was accepted. The world went silent. The moment of calm before the storm.

One second that felt like forever. Lucien stepped forward, moving through air that felt like jelly, one hand flung outward, trying to stop it in time.

"Don't!" Lucien screamed, tearing the reins away from his father for a second and flinging up the strongest ward he knew. The sudden ripple in the air tore away his words as Sebastian simply... detonated.

Ianthe threw herself forward and clung to the edge of the second floor, her legs dangling in midair as the staircase sheared out from under her. Slamming the gauntlet onto the floorboards, she tried to find purchase, but her hands were slipping, slipping...

"Help!" she screamed as part of the ceiling gave way, dropping behind her into the foyer. The chandelier landed with a fierce crash, spewing glass all across the tiles.

The world wouldn't stop moving. The first ripple had almost torn her feet out from under her, but she'd felt it grow as power radiated outward. An earthquake that gained magnitude, the further away it swam...

A pair of pale silvery skirts swished into view. A young woman staggered out of the shadows, her hair a shining gold halo of curls around her head, and a linen blindfold covering her eyes. "Hello?" the girl called. "Where are you?"

"Here!" Ianthe gasped, trying to drag herself to safety. Nails wrenched themselves up out of the timber floorboards as the house shuddered.

The young woman moved with unerring accuracy, scrambling onto her hands and knees and grabbing Ianthe by the gauntlet. "I wish this bloody floor would stop shaking!"

The stranger was taller than she was, but lighter of figure. Her skirts slipped on the floors as she tried to haul Ianthe up.

"Me too." Ianthe kicked a boot up onto the edge of the staircase, and with an enormous wrench of effort, managed to roll herself onto the second floor. The pair of them sprawled there in a heap of skirts, panting, as the entire building shook and shivered.

The worst thing was, she could feel the torrent of power building. Something was barely containing it, but that something was about to give, and when it did...

"We've got to stop him," the girl gasped.

"Who?"

"Sebastian." The young woman turned around, stumbling against the wall. "I can see more sparks, but I don't think they're strong enough to hold back the storm. I don't even think I am, but I have to try! You have to take me to him!"

It sounded like utter gibberish, but Ianthe darted another glance at the blindfold. If she wasn't mistaken, that was a sure sign of a Cassandra. Taking the girl by the arm, they staggered along the hallway. "What's your name?"

"Cleo Sinclair."

Sinclair, Sinclair... Where had she heard that name? Then she realized. The Earl of Tremayne was a Sinclair. Ianthe stopped in her tracks, almost wrenching the girl off her feet. The shaking of the floor drove both of them into the wall.

"I mean, it's Mrs. Cleo Montcalm now, I suppose. I keep forgetting that I'm married. And stop looking at me like that. I can almost feel your eyes upon me. I'm sure you've had dealings with my father, but right now, there's no time. Sebastian's going to destroy half of London if I don't get to him in time."

"Sebastian's your husband?" A piece of plaster tore itself in half along the ceiling, and Ianthe dragged Cleo forward, trying not to fall as that section of the roof crashed to the floor. One by one, windows were shattering somewhere in the building.

"Yes. You would be Miss Martin, I presume?"

"How did you know?" Suspicion reared its head.

"I *saw* you. This whole affair set my precognition off, and I kept hearing your name and seeing your face. It was so prominent it was blinding the rest of my senses. I knew I had to find you. You're the only one who can stop this, I think."

Two brothers enter that building... Only one of them comes out...

Which meant either Cleo was going to be a widow very shortly, or Ianthe was never going to get the chance to be anything more than Lucien's Anchor. "Here," she said, dragging the young woman faster. Pieces of rubble jumped and shivered across the floor as a tremor began to shake the very earth itself. "It's intensifying."

Silence.

No wind. No air to breathe. Just pressure.

A vacuum of nothingness.

Lucien's ears were ringing. He took a step forward, power roaring through him and diverted through his outstretched hand into the Prime. Glass crunched beneath his boot, having given up the ghost in the first blast. The wall between the cell and the sunroom had blasted outward during that first intense wave as the Prime sought to contain the raw force erupting from his son.

Lucien's brother.

He recognized little of himself in the other man. No, Sebastian was cut from Drake's image, whereas he himself bore more of his mother, Lady Rathbourne. When Sebastian looked up, his eyes narrowed with hatred upon the woman that Drake was protecting, Lucien finally saw something that he recognized.

The loneliness. The ache of betrayal. A brother who had known some of the same miseries that he himself had felt.

"Can't... hold him... much longer." Drake grit his teeth. The sheer amount of power that he was grounding was extraordinary.

"Then let him kill her," Lucien shouted, though his voice sounded strange and empty. *He* was starting to feel empty. One of the rings on his hand shattered as he drew too much power, letting his father absorb it.

The Prime's startled eyes shot to his, but defiance formed there. "No. That task... is mine. Not his... No son should have to... kill... his mother."

Drake had been straining beneath the lash of raw fury, but at the words, somehow the Prime found an inner strength that began pushing back against the strain. Somehow he was containing it.

That sensation of feeling watched heightened. An eerie sensation trailed down Luc's spine.

Shouts. Ragged confusion. Then something slamming into his side as Morgana drove herself against him, sliding the knife into his side.

"Your sacrifice, my lord," she whispered, her green eyes meeting his.

Agony erupted. A wash of red flooded Luc's vision, making him see double, until it felt like he stood in two places. In one world he staggered across the floor with glass crunching beneath his boots, a cold throb erupting from just beneath his ribs; in the other world, there was an aching feeling of nothingness, just icy stonewalls and a shadowy figure turning around to face him, its hands lifting to drag the black hood back from its face.

"There you are," something whispered in his mind. Its mental claws locked tight over him.

Lucien screamed as all of his old nightmares took shape and form.

When he blinked, he was no longer standing in the sunroom. The two worlds became one. Instead, he was screaming within a prison of nothingness, the grate overhead revealing a small, insipid moon that looked oddly wrong, and the walls shimmered with a haze of heat, as if they were not truly there.

Voice raw, he came back to himself. "Where am I?"

The shadow revealed its face. The demon stood there, wearing a mask, and a topcoat with tails. The thin eye slits gleamed black, as if the holes fell into infinity, rather than reveal its eyes. It smiled, the mask stretching into a contortion that echoed its expression, and chilled his blood.

"My prissson," the demon rasped, "in your mind." Both hands speared wide. "This is where I dwell. Where you casst me, once my s...sservice was done."

No. A cold sweat gleamed along his skin, and Luc took a step back. "How...?"

The demon advanced without taking a single step. "Do you remember my name?"

Lascher. He didn't dare utter it. "I banished you."

That smile spread. "Yesss. Here. Always here. Did you not know that I have been watching you? All this time?"

A bubble of power spun to life, balanced on the creature's fingertip. Within the opaque globe, Lucien saw himself and Ianthe entwined upon their bed. Her pale skin gleamed against their dark sheets as her body arched in ecstasy and she threw her head back.

Lucien smashed the bubble, and it dissipated like smoke. "Not her."

It can't hurt me, Lucien told himself. *This is a psychic plane that it's created somewhere within my mind. I'm not really here.* "You cannot step through into the physical world."

The demon laughed. Between one instant and the next, it vanished, and then it was standing directly in front of him. One hand lashed out, catching hold of the back of his neck. Their bodies pressed together, and the demon reached out and licked his cheek.

It burned like acid. Lucien gasped, trying to push it away, but all he could hear was that mocking laughter. Its grip was iron. The press of its body mocked him, and the fingers that glided down his chest clenched in his shirt, driving through what felt like the first layer of skin covering his heart.

"This is where I rule," Lascher whispered. "You are not the strong one here. I am. All I needed to do was wait for you to open yourself up psychically, wait for blood to ssspill." It leered closer, its breath smelling faintly of cinnamon and burnt spices. "Have you not dreamed of me?" A poisonous whisper. It conjured memories of nightmares too horrible to remember. "Yes," it taunted. "That one."

Red silk sheets. Naked flesh. The creature entwined with his body, its skin sinking into his, its mouth on his, their bodies slowly becoming one until Lucien lay alone, blinking up at the ceiling with black eyes...

No. *No.* He wouldn't remember. This wasn't happening. The demon couldn't take from him; it was only granted power when he willed it.

"Are you certain?" Lascher taunted; its body pressed against his. The movement dragged him back into the nightmare...

Ianthe. Lucien threw the thought out there, clinging to her memory. Of the perfume she wore, the feel of her skin, the taste of her smile... It grounded him a little.

"She's lovely. Perhaps when I'm in your body, I'll get to enjoy her too?"

Rage spiraled through him. Somehow Lucien caught the creature by the throat and shoved it back against the icy walls. They throbbed and the demon flinched. Lucien found some strength in that. "You'll never touch her. Never!"

This... this was his boundary. Fury gave him strength that hadn't been there before. Suddenly, he felt like there was distance between them. He felt like himself again.

But how did he get out of here?

A whisper of skirts brushed against him. "Lucien!" A hand slid over his sleeve. There, but not here. "Lucien, wake up! Here! Take my hand!"

And then Ianthe shimmered to life beside him, her hand curling through his. Her figure was as opaque as the vision the demon had shown him.

She was blind to the demon beside him. Blind to this world. But somehow she stood on the threshold of it. The lilac color of her skirts seemed so bright, so vibrant against the cold, dark walls of this inner prison, even though she was not wholly here. Lucien could see right through her, but her touch... that anchored him. Suddenly, the ground felt real beneath his feet. Flashes of sorcery crackled off wards around him, and he saw Drake with his hands outspread, his rings sparking and smoldering as he flung sorcerous weaves at his ex-wife. Morgana retaliated, stumbling back in a rush of red skirts, staggering as both Drake and Sebastian hammered at her. It all swam around him in an eerie dream-like sequence, the figures moving so slowly as they ducked and threw battle globes at each other.

Only the weft and weave of sorcerous power held any weight to it, any significance in this world. Battle globes met each other, erupting in violent coruscations of red and blue.

The only thing that looked real was his body, gasping on the floor, and Ianthe curled over him, holding onto his hand, while she frantically tried to staunch the blood.

Holding his hand, even now.

"Ssshe's the only thing holding you back," Lascher said spitefully. It reached out, gripping Ianthe's wrist.

Ianthe screamed. "He's mine!"

"The only thing holding *you* back," Lucien corrected, shifting so that his body was between them. He felt stronger now. "You have no hold over me. She does. She owns me; body, heart, and soul."

The demon hissed. A malicious cloud seemed to be building behind it, little sparks of malevolent green lightning crackling within.

"Lucien," Ianthe called to him. "Come back! You belong to me."

One last look at the demon, and then she was dragging Lucien back, through some sort of hazy tunnel, Lascher receding into the distance.

The demon hissed and flung the cloud at them. Lucien thrust up his hands, but it passed right through him, a sting of icy needles that tore at his skin. Ianthe, however, screamed.

As if it were cutting her apart inside.

Drake staggered, torn between opposing forces as Lucien's spine arched off the floor and he screamed. Sebastian was on his hands and knees, swaying and bleeding from the nose and ears. He didn't know which son was in worse condition. Standing halfway between them, he eyed Morgana.

"Lucien?" he called.

Ianthe ground her teeth together, blood dripping from her nose as she lifted her face. "I've... got him."

A black haze enveloped her. Then she screamed as Lucien gasped, his eyes springing wide open.

"No!" a woman cried out. Eleanor.

Just a split second where his attention had been misdirected. Enough time for Morgana to make her move.

She held the tip of the Blade to Eleanor's throat, draping his lover's weakened form back against her. "Don't move," she spat.

Drake held both hands out in a gesture of surrender. His eyes met Eleanor's. She looked confused, weakened. *Fight back*, he wanted to yell, but Eleanor's magic was silent. She was never submissive, never this quiet. Eleanor was a raging lion when someone threatened those she cared for. It made his heart drop like lead. What had Morgana done to her? "You're facing a dilemma, Morgana. If you hurt her," he promised, his voice darkening, "I'll kill you. Let her go, and I might spare you."

"I'm the one with the Blade! Don't speak to me like *you* hold the power here!" Morgana gestured the tip of the Blade toward him, then shifted it toward Sebastian when their son looked up. "Don't you move either, you treacherous brat."

"Morgana." Drake held his hand out toward her and took a slow, steady step. "It's done. You're surrounded."

"It's done when I say it's done—"

Sebastian launched toward her.

His son's sorcery was burned out, leaving him weak and unsteady, but he moved with deadly accuracy.

"No!" Drake screamed, but it was too late. Sebastian collided with them just as Morgana drove the Blade home.

One final time.

Sebastian ground his bloodied teeth together, holding the blade sheathed in his side and his mother's hands around it. This time, there was no warning. Expression ripped its way through the room, focusing in on the Blade itself. The pressure built, and Drake barely flung up a ward large enough to contain it.

Red light exploded as the Blade's magic sunk in upon itself, stretching the very fabric of being, and then it collapsed. Sebastian's power threw him and his mother apart, taking Drake with it.

When Drake blinked and came to, he was lying beside Eleanor. Some part of him remembered crawling toward her before the blackness overtook him. "Ellie?" he whispered. "Get up. We need to get moving."

Those gold-ringed blue eyes met his. "*Nur. Megurrh.*"

"What's wrong?"

The room began to tremble. The entire floor felt like it was going to drop beneath his feet. Their sorcerous duel must have weakened some of the supports below. "Ianthe, get Lucien out of here!" Drake threw over his shoulder, then curled over Eleanor. There was blood on her back—a blow directly from the Blade, which sent a chill through him. The only way to heal such a cut was by using the Chalice to mix a healing potion. *If* they got to it in time... The slow steady trickle of blood wet his hands.

"Ianthe's not breathing!" Lucien yelled back.

Everything seemed to turn on its head. Drake glanced behind him. Ianthe flopped like a doll in Lucien's hands, but Lucien looked fine. Strained and pale, but he was only bleeding a little.

Drake glanced back at Eleanor, who lay on the floor, and Sebastian, who was grappling with Morgana, torn between too many opposing forces. For the first time in years, he didn't know what to do.

Or who to protect.

For they all meant something to him. And he was terribly afraid that he would have to make a choice...

CHAPTER THIRTY

'A Soul-bond is formed between two lovers, and it ties their life-spans together as if they were truly but one...'

—- Lady Eberhardt's transcription on Soul-bonds

"IANTHE?" Lucien whispered, his voice tight and dry. "Ianthe. *Please*. Please come back. Breathe, damn you!"

The floor shuddered beneath them. Something fell. Somewhere.

But he shut the world out, pressing hard on her chest. Power was a faded ember within him, almost burned out, but at the periphery of his senses, he could sense the faded gold spill of the bond that connected him to Ianthe. It unraveled with delicate slowness as if she were slipping away into a place he couldn't follow.

"No," he whispered, bending forward to breathe into her lungs. Her mouth was soft and unresisting. Whatever the demon had flung at her had been a psychic storm of immense proportions. Ianthe had held firm, focused on dragging him out of that inner prison, rather than on protecting herself. It had worked. Lucien had blinked and found himself falling heavily into his own body, flesh weighing him down, but the cost of it... He didn't think he could bear the cost of it. He reached out with unsteady hands, stroking her face, trying to hold on, with everything that he had, to that dwindling thread of gold.

Their link.

Their bond.

Her.

She wasn't breathing. And she was colorless, all of the beautiful, incandescent colors that flickered around her constantly, fading to nothing.

It choked him, as if, without her breath, his own could not release. The shimmer of magic around her dulled a little, the vibrant white glow softening as if there were nothing to sustain it. Like a hot coal slowly fading in a cold grate, all of that heat, that energy, compressing into the heart of her, and then... flickering out.

"Please," he whispered, stroking a rough hand through Ianthe's hair. Her head lolled to the side. "Don't you dare do this. Don't you leave me."

Leaning down, Lucien pressed his mouth against hers, giving her the type of kiss that he'd never dared. One that gave her his heart and soul, tasting the lax fullness of her mouth. "You win," he whispered, hands fisting in her hair and heat flushing his eyes. Finally reduced to begging. "You win. I'm yours. Everything that I am is yours. *I love you!* Just... don't you dare leave me."

The link between them unraveled. Somehow he snatched at each end of it, holding on with sheer force of will as the pull of her own soul stretched back toward a pool of obliterating darkness. The pain burned him to ash, tore him apart, and burned him again, but he wouldn't let go. His teeth slammed together so tightly that he could feel the ache even through the lash of power. It scalded his senses, left him raw and scabbed over, where he'd finally begun to rebuild against the sensitivity of it.

But he didn't let go.

Instead, he drew the vast depths of his power into himself like a man taking in the deepest breath he could. Finger trembling, Lucien traced one of the forbidden runes between her breasts. It erupted into scarlet light, and Ianthe's body jerked as he turned the same gold-tipped finger to his own heart, transforming the bond that they'd begun, so long ago, it seemed.

Power exploded in a violent coruscation around them as the bond between them snapped back into place, twice as thick, each lashing tendril of power binding them together like a web.

He didn't think he could hold it. A force stronger than his own dragged him after her, slipping inexorably toward that pool of oblivion.

A small psychic touch brushed against him, a tiny little thread adding to their bond. Something alien, but something he recognized instantly. *Louisa.* Reaching out with powers as yet undeveloped, as if she'd sensed her mother's need, even over such a vast distance.

And both of them catapulted back into reality, slamming harshly into their own bodies.

Ianthe's eyes shot open, golden power streaming from them, and a dry, hollow scream sounding in her throat. Lucien held her in his arms, pressing his face against her throat, whispering, "*Please,*" over and over again as he rocked her.

She fell into sobbing, and Lucien curled her against his chest, feeling raw inside. *Thank God.* He looked up to the heavens, barely able to breathe through the enormity of the emotions surging through him.

The room trembled.

Drake snatched at his sleeve, concern in his eyes, and his face stained with dust. "We have to get out of here," he said, balancing Eleanor Ross in his arms. "The entire house is going to collapse, I think."

In the end, it was a choice that Drake did not wish to make.

His lover in his arms. His son and the daughter-of-his-heart stumbling behind them as they fled the building.

Morgana and the son he'd only just found were left behind.

I'll go back, he promised himself as they fled. *Go back and save him...*

His heart bled, but he got them out, just as the house collapsed. Half of it sheared away, burying itself in rubble. The half where Eleanor had been held. Drake turned back to it, knowing he was too late to enter, knowing he couldn't save this last son.

You failed. You failed him. Just as Lady Rathbourne had once prophesized.

Others were there. Lady Eberhardt, setting the situation to rights with a brusque take-charge manner; and Bishop, the only son who he'd spent much time with, watching him with those dark Sicarii eyes, as Drake turned to stare at the house.

"It's better this way," Bishop told him.

They understood each other. They always had. Nobody should wield that much power. Nobody with only the gifts of Expression. It was dangerous. The whole of London would burn.

But Drake mourned, not as a Prime, not as a man who knew the dangers of such things, but as a father who remembered, once upon a time, the words that his lover had once told him:

Three sons, three sacrifices.
When you first lay eyes upon them all, the end will begin.
You shall be their deaths. You shall turn their graves.
And the whole of London shall burn, if it does not come to pass.

"I tried to stay away," he said, weakly. "I tried."

"I know," Bishop replied, and for once, his bleak eyes showed symptoms of sympathy.

CHAPTER THIRTY-ONE

Minutes before the collapse...

"SEBASTIAN?" CLEO CALLED, taking a careful step forward into what she suspected was the hall. Miss Martin had left her side as soon as someone screamed, leaving Cleo to shuffle her way along, tripping over pieces of rubble.

This way, said her senses. *Go this way.*

Voices called as others moved away from her. The entire building shook, but everything in her screamed to keep going.

Someone was coughing nearby. "Bloody hell," Sebastian spat. "What are you doing here?"

Relief flooded through her, and she hurried forward as much as she could. "You're h-hurt?" It was partly a question.

"Cleo." A hand caught her wrist, and then she was being dragged sideways as Sebastian listed toward the wall. His voice was raw, cracked. "You've got to get out of here.

The roof's... coming down. The whole building's... coming... down."

"I know," she told him, because she'd *seen* it. She was more concerned with him and what else she'd seen. "You're bleeding. Where? Where are you bleeding?"

He hesitated, but she was shoving aside his clothes, trying to find the source of his forthcoming death. She could stop this. She had to stop this!

"You need to get out of here."

"Not without you," she told him, even as a nearby wall collapsed, taking with it part of the roof. Cleo cried out, her hand curling through his in fright as something sharp slashed her cheek as it flew past.

"Cleo." There was a world of information in that one word. Sebastian slumped back against the wall, his voice sounding strained. His legs gave way, dragging him down—and her with him. "It's done. T-the ceiling collapsed upon her."

"Who?"

"Morgana." He wheezed. "It's done. She's done. I finally... did it."

"If we don't hurry, then the ceiling might collapse on us too!" As if to punctuate her words, something fell with a heavy crash nearby. Cleo gasped.

"I don't think... that I'm going... to be able to manage." Sebastian pressed something into her hands. A ruined piece of knife. It felt plain, heavier than expected, after all this fuss. "Take this... with you. I destroyed it, but... make sure... it's melted down."

"No!" She caught his coat by the lapels as Sebastian slid down the wall, and she landed on her knees in front of him. The knife tumbled into her skirts. "No! I won't let this happen!" Hot tears wet her blindfold. "I won't!"

Strong fingers curled around her wrists. "You've seen it... haven't you?"

The entire building was shaking. She screwed her eyes shut behind her blindfold, pressing her forehead to his chest.

"Cleo, it won't stop bleeding." He sounded like he was explaining something to a child. "She stabbed me with the Blade. It's the type of wound that cannot be healed... or so they say."

Cleo tore at her skirts, wadding them up and pressing them against the hot, weeping slash at his side. She couldn't stop crying, but she was determined, even if premonition had been willfully silent on this topic. In every vision she'd seen, every twist of the future that she'd tried to imagine, all she'd ever seen was herself crying over his body when he finally stopped breathing.

"I won't let it happen! I won't!"

"Cleo, you need to get out of h-here." He was slurring now. Hands cupped her face, his trembling fingers holding her in place. "I don't want to... die... knowing that you're still in here."

"Well, you'd better help me get out then, hadn't you?" she demanded. "Because I'm not going anywhere without you." Her throat closed over. "You tried to stop them from killing Mrs. Ross, didn't you? This is my fault. This happened because I demanded that you save her!"

"Hush. Hush..."

Cleo shook her head. "If I hadn't demanded such a thing, you wouldn't have been there." She was flat out sobbing now. "I'm so selfish!"

"No. No, you're not." He was whispering now, still holding onto her face. "You're the most amazing person I've ever met. It was worth it. I'm finally free, Cleo."

"Bastian—"

"Hush." His voice sounded closer, his thumbs stroking her cheeks. "Just hush. Just give me this. Once."

And then his mouth brushed against hers, his breath teasing her lips. Cleo froze in shock as Sebastian finally kissed her, so sweetly it almost took her breath away. A simple touch, but one filled with so much yearning, so much need...

She could feel the tingle of premonition itching over her skin. *Not yet!* She wanted this to last, wanted—

A vision speared through her; a way in which she could save his life. She could see the threads of sorcery dancing through her own fingers, see how she could save him! Repercussions stretched out, consequences echoing with a warning cry, but she didn't heed them. She had done this. Now, she could undo it. All she had to do was—

Sorcery wove into a fine thread between her fingers. Cleo struck with it, pressing her hand over his chest and forcing that fine web to curl around his heart, binding it to hers as his mouth tore from her own. Something wrenched in her chest, and Sebastian screamed, his body arcing off the floor and pressing up into the palm of her hand as she threw everything she had into this last, final spell. A way to bind him to her, so that not even death could steal him away.

It hurt. Gods, it hurt. She was screaming too, her heart resettling in her chest before finally smoothing into a steady, deliberate rhythm again. Something soft pressed against her face, and as she came back to herself, she found herself lying atop him, her head resting against his chest.

His heart beat beneath her ear, a rhythm that synced perfectly with hers.

His wound was wet and bloody beneath her hand, but sealing slowly. It was a wound that would never fully heal, would always form a weakness for him, but one which owned no mortal effect upon him, at least, not for now.

As for the rest... She had time to think, time to work out how to deal with it... all of it.

"What... have you done?" Sebastian whispered hoarsely. His hands gripped her upper arms, almost painfully, as if he was frightened. "Cleo?"

"I've saved your life, Bastian."

No matter what the consequences were, She wouldn't regret a thing.

"Now help me get out of here."

CHAPTER THIRTY-TWO

IANTHE BLINKED in the soft morning light, trying to remember where she was. The room was abnormally bright, searing her senses. Lifting a hand to her eyes, she moaned in pain. It felt as though every muscle in her body had been pounded between a hammer and anvil.

"Be still," a dark shadow murmured. Drake appeared in her vision, impassive in black. "You're not to use your sorcery for a very long time, do you understand me?"

"M-my sorcery?"

A hand cupped her forehead, a wash of warmth seeping through her and filling her with strength. Ianthe shivered as her body soaked it up, clinging to the rush of power like a drowning man.

"You exerted yourself immensely," Drake's voice was grave. "From the sound of it, you completely stripped your body of energy in order to protect Lucien, and the demon's psychic assault nearly killed you."

"L-Lucien?"

Drake eased her back onto the pillows and sat on the edge of the bed. "He's safe and well. Far better than you, actually. He forged a bond between you, Ianthe, against your will. A bond far tighter than anything that you wove before. You will never break it. You will carry it with you until one of you dies, and then most likely, the other will follow. A Soul-bond." Drake's dark lashes fluttered against his cheeks as he looked down, his fingers still in hers. "He said you were dying."

Coldness spiraled through her chest. Faintly, the image of being surrounded by nothing but darkness flashed into her mind, followed by a voice screaming at her to come back. Reaching out, it held her there, trapped between life and death.

"What he did is illegal."

The words were a slap in the face. "Not if I chose to accept it."

"Did you?" Drake's piercing gray eyes locked on hers.

"Yes," Ianthe lied boldly. "We had a telepathic bond. I knew what he offered."

That steady gaze never looked away. She fought a blush.

"He is a changed man," Drake said. "You are changed too."

"Change is not always for the worst."

"No." He smiled faintly, but it looked like an effort. Someone scratched at the door. "Ah. There's someone else who wants to see you. Two someone's, in fact."

The door opened and Thea stepped inside, her face pale and her hand curled around—

"Louisa," Ianthe whispered, pushing herself upright and opening her arms.

"Mama!" Her daughter's composure broke, and the little girl darted for the bed, wrapping herself around Ianthe as if she'd never let her go. There was an odd sense of rightness about the motion, as if Louisa's presence had somehow made her whole and she had not realized that a piece of her was missing until now. Ianthe drew back, frowning.

"Someone Expressed herself for the first time," Drake said, his smile set in stone and his hand gentle on Louisa's head, so as not to frighten her. "She sensed your need somehow and reached out to help her father bring you back. She is part of your bond, just not as tightly laced as the two of you are."

That spoke of precognition, perhaps. How else would Louisa have sensed what she'd needed to do? Ianthe's heart grew heavy. Her daughter was far too young for the weight of sorcery, but she forced a smile and kissed Louisa's cheek. "We shall have to begin teaching you how to control yourself then."

"May I?" Drake offered. "I have no apprentice, and someone else needs your full attention."

Ianthe's gaze lifted to Thea. The girl's eyes were full of heartbreak. Ianthe held out her hand and dragged Thea onto the bed with them. Her arms curled around both girls. "None of this is your fault," she whispered, kissing Thea's hair. "It would have happened regardless of what you did. I tried to wrestle with a demon on a psychic plane that it had created." She tried for brevity. "So lesson learned: Stay as far away from demons as possible, Thea, and don't ever think yourself a match for one when you're playing by their rules. They pack one hell of a wallop."

No such luck in diverting her apprentice. "Lucien said you weren't breathing."

"A great deal happened at once, I believe. He probably overstated the gravity of the situation." Ianthe met Drake's dark gaze over the top of Thea's head, and he nodded, just faintly. Louisa's hand curled tightly in hers. There was no fooling her daughter. Not if she'd sensed it.

"Lou, would you like to learn sorcery with Drake?" Ianthe asked, setting both girls beside her, their backs to her pillows.

"Do I have to live with him?" Louisa asked, suddenly fearful.

"No. No, not yet. You're to live with me." *And Lucien.* But she suddenly wasn't certain of that answer. She could sense him somewhere within the house, but when she reached out—

Ianthe winced. Her head was pounding. The entire world seemed washed in too much light, too much sensation. Was this how Lucien had felt?

"There is plenty of time," Drake said, reaching behind Louisa's ear and producing a penny, of all things.

"That's sleight of hand." Ianthe rolled her eyes. "Not sorcery."

Louisa giggled as Drake vanished the penny then held both hands up, as if to dispute her.

"And it gives me leave to visit every week," he said. "To see how my granddaughter is doing. We can have her lessons then."

No doubt he intended to keep a close eye on all of them.

Ianthe sighed. "Two young ladies threatening to set my house on fire. Whatever am I to do?"

The jesting continued, but Thea held herself somewhat absent. Ianthe reached out to squeeze the young lady's hand, to try and chase away the shadows in her apprentice's eyes, as Drake tried to show Louisa his penny trick.

"I will never use Expression again." Thea's promise was raw.

It ached that this lesson had been so brutal.

"I am glad to hear it." Ianthe paused. "We shall take it slowly. I'm certain Louisa will need someone to help her adjust to all of this. It has been a trying experience for all, but mostly her. She will need you."

"You want me to stay?"

"Oh, Thea. That was never in any doubt." But she realized, looking at the girl, that it had been. Just not in Ianthe's mind. Had she ever been so young herself?

Her smile faded. Of course she had. "I tell you what, why not let us make this formal? I shall draft a document to take you on legally as my ward. I must do so for Louisa; you might as well become sisters in truth."

Thea swallowed hard. "Thank you."

As she hugged the girl, Ianthe caught Drake's eyes over the top of Thea's dark hair. He nodded, just once, but it was nice to know she was finally mastering the art of being Thea's tutor. There was so much more to it than spell craft, wards, and lessons.

"Girls, I promised you could see Ianthe when she was awake. Now, perhaps it's time to let her rest? It's been a strenuous couple of days. Maybe you could scurry down to the kitchens and see if you can get her something to eat?"

"Kisses first," Ianthe said, dragging Lou into her arms. The little girl clung to her, and Ianthe breathed in the sweet scent of her hair. "*I missed you*," she whispered, "and I promise we are going to have a lot of catching up to do once I've gotten my feet back under me."

Then she snagged Thea into the embrace, kissed her on the forehead, and told them to hurry and fetch her some breakfast, as she was now ravenous.

The door closed behind the two.

Ianthe swallowed. "I still feel like I don't know what to do. It terrifies me sometimes."

Drake crossed to the fireplace to give the coals there a poke. "That feeling never goes away, Ianthe. I think it's part of being a parent."

He wasn't saying something. "How is Eleanor?"

"Lucien's wound wasn't bleeding like Eleanor's was, strangely enough. We used the Chalice to heal her stab wound, but... the doctors believe she's suffered an apoplectic seizure. She cannot speak. She can barely feed herself, or dress herself, but she's there. I know she's there. I see her in those eyes when she looks at me, as if she wants me so desperately to understand her." He fell silent, toying with the hilt of the poker. "They think Ellie would do better if I committed her to a treatment facility."

"Oh, Drake," Ianthe whispered. "What are you going to do?"

"I am going to keep her here. I will look after her myself. I owe her nothing less. She... she only went into danger in order to protect me."

"And the Order?"

Drake turned toward her, face implacable. "I cannot remain Prime. I cannot split my attention between the Order's needs and my own anymore, and I'll be damned if, for once in my life, I don't give the right priority to those who need me, to my family. I intend to resign."

Ianthe's eyebrows arched. That was unheard of, but then, what man *would* resign from a position of such power?

"But what about Morgana? What about Tremayne? The Relics?"

"Morgana is dead. The house collapsed and she never emerged. Some of my men are excavating as we speak, but I expect that thorn in my side to have been buried. Tremayne, however, remains a problem. The second the tides of the battle turned against him, he commanded his remaining imps to overrun Agatha and Bishop, and then he fled. Bishop intends to hunt him down. The Relics? Well, Bishop still has the Chalice that Agatha gave to him, and the Blade was destroyed in the conflict. I'll set him to hunting for the Wand too. Morgana shall have hidden it somewhere, I presume."

She knew him too well. His bland recital hid something that he didn't want to discuss. Too bad. That was part of having this little ragtag family of theirs. "And Sebastian?"

Drake's gaze slid to the window, staring at nothing. "No sign of him. I suspect we will find him once the excavation has been completed."

"Oh, Drake, I'm so sorry."

"I knew it was too good to be true. I'd grieved for him for so long, that when I realized he was still alive..." His stiff, proud shoulders wilted slightly. "I—I couldn't save them all. I couldn't get to him in time, and Morgana... she stabbed him with the Blade. He would have bled out." He sounded as though he was trying to convince himself. "So you're asking the wrong person what it's like to be a parent. I'm the failure, Ianthe. Not you."

"You were never a failure, Drake. Not to me."

He smiled at her, but it was empty. "Thank you. And now that you've seen straight through me, I must return the favor. You haven't asked about Lucien."

How well they knew each other. "You told me he had bonded me. I assumed he was all right." She thought about it, feeling that faint psychic touch against her. "No. I know he's all right. Limping slightly and favoring his right foot, but the wound in his side seems perfectly whole."

"Do you wish to see him?"

Yes. Always yes. Lucien had become her entire life, filling her world with him. She couldn't wait to settle into an ordinary life with him and watch him love their daughter, and hopefully one day, herself. "Tell him I'll meet him in the orangery. Just let me dress first."

Lucien paced on the tiled floor, tapping his hat against his thigh. A little quiver plucked at the bond that he would wear forever, like fingers rippling over cellists' stings, and he turned, his breath catching at the sight of her.

Ianthe took a hesitant step inside the orangery, dark circles still shadowing her eyes. Her skin was pale against the lavender skirts she wore, but he thought, in that moment, that he'd never seen her so beautiful. Perhaps the near loss of her only served to emphasize how precious she'd become.

They stared at each other for a long moment; then she breathed out a faint laugh that barely hid a tremble. "I must look a sight."

"You do," he said hoarsely. "You look beautiful."

Faint color flickered over her cheeks. "I told Drake that I agreed to the bond," Ianthe blurted. "I know it wasn't what you wanted, but thank—"

He took that final step toward her and wrapped a hand around the back of her neck. Dragging her against him, he stole her words with his mouth.

Ianthe gasped, and then her hands locked in his collar.

A kiss to steal his senses, to sign his fate. It terrified him to think of how close he'd come to losing this forever. Kissing her had become more than a pleasure, but a sign of intimacy, a sign of surrender... That foolish bet sprang to mind. How arrogant it seemed now. A play of power between them, when they'd both been wary. He gave her that power now, gave it wholly and without doubt, surrendering everything that he was into her hands. One of them broke the kiss—him or her, he wasn't certain—and they stood against the wall, panting.

"We cannot break this bond," she whispered, still holding onto his collar.

"Do you wish to?"

Ianthe looked up, her heart in her eyes. "No. But y-you—"

"I have no regrets, Ianthe." His thumb stroked her cheek. "I want you to know that. I consider myself the luckiest man alive right now. I love you."

Ianthe looked up shyly from beneath her sable lashes. It ached that he could see the pleased sense of shock in her, as if nobody had ever told her such a thing. At least there was no doubt. She trusted him, believed in the words he was telling her, and he knew then that he would have to keep telling her such a thing over and over until she forgot all of the times she had been told she was not worthy of such.

"I love you," he repeated, his voice firming. "And I'm going to marry you. We can be a family—you, me, and Louisa."

"And Thea."

"And Thea. I had nothing, nobody. That's the truth of it. My life was dust, Ianthe, until I met you."

"The first time? When I came to arrest you." She tried to make light of it, and he realized she was still a little uncomfortable with this outpouring of emotion.

"The first time," he corrected, "when you walked into that grotto, gowned in white silk with a filigreed mask hiding those beautiful eyes. That was the beginning of us. You stole my breath. I just never realized that you stole my heart too. I mean to have all of your nights, Ianthe, and I shall give you my days. All of my days. And all of my heart." His voice roughened. "I didn't... I didn't realize how much you meant to me until you collapsed. I suspected, of course, but that moment... Nothing in my life has ever meant as much to me as you do. As Louisa does. I want you to know that."

Ianthe swallowed. "I hardly know what to say."

"Say you believe it. Say you deserve it."

Those violet eyes met his. She was hesitant. "I believe it. I deserve it. And I love you too, Lucien. I never dared admit that until yesterday, because I was frightened that it could be taken away from me."

"Nothing can take it away from us. We live together, and eventually, we shall die together, our breaths as one. Come here." He leaned down to kiss her. It was the sweetest sensation in the world, feeling her heart beating in time with his own. The kiss drifted on for long minutes, a slow and steady exploration, as if they had all the time in the world.

"To forever then," Ianthe said breathlessly when she finally drew back.

"All our days and nights," he agreed.

And for the first time in her life, Ianthe believed in such a promise—he could feel it light her up within, soaking through their Soul-bond and filling him with it too.

Forever.

EPILOGUE

MORGANA COUGHED the ash from her lungs and then quivered, lying still for a moment to catch her breath—and her bearings. Something weighed her down, and the world was blackness and rubble. Every inch of her hurt, as though poison raced through her veins, scalding her from the inside out. And... and she couldn't seem to feel her toes. No, not just her toes. Her entire lower half was nothing more than numbness.

Her own son had betrayed her, and the girl, Cleo, had something to do with it. Drake had won, or no, not quite... She'd had one last hand to deal, and it was a winning hand, but where... Patting around, her heart erupted into panic. Where was the Blade? Where was her trump card?

Morgana scrabbled beneath her smoking skirts and found the hilt of the Blade there. Relief flooded through her. Her smile was a thing of vengeance. They thought they had beaten her, but she still had the relic, and now they would presume themselves safe.

After all, when one's greatest gift was Illusion, sleight of hand was but a mere trick. Sebastian's power might be brutal, but the kitchen knife that she'd wielded last night had borne the brunt of it, not the Blade hidden in her skirts. All she'd had to do was make sure the ensuing explosion felt powerful enough to hint at the destruction of a Relic Infernal.

Still, she wasn't certain how she was going to manage to get out of here.

She tried to move her legs, and... nothing.

A new fear enveloped her.

No. Not this. This would *not* be her price to pay, it would not be.

She fought long and hard, straining to force her weakened body to obey. The heavy beam across the middle of her back had no give to it, and the exertion left her panting, clutching hopelessly at the treasure in her hand, a treasure that was ultimately worthless if she couldn't force herself to escape this physical trap.

Her magic was useless, drained in the encounter.

Her body was useless.

"Damn you," Morgana cried, her forehead resting against the timber floors and a hot tear scalding her cheek. "You fucking useless piece of flesh. You bleeding little whore." Her uncle's favorite words to use against her, and she used them now to inspire that inner rage that always burned, but even her own innate fury could give her no release. "Get up!"

The door opened with a creak.

Morgana froze.

A pair of men's heeled shoes came into view and a tall shape materialized, wearing a long black cloak with a hood. His face was somewhat obscured, and she blinked away her tears, trying desperately to make him out.

The ominous click of the heels came closer. Morgana's breath caught in her chest, but it didn't matter. She was helpless.

That was when she saw his face, that bland marionette mask beneath the hood with spells of Illusion carved into the papier-mâché. Her eye wanted to follow the runes that burned with a brassy gleam, but she forced herself to meet his eyes, ignoring the flicker of an image—a young, handsome man—that the spell suggested to her weakened mind.

Those empty, black holes gleamed with nothingness. Every person who passed this man would see a different face in their mind. Nobody would be able to describe him. Only she, who knew Illusion, could see through it.

"What are you?" she whispered, forcing herself to swallow. "Show me your face!"

"I find it interesting that you think yourself in the position to make such demands," the stranger said. The words burned into her mind, as if they'd bypassed her ears entirely.

Her heart hammered, her blood seeming to freeze in her veins. She'd heard that voice before. She'd *commanded* it, so many years ago, when she, Drake, and Tremayne began to dabble with the Relics Infernal. Her fist clenched around the hilt of the Blade, but the creature merely laughed.

"Yessss," it whispered and reached up to remove its mask of Illusion. "Now you are beginning to understand."

Slowly, the mask lowered, and Morgana squeezed her eyelids tightly together. She did not want to see it.

"Look at me."

She shook her head.

"Look at me, or I shall remove your eyelids, so you may never look away again."

That made her open them.

Noah Guthrie's body. Or it had been once.

The creature squatted in front of her, his trousers straining over his thighs. His eyes burned holes of fire in his handsome face. He was beautiful, stunning, his skin made of pure alabaster, as if carved by a Renaissance master. Except... Except for the faint flaws, the sheer *inhumanness* of it. The skin on the middle of its forehead smoked and began to peel, a sigil of burning light branding itself there. A sigil she never, ever wanted to see again.

Morgana froze, turning her eyes away from the sight. She couldn't breathe. All of her life, her dreams, her ambitions... destroyed. She knew it already. And now she was at the mercy of a being who could, and would, do anything it wanted to her. Helpless. She knew that feeling so well. She'd spent years fighting to put herself in a position where she would never be helpless again, but the world conspired against her.

"I see you remember me."

How could she forget? It was the first creature they'd ever summoned from the Nether Reaches, a plane of existence that some termed Hell. Their audacity had been met by a being of power that had stared at them as though it were committing their faces to memory.

Tremayne had crowed, as if the world had been handed to them on a platter, but Drake had grown still. And Morgana had hovered between both emotions. Here was the world—power, revenge, and everything she'd ever wanted—hers for the taking... But meeting the demon's eyes felt like staring into an abyss that had suddenly opened beneath her feet.

The creature smiled, an expression that made her feel like a cold claw was trailing down her spine. "What can I do for you? Mastersss?"

"Tell us your true name," Tremayne had demanded. A name was power, or so it was spoken by all the mystics. "You are bound by these relics. You must obey me."

It had been a little too easy. The creature blinked. Its eyes narrowed, a muscle jumping in its jaw, and then with a snarl it had spat: "Lascher."

"We can never do this again," Drake had told her, later that night. "We have to destroy the Relics."

"But—"

"I caught a glimpse of its mind, Morgana." His voice had been tight. "For all its subservience today, it was furious. It wanted to destroy us, to rein upon us agony that would break a man's mind and tear him limb from limb, then do it over and over. We can never *bind that creature again."*

"But with the relics, we can control it."

"Do you believe that?" he'd asked, turning to face her.

And she'd doubted, just enough to agree to his plan to steal the Relics from Tremayne and replace them with illusory ones.

Over the years, she'd come to regret that decision, declaiming it as weak, but now, now that she stared up into those merciless pits of eyes... "What do you w-want with me?"

"What I've always wanted," Lascher replied. "It has been a mere flicker of years for me, a blink of the eye, but for you it has been many. Your flesh is sagging and eating itself alive from the inside with age. You are weaker and vulnerable." It poked her directly in the thigh, and to her horror, Morgana felt nothing. "I could tear you limb from limb, just for the audacity in summoning me, but I want more." It leaned closer. "We have an enemy in common, you and me. A powerful enemy."

"Who?"

"The one you call the Prime. He is too powerful for me to confront. Serve me," the creature replied, reaching out to stroke her tearstained face with his gloved hands, "and I may not kill you."

Never deal with a demon. Never trust them. Never believe what they can offer you. The only way to approach them was with the Relics Infernal in hand.

But what choice did she have? She couldn't feel her legs and her magic was weakened inside her. She needed to regain her strength, and even then she might not be able to fight this creature off.

"I can help you make them pay," it whispered, and the whisper slithered all the way through her veins. "I can help you bring that son you spat into the world to heel. I can help you make him crawl."

Yes, her heart thundered, while the little part of her that often offered counsel hid in its corner of her mind.

"I can give you back your legs," it promised, and Morgana's tears welled again, against her will. "I will even allow you to keep this." He slid the Blade closer to her fingers with the tip of his shoe.

"What is your other choice?" it taunted. "Lie here and rot whilst your enemies dance on your bones? Perhaps you will die before others find you, others who find your weakness... appealing. Or perhaps you will not."

There was no choice, not truly. Morgana grit her teeth. "What is your price? What do you get out of this?"

"The same thing you desire. Vengeance. To crush those who thought to harm me beneath my heel." He lifted a hand to his flawed cheek, to the marred flesh there, looking thoughtful. "And I am not fully here. Something happened when you used the Blade. I was brought only halfway into this world, my vessel torn from me before I could overtake it."

She'd used the kitchen knife to stab both Lucien and Sebastian, not the Blade. If he ever found out... "Then how—?" she blurted, gesturing to the body it wore to distract it.

"This?" It traced a proprietary finger down its suit. "Tremayne found this for me several months ago. It serves as a vessel until another more suitable one can be found. I can only use it for short periods of time, however, as the body weakens too swiftly. I need a stronger vessel, one that commands sorcery on the highest level and doesn't burn out so swiftly."

Several months ago. Her ally had never mentioned anything about *this*, but then Tremayne had somehow gotten his powers back after the Order's Council had locked them away from him.

"Tremayne made a deal with you," she said.

The demon smiled. "I made a deal with Tremayne."

"Then what can I do for you? You want a body?"

Lascher's lip curled. "I want *the* body that was promised to me. Rathbourne. I want the woman gone—his woman. It stands between us. Kill her, and I shall still have a link to Lucien. If you bring the three Relics Infernal together, then the spell that should have been completed with the Blade shall overwhelm him."

Her mind worked quickly. "What about Sebastian? You could take him as a vessel. He's strong, stronger than Rathbourne, even."

The demon considered it. Its expression shuttered. "No. No, there is... someone who stands between us. I would not rise against her, not yet, and I have no link to your son. He has never summoned me. Give me Lucien. Once I have a vessel, I shall have the power to do my will. I want you to assemble the Relics Infernal and call me into being. Then we shall destroy the Prime. Together."

Yes, a part of her whispered. If she gathered the relics, then she could do as this creature wanted... and then use the power of the relics to wield *him*. "How do we destroy him? Drake is powerful..." Especially if he could challenge a demon like this by himself.

"I would have you wield a weapon against him that is of his own making."

Morgana frowned.

The demon leaned closer, its breath scalding her ear. "Sebastian is the key. Wield him. Break him. Use him. And destroy the father."

In the end, there was no choice. "You have a deal," Morgana whispered. "But how do I control Sebastian?" The ring had burned through her finger, taking the flesh with it and leaving the stump cauterized.

The demon smiled. "Oh, I have an idea about that."

This dream was new.

Cleo sat at a small table in a room with no walls, a room of infinite dimensions. The black and white checkerboard of floor tiles seemed to stretch into the distance where mist obscured it, and the ceiling was made of the evening sky with the rosy taint of sunset darkening to midnight from one end to the other. Stars and constellations gleamed, and yet, seemed somewhat watchful.

She looked down. She could see her hands, which meant no blindfold, and she knew, in a deep part of herself that she was both awake and yet not awake.

"Your move," said a hollow voice across from her, and she realized there was a cloaked figure sitting there, draped in midnight silk. It could have been man or woman, she wasn't certain. At this moment, it seemed difficult to even guess if it was human.

"My move?" There was a chessboard between them with intricately carved figures. If she looked closely, she could see the faces on the white figures were people who she knew from previous visions: Miss Martin, Lucien, the Prime, and two others she didn't know—a young man as bishop and an older lady as one of the knights. The White Queen had a blindfold on, and she was guarded by Sebastian, whose face was rendered above the White King.

Clearly the board was meant to represent the battle between the Prime and his enemies, but she hadn't expected to be the one making the moves.

"Of course you make the moves," the entity opposite her intoned. "You're the one who can see the future."

"But these aren't pawns. This isn't a game."

"It's always a game. What you mean is that each move has a consequence you don't want to pay. Now make your move."

Her hands began sweating in her gloves. The Black Queen wore Morgana's face, and the Black King was her father. Both of the Black Knights had circled the White King and were threatening one of her pawns. She couldn't see who it represented, but she knew she had to save it.

Reaching out, she hovered over Sebastian. A little tingle of wrongness echoed over her skin. It was instinctive to reach for him, but she trusted her senses. Slowly raking her hand over her pieces, she felt a little quiver against her prescience, a tingle that echoed over her skin.

Cleo swallowed hard and moved her bishop.

"Interesting move." The entity wore a smile. He—and it was definitely a he now—crooked a finger, and his black bishop slid toward hers, stopping directly in front of it.

The black bishop was a woman, one glancing over her shoulder, even as she hid something within her waistcoat. She wore men's attire with tightly fitted breeches, but her figure was most certainly feminine, and her hair was knotted into a crown of plaits. The only abnormalities were the shackles at her wrists.

"Who is she?" Cleo asked.

"You shall discover her identity soon enough." The entity bowed his head to her. *"Until we meet again, Cassandra."*

The world spun, the room vanishing around her, and then—

With a gasp, Cleo sat bolt upright in her bed. Her heart was thundering in her chest, and the familiar rustle of the linen bindings over her eyes reminded her of where she was—safely nestled in a bed at the inn that Sebastian had removed her to before he'd retired to his own adjoining room. He was hurt, his senses obliterated by the backlash of power, his hands torn and ruined, and his wound newly healed, but he wouldn't allow her to see to him, the fool. Whatever she'd done to him at the house had disturbed him.

With a sigh, Cleo lay back down, drawing her covers up around her chin. What on earth had that dream meant? It belonged not to the realm of precognition or foretelling, but had felt as if it had truly been real.

Something moved, a slow creak, as a floorboard shifted beneath a stealthy foot.

Cleo froze.

"Hello? Is anybody there?"

Skirts swished, and then a hand clapped over her mouth as she tried to scream. "Surprise," Morgana whispered in her ear. "I think you should come with me and be quiet about it. I wouldn't want to have to cut my own son down when he sleeps so heavily in the next room, his mind and body battered by exhaustion." The hand pressed firmly over her mouth as Morgana leaned down to whisper in her ear. "Don't make a sound, or I'll kill him, I swear. Do you understand?"

The hand over her mouth lightened until only a silencing finger pressed against her lips. Cleo thought about her options, her heart hammering in her chest. Sebastian *was* injured. She'd almost had to carry him up the stairs herself, his power bleeding all over her and every step earning a wince from him. He was in no state of mind to deal with an intruder, even one without power.

And she had the suspicion she was not going to be harmed. Morgana wanted something from her.

Cleo nodded.

"Good," her kidnapper gloated. "Now come with me."

"White Queen in check," whispered the entity, in her mind.

Want to find out what is going to happen to Drake and his other two sons? The story continues later this year with Bloodbound... Read on for an excerpt...

COMING 2016...

If you enjoyed Shadowbound, then get ready for Bloodbound! Book two in the Dark Arts series, it will be available in late 2016, so make sure you sign up for my newsletter to receive news and excerpts about this release!

Can't wait for more Dark Arts action and romance? Check out my London Steampunk series. I recommend starting with Kiss Of Steel. Not only is it the first book, but it also features a cocky, bad boy anti-hero who captured my heart from the very first moment he came onscreen. There's humour, heroes to die for, dangerous plots, sexy corsets, kick-bustle heroines, duels, steamy kisses (not-just-kisses), and vampires. They may not be your regular sexy vampires either.

Thank you for reading Shadowbound! I hope you enjoyed it. Please consider leaving a review online, to help others find my books.

Not ready to leave the London of the Dark Arts? Read on for a preview of what's next for Adrian Bishop...

COMING 2016

BLOODBOUND

BOOK 2: THE DARK ARTS SERIES

It should have been an easy task...

Miss Verity Hastings has a little trick: she can find anything, no matter where it's hidden. It's a skill that's kept her safe and fed all the way from the orphanages and workhouses of her youth, and makes her valuable to the sorcerous Hex gang she runs with. But when she steals a mysterious relic for a masked man, she knows the con is on her this time. In order to protect herself, she can turn to only one man: Bishop, the sorcerer she stole the relic from.

Sicarii assassin Adrian Bishop is rarely surprised anymore, but when a rather enticing little handful turns up on his doorstep claiming to be his mysterious thief, he doesn't know what to think. He needs the relic back, no matter the cost, and he's not above using Verity to find it. But as Verity begins to sneak under his guard, for the first time in years there's a ray of light in his dark world. He will do anything to protect her–anything–but can Verity ever love him once she learns the truth of his dark talents? And will he be able to protect her from the trap he sent her into himself?

London, 1880

ADRIAN BISHOP woke quietly, his eyelids fluttering wide, and his skin tingling as if every sense of his was suddenly on fire. He held his breath, listening intently to the cold, dark silence of his house. Nothing moved. Not a whisper, not a creak, not even a mouse.

Except...

Someone stepped through one of the invisible wards he'd set throughout the mansion. It clung like spider silk to their body, giving him an instant beacon of awareness: the intruder was in the second guest bedroom, with its simple furnishings, and the revolving fireplace that hid a staircase that led to a hidden room. Whoever it was, they moved with deliberate purpose, as if they knew exactly where they were going, and most likely what they were looking for.

It was almost impressive, the stealth with which they moved.

Sicarii, then? Like himself?

Highly trained, the Sicarii were the lethal edge of the sorcerous Order of the Dawn Star, and only one man - the ruling Prime - knew all of their identities. Most Sicarii did not even know of each other's existence, as they used masks to meet. Their purpose was absolute–protect the Order, serve the Prime, remove all threats... Most importantly that last one. It was lonely, bloody work, but he'd known nothing else, all of his life.

Bishop eased back the covers, slipping naked from his bed. He dragged on a pair of the loose black trousers he wore for training purposes, and started gathering together his power. Energy slipped and slid into his skin, the temperature of the room plunging abruptly to freezing as he prepared himself, drawing power from the world around him. Heated breath spilled in a fine mist around his mouth, as he passed in front of the windows, and the faint, silvery moonlight. All in all, it took him six seconds, and the task was done in complete silence.

Another ward tripped, just as the downstairs clock began to chime midnight. BONG. BONG. BONG. There. He closed his eyes, head tilting upwards, as the clock droned on. His thief had found the fireplace, which meant he had no time to spare. Forging a knife made of raw matter, he cut his hand, and pressed it against the plaster walls of the house.

"Hecarah as di mentos," he whispered, breathing a spill of Power into the words. The words meant nothing; ritual was the key in training his mind to accept simple codes, and he had chosen his words wisely so many years ago.

Nothing happened, but he could sense the house coming alive, awakening to his touch, and anticipating his commands. It too, felt like it held its breath.

Above him, the thief paused, just for a second.

And that was when he realised that he was facing a master adversary. The house wards were inverted. Nobody should have felt it waking, but from the sudden fierce patter of footsteps the thief had given up all pretence of stealth, and was opting for speed.

Done then. Bishop moved like a wraith. The tracking ward jerked forward, almost as if it were leaping from place to place–which caused him some consternation–but he was swiftly gaining as he thundered up the staircase. The thief might be heading directly toward the object of their desire, but they were moving in a straight line, and certain obstacles, walls for example, kept interfering.

His blood was up, the fierce hunting edge keening through him. Death rode him hard, hungering for a taste of blood, and Bishop forced it back within its leash. Some sorcerers found power through blood or sex rituals, but only a kill gave him that edge, that sweet ride of power, like an aurora awakening in his veins. He could tear London apart with but a thought following the hot gush of blood, but such power came with a weakness: the hunger for the kill grew every time he took a life. One day he would be a dangerous force to be reckoned with, the sweet addiction stronger than his will, and then another of the Sicarii would be sent to remove him.

But he was not there yet.

Racing silently up the hidden staircase, Bishop saw the faint bobbing glow of a mage sphere through the partly opened panel that led to his secret room.

Bishop threw himself into the room in a roll, beneath a hastily flung ward that would have smashed him back through at least three walls, and came to his feet just in time to face a masked adversary.

No time to think. The rosy mage globe spun into twelve that circled the thief's head, and began to spin faster and faster. One shot directly toward him, and he flung both arms up, crossing them at the wrists, as a single protective ward formed around him. The globe the thief had flung burst into heated, liquid light that bathed the thin shimmering ward around him, and then dripped to the floor. Molten sparks burned straight through the timber floorboards.

"Well," said the thief, in a faintly amused, very feminine voice, "I see the rumors of your skills were not exaggerated."

His first shock of the evening–the Chalice that he'd sworn to protect with his life was already hanging from her belt. It gleamed silvery against her all-black man's attire, along with a dozen small devices of unknown origin.

It should have taken her nearly ten minutes to crack through the safeguards on his safe: a safe that hung open on the wall, it's heavy steel-lined door hanging limply from its grooves.

"I don't believe we've had the pleasure," Bishop replied, straightening, and letting the silvery gleam of the ward disintegrate with a static crackle. It would take but a thought to reform it.

A faint smile curled over the woman's lips. Her chin and mouth were all that he could see, apart from the gleam of green eyes behind her black lace mask. The battle globes spun lazily around her head, warming her creamy skin, as she slowly circled him. The entire effect was... provocative. "And here I thought you a stranger to pleasure? Or so they all say."

Bishop didn't move. The only way out was through the doorway that stood directly behind him. His smile was cold. "I'd be careful about listening to rumors. Sometimes I start them myself."

"Oh, I know," she whispered, her eyes alight with humor, as she sauntered slowly around the room, crossing one foot over another. "Let's just say I've spent the last month learning everything there is to know about you. I've watched you paint these walls with your blood wards, trying to protect against thieves. And I've watched you move quietly through the house each night, restless, unable to sleep. All alone at night, in this dark house. Why do you send your servants away? Do you not want them seeing the mess of your body that you hide beneath your clothes? Or perhaps you're afraid they'll hear your nightmares? It's the one mystery I haven't been able to crack yet."

Bishop's gaze flattened.

"Didn't you notice me?" Her smile was positively wicked. "And here I thought you had eyes in the back of your head."

Every muscle in his gut tightened, and he took the time to re-examine her. He was very, very good at what he did. The fact that he hadn't noticed the surveillance made him wonder if she was better.

Or perhaps not better, no, perhaps he'd been distracted, more to the point. His nails dug into his palms. What had she seen? Had she any idea what plagued him?

No. No, she couldn't have. Or she'd have used it against him.

Both of them faced each other on light feet, their bodies tense with implied movement. A pair of cuffs circled her slim wrists, and a black corset buckled over her thin shirt. Those slim hips were encased in a pair of trousers that were positively indecent, but she looked lean and strong, and she moved with a kind of supple grace he'd rarely seen before.

"Who are you?" he asked.

Just who is Bishop's mysterious thief? Find out in

BLOODBOUND, *coming late 2016...*

ABOUT THE AUTHOR

Bec McMaster is the award-winning author of the London Steampunk series. A member of RWA, she writes sexy, dark paranormals, and adventurous steampunk romances, and grew up with her nose in a book. Following a life-long love affair with fantasy, she discovered romance novels as a 16 year-old, and hasn't looked back.

In 2012, Sourcebooks released her debut award-winning novel, *Kiss of Steel*, the first in the London Steampunk series, followed by: *Heart of Iron*, *My Lady Quicksilver*, *Forged By Desire*, and *Of Silk And Steam*. Two novellas–*Tarnished Knight* and *The Curious Case Of The Clockwork Menace*–fleshed out the series. She has been nominated for RT Reviews Best Steampunk Romance for *Heart of Iron (2013)*, won RT Reviews Best Steampunk Romance with *Of Silk And Steam (2015)*, and *Forged By Desire* was nominated for a RITA award in 2015.

When not poring over travel brochures, playing netball, or cooking things that are very likely bad for her, Bec spends most of her time in front of the computer. In 2016, she debuted the Dark Arts series with *Shadowbound*, as well as the second London Steampunk: The Blueblood Conspiracy series, with *Mission: Improper*.

Bec lives in a small country town in Victoria, Australia, with her very own Beta Hero; a Staffordshire terrier named Kobe, who has perfected her own Puss-in-boots sad eyes–especially when bacon is involved; and demanding chickens, Siggy and Lagertha. It's possible she has a minor obsession with *Vikings*, and *The Originals*.

Connect with Bec at www.becmcmaster.com, Facebook, and Twitter. For news on new releases, cover reveals, contests, and special promotions, join her mailing list.

ACKNOWLEDGMENTS

Ten years ago this dark gothic world crept into my head, and it all started with Drake. I could never quite get that story right until now, but it's crazy what a few simple tweaks to the plot can unleash in your mind!

I enjoyed every second of writing this book, but as with every project I take on, I couldn't have done it without a lot of help from these amazing people:

I owe huge thanks to my editor Virginia from Hot Tree Editing for making this manuscript so clean, my wonderful cover artists from Damonza.com for bringing Ianthe and Lucien to life, and Marisa Shor from Cover Me Darling for the formatting. Also special thanks to my beta readers Kylie Griffin and Jen Brumley for asking all of the pointy questions. To the ELE, and the Central Victorian Writers groups for keeping me sane! Special thanks to my family, and to my other half—my very own beta hero, Byron—who encourages and supports me every step of the way. You're forever banned from reading out passages in that 'voice' you employ, but I love you anyway.

Last, not least, to everyone who read/loved/reviewed or talked about this book, you guys are awesome! I hope it was worth the wait!

Made in the USA
Lexington, KY
29 August 2019